The Silver Dolphins Saga:
Book One
Of Life and Love

M.M. Scott and V.Y. Mummert

An Arisdale Arts Book

Pennsylvania

Dedication

I dedicate book one of The Silver Dolphins Saga: Of Life and Love to all the loves in my life: my family for their support, those who call me friend, my acquaintances and most of all the love of my life, my husband for being my light, my love, and friend.

Thanks to my little sister, collaborator, and co-author, Victoria Mummert. Combining our characters together has created a stronger and vibrant tale. Her love of bunnies and her soul inspired the creation of Snow Artichia. My older sister Denise for encouraging me to draw and for being an inspiration to me. Her love for dolphins and Egypt inspired me on the design of the Silver Dolphins, and the design of Fandia, Katenna, and Artilone. My mother Margaret for her incredible strength and pure heart. Thank you for making me who I am.

I thank the Deviant Art community for their kindness, friendship and support: Spaghetti-Mayhem, TheArtisticPony, NinjaTanner, Plenilunij-Lee, Kayly101, DaRkN3X, MistGod, Shelthedreamer, Agent-LaDue, Marek816, Viruleince, MasqueradeOfTheNight, and many more.

A special thanks to Spaghetti-Mayhem for taking time out to consult with me about the book and give me helpful insight into reworking the beginning.

A thank you to everyone who helped with editing and working with me to make this novel complete.

The passion for sharing this story is fueled by the fire of my own gratitude to be alive and for every soul that enters my life. I grow stronger because of you. Even if that time is brief, I will always love you, and I thank you for adding to my life with your own journey.

❧Contents❦

When Two Become as One

"A valuable lesson was taught to the world about living a life in the light of love. This must be shared and never forgotten. For change to occur all of life must heed the call. Love is a driving force that causes us to go to incredible lengths. Of all emotions, love is the most powerful and has many meanings and forms. We can be a person who lived a wealthy life, but if there was no love given to the self or others, we gain nothing from the emptiness of possessions. Forgive and forget, be understanding, and share a moment of your time. These simple gestures of kindness can change another's life and your own for the better. One must live their life in the light of love, to ever be able to say they lived at all. Distance is no obstacle to love. Through our thoughts and prayers, no one is ever too far away. The voice of love is like a whisper on the wind, and can reach the heart of the soul who is in the same place within themselves, where you live within yourself. A strong bond is formed as two become one. For the heart that longs to sacrifice all for the sake of love, there is no greater power than that."

-Sara Phoenix

Prologue - Irana's Torment

Irana could feel the chilling grip of darkness welling up inside her as she wept over the crypt of her beloved husband. She was told his death was natural; however, a voice inside her screamed in protest. The voice was not her own. It sounded like a nightmarish choir of distorted voices that refused to stop speaking and could not be ignored. She wasn't sure if she was going mad or if the loss of her husband was too much for her heart to bear. The voices repeated in her mind, replaying their words in an agonizing loop.

"He was murdered and you know that. They are coming, the ones who killed him. Give in to your desires and let me help you get revenge. Let me end your suffering. Give me control."

A single torch and the occasional flicker of lightning from the window lit the room, giving an eerie definition to the tombstones. Thunder roared overhead as if her cries of agony reached the heavens and were given voice. She knew revenge was not the answer. She was not an evil person, or was she? With all the fatigue and anguish weighing on her, she was no longer sure if life had been a dream all along. She touched her fair-skinned cheeks with the palms of her hands. Perhaps this is her reality.

"No, this can't be real!" She grabbed fistfuls of long blue hair and pulled hard, radiating sharp pain across her scalp, as if doing so could tear the madness from her mind. The harder she fought the voice, the louder and more insistent it became.

"Let me end your suffering. Give me control."

Her blue eyes darted across the marble stones. She wanted to puncture her eardrums and make the voice end. She knew that would not work. Her dreams repeated the tragedy every night. She saw her husband being poisoned by an elder race with a long snout and tail. She helplessly watched her beloved Charles dying in agony, and she could hear the voice calling to her.

"You are queen, there is nothing you cannot do!"

The voice said it could end her torment, and yet her torment was the voice. She hadn't slept for the last two days, and in her weariness, she thought about doing as the voice demanded, giving in to the insistent pleading.

"Give me control."

She ceased her struggle against the voice and was aware of another presence within her mind. She watched herself moving, rising from the floor to stand, unwilled by her own thoughts. She approached the tomb guard, who saluted her as always. She pulled the sword from his scabbard and stabbed him. Red oozed from his midsection, his face twisted in question as he dropped to the floor. The awareness within her was delighted and knelt to draw an intricate pattern on the floor in the man's blood. She heard herself chanting words in an unknown language. She rose and left the room. She didn't like what she witnessed, but now she was free from the torment. Maybe now she could finally rest in peace.

Chapter 1 - Dreams

In the depth of his peaceful slumber, drips from on high cascaded down, blooming ripples emerged upon impact and rolled across the surface of the once still and quiet pond. Golden eyes watched the rhythmic pulse, soothing, grounding, enchanting. He floated off the ground in a seated position, as one with the earth that flowed through and around him. Softly, growing in tone, as the ripples disturbed the rest of the water's surface more frequently, voices speaking in unison were heard.

"We are sorry . . . if we had known . . . suffering will rise as the light fades. Seek the inner light."

Disturbed by the phrases, Justin sat up fast, heart racing, breaths deep, mind frantic with the wonder of what he had just dreamed of. His brown-scaled hands rubbed his eyes a moment before he attempted to leave the warm comfort of rest. Groggy from the sudden wakefulness, he pulled himself from the crimson silk sheets of his feather bed and stumbled upon the carpets to his wardrobe closet. The sun was rising and lit the room gently with a golden hue.

From what he recalled, his father had nothing pressing for him to do. He wanted to go fishing before the winter season took hold; today would be the perfect day. He selected casual attire for the venture though he still looked dapper in this compared to the common folks' version of relaxed garb.

He paused, considering the dream once more. "How odd to dream of a pond then wish to go fishing," he said in a deep and refined tone. He released a small chuckle as he carefully pulled on pants over his sickle toe claws. A difficult task for a Velociraptor; however, Arisdalians wore metal guards on their talons at night and sometimes in social functions.

These allowed him to dress with greater ease. There was nothing worse than tearing up one's bedsheets, clothing, or even loved ones by accident.

The pants were fastened together with a button at the back, above his tail. He looped a gold and green-gemmed belt through the pants and fastened it. He pulled out half boots and wrapped them around the pant legs, fastening gold bands shut at the top and bottom, above his ankle. He placed similar style gauntlets on his arms. He slipped on a green and gold-lined shirt then shifted himself to stand before his mirror. Narrow angular eyes searched his reflection to ensure the attire was in order, and that his brother Agar hadn't used his unique lightning magic to adhere personal clothing items to his shirt again. He laughed once more. However, that was a terribly embarrassing memory all the same. He could still hear the guards' laughter in his mind as he walked obliviously through the castle that day.

He ran his hand through his great mane of sandy-tan head feathers to realign them as they were disheveled from rest. He paused over one that was new growth and sighed. Feathers were nice to have but were a lot of maintenance, especially for the grand mohawk that sat atop his head. Rather than make a mess of his clothing he let it be and would promptly seek one of the castle caregivers to aid him later. He reached for his tail, bringing it closer. He inspected the feathers that lined the tip. They appeared in order, and he let his tail go, swaying it behind him as he checked himself once more.

He smiled, white fangs gleaming in contrast to the dark brown of his skin. He rubbed his four-clawed hand against his sandy-tan jaw and nodded in satisfaction. He turned and walked purposefully on his digitigrade legs to the bedroom door. Upon exiting his room, two guards on either side of the doorway saluted and remained so until he had well passed them. He turned and acknowledged their presence with a hand to the heart and a slight bow of his head. After the gesture of appreciation was given, Justin turned back and walked forward with guards trailing behind.

At the end of the granite stone hall, before the door to the study, was one of the royal guards, elite soldiers of which there were eight. There was only one window at the end of the long hall, and that was not enough to adequately light the area. The warm glow of candles lit the remainder of the passage. The rays that peeked through the window darkened the guard making it hard to see him, though his white and gold armor and red cape were outlined by the caressing glow of dawn's light and defined his rank. His father must be in the study for one of them to be there. The guard was facing him and not at his station as he approached, which meant he wished to speak to him. Justin paused before the green-scaled stegosaurus that saluted him.

He returned the salute with a bow of his head. "Captain Severos, my good friend, what brings you to greet me?"

"Highness," Captain Severos replied lowering his head, "King Johanas rose early. He is in the study reading a missive that arrived from Delphi this morn. He wished for you to attend to him as soon as you are able."

"Truly?" Justin replied with an arched brow. "What did this missive say?"

Severos shook his head. "I know not, Highness."

"Ah, very well then. I shall see to him now, I thank you."

Captain Severos saluted once more then turned to knock on the mahogany study door before opening it for him. Justin often wondered how the man navigated halls and rooms with the four spikes that lined his tail, yet Severos never damaged or knocked over anything in all the years he had known him. Much like their claws, spikes and horns were also covered in protective metal. In combat, those covers would be removed; however, a fight of that level was something of dreams and fairytales. The first and last known battle was against the humans of Flourisha three hundred years ago, long before his and his father's time.

"Father," Justin said with a bow of his head. "You asked for me?"

"Ah, my son. I did indeed," he gestured for him to enter and stand beside him at his desk. "We have received a missive from Delphi of great importance."

Justin approached his father whose green eyes were alight with anticipation as his son peered down at him. He disliked being taller than his father, who he mirrored in appearance rather closely except for the king's rounded eye shape, and his first few head feathers were curled. Justin himself had a slightly pointed snout tip that was an inherited trait from his mother, but fate had also considered making him a few inches above his father, and many others as well. He was on the high end of Arisdalians' average height of six foot five, reaching seven foot in his natural stance. Seven and a half if you counted his mohawk. Straightening his digitigrade legs allowed him to reach eight and a half feet tall. He liked being able to tower over the masses for the sake of intimidation and power, but at the same time, was tired of constantly looking down. He smiled at his father. "As Severos had informed me, pray what does this missive say, Father?"

Johanas nodded. "King Charles and Queen Irana Delphi have invited us to their kingdom in hopes of forming an alliance as well as a source of trade."

"Truly? If we were to achieve this noteworthy task, 'twould bring honor back to great-grandfather King Mishiku Arisdale after he freed humans from slavery. Perhaps even end this two thousand year hatred of each other." His vertical slit-shaped pupils dilated, and his head feathers briefly rose as he thought, then lowered to their relaxed position. "'Tis grand news indeed, Father."

"As you know Arisdales always attend affairs of state to this degree in person to show that we are committed to the cause and to demonstrate that we are not afraid. 'Twould be a good experience for you as a future king as well," he said placing his hand on Justin's shoulder.

"Father, while I am in no hurry to take your throne, I am greatly honored to join you on this monumental occasion. 'Tis indeed an experience of a lifetime."

"Hey, what about me?!" a whiny voice replied in protest.

Justin looked down at where he heard his adopted brother's voice, watching the elder race white tiger intently as he began to become visible. "By the gods, Agar! 'Tis an exaggeration of many occasions past to now say that you ought to know better than to spy on others, and yet here you are. Your magical gifts are no excuse for spying on father or me."

"Why did you leave me out then?!" Agar huffed and folded his arms, his white and black striped tail whipping behind him.

Johanas sighed and rubbed his brow. "Agar, I was planning on speaking to you after I talked to Justin. I wished to know his thoughts before committing us all to go. Heaven knows Queen Katenna might appreciate the experience for you as well," he said, followed by a laugh.

"Yeah, yeah," Agar replied dismissively with a wave of his hand. "I'll go! This will be fun!"

The door opened and Justin smiled warmly at the sight of his mother entering the room. She had a spring in her step, no doubt she was aware of the missive's words.

"Ah, and all my boys are here," Anelda chirped, touching her yellow beak with her clawed hand, her aqua eyes gleaming with enthusiasm.

"Mother!" Justin replied hugging her tenderly, his snout buried in her white feathers. "I can only imagine your joy right now. 'Tis what you have been working so hard for."

Anelda brushed back her pink head feathers and smiled, "Oh yes, my son, I am pleased beyond words!" She turned to Agar and patted him on his head of black hair. She embraced him tightly. "A rascal as always, I see. Do not ever doubt our love for you, Agar."

"How did you know? Ah, who am I kidding? You always know, Mother," Agar quipped.

"General Dilos is quite upset by this turn of events," Johanas interjected. "I value the man's opinion; however, he tried to convince me that 'twas a trap. Honestly, I do not see it. I am bringing most of the royal guards and a few from each of their charges, you two boys with your elemental magic, and, of course, the Elemental of Wind, Yarway. With three Elementals of Light at our side, there will be little to worry about."

"Delphi will regret a trap!" Agar said with determination and a spark of electricity from his hand. "No one is hurting my family!"

"I highly doubt a trap as well," Justin replied calmly. "Delphi does not have the forces to go to war with Arisdale, even if they allied with the other human tribes, 'twould be a small victory to assassinate a royal family that has a stable government with the Elder Council to take our place. Let us not forget our alliances with other great nations such as Egyptalia and Volga. They would be eradicated in little time, and of course, be quite fortunate to even succeed in an assassination attempt with us beside you, as was said."

"This is why I wished to speak with you first, Justin. I pray you understand, Agar."

"Yes, Father," Agar said bowing his head, "everyone knows Justin is the deep thinker in this house!"

"You both flatter me," Justin replied running his hand through his head feathers.

"Flattery that is thusly earned, my son. You make us proud. Agar," Anelda said expecting a retort, "you know that we are proud of you as well for the values you have."

Agar smiled. "That I do, Mother."

"When are we to leave for this venture?" Justin asked his father.

"On the morrow, this will give us time to convene with the elders and plan our negotiations. The journey ought to take three days by sea."

Agar groaned. "Three days on a large pile of wood, the only safety between me and the water."

"Straight to the negative then, Agar?" Justin asked. "You will be perfectly safe on a ship."

"Oh, Agar dear, do not think like that, all right? Justin is correct, everything will be fine," Anelda replied giving Agar a firm hug. "Although you will need a bath before we arrive, dear. Pray do not fight me on that."

Agar's face washed with panic. "No, no, no! I just had one a day ago, pray!" His large ears drooped and he stared at her pleadingly making a begging gesture to her.

"Agar, there will be no further argument on this," Johanas replied sternly with a shake of his head.

Agar huffed a sigh and crossed his arms. "Yes, Father."

A knock came at the door. Aunt Galena entered the room with a smile, and Yarway followed behind her. "Ah, here you all are. I heard there was some excitement with a missive this morn'."

"Oh yes, sister!" Anelda replied embracing Galena, whose yellow head feathers tickled her beaked snout. "My dreams may finally come true! The completion of the humans' injustice, and the unity of all races of Flourisha."

"Oh, that would be grand indeed! I am so happy that your hard work is finally coming to fruition!"

"I want you to come with us, dear sister!"

"I am grateful for that, Anelda, but perhaps I should stay here and be your representative in case something comes along while you are away. The last thing we need is an incident with a human whilst you are out trying to form lasting peace," Galena said with a firm nod.

"Ah, yes, an intuitive notion, Galena," Johanas replied.

"Oh well, perhaps once things are settled there we can visit Delphi again and you can come then," Anelda said.

"Indeed so, sister!"

"Yarway, I thank you for coming as well. I pray you will be able to join us to Delphi? Your past will not affect your ability to be cordial?" Johanas asked him.

The elder race red fox smiled lightly, bowing low at the waist. "Of course, Your Majesty. I owe the Arisdales much in return for the kindness you have bestowed me all these years." His blue eyes dropped to the floor then rose back to meet the king's. "Though I lost my family to bandits, I do not hold disdain for all humans, only those who chose their actions that day."

Johanas nodded. "Splendid, Yarway. You are a welcome guest in our home and we greatly appreciate your service."

"Hey, who's hungry?!" Agar blurted out.

Justin laughed, "Agar, heavens, what are we to do with you? Come then, brother, let us get you fed before you wither away, yes?"

"Yes!"

Johanas shook his head. "One day, Agar, one day you may act a prince, and till then, I will pray," he smiled. "However, I am in agreement, shall we?"

Justin replied with a nod and ushered his brother out the door with him.

"Justin?" Johanas called to him.

"Yes, Father?" he asked glancing back.

Johanas pointed to his shirt. "Pray, was there something else you had planned for today?"

"Ah, yes, Father. I was hoping to go fishing though there are plenty of days ahead for such a thing. Perhaps we can find time in Delphi before we return home."

Johanas wore a broad smile. "Certainly, Justin, I would enjoy that."

Justin returned the smile. A day fishing with his father was a rare occurrence. The life of a king of a vast kingdom was filled with responsibilities.

Together they dined in the castle ballroom, happily discussing the upcoming venture. Meetings with the elders followed, and as expected, the royal guard, General Dilos Manning, held strong to his objections.

Tired and stressed after the long day, Justin met with Agar and Yarway in the castle gardens, a favorite place of his to sit outdoors within the confines of the protective castle walls. The sun was setting and its fiery cast slowly faded as they spoke.

"You know I never said this, but I often wished they had taken me too; the bandits, I mean," Yarway said releasing a heavy sigh and lowering his head.

Justin's head feathers rose with his words. "Truly, Yarway? I cannot fathom the depths of your pain, but life is precious, and we all have a purpose in this world before we must part."

"I know, Justin, if it weren't for you and Agar, I wouldn't have seen that purpose at all. My wife, my daughters, I miss them."

"Yarway, my man, we are grateful to have you with us!" Agar replied. "Just look back at all we have done! The fun we had in training and with our magic!"

"Heh, yeah. Lots of fond memories for sure," Yarway replied with a smirk.

"Many more to come as well, hmm?" Justin replied looking up into the vast sea of stars. "I wonder what memories Delphi will bring."

Chapter 2 - Cursed

Time seemed to stand still as Miral and the castle staff received the grim news. King Charles Delphi had passed on to the World of Light. Tear-filled sobs and mutterings of denial resounded through the main hall in mournful song.

She heard a man in the crowd shout, "The king was young and healthy. How could this happen?!"

She couldn't see who spoke past the wall of other servants, but had pondered the same question as she brushed blue hair from her fair-skinned face. Intrigue and conspiracy theories spread through the masses quickly. The elder races were the first to be blamed. Rightly so, all their kind ever did was keep humans under their fist; however, she didn't believe all of them could be cruel. Though she had no way of knowing.

"The elder races assassinated the king!" an unknown man shouted.

The hall erupted with shouts of multiple raised voices and bickering ensued. Miral felt overwhelmed and left the castle to sit on the sandy shores of the Island of Delphi and watch the sunrise. The golden rays of warmth were comforting and sparkled as waves rolled towards the shore with soothing melody. Several seabirds landed beside her and picked the sand looking for food. She smiled as they fearlessly scavenged around her.

"Miral! I knew I would find you here."

The seabirds took flight at her father's voice. The frightened beating of wings left plumes of feathers behind that danced in the breeze, one landing almost purposefully within his head of deep blue hair, his eyes shining like polished sapphires. She shared his hair and eyes, as was true for all Delphinians.

With a warm and comforting smile, he sat close beside her and wrapped an arm around her shoulders. "I don't know how you do it, Miral, but ever since you were a baby, animals just walked right up to you and no one else."

Miral smiled at him. She liked that they did but did not know how either.

"Your mother attracted them for a long time too, then you somehow took over!" he chuckled. "They must admire your shared beauty as much as I do." He gave her a kiss on her forehead, his short beard brushing against her skin. He sighed. "This is really hard to believe, isn't it?"

"King Charles was a good man. I feel sorry for Queen Irana," she replied quietly.

"What's on your mind, sweetheart? I know that tone."

"Mother."

"Ah, the death of another has a way of reminding us of the past. Sonya," he said in a hushed tone, laying his head on hers, "we will see her in the World of Light once our journeys come to an end. You know she is watching over you, right?"

"Yes, Father, I do."

"Good girl. There is no end, only new beginnings." He gave her a comforting squeeze before looking at her with his warm smile. "Shall we pray?"

Miral nodded in reply and together they prayed with the song of mourning. A hymn that was sung for grieving to the Goddess of Light, Fandia, and the sacred Silver Dolphins.

"Silver Dolphins, light of the world, free my heart from sorrow. Silver Dolphins, I am in mourning, take my heart and lift up my soul."

"Feeling better now?" he asked her.

"Yes, I am. Thank you, Father."

"We best get back to the castle and to work before we're in trouble."

"You're right."

They stood, dusted sand from their clothing, and proceeded to Castle Delphi. The white marble walls shone with splendor despite the darkness that now loomed within its halls. Guards at the oak double doors looked them over before allowing them inside. Her father gave her a final hug before departing to his workstation.

Miral's duty today was to dust the castle library. A task that certainly took a day's work. She stopped at the supply closet to grab the cloth and waxes she needed for polishing. People were still speaking in hushed tones to each other about the news. Guards watched them all carefully and even swatted a man with their sword hilt when he stopped working to chat. She made her way with haste and began her work with care. She was blessed to have this job at all.

Near the end of her task, her wandering thoughts were interrupted by the sounds of two women chatting as they entered the library. Miral was on the second floor and listened to them as she worked.

"I think I know what happened!"

The voice belonged to Madrelin. She was the headmistress of the castle cleaning staff. She was speaking to Helen, the librarian. Her father often talked to Helen at length, she was a kind lady compared to Madrelin and never made Miral feel unwelcome.

"Oh, out with it!" replied Helen.

"I overheard King Charles and Queen Irana speaking in his private study the other night," Madrelin whispered while leaning in close to Helen.

Madrelin always spoke with a boisterous voice. The weak attempt to whisper was still loud enough to be heard by Miral in the echoing hall of freshly-dusted books.

"He was talking about a book he received as a gift titled, 'The Truth of Times,' or something like that. The author claimed the forbidden word was only made so by the elder races to prevent us from speaking it."

Helen gasped. "Did our king speak the word then?! Did it drive him to madness?! Did it kill him?!"

Miral turned away from her polishing and set the jar of wax and cloth down on the stool and crouched in front of it. The conversation had become rather frightening and begged for full attention. She covered her mouth with her hands and listened carefully.

"Aye, he had and the queen as well!" Madrelin replied with hands gesturing wildly. "Nothing happened, not to either of them! The book was right! The elder races must have kept it from us to keep us from our gods!"

"The nerve!" Helen said thrusting her arms down in frustration. "Who was the author of this book?"

"A scholar named Lord Azan wrote the ancient tome. Within he said the word *shadow* or *shadows* was a call to our divine goddess. We lost her favor when the elder races stopped us from speaking it. Then they had the gall to blame us when she disappeared from the World of Life two thousand years ago! Just because we were new to this world, they picked us to take the fall, to become their slaves, and their entertainment! They claim to have given us freedom three hundred years ago, but they continue to keep us subjugated! This is proof!"

"Curse those beast-men! How did the king die if it was not from saying . . ."

"Don't be afraid, Helen, just say it! Shadow!" Madrelin replied with her arms raised.

Helen jumped with fright. "Ah, so you have said it, and you're fine? Well then, shadow."

Goosebumps prickled Miral's skin as she heard the two gossiping women speaking the forbidden word freely. *Could Madrelin be right?*

"There you are! Well done, and now you too will be safe and protected! Perhaps the true goddess will return and grant us her favor over the elder races!" Madrelin cheered. "The queen has been rather odd of late, though. She goes about muttering to herself and repeats that an elder race killed him. Perhaps they found out that we know the truth and acted to stop us as the others have said!"

"What about the queen then? She is acting frantic. Has she not gone mad from fear as the other records claim occurs from speaking that word?"

"Helen, I think the elder races did that to her! Probably was Arisdale. They have the most to gain from our island, greedy vicious beasts that they are."

"That is true, Madrelin. What about you? Are you safe? Am I safe?!"

"The king and queen were the only ones in that room. The assassins must not know that I heard it as well. We must be careful though and spread this knowledge to the others quietly lest we meet the same fate!"

"Oh heavens! How would they have found out about the book?"

"They have that cursed magic like Akemi. I'm sure King Johanas Arisdale and his offspring Justin are watching Delphi . . ." Madeline said as she looked upwards.

15

Miral leaned back against the stool so she would not be seen and cringed when she knocked the wax jar off it. Madrelin's eyes found her and locked to her with a steely gaze.

"Maybe she knows something of that," Madrelin grumbled softly to Helen. She ascended the stairwell and stood before Miral with her arms crossed. "Akemi, finding it better to eavesdrop than to do your work?"

"No, I was working when you came in, but I hadn't heard anything, I swear!" She disliked lying but after all that was said, especially about cursed magic, she wasn't about to admit she heard it all.

Madrelin's face scrunched into a sinister cast. "Well, since you're obviously done and have nothing better to do, why don't you get supplies." She held her hand out with a folded paper. "Go to town and retrieve these items from the general shop."

"The . . . but they don't . . ." Miral stammered, biting her lip.

Madrelin rolled her eyes and huffed with annoyance. "I know and I don't care, go now!" Madrelin demanded shoving the list into her hands quickly while taking care not to touch her. She spun on her heel, her hair whipping around and stormed off while mumbling to herself.

Miral trembled slightly and unfolded the note. The list included soaps and cloth. Miral collected her cleaning supplies and headed to the closet to put them away. She didn't want to go to the store alone; however, her father was not at any of his usual stations. *Why wasn't he? Where could he be?*

Miral sighed. Madrelin enjoyed tormenting her, it was something she had come to expect. She stepped past the double doors, opened for her by the castle guards. It was a chilly day in Delphi, but the breeze felt refreshing as it blew past her, tossing her hair behind her like waves of the ocean. Palm tree leaves danced in the air. White colored seabirds cried out as they circled the market sector of town. The sky was a lovely shade of blue. The clouds were fluffy and soft. The wonderful scent of tropical flowers filled the air. Miral took a deep breath in through her nose and held it a moment. She would spend every day outside marveling at the wonders of life if she could. She looked at the dark form of her shadow on the ground before her. All the talk of the forbidden word left her skittish, her muscles rigid with tension.

She paused outside the door to the general shop staring at it with shifting eyes. The day appeared to be carrying a theme, and the theme was fear.

"Goddess Fandia, bless me," Miral whispered as she pushed open the door. The small bell over the door dinged, the soft sound more like a loud gong to Miral in her troubled state. The shop was full of supplies and nonperishable items. Its old and weathered keeper stood behind a long, waist high, oak counter. His face bore a look of shock.

"Akemi! Get out of my shop!" Harris shouted glaring at her menacingly with narrowed eyes and wrinkled scalp that was balding in the center.

"But I was sent by the queen's . . ." Miral murmured holding the list up in trembling hands. *Why did Madrelin send her? Nothing was going to be accomplished here, other than her own humility.*

"I don't care! Out now!" he said clenching his fist. His seething boiled over and he waved his hands wildly. "First, my wife dies from your mother's disease! Then you destroyed our home with your curse!"

Miral trembled under his gaze and stared at the circular-shaped scars on his arms, the remnants of the plague he survived. "It wasn't on purpose, none of it was. We never meant to hurt anyone."

"Well, you both had!" he said grinding his teeth. "Your mother must have bedded an elder race! That is how she brought the plague to us and that is how you developed their magic!"

Miral jumped in surprise. "No! Mother would never betray father!"

"How would you know?!" he said slamming his fist onto the wooden countertop, causing a jar to nearly topple over. "No human in history has ever had an ounce of magic! She was from Fovran! Everyone knows that land is mostly elder races and small communities of humans and half-breeds! How else do you explain your elder race curse, half-breed?! Out now!" he said pointing to the door, appearing ready to jump over the counter and toss her out himself.

Miral shivered and slowly backed out the door. *Elder race half-breed? That was a new and farfetched idea, but she had no other explanation for her unique curse of water magic. He didn't mean that, he is just upset, who can blame him after what happened.*

"He told you to get out!"

She felt a hand grab her shoulder and yank her backward. She stumbled and fell onto the hard cobblestone road. People erupted into laughter all around her. Miral looked back to see who had pulled her. It was the shopkeeper's son, Jed. She felt tears welling up in her blue eyes and looked away from him. She fought hard to keep herself from crying.

The people suddenly stopped laughing and murmurs spread through the crowd.

"What is one of them doing here?!" a man sneered.

"Need help, miss?"

Miral turned to the voice. It belonged to an elder race timber wolf. The elder races were various types of anthropomorphic animals with digitigrade legs and said to be the first creations of the Goddess of Light, Fandia. The wolf beside her had a furry human-like wrinkled face and bright yellow eyes, short white hair, fluffy brown and tan tail, and long ears that sat on the sides of his head and bent backward. He wore long baggy black pants and a green tunic. She stared at him transfixed, trembling with uncertainty. Jed swung a fist towards the wolf, but the elderly man caught his fist in his hand without taking his gentle eyes from her.

"Miss?" he asked once more in a soft and soothing tone, offering his hand.

Miral wasn't certain if she should accept his help after all that Madrelin had said but she didn't wish to remain in this situation. Besides, everyone deserved a chance. She took his hand and let him help her to her feet. The wolf turned to look at Jed. His eyes were piercing and made Jed shrink back slightly.

"May the goddess's light bless you," he said with a nod as he ushered her away from them.

Chapter 3 - Prophecy

She remained quiet as the wolf led her to the outskirts of town to the sea, trembling as she let him whisk her away, but something about him also made her feel safe as if he radiated a soothing energy.

"Are you all right?" the elder wolf asked her.

"I am, thank you," she replied in a lowered tone once they stopped walking and sat on the warm sands.

"Good, Yarlin will be along shortly," he said sitting beside her and staring at the ocean, eyes full of longing.

"My father? Why? How? Who are you?"

He turned to her and smiled. "I am a friend, don't you worry," he said, turning to look back out to sea again. "Delphi is a special place. I have always felt her presence here."

"Her presence?"

"The Goddess of Light, Fandia." His eyes returned to the look of desperation when he spoke of her.

"The Goddess of Light," Miral replied softly. The people of Delphi believed that if the goddess were real, she should have aided them. Why should they suffer under the fist of the elder races that once enslaved them if she were real? Why should humans believe what they did? Now with the book that King Charles had, that fire of disbelief burned brighter, and Madrelin would spread it. *Was Fandia a false goddess?* Her father told her to never lose faith in Fandia and the Silver Dolphins. She never would.

"Why did you help me?" Miral asked.

"Why not?" he replied. "You are not deserving of their disdain."

"But you're a . . ." she lowered her head not wanting to say the words.

19

"An elder race? That is just a label. We look different, but we are not different at all, Miral."

Miral jerked her head up. "How do you know my name?!"

He smiled at her. "I know many things."

"Miral!"

"Father?" Miral called as she looked behind her.

Her father stared at the wolf next to her with mouth agape scratching his head.

"You got my message," the wolf said, standing and reaching out his hand.

Her father looked at the tall wolf, studying him before shaking his hand. "You . . . I thought the message was from Miral."

"Greetings, Yarlin. I am sorry for the deception. Allow me to explain," he said with a nod. "I am here to deliver a warning to Miral. I wanted you to be here with her."

"A warning?!" Yarlin asked with a wrinkled brow.

"I am a prophet. I have foreseen a fate that involves your daughter."

Yarlin looked at the wolf with an arched eyebrow. "It's because of the wolves of Glenn that we humans gained freedom from the thousands of years of slavery and oppression the elder races placed on us. With the prophecy given to us we rose up as your kind told us we could three hundred years ago, and fought back against Arisdale. So, I will hear what you have to say."

The prophet smiled and bowed his head in respect to Yarlin. "In the days ahead, darkness will befall the kingdom of Delphi. She must flee from here at once."

"Darkness, Miral, why?" he asked.

"It's the water magic isn't it?" Miral asked rubbing her arms before crossing them.

"That is part of the why, and your water magic is not a curse but a gift, Miral. A blessing from the Goddess of Light."

My water magic is a blessing? She blinked with her thought.

"Now then, I know this is hard to ask of you, but I need you to go to the Kingdom of Arisdale."

Yarlin's blue eyes grew wide. "What?!" he exclaimed, running his hand through his hair. "How is that any better than being here?!"

"Stay and you will both meet your death for certain," he said. "Go to Arisdale and ask for the Elementals of Light. She will be safe in the kingdom of the earth under the guard of the protector." The prophet nodded to their silenced stares and turned to leave. "The goddess goes with you, trust in her."

Yarlin caught his arm. "Will you not go with us? It could help us plead our case to Arisdale!"

"I cannot," he replied, lowering his head. "My presence will only bring you more trouble."

Miral thought about his words and trembled. "Darkness is coming. I heard someone speaking of a book King Charles had that proclaimed the forbidden word was a lie, a trick of the elder races to keep us from the goddess."

His eyes grew wide. "Then it has been spoken," he said hanging his head. "Pray, what book?!"

"She said 'The Truth of Times' written by—"

The prophet lunged and covered her mouth. "Don't say his name!"

"Get away from my daughter!" Yarlin snapped shoving the man back.

The wolf stepped back slowly with hands palm up. "I mean no harm, but that word and that name are not to be spoken aloud, not even by the elder races. That book is a lie and it's dangerous, Miral. I pray you believe me." He nodded to them once more, turned away and walked into the setting sun towards the harbor.

"Father," Miral cried with a trembling voice, "I'm scared!"

He squeezed her tightly in an embrace, his beard rubbing her forehead. "Everything will be all right. Come now, I don't entirely trust him. Perhaps we should leave here anyway. I have been saving up so we could go somewhere no one knows about us. Arisdale though, any place is better than Arisdale."

"I could have a better chance in Glenn Harbor, but only if . . . only if I can hide my curse. I don't think I can! When you are gone, I'll be alone forever." Tears rolled down her cheeks, splashing as they landed on her pale folded hands.

"Miral, sweetheart, don't think about things like that. I'm not going to leave you anytime soon, ok?"

She wiped her tears away with her hands and stared at him. "I pray so, Father."

Chapter 4 - Nightmares

Miral sat at her vanity holding her brush and combing her long blue hair. This would be the last time she would sit in her small room at Delphi Castle. The thought of leaving was exciting her. A fresh start, a new home! It was the season of autumn and on the lush tropical island of Delphi, every season was the same, with only a slight temperature difference occurring as they approached winter. She had heard stories from minstrels of far off lands where trees would change their leaves from green to shades of yellow, orange, and red. Of frozen water that fell from the sky. It sounded enchanting, and she wished to see it all.

Miral looked into the mirror, her stomach churning, wide blue eyes staring back. Why was she warned to leave for safety? Her father insisted that speaking of the prophecy would only cause more trouble for her. The townsfolk were already superstitious and quick to judge. Madrelin likely told everyone she favored about King Charles and the tome by now, spreading the forbidden word and the author's name around. She would just be blamed for the darkness when it came.

She wondered whom the protector was that the prophet had mentioned. *Someone from Arisdale could help her, protect her?* The notion was rather absurd. *What did she need to be protected from? What was the darkness?*

Miral yawned and shook her head to clear the thoughts as they raced about. She stood from the vanity to lie down on her bed. Soft rolls of thunder broke the silence. Rain pattered hard against the stones of Delphi Castle. The sound caused her to shudder . . . the rain . . . just like that horrible day. She took long deep breaths. Her eyes grew heavy with each inhale and exhale, and she fell asleep the moment she closed her eyes.

Miral opened her eyes, torn from peaceful sleep by the insistent urging of her father's voice. The sun dimly peeked through the windows of her small room, but she could see that he was bloody and frantic as he shook her.

Between gasps for air, he urged her from bed. "We must go now! Put this on quickly!" He handed Miral her mother's old ginger and white dress and turned away looking out the door into the hall.

"What is happening?!" Miral asked as she turned her back to her father pulling her nightgown off and frantically slipping the dress on, pushing her arms through the long puffy white sleeves with pink cuffs.

"No time to explain, the prophet was right. Hurry along!"

She tied the pink scarf belt, and her father pulled her by the arm, through the halls of Delphi castle. Outside the servants' quarters, there were trails of blood on the ground, but no bodies. She secured her mother's gold and red gemstone brooch at the collar while her eyes darted around the blood-spattered white marble walls. She gathered her hair into a high ponytail, wrapping a pink ribbon around it, and tying it tight. Her mind raced with thoughts of what could be happening as they ran. Distant sounds of battle and screams of terror blended like a deranged choir and echoed through the hall. She felt as if her chest was squeezed in a tight embrace with the sounds.

The queen's advisor Gostre was directing panicked people where to flee. Miral saw that he carried his dueling sword and frowned. She thought about helping them with her magic but froze. Her father pulled her down a hall away from where Gostre had sent the others. The wall leading to the front gates was painted with smeared red handprints. The ground of the corridor was carpeted down the middle with slick crimson goo. The coppery scent of blood grew heavier in the salty air. Her father seemed to know what was going on. Perhaps he was afraid of her being blamed for this and wanted to avoid the others. She was snapped out of her thoughts when her father abruptly pulled her back. He had stopped a few feet away from a large pool of blood on the ground. The dread on his face was unlike any she had ever seen before.

"Father, what is wrong?! Tell me something!" she cried, gripping his arm with white knuckles.

23

He remained silent eyeing the floor intently. A quiet curse escaped his lips.

A Delphinian soldier jumped in before them. "I'll cover you, go now!"

She didn't recognize the man with his helmet and red-stained face. The soldier approached the large glob of red, battle ready and with caution. She didn't understand why they both were afraid of the large puddle on the ground. It was just blood, like on all the walls and floors they had passed to come this far.

Yarlin pulled her in a sprint past the soldier. She looked back over her shoulder, and her curiosity was answered when she saw two dripping outstretched human-like arms rise from the puddle. An eerie high-pitched cooing sound emitted from the creature as it rose from the floor into a blob. The thing pulled the man into its undulating mass. The soldier was gone in an instant, shrieking in pure terror as he vanished. The monstrosity sounded as if it was giggling with delight as it slid after them. Behind it was all that remained of the soldier. Blood-soaked bones and armor. Miral's eyes went wide with fright. She wanted to scream, but her breath was constricted in her chest. *What is that thing?!*

Miral and Yarlin exited the castle's double doors with the demon following close behind. A group of guards ran past them and fought against the sickly mass. Yarlin urged her to keep moving, but Miral glanced back at the battle behind them. One guard fell swiftly as one of the gooey tentacles wrapped around his midsection cutting the man in half. Blood spurted and blanketed the ground. Even as they fled distant from the horror, screams of agony cut sharply through the air. Miral turned her head forward as shouts erupted from in front of them as well.

Masses of people were fleeing from the village harbor towards the castle in a mad dash while screaming, "Arisdale is invading!"

Arisdale invading?! The prophet had said Arisdale would be safe. Now she wasn't so certain, and her father looked to be sharing her worry in his frightened eyes. The prophet was an elder race wolf. Perhaps he was trying to goad her into going to Arisdale of her own volition.

In the distance, Miral could see a large ship and two smaller ones headed toward the docks. The large ship was by far the biggest vessel she had ever seen. The ships had crimson and gold sails and a golden bird on the front sail. The crest of Arisdale. It was true, they were invading!

Yarlin shouted and swung his arms in hailing. "No, don't go to the castle, there is a demon inside!" The madness that spread among the masses caused his pleas to go unheard.

Miral saw Jed approach her from the corner of her eye, jogging at a brisk pace. He shoved her hard once he was before her, causing her to fall to the ground.

"This is your doing, Akemi, once again; you and your elder race blood!" Jed spat, and then ran on towards the castle with his father.

"That isn't true! I haven't done anything!"

"Miral!" Yarlin cried out to her.

Miral stood and looked around frantically for her father but could not find him through the stampede of people. "Father!" she cried in desperation.

"Meet me at the outer docks!" he shouted.

His voice was faint, but she did as he said and ran towards the outer docks. They could still escape Delphi without being caught by Arisdale if they slipped out there.

Chapter 5 - Arrival

As the Arisdalian ships pulled into the docks of Delphi's harbor, it was quite apparent that something was amiss. The harbor was emptier than they were accustomed to in the early part of the day. What people were there ran quickly towards the castle when they caught sight of the ships.

Colonel Fai Martizar, an elder race dragon from Volga and the highest-ranking royal guard who attended them, stepped up to the plank and scanned the horizon with her green-blue scaled hand over her eyes. She turned to face them with a look of uneasy concern. "I don't like this, Majesty. I think it best if you remain within the cover of the ship until we learn what this is ab—"

"I beg your pardon, Your Graces," a Delphinian man shouted as he approached them with several guards trailing him.

Johanas narrowed his eyes. The man was dressed in silk robes. "Pray, you have a lot of explaining to do."

His six royal guards tightened a line before him allowing him only a glimpse over their shoulders at the approaching man.

The short and portly man quickly knelt. "Yes, a thousand pardons for what you witnessed and, of course, for being late to attend you, Your Graces. I am Ambassador Markien."

"Pray, what have we witnessed exactly, ambassador? I have never seen humans running in terror from us, surely obscenities and other vulgar behaviors, but never this."

"The queen wished to know the real feelings of her people, so she had not informed them of your pending arrival to gauge their reaction to your sudden visit."

His guards tensed, as did he and his sons. "To gauge their honest reactions, you say?" Johanas retorted. "I know not what your monarchs were thinking in this, but 'twas a foolish thing to do! By the gods, this misunderstanding could have ended in the unnecessary injury to her people or one of us! Then where would we be but back where we were or worse?"

The man lifted his red eyes to meet the king's. "Of course, Your Majesty is quite wise indeed. We had not expected this level of panic. All will be well though I assure you. The people have gathered at the castle and are being promptly addressed and sent on their way as we speak."

Johanas stared at the man with skepticism. "I will send two guards with you to ensure your words are justified. If they return and swear to me the truth of what you say, then I will attend you."

"As you wish, Your Majesty," the man said as he stood and bowed.

"Allow me, Your Majesty," Colonel Fai quickly replied with a salute. "I will take Major Clement with me, sire."

Johanas nodded in agreement. "Very well, return swiftly and safely."

The royal guards turned to salute in unison, spun on their heels, and descended the plank to follow the ambassador back to the castle. He watched as they faded into the horizon then turned to look at everyone present. The low-ranking guards were outfitted in white and iron-edged armor. Gold was reserved for royal guards and the royal family. Justin, Agar, and Yarway were dressed in suits of white and gold armor with more ornate decorations than the royal guards. Justin had green gems, Agar orange, and Yarway purple, each based on their elemental power. General Dilos Manning and Captain Severos Miragaia remained in Arisdale to protect the people in their absence. The royal guards with him were all excellent soldiers, chosen by himself and some by his father, King Roryian Arisdale.

"What say you?" he asked them all.

"He appeared to be honest, Father," Justin replied. "Though I agree with you that there are certainly better ways to understand the feelings of your people."

"Oh, perhaps the Delphinians are just afraid and as such, simply made a poor choice of judgment," Anelda murmured.

"I hope so! Sure is making my fur stand on end," Agar replied. "What about you, Yarway?"

Yarway nodded. "Humans are odd."

The four royal guards nodded in agreement to all that was said.

"At least the trek to the castle is not a long one. We should have our answer soon enough," Johanas said with a shrug. "I will be quite cross to have come all this way for naught." He glanced at his son who was staring absently towards the castle, red cape flapping in the breeze, his eyes searching as if watching something unseen. "Justin? What has your focus so, my son?" Despite his words, his son continued to search.

Justin blinked as Johanas touched his arm. "Father, I have seen the magic energy of a water elemental. 'Tis curious to find that presence here; however, perhaps there is a visiting elder race with the gift. They are moving from the castle towards the harbor."

Yarway and Agar perked up and followed Justin in the sightless search. Johanas wondered what it was like to be able to see magic, the color, the energy, as his son did. Certainly took a lot of time and adjustment to become accustomed to living with one elemental, though Galena was never troublesome and a great aid with her healing magic. When his son was given the gift of earth, things took a drastic and trying turn. Five years later Agar was bouncing off the walls of his home, and that was by no means an exaggeration.

"Father!" Justin boomed with excitement. "They are near the harbor over yonder and may leave!" He pointed to the north. "May I go speak with them? I mean if all is well here, and even if 'tis not so, 'twould be regretful to let the opportunity to meet with a water elemental pass. I would love to combine powers with them to help for once, rather than . . . well you know, destroy something."

Johanas blinked in surprise. "Justin, if all is well we should not keep the king and queen waiting."

His son folded his hands together in pleading. "Father, pray, let me speak with the Elemental of Water! I will not be long. You can start without me. I am a good negotiator. I am sure I could convince them to meet with us at a later date."

"Oh, Johanas, let him go do this," Anelda said smiling at Justin. "You do wish to collect all the elementals together in one place, do you not?" she giggled.

"Ah, well, I am eager to see what we can all do together! Sara Phoenix said such a meeting does not exist in recorded history," Justin said with a bright smile.

Johanas sighed, "Very well then, Justin. Make it quick and come straight away," he said, then glanced at Agar whose eyes darted from Justin to himself. "Agar, you are staying with me."

Agar drooped his ears and nodded. "Aww man, ok."

"You have my word, Father!" Justin said with a bow.

"Take two of the colonel's guards with you and be safe, my son."

"Thank you, Father!" Justin walked down the plank and headed to the north end of the harbor with two guards behind him.

Chapter 6 - Fate

The outer docks were vacant of the usual people; fishing poles and nets were left behind, and merchant carts were abandoned. The eerie silence prickled her skin as she searched for her father. "Father! Where are you?!" Miral gasped and covered her mouth when her eyes fell upon a towering, broad-shouldered and muscular Arisdalian in ornate armor beyond some crates. Two shorter Arisdalians in simpler iron-lined armor flanked him. They were all different species, but certainly from Arisdale. She stepped back and hid in the darkness of the sheds, but the taller one turned swiftly in her direction as if he already knew she was there. He marched his digitigrade legs at a determined pace towards her, and the two that were with him followed behind.

"Halt there, maiden. I mean you no harm," the dark brown Arisdalian said in a deep, authoritative, and aristocratic tone. His long feather-tipped tail swayed as he walked, and his sharp sickle-shaped toe claws clacked against the cobblestone road. Each rhythmic step he took rattled her nerves. Miral's instincts begged her to run, and she dashed between the narrow spaces of two harbor sheds and out the other side.

"Just like the stories!" she blurted as she ran with all her might, praying her father was nearby. The elders had told stories of the ferocious Arisdalian Velociraptor, who would hunt human children at night, coming to take them from their beds as they slept to eat them. The people often told stories of their species' crude and violent nature. She wasn't sure if any of them were true; however, now she would learn the truth for herself. She stopped fast when the brown Arisdalian man stepped out in front of her, grasping her shoulders with his black-clawed hands. He was alone.

"Pray maiden, allow me to speak with you," he said exasperated, removing his large hands from her and holding them palm up before resting them to his sides in a gesture of peace.

She froze, feelings of awe and terror blending together at the sight before her. She backed up slowly and cautiously, her trembling hands clasped together over her chest. Arisdalians were wicked in appearance! Large claws, sharp teeth, and so tall! He said something to her, but she had not heard him. She knew the dread she felt had destroyed any clarity in her mind. Fear of whether or not she would survive this unexpected encounter overtook her.

She remembered the elders saying that the Velociraptor was fast and agile and if you were to face one, how to read them. If the killer claw is erect, they intend to attack. If their crest of head feathers were raised, they are scared or threatened. The points of the sickle claw were touching the cobblestones. She craned her neck to look up at him, and he appeared to be calm since his big Mohawk style of sandy-tan head feathers were not standing on end. She stared into his intimidating eyes taking them in thoroughly. They were large, angular and rather handsome in shape. His irises were a golden yellow with orange accents, which made them appear as if they were on fire. The darkness was broken up by a sandy-tan color that ran through his lower jaw, and down the middle of his neck. She found herself at a loss for words and simply stared at the giant dinosaur while trembling. He was staring back at her with an intense gaze, and she was not certain, but a look that could possibly be confusion adorned his face. She saw the corners of his mouth pull back into what looked like a smile, and his eyes softened and appeared to be smiling too.

"Maiden, I am terribly sorry if I scared you," he said in a lowered tone while bowing his head. "I mean you no harm."

The rows of serrated teeth that lined his jaws glistened in the sunlight contradicting his words. Miral felt as if she was prey being stared down by a hungry predator.

The man spoke in a sing-song voice, calm and fluidly. "After we arrived here I felt your magic energy and decided to locate you before meeting the others at the castle. I wish to extend the greetings of the king and queen of Arisdale, and to inform you that, and if you desire, you may meet with us, and talk," he said with another bow of his head. "We extend the same courtesies to all Elementals of Light. Though I must say I am amazed to have found a human with elemental magic, indeed the first in recorded history, maiden. I ramble. However, I thank you for hearing me out."

He paused swinging his sandy-tan feather-tipped tail back and forth, his crimson cape moving with the sweeps. "Pray, if I may ask, why did you run away in terror?"

Miral stood rigidly still as she listened to him speak. He sounded honest and non-threatening; however, she wasn't at all sure that she trusted him. A gust of wind billowed a rectangular cloth that hung from his gold, green-gemmed belt. The cloth was emblazoned with the royal crest of Arisdale: a golden bird with two longer red tail feathers. Perhaps he was a high-ranking guard. "You're an Arisdalian," she replied.

The man straightened, which only made him appear taller than he was before. He looked at her with his head tilted slightly to the right. She wondered if that helped him to see better past his long snout.

"That is the obvious observation, maiden. I know we are not on the best of terms; however, any tales told to cause panic on this scale are grossly exaggerated, I assure you."

Miral blinked and stared at him in bewilderment. It is hard to process the soft and caring tone he used without his other menacing features taking over and making him appear intimidating instead. "Well, there are some terrible stories, but we all think you're invading, so I ran," she said while pointing back in the direction of the harbor. She really wanted to go find her father instead of speaking to this mountain of a man, but she was too rigid to move.

"Invading?!" he exclaimed, his head feathers spiked upward then settled back down. "Heavens, I assure you we are not. We were invited here by your king and queen to establish relations, trade, and hopefully peace," he rubbed his lower jaw with his four-clawed hand. "Ah, maiden, forgive me. I have delayed too long and must take my leave. I pray you consider what I have told you. I thank you for your time, and pray we meet again," he said with a bow and turned to leave.

"Wait!" Miral cried out, shocking herself with her own outburst. "Don't go to the castle!"

The Arisdalian man turned to address her with a wrinkled brow. "I do not like your tone with those words. Pray, explain."

"I work in the castle with my father. We fled because of a prophecy that was given to me, and there is a demon eating people in there! It chased us outside, and I don't know where it is now, or my father!" Miral said, tears welling up in her eyes.

The man tensed, his head feathers rose once more and remained on end as his eyes widened. "A demon?! Eating people?! Goddess Fandia be blessed! I must be going then!" he said in a wavering tone and turned back to leave once more but stopped and looked back at her, his head feathers relaxing. "Prophecy, I would much like to hear about this at another time. If you wish to leave this place, go to the largest ship. Explain to the guards that you had spoken to me and who you are. I pray you find your father as well."

He left at a fast pace turning the corner he came from and was gone. She breathed in deep to calm herself. Having spoken with him, she wasn't even sure who he was.

"Miral!"

She faintly heard her father calling her name and ran to his voice. "Father! Where are you?!"

She heard a woman scream and gasped. Her father was backing up with hands held before him. Helen was behind him, and the blood demon was inching up to them, cooing and giggling as it reached its tentacles at him in a teasing manner.

"Run, Helen!" Yarlin shouted.

Miral saw Helen glance her way briefly with a look of remorse before she ran down the alley to her right. Her father continued to back up and was a couple hundred feet away. Her mind screamed to run to him and yet made her freeze in horror at the sight of the creature. She followed her mind and ran to her father not knowing what she could do to fight the thing without her magic.

"No!"

She was jolted to a stop after the deep voice of a man cried out. There was pressure on her chest. She looked down at her mother's brooch, which was pressing painfully inwards as if it wanted to go through her. She heard the clicking sound of claws against cobblestone behind her. The same Arisdalian man she met just a moment ago paused beside her. He raised his hands before him and a green glow surrounded him, then her, and finally her father. There was a familiar pulsing energy radiating from it, the same energy she felt with her own magic.

"What good do you think 'twill do to run in there!" he scolded.

He stepped out ahead of her and stomped his foot hard into the ground. The cobbles loosened from the impact and fractured with the force. They rose into the air, pausing before his outstretched hand. He thrust his arm forward and sent the rocks at blazing speeds into the blood demon. They punched straight through the being, slamming hard against the wall of the stone building beside it with loud cracks. The creature remained intact laughing with a gurgle and began poking at the green glow around her father. The magic force had protected him from the demon's tentacles; however, the thing kept jabbing at the glow until it dissipated, then stopped.

"Miral, go with him," Yarlin cried as he stared at her. "I love you, sweetheart!"

The blood demon cooed in reply and drove its gooey tentacles towards her father's chest.

The Arisdalian man spun towards her blocking her view of her father and pulled her tightly to him. "Pray, do not look!"

She fought the man's embrace, but he was far too strong. She could hear her father's screams and then there was silence. "Father! Father, no!" Miral yelled fighting to look past the wall of a man. "No!"

"By the gods!" the Arisdalian exclaimed in disbelief as he hefted her up in his arms and ran from the blood demon.

"Let me go! Let me go now!" Miral cried and screamed pounding her hands against his breastplate. "Father!"

"Pray, maiden, would you cease doing that?!"

Her pounding slowed until she stopped and clutched his armor tightly, crying in racking sobs. She had just told her father yesterday that she would be lost without him, and now her worst fears had come to pass.

"I am terribly sorry. I cannot fathom how you are feeling right now, but I can certainly sympathize," the man replied in a sincere tone. "There was nothing more we could have done. Magic attacks were worthless against that thing."

"I don't care! I won't leave him! Let me go!"

"I am sorry, I will not. My conscience will not allow me to leave you there to die. I shall respect the last wishes of your father and bring you with me, by your will or not."

She cried as he spoke, the pain in her heart demanded more tears. Her helplessness against the demon that killed her father and this man who held her in an iron grip frustrated her. She looked over his shoulder and saw that they were headed away from the harbor and towards the castle.

"No, no don't take me back in there!" she screamed pounding on his breastplate once more.

"Maiden, I have little choice in the matter! My family and friends are in this castle. I can feel the magic of the other Elementals—"

He stopped running abruptly before the stairs to the castle doors. His eyes wincing then growing wide as they darted around at something unseen. His head feathers danced in waves as they lifted and fell. At the same time, she felt the odd sensation of heaviness and heartache roll through her.

"What was that?!" she asked.

"Gods no, pray, do not be dead, Agar, Yarway," he murmured with a quiver in his voice. His face softened and then scrunched tightly, teeth bared, head feathers remaining tensed. He set her down gently. "Stay beside me," he demanded, as he climbed the steps.

Miral stood still trembling as she looked at the blood-stained walls and ground. She felt his large hand grasp her left arm and tug on her.

"Come now!" he ordered.

She cowered at his barking tone and followed behind him unwillingly. He was strong, and she wasn't able to fight being pulled along. She didn't even know his name yet, but he now knew hers, even if he didn't say it. She wanted to ask him what his was but kept her silence as they entered the eerie castle.

Chapter 7 - Darkness

Once within the darkened castle, the towering Arisdalian whipped his head from side to side taking in the sights and sniffing the air. The smell of blood and death was potent, and Miral felt nauseous. She wondered how bad that smell could be to someone with a snout like his.

She peered up at him and in the darkness, she noticed that the gems on his large shoulder pads gave off a brilliant green light that slowly pulsed brighter, dimmed, and then pulsed again. When he turned towards her and gazed down the hall to the right, she saw that all the crystals on his armor had the same rhythmic glow. Ethereal gems, she knew about them but had never seen them set in armor before. They were only used for lighting in Delphi castle. There were several lanterns of clear ethereal gems along the walls as they walked on.

The man pushed forward through the oak double doors ahead of them, still sniffing the air. They entered the throne room, and a gruesome scene unfolded before them.

"Queen Irana?!" Miral muttered.

The Arisdalian man turned his eyes to her, they were set in a glower, but quickly turned their focus back to her queen.

"Finally, the oldest Prince arrives! Why have you kept me waiting? I was most eager to meet you dearest, Justin," Queen Irana Delphi said, followed by a bellowed laugh.

Miral gasped. This man who has been toting her around was the Prince of Arisdale. She folded her hands together before her as she blushed.

The woman did not look like the kind queen she had come to know and love. She appeared wicked and lifeless now, and her formerly blue eyes were glowing red. Miral stared dumbfounded at two Arisdalian guards in white and gold armor that stood beside the queen protectively.

"I see you brought me a gift as well!" she said gesturing to Miral. "How kind of you to return my servant to me!"

Miral stared wide-eyed at Irana and grabbed hold of Prince Justin's arm tightly. *A gift?!* She gasped, the prince didn't react to her impulsive move. His focus was deeply set on the scene ahead of them. She let go of his arm twiddling her fingers together and looking to the ground.

"Mother, father?!" Justin cried out. "Pray, Colonel Fai, Major Clement, why are you just standing there?!" he shouted in a scolding tone.

Miral followed Justin's gaze to a white elder race bird with pink colored head and tail feathers, and an Arisdalian man with green eyes that closely resembled the prince. They were on the ground next to Queen Irana. The king and queen of Arisdale, they were bloody, and weakly gazed up at their son.

"Justin, Agar. Get out of here now!" his father groaned.

Miral looked across the room. All the Arisdalian guards, save the two beside the queen, were dead. A red fox lay lifelessly on the floor. An elder race white tiger was standing with daggers drawn to their left. She could have sworn he wasn't there when they walked into the room. The ground around the throne room was scorched in places. Queen Irana's black dress was also burnt, in tatters, and soaked with blood from deep gashes in her flesh. A pool of blood grew at her feet. It appeared as though they had all attacked her, but the mortally deep wounds hadn't affected her. *How could she defeat so many and still be standing?*

"What is the meaning of this?!" Justin bellowed. A small quake rumbled the ground with his words.

Miral folded her hands together over her heart. She hated the idea of being inside the castle more now than before.

"I would tell you, Justin, but that would ruin my fun!" Queen Irana mocked, her face bearing a twisted smirk.

Justin glared into Queen Irana's unnaturally glowing red eyes. A deep guttural growl rolled through him causing Miral to shiver with goosebumps.

"Fun?!" Justin shouted in reply. "You truly think this is fun?!"

"You met the Virabis, yes? Did she entertain you as I asked her to?"

"Virabis, my Queen, that thing killed my father!" Miral replied with a lowered head and sobs. "Why would you ask for that?!"

Irana smiled. "Of course, it had, dearest. Why?" Irana laughed. "Because I can, just like I can command the king's two guards here! They did an excellent job convincing him it was safe. At least, until he smelled the blood, then I had to be forceful."

Miral stared blankly at Queen Irana, her voice stolen by the grief the spoken words conjured and was replaced with sobs.

"She has dark magic of some sort, brother," the elder race white tiger interjected, looking up at Justin.

Justin remained silent, keeping his gaze locked on Queen Irana as she paced across the room once more. Beneath her sobs, Miral wondered why the elder race tiger had called the prince brother, and why did he say that the queen had dark magic?

"I know what you're thinking right now, dearest. You're planning the best way to attack me." She looked down and held her arms out to her sides. "You see clearly that I have slain all your guards, and this pathetic Elemental," she teased lifting her head slowly to meet Prince Justin's eyes. She smirked. "Abandon that thought, dearest, I am more than prepared to deal with you!"

The green glow of magic surrounded Justin as he charged forward growling. A flood of people swarmed in front of Queen Irana forming a tight line. Justin halted and stared with narrowed eyes at the row of civilians.

Madrelin, Helen, Gostre, other castle staff and even children stood with the two Arisdalian guards as a shield before the queen. *Whose side should she be on now?* Her queen frightened her and so did the prince. She felt herself moving forward, but Prince Justin shot his arm out in front of her.

"No!" he scolded keeping his eyes on Queen Irana.

"Come now, dearest, let the girl make her own decisions, hmm? She would make a great guard. A shame I hadn't considered that before."

Miral stepped back. "I won't fight, and I won't hurt anyone ever."

"Sure, dear, sure, don't fight. You will make things easier for me then."

Justin raised his hands as if he was going to cast his green glow once more, but nothing happened. Miral saw his eyes crease as he lowered his hands.

Irana glanced at Justin with a smirk. "What is the matter, dearest? Your protection magic is not working on my minions? No longer willing to attack because of hurting them? Did I guess right about your moral weakness?" she teased.

Justin growled. "You are a coward, Irana! I can see the lifelessness in these people's eyes, the dark magic that surrounds them. Are you afraid to face me?!" he bellowed, and the room rattled with a quake once more raining bits of rock and dust down from the ceiling.

"Afraid of you? Don't make me laugh, dearest! I'm simply having fun with you while I can! So, I take it you won't risk these pathetic whelps' lives even if I should . . ." Irana rounded on his parents, a scythe made of black and glowing purple wisps formed in her hands, "kill them?!"

Justin thrust his hand out once more, and the magic green glow surrounded his parents.

"Justin, you have to know that we are proud of you and your choice. We love you both!" Queen Anelda cried embracing Johanas tightly.

Queen Irana grinned. "Isn't that sweet," she swung her scythe and struck both with a slash through their bodies. The green glow dissipated, and there was no blood. The shadowy weapon passed right through them as if cutting at their souls.

They all watched in horror as the king and queen fell lifelessly to the ground beside Queen Irana.

"No!" Justin roared. "I will kill you!"

Miral tensed and placed her hands over her heart. A strong quake rattled the castle with ferocity. More dust and bits of rock rained down in various locations.

The elder race white tiger reached out for Prince Justin, who lunged forward to attack. "Justin, no! Come on, let's go!" he urged in tears, locking his arms around his brother, and struggling to pull him back. "We can't fight her, we already tried that!"

"Let me go, Agar!" Justin bellowed.

Agar urged him on more insistently. "These are innocent victims, and you will not wish to hurt them! Let's go now!"

"Get them!" Irana said pointing. The line of people ran forward, more that were hidden on the sides of the room joined the flood.

Justin relented, spun, and took Miral by surprise as he swept her off her feet and helped her onto his back. "Hang on to me!"

39

Miral wrapped her arms around his neck and locked her legs together in front of him as he ran out the door with the elder race tiger he had called Agar.

Chapter 8 - The Protector

Justin saw the herd of people pouring out of the castle through his wide peripheral vision. He knew it would be best for their escape to keep the people contained. With his will, the energies of his earthen magic were channeled into the ground. He raised his hands, the ground cracked and split in front of the gate to the castle as he envisioned it. He thrust his arms into the air as he passed the gate and a wall of earth jutted up from the ground behind him, blocking the opening. The lady that clung to his back tightened her grip. Witnessing magic was certainly new to her.

"Very nice touch, brother," Agar said. "You still make me wish I could do things like that!"

Justin smiled at Agar briefly. His brother never liked negative or depressing situations, jokes were a sort of comfort to him. His eyes darted forward as a glint of light fell within his visual range.

"Archers!" he called to Agar before leaping, spinning to the left, and dodging a volley of arrows from men that were hiding ahead of them.

Agar vanished in a flash. The energy of his lightning magic surrounded him as he moved forward, hidden from the eyes of the archers.

Justin launched himself ten feet into the air, pushing against the earth below by manipulating the magnetic field to keep him high and moving forward. He willed his magic to form a barrier around himself and the lady named Miral. The channeled spell completed and a green glow shielded them. Arrows were reflected off the translucent wall by the earthen tips they bore.

The momentum of his speed as he flew brought him forward and above the archer to the left. He targeted the man on his descent pointing his left foot ahead with sickle claw erect. He aimed to slash the man's shoulder, leaving a harmless bloody gash. Justin hit the ground. A loud crack and flash of light erupted beside him. It was Agar, and his spell sent the other archers hurdling through the air a few feet from him. Miral tightened her hold with a death grip again, causing him to glance back into her rounded eyes.

"Are you all right?" he asked.

"Yes, I'm ok," she replied.

His relief faded when a sea of humans appeared in every direction, swarming their location. "Curses, get down!" Justin said stooping slightly so she could hop down from his back.

He channeled his protective barrier once more, shielding his brother as well. "King's guard," Justin called to Agar.

They each stood to a side of Miral in a defensive formation they learned in training and fought against the swarm as they trickled in while pushing forward to the ship. Justin's powerful shoves, fueled by his innate gift of earth magic sent attackers hurdling into others, knocking them down on impact. Agar clapped his hands together emitting that same loud crack and burst of light as before, sending attackers flying.

Justin wrapped his arm around Miral, moving her with him as he swept his leg in an arc and kicked a group of mindless assaulters. A sword swung toward her, and he stopped the weapon in the air with a thought, latching on to the magic within the earthen metal. With a push of his hand, the sword was torn from the man's grasp and sent flying to be embedded in a wooden crate. He turned towards a soldier in iron-plated armor charging him and lifted the man into the air as he raised his hand. He thrust it out. The man soared back into a group of other armored guards. He extended his hands once more and sent the entire pile of them flying back farther.

"Justin!" Miral cried in alarm grabbing hold of his arm.

He froze with the panicked sound of her voice and turned his head to briefly look in the direction she was pointing.

"The Virabis!" Miral said with a quiver, her grip on him tightening.

Justin watched the mass of undulating red moving towards them consuming whatever innocent soul was in its path. "Hellspawn of darkness!" he said apprehensively fighting back the swarm. "Definitely time to be going!"

"That is an understatement, big brother!" Agar replied.

Justin and Agar redoubled their efforts to part the sea of Delphinians. There was nowhere to go, and the mass of mindless souls was growing in number. Justin struggled to fight them all back. He took blows from multiple fists, and exhaustion was beginning to take its toll.

"Your highness! The ships!" Miral called pointing to the harbor.

Justin whipped his head around to look towards his ships and saw them beginning to pull out to sea. "By the gods! I am both angry at them for retreating and yet glad that they are, and I am not sure which is better!"

Agar chuckled. "Look at it this way, brother, it certainly makes getting off this island a bit more entertaining!"

Justin rolled his eyes but laughed slightly at Agar's remark, which died as sigh took its place. "Agar, we must take some risks if we are going to make it in time. Goddess, forgive us," Justin said with remorse.

Agar frowned and drooped his ears. "You got it."

"What?!" Miral replied in shock.

Agar stopped to channel a spell, his eyes closed in focus. Miral's hair lifted into the air weightless with the increasing static around them. Sparkles of light flickered around them, and a buzzing sound grew louder. Rumbles and claps of thunder rolled overhead. Bolts of lightning streaked down and danced around them. The might of the electricity repelled attackers away as it connected with the ground with an explosive crack.

Justin knelt. "Climb up!" he commanded Miral.

She quickly laid against his back once more. He lifted her and sprinted forward. With a quick glance behind him, he saw the Virabis gaining on them. He watched in horror as the monstrosity plowed forward through the mass of Delphinians, blood spraying in fountains as it passed through them. He heard the eerie sound of a woman's laughter coming from the creature. It looked bigger than the last time he saw it, taking on a slender, tall shape, rather than a blob.

"What is that thing?!" Agar asked in a panicked voice.

"I do not know, brother!" Justin replied, wrapping an arm around Agar and lifting him. "Hang on tight, maiden!"

He felt Miral tightening her grip as he leapt from the edge of the wharf, narrowly escaping the Virabis's arm-like appendages as it reached for them. The ship was easily forty feet from the dock now, but for him, getting to it was a simple task. His magic connected with earth from the shore and the sea below. He pushed against it using magic energy to float. The monstrosity stopped fast at the edge of the wharf emitting a scream.

Justin reached his hand towards the ship and used his will to grab hold of a pulley attached to a rope that he knew would be there. He used that rope to swing from the ship before while training his magic capabilities at sea. The pulley and rope extended and remained there as if waiting for him to reach it. He grabbed hold of the rope with both hands; it fell slack as he released his magical grip, and his momentum swung them towards the ship.

Agar raised his arm in the air as they sailed towards the ship. "Wee!"

Justin couldn't help but laugh at his brother. *'Twas the simple things in life that amused Agar so.*

The ship crew watched with wide eyes as Justin braced for impact with the ship using his feet, landed on the side with a loud thump, and climbed up. Once on the ship deck, Justin knelt so Miral could drop down. They turned to take in the horrible scene they just escaped from. The brothers stood rigidly with clenched fists and angered eyes.

Justin turned away from them and stood tall with hands on his hips, head feathers fluffed up. "Which one of you thought 'twas a good idea to leave your monarchs behind?!"

The ship crew fell to their knees trembling before Prince Justin.

He looked at the helm of the ship and narrowed his eyes. "I demand an answer!"

The crew remained silent with heads hung low.

Agar approached and stood before him. "Brother, I am angry too, but you need to back down, ok? Remember what —" he grew quiet and squeezed his eyes tight, "what mother would say. You're falling into rage, ok? Pray, let me take care of this."

Justin growled, turned away from them, sat on the deck, and closed his eyes. He knew Agar was right. With slow deep breaths, his head feathers relaxed, and he continued the soothing meditation as his mother taught him; however, in the stillness of his mind the grief returned. Doubts about whether he truly had done all he could, if his nature had failed him, entered in like roaches in the dark, greedily taking advantage of the fear that now took root in his mind. He knew fear was a dangerous entity, and it had to be faced, dealt with, before it could grow and take control.

Chapter 9 - Anger

Agar cleared his throat. "All right, we have a ship to run and a home to get back to quickly!" he shouted. "Justin is in command now, and I'm sure you understand what that means. We may have to fight our way back so prepare your arms. Get to it or I'll shock all your arses into motion!" Agar said with a sparking clap of his hands. He turned to look at the beautiful young lady his brother brought to the castle with him. He brushed a strand of black hair from his eyes and bowed to her. "Prince Agar Sabier Arisdale, fair maiden, and who might you be?"

She curtsied. "Miral Akemi, Your Highness."

Agar smiled wide at her. "A lovely name for a lovely lady." He grinned when he saw her cheeks flush red. Humans had a funny way of showing embarrassment; however, it was flattering on a lady. A loud crack erupted behind them, and they both turned to see what it was.

Justin was on his knees punching the wood deck with his fist. The force broke through the cedar deck of the ship with ease. He was growling furiously, punching multiple holes into the wood. His older brother was never able to manage his anger well; however, he was calmer and more caring than the Arisdales that came before him. The velociraptor family line has always been known for aggression and easy anger. Being an elemental is what set Justin apart from his ancestors; he had no choice but to control his anger better. The punching ceased, and he trembled, followed by sounds of muted sobbing.

"W . . .Wait!" Agar called to Miral when he saw her run to Justin.

She threw her arms around his neck, embracing him from behind and crying along with him. "Justin, I'm so sorry!"

Justin placed his hand atop hers squeezing gently. His sobbing grew more intense. "As am I for you, milady."

Agar joined them embracing both in a hug, and together they cried tears that needed to be shed. Miral must have lost someone as well for her tears sounded just as painful. His ears twitched when she began to sing the song of mourning.

"Silver Dolphins light of the world, free my heart from sorrow, Silver Dolphins I am in mourning, take my heart and lift up my soul."

They cried for some time before Justin calmed, taking a deep breath before speaking. "To all those who are lost. May they find their way to the light." He stood and bowed his head to Miral. "Thank you for your kindness, milady . . . ah, heavens," he said while running his hand through his head feathers, "we have yet to be properly introduced. I am terribly sorry for my lack of proper protocol at our meeting. Things were rather confusing and frantic at that time."

Agar shook his head with a smirk. "You forgot to introduce yourself first? It really must have been crazy."

"'Twas indeed. I will explain in a moment, Agar." He turned to Miral and bowed. "I am Prince Justin Arisdale," he said in a lowered tone.

She curtsied to him. "Miral Akemi, Your Highness."

Justin nodded. "A pleasure to make your acquaintance, Lady Miral."

Miral twiddled her fingers together over her dress. "I uh, want to thank you for helping me. I am sorry for being difficult."

Justin smiled. "'Tis all right. I am sorry for frightening you, even though 'twas not intended."

"This is a story I have to hear!" Agar interjected.

Justin shook his head with a brow raised and Agar knew that particular look was given to him whenever he was too impatient.

"The people of Delphi had not been informed of our planned arrival, and as such were panicked with the idea that we were invading. That includes Lady Miral," Justin said gesturing towards her. "She was looking for her father when I found her."

Agar's ears slumped. "Oh. I am sorry, Miral. I remember you mentioning that to Irana. The Vir . . . Virabis, yeah that's what she said. I wonder if I could have shocked that thing to death!"

Agar stared blankly when Justin turned away and began pacing across the deck of the ship, slowly at first then faster. The remaining ship crew watched their monarch silently as he did, appearing afraid to breathe let alone move. As Justin's head feathers rose and remained taut, he couldn't help but feel like he said something wrong. Agar tensed. "Hey, Justin? What is on your mind?"

"Magic was useless! I failed her, I failed all of them! I thought I was ready for battle! I was overconfident with my power all my life! Perhaps you could have done what I could not, Agar," Justin's footsteps thundered across the deck as he paced. "I was too weak! I could not save her father or even my own!" he barked, and a low rumbling growl preceded his words. "I also allowed my heart to stand between my parents and me! I just stood there and watched them die!" Justin seethed as he clenched his fists. "I should have been there with you, Agar! Then Mother, Father, Yarway and our guards would still be alive!"

"What do you think you could've done differently?!" Agar shouted back. "I was there!" he pointed to himself several times. "The only reason I'm still alive is because I hung back and attacked from a distance! If I had been up front, I wouldn't be here either!"

Justin turned his gaze away from Agar and stared with narrowed eyes back towards Delphi. "I am the Elemental of Earth! I could have done something! I chose my actions poorly."

"You know, I'm glad there was a wall of defenseless people between you and her! All you would've done is gotten yourself killed! Your heart saved your life back there, you damn idiot!" Agar turned and looked at Miral briefly then gestured towards her. "I'm sorry you couldn't save her father, but you saved someone today! Doesn't that matter?!"

"Majesty!"

"Hey!" Agar yelled, waving his arms at the lookout that shouted. "Don't bother him now!"

"I am already bothered, Agar," Justin groaned. "Pray, what?!"

The lookout was a skinny and short Arisdalian about Agar's height. He slid down the mast and bowed quickly before speaking. "Queen Irana is not pursuing us, Majesty."

"What?!"

Justin's exclamation had sounded more in surprise than in question to Agar. The ship was understaffed and would be vulnerable, and even with additional escorts, they were easy targets. He watched as Justin shielded his eyes from the morning sun and scanned the horizon.

"By the gods!" he exclaimed. "She could have killed us back there if she wished it! You know that, do you not?! This is a game!"

"A game?" Agar asked uncertainly.

"She said it herself," Justin shouted, "telling us the meaning would ruin her fun. Her fun!" he exclaimed in a rising tone. His fist was clenched, his head feathers standing on end. "She sent that Virabis to 'entertain us' as she said. 'Tis not entertaining to watch a man die like that! The death of our family and friends was fun!" he shouted lowering his head and looking away from them. "She does not fear me!" He snapped his head back a moment later with a fierce determination in his eyes. "I will have my revenge! I will bring the weight of Arisdale upon her!" he roared and spun towards the helm. "Turn this ship around!"

"Justin! What for?!" Agar asked with wide eyes. The look on his brother's face was frightening—the anger in his eyes dense like a blanket of fog. His mind raced for answers. *Mother knew how to calm him. What would she do now?*

"I will show her the might of my family name!" Justin bellowed with raised fists.

Earthen items on the ship rose from their resting places, the armored crew and Agar were lifted into the air to float. Miral clasped her hands tightly around her mother's brooch as it lifted from her dress.

"I will raze all of Delphi to the ground with my own hands!"

Miral lunged for Justin's arm. "You don't mean that!" she cried, tears streaming down her cheeks.

Agar's face flushed as he watched Miral. The crew looked to be in shock as well. Right now Justin was trapped in rage, a phenomenon that all elementals become aware of at some point in their life. Touching him in that state was a dangerous venture.

Justin jerked his head to look at Miral and as she held his arm, his tense eyes, feathers, and wrinkles relaxed. His face shifted into a slack expression as he stared back at her silently.

Agar and the crew dropped back to their feet, and earthen items clanked as they rained down upon the deck. Miral released his arm as he backed away from her slowly. His narrowed eyes continued to regard her warily. He turned to leave them, stopping briefly to look back at her once more before continuing. He walked to the double doors beneath the helm and paused.

"Remain on course to Arisdale," he ordered in a barely audible tone. He opened the doors and went inside, shutting them behind him.

"How did? How did you calm him down?!" Agar asked with raised brows.

"I don't know!" Miral replied with a quiver in her voice.

Chapter 10 - Elemental Rage

"It's my fault, isn't it?" Miral cried softly to Agar.

Agar shook his head and sat beside her. "No, if he were there he would've been upfront with the guards, father, mother and Yarway. He would've died or been used for whatever she is planning like she did with our own royal guards. His meeting you, helping you, it saved his life, Miral."

Miral wiped her eyes with her sleeve and smiled at Agar.

He winked and smiled while his black fur-tipped tail lifted happily from the wooden deck and down again several times. "So why is a lovely lady like you following us anyway?"

"It wasn't my choice! Just-the prin-I mean he forced me to!" Miral puffed defensively, "but a prophet did tell me to leave Delphi and go to Arisdale yesterday. I have no home anymore. What else can I do? I have to find a place to live. Somewhere I can fit in."

"You didn't fit in?"

Miral hung her head. "The other Delphinians feared my magic, that I have it and don't understand it. The elder races hate me because I'm human. I don't really belong anywhere. It's why we stayed where we were. No place would've been better."

"I see. I never really thought about what a human with magic would be like to other humans," he rubbed the fur under his chin. "I imagine they had all sorts of cruel, superstitious theories, right?"

Miral just acknowledged him with a nod of her head.

"What did they say or do?"

"I was barred from places, pushed so I fell, called a half-breed and treated like a disease. My mother was too." She twiddled her fingers together. "They are just scared, it's not their fault."

"Forgive me for saying this, but you seem awfully empathetic. These people give you such a hard time, and they obviously hate you. But you don't appear to hate them in return. Don't they make you even a little bit angry?"

Miral winced at his words but remained silent.

"You know what happens when you feel really infuriated, don't you?" Agar asked her.

Miral's face flushed with heat as memories of her first rage with magic flooded her mind. Her chest grew tight as she fought back tears.

Agar looked at her with a fixed stare. "I thought so. You are far too passive," he said. "It's obvious what happened."

Miral's heart fluttered, and a frown creased her face. He was right, though. It was because of that day.

"I'm sorry. I won't ask any more about it, although you can tell me if you want to. I just figured that's why you don't like to be angry."

She nodded and offered no reply, then hugged her knees tightly to herself. He was very perceptive and able to understand her in seconds.

Agar hung his head. "Miral, all Elementals know what that was like. This occurrence isn't new to us. The first recorded history of elemental rage goes back to the dawn of our existence on Earth. Being a child with that much power and responsibility and not knowing it until rage caused you to lose control is hard," he said drawing his dagger and stabbing the deck with it near the holes Justin had punched into it. His ears drooped, and he breathed deeply. "You are first aware of your power the day something goes wrong. The day anger showed you and showed everyone who you were. Right?" he asked.

Miral nodded, and tears painfully flooded her eyes.

"I don't like to talk about it either." Agar shuddered while fighting back his own tears. "I only ever told Justin, and as far as I know, he has never told anyone. Sadly, everyone in the kingdom knows what happened the day Justin found his powers. He can't keep that a secret."

Miral was unable to bring herself to ask the question in her mind. Agar must have seen it in her eyes, though, as he had acknowledged her with a nod.

"Earth magic and civilized people, they don't mix," he explained in a lowered tone. "Arisdale is full of gold mines. We are the center of trade for all of Flourisha," Agar said with hands wide. "That is why we have so much refined gold on our armor. It is the pride of Arisdale and one of the reasons why the kingdom is so prosperous. As you can imagine a quake near a mining site," Agar cringed. "That just doesn't end well for anyone."

She gasped and stared silently at him with her hands over her mouth.

"Justin threw a young child's temper tantrum near a mining site father was visiting. His rage exploded within seconds and spiraled out of control. You know kids, right? What can you do?" he shrugged while smirking briefly then rested his head on his knees. "I'm not innocent either, Miral, but a lot of people died that day," he whispered with a grimace. "It's why Justin will not use violence to solve problems. There has to be no other recourse. He will not kill if he doesn't have to. He blames himself for not breaking his own promise, not killing the wall of people Irana placed between her and us. There were children in that group, though," Agar puffed a breath. "Somehow she knew that would work."

She had stopped herself during her rage before anyone was badly hurt. What could have happened if she had not been so afraid?

"Arisdale is used to having earth elementals, there has always been one in the kingdom since it was founded," Agar continued. "They tested the structures of buildings to ensure they were sound enough to withstand the quakes for as long as possible. The castle and town have not endured many quakes, though. After the first event, every earth elemental learns to either control their anger or leave the land if they can't. Justin struggles to control his. He is emotional and freely expresses as he chooses. Father couldn't have his only heir leave, so our Mother taught Justin to be in control. She spent a lot of time with him, almost always by his side. He did well all these years till now, but the people still fear him, Miral."

"Because of his magic?"

"His magic, his height, his girth, his eyes, his strength; the guy is a mountain, and he is intimidating. Isn't he?" he asked looking at her quizzically.

Miral fumbled with her hands together in her lap, unsure of how to answer that. "Y-yes, very much so. I was so scared when I first saw him, and everything that happened since hasn't helped."

Agar nodded at her. "That is usually the reaction he gets anywhere he goes. The magic turns caution into fear quickly. Until you get to know him, it can be hard to determine what he is like." Agar leaned close and whispered, "Don't tell him I said this, but the people also think he's too soft."

Miral looked at Agar with wide-eyed surprise. "Too soft?!"

"Soft of heart," Agar replied quietly. "He is unique for an Arisdalian, Miral. If you met father instead, things would have happened differently for you. Justin is both frightful and tender. He does have father's explosive temperament. All of mother's lessons and attention helped him control his anger, but the results of that and life circumstances created a very altruistic and emotional man."

"The way you say that makes it sound as if that is a bad thing."

"To Arisdalians it is a weakness," Agar explained. "Justin's ancestors sat on the throne for generations. There is a long legacy to live up to. The past kings were tough and often ruthless. They were respected for their authority and strength." Agar leaned in to whisper to her and tugged on his long ears. "I hear everything, Miral. All I have to do is hide with my magic, and I get all the gossip! I heard plenty of talk about Johanas becoming too soft after marrying Anelda. Justin is gentler and more loving than his father. You will get to see that side of him soon, I'm sure," he sighed. "The people are afraid of what he will bring to Arisdale with his shortcomings."

Miral blinked. "Shortcomings?"

"He tends to be overprotective and overdo things. Too much kindness for kings is a bad thing," Agar frowned and looked back where Justin had gone. "He can't ever know all that. It would hurt him too much." Agar paused and squeezed his eyes shut. "And mother is gone. She was so good at calming him, and I am terrible at it! I am an instigator by nature as you saw."

"I will never say anything, Agar. I promise," Miral replied.

"Thank you, Miral."

Chapter 11 - Life is a Garden

Within the dimly lit cabin of his family's ship, Justin sat in meditation, searching for answers and truths within his mind. He drowned out the background noises of muffled chatter, footfalls of the crew, sloshing of ocean waters and the moaning creaks of fragrant cedar.

One by one the emotions buried beneath the surface were freed in tears and contained his anger as mother had taught him. If he had a way to keep that anger controlled and released inside without meditating, rather than letting it explode as he had done many times before, things would be better for everyone. Try as he might, though, his anger demanded immediate release despite his fear of consequences. *The curse of being a raptor. Quick to anger and quick to strike.*

He composed himself and left the office to join Agar and Miral. He hoped that the lady was not so scared of him now that she would never trust him. It was bad enough that Arisdalians had formed expected aggression towards humans so long ago. The truth of that was clearly displayed on her face when they met. He and his mother fought to change that, and he did not wish to ruin all that work with his uncontrollable rage. Perhaps there was a solution, and maybe the human lady he saved had the answers. Whatever she did, it worked to calm him in seconds.

Justin approached Miral and Agar, who stood to address him. As he had done before, he gave his voice a sing-song quality. "I am sorry," he said with a slight bow of his head. "I failed. I let my anger get the better of me." He looked at Miral with a small smile. "I do not know how you calmed me with just a touch, but I thank you for that. I could have gotten us all killed, and no one would have known what happened.

"There is also the fact that the people of Delphi are innocent, and they too would have suffered for their queen's actions, after sparing their lives in my escape. I would have betrayed everything that I am, and everything that I believe in so deeply."

Miral smiled at him with bright eyes. "It's all right."

Agar patted Justin on his back. "Don't overthink it, big guy. I don't think it would have been enough to stop Irana though. Not after what I saw."

"What did you see?" Justin asked him, sitting on the deck floor. "To me she appeared mortally wounded, yet quite alive and well, and I cannot fathom that." He looked at Miral. "I would not mind hearing your side of the story as well, and that prophecy you mentioned."

Miral nodded to him in reply.

"Aye," Agar replied, "first the guards assaulted her after she had dropped father and mother to their knees before her. That scythe appeared in her hands and even though they stabbed and slashed at her, in one swing through them, they all dropped dead!

"Her strength was surreal, kind of like yours, brother. Yarway and I attacked her. He moved in close with his blazing speed and sent a wind gust to move her away from mother and father. I cast lightning before he reached her, and she looked pained, but kept her stance and focus on Yarway. No living thing can stand after a single lightning bolt! You know that, brother!" Agar paused, his face and eyes scrunching, looking as though he was fighting back tears. He shook his head. "Yarway was-he couldn't-she killed him too," he cried, rubbing his eyes and taking a deep breath. "Irana mocked them for wanting to make peace with humans. Told them that humanity would rise to arm and strike down the elder races," he punched his fist into his hand. "She told me to stay put unless I wished to die as well. She said she would prefer it if you were there to watch me die first, Justin. I knew I had no chance. Nothing worked! It was like getting that stubborn Elder Nyros to agree with what I'm saying!"

Justin shook his head at Agar's example and grumbled to himself. "Irana wishes to see the conflict between us remain. Why?" He turned his attention to Miral when he sensed her nervousness rising with the conversation. Her scent changed, and she was fidgeting. "I never heard of Queen Irana possessing dark magic, or anyone for that matter. Lady Miral, can you think of any reason why she would change or when she did?"

"King Charles died two nights ago, that is when she became distant for the first time. Muttered to herself at times. People were saying she was going mad with grief."

Justin's head feathers spiked. "King Charles died?! How so?"

"They said it was a natural death."

Justin stared at her with narrowed eyes. "'Tis far too coincidental to be natural. Do you agree?" he asked Agar.

Agar agreed with a nod. "We got word that they wished to speak with us on peace, agreed and then set sail the day before he died. That is far too odd!"

Justin gestured to Miral. "There was no word at all to prepare for our arrival, I assume, least that is what the ambassador told us. 'Twas to gauge the honest reaction of the people. However, Irana did not seem to care about her people at all."

"There is one other thing," Miral said wringing her hands together.

Justin arched a brow. "Pray, what is this other thing?"

"I overheard two ladies while I was working. They said King Charles was given a book called 'The Truth of Times.' The prophet warned me never to speak the author's name aloud. The look in his eyes was frightful," Miral said with a shake of her head.

"Never speak his name? 'Tis odd. Carry on, Lady Miral."

"They said the book discussed the forbidden word, and that it was made forbidden by the elder races to keep us from the goddess."

Justin's eyes grew wide, and his head feathers spiked upward. "The forbidden word?! The one that is claimed to drive one to madness upon uttering it?"

"Yes. The king and queen said the word and so had the two ladies. They were both in that line in front of Irana, and Helen, she was the one with my father before he . . ."

"Pray, you had not spoken this word had you?" Justin asked with an authoritative tone, his eyes locked on hers.

"No!" she exclaimed, shrinking back from his interrogating stare. "I swear I did not!"

"I believe you, Lady Miral. There is no lie in your words," Justin affirmed with a nod. "I had to be sure, though, as much as I would regret ever having to do this as a king, one who has spoken the forbidden word is detained for a long duration. In that time, they are watched and questioned to determine their sanity, for the safety of all, of course. Terrible crimes have been committed by those trapped in madness. I would not wish for this to happen to you, and as such, I think it best that this incident kept between us. The people of Arisdale will be quick to judge you despite my faith in you, because of what occurred," Justin sighed heavily. "By the gods, Dilos will be seething that he was right; however, I cannot see this as an elaborate trap either unless the Queen has indeed gone mad from uttering the word." He paused and continued to rub his jaw. "There is still the matter of her new-found magic, however."

"The prophecy!" Miral exclaimed. "I was told by an elderly Glenn Woods wolf to flee Delphi because darkness was descending upon it. That was yesterday. She didn't have dark magic, at least that I knew of, until after that. Though I have no idea where she got it from."

Justin's eyes wore an intense gaze. "Perhaps. Was there more to this prophecy?"

"He told me I needed to go to Arisdale, find the Elementals of Light and under the guard of the protector I would be safe."

"Well, you found us!" Agar replied. "What's left of us, that is."

Justin sighed, "Yarway . . . there will be a new Elemental of Wind now."

"What do you mean?" Miral asked him.

Justin raised his hands palm up. "The Elementals of Light, of which there are eight. Only one representative of each element exists at a time. When one dies, a new and unknown person is granted the gift and their age does not matter. I am not sure how or why it works this way. It has been so for thousands of years," he said with a shake of his head, "and no one knows the purpose for the Elementals existence. Some theories say they were the elite guards for the goddess; however, with no goddess to protect, it remained just that, a theory."

Miral nodded her understanding.

Justin tilted his head to the right. "Under the guard of the protector? I have never heard that before. I wonder if there is a reason for you to be guarded, or if 'twas merely a means of making you feel better about seeking aid in Arisdale. He did not inform you of what he was referring to, I take it?" he asked her.

"He didn't," Miral replied with a shake of her head.

"Curious," Justin stated while rubbing his jaw once more. "Well, all my questions of that nature have been answered as best they could. I wager the forbidden word has a part to play, but I have never heard of one obtaining dark power from it before." He thought about the dream he had the morning before they left, after what occurred in Delphi, and with the prophecy, it no longer felt as if it was merely a randomly conjured vision from rest. *Suffering will rise as the light fades. Seek the inner light.* "Anything more you wish to ask me?" he said looking at Miral with a gentle cast to his golden eyes.

"I have so many questions! I'm not sure where to start."

"We have a long journey ahead, and there is little else to do than talk or play games," he said, his voice growing deeper with his relaxed tone. "Start with the first thing that comes to mind and we shall see where it leads."

"You said your family came to talk about peace. Why has it been so difficult to unite our races?"

"Ah, yes. The problem lies on both sides, Lady Miral," Justin replied. "See life as a garden, and those who hold to the old convictions are weeds. Once one rises to sow its seeds, more will quickly rise along with it. The battle to free the garden of weeds becomes an ever constant, and self-perpetuating problem with no easy solution. It takes an ever vigilant eye to keep after the weeds. With considerable time and effort, the problem can be maintained, but never controlled. Such is a physical impossibility."

Agar raised his hands in the air in a sign of surrender. "All the weeds would have to give up and stop blooming!"

Justin laughed, "Indeed; however, there are those who refuse to abandon their beliefs. They are the ones who fan the flames and keep the conflict alive," Justin said heaving a sigh afterward. "No doubt you heard old tales of human merchants who have been locked away and tormented under false accusations until another unfortunate soul happened along to take his place. Since the amusement was gone from torturing the former," he said with a firm shake of his head.

Miral frowned and nodded to him.

"For some the mind of darkness fuels them, and there can be no other way," Justin said shrugging. "Of course, Arisdalians can live to be two hundred years old. This makes them harder to change, and the elders also like to stay in control," he clenched his fist. "I often wonder why there is kingship at all!"

"The King is just a figurehead and symbol as things stand now," Agar interjected. "They overruled everything Johanas ever tried to do. They never even took the time to consider his words! As if every valid point had no meaning to them," Agar seethed rubbing the back of his neck. "Should war come the elders will not be standing in the front line leading the armies. That will be the King."

Justin looked off into the distant horizon. "I like the system. I do not believe one man should have all the power. The elders make things difficult when they fill the youth with their old views, which allows the path of hate to remain open," he said, turning his head to look at Miral once again. "However, as I said, this problem is on both sides, and as such will continue unabated. Now more than ever with Irana's single act against us!" Justin looked down and closed his eyes for a time then raised his head and looked at her. "Miral, I apologize in advance for any actions or words held against you. I intend on making it clear that disrespect towards you will be viewed as disrespect towards me, and is, therefore, punishable."

"I wouldn't want people punished for how they act because of me," Miral replied with hands folded before her.

Justin smiled at her warmly. "You have a beautiful soul, Miral, and your concern is moving; however, as I said earlier, I need to quell any indiscretions quickly, lest I have an insurgence on my hands."

Agar nodded. "Such is the pitfall of the crown. Needing to do what must be done for the better of all, even if it means hurting another."

Justin placed a hand on Agar's shoulder. "Indeed! I will take no pleasure in it, milady, of that you have my word. My father ruled justly, even in the handling of punishments. I will do no different; however, I will do better," he said. "I plan to find a constructive way for these individuals to uphold their punishments. If they refuse to change, I will have no choice but to exile them."

"Exile?!" Miral replied in alarm.

"'Tis not something I ever wish to do, but as I said, I will give them ample time to accept change. Beyond that I will not tolerate indifference for the sake of letting one remain and grow more weeds."

"Ok, I understand," she replied.

The lady has a very forgiving heart, one filled with the care and concern of others, those she doesn't know, those who would likely hurt her in a heartbeat, and he wondered if she felt the same level of concern for herself. He was distracted from his thinking with the soft and songlike voice of Lady Miral.

"How did you become brothers?"

Justin smiled wide at her. "That is a good lighthearted story. I can think of no better way to pass the time till nightfall."

Agar nodded with enthusiasm. "Aye!"

Justin's voice rose to a higher tone with his excitement. "Mother and Father brought me with them on a royal affairs trip to Egyptalia fifteen years ago. I was ten years old and overconfident with my magic. I always had a desire to lose the guards that watched me, even at home. I wished for freedom from their eyes, and I managed to wander off on my own to explore the sites," Justin said with a sparkle in his eye as he thought back on that day. "I caught Agar in the market square stealing from a food cart. 'Twas an incredible sight to see. Agar, as the Elemental of Lightning, can vibrate the air in such a way that it renders him invisible to the eye," he said gesturing with his hands in the air.

"Oh!" Miral responded placing her hand over her heart.

Agar winked and smiled impishly at Miral.

Justin shook his head at Agar with a smile. "I decided to follow him because I knew he had magic," he continued. "When I confronted him at his hideout, he was afraid I would turn him in. He appeared to be malnourished, had fleas, and stank to the hells!" He chuckled and mocked a gesture with his hand fanning his nose.

Agar glared at him briefly through narrowed eyes, but eventually laughed as well.

"Agar was an insolent youth, and hard to talk to," Justin said while patting Agar on the shoulder. "He was hiding behind a large boulder, so I lifted it off the ground from where I was standing with my magic to show him he was not alone. He agreed to hear me out. We talked at length, and I learned that his family from Zeiram, out of fear for their lives, abandoned him because of his wild lightning magic."

Miral gasped and looked to Agar. "I'm so sorry."

"Thank you, Miral."

Justin smiled at them. "I wanted a sibling so badly. Mother and father were never able to have another child live past infancy, once they were born. Life denied them the chance."

"Oh! Why did they never live?" Miral asked him.

"'Twas an odd occurrence that we never understood. I was not the first of their children or the last; however, I certainly feel blessed to be alive, and yet cursed."

"I am sorry, Your Majesty," Miral murmured.

"Thank you, Lady Miral."

"Pray what happened next?"

Justin nodded. "I brought him to my parents and pleaded with my father. Mother adored him! She insisted they take him in, and father did not hesitate to agree. Of course, I was scolded fiercely for worrying them and wandering off," Justin sighed. "Mother was always open with her love for everything, and everyone. She was the spark of hope in uniting our races . . ." he said trailing off into a silent stare.

Agar placed his hand on Justin's shoulder. The two shared an exchange of looks, full of words left unspoken.

"She sounds truly incredible," Miral said folding her hands before her. "I do wish I could have met your parents."

"I wish you could have as well," Justin replied in a lowered tone. "She would have adored you."

Miral blushed at the compliment.

"I also wish I could have had the honor of meeting your father properly. Pray, what was his name?"

Miral's eyes misted with tears. "Yarlin."

"A fine name," Justin replied.

She smiled at him, wiping tears from her eyes. "Do you have other family in Arisdale?"

"Yes, my mother's sister, Galena lives with us. She looks very much like her, except for yellow head feathers. My aunt is the Elemental of Holy, and she shares mother's deep love for all things," Justin chuckled. "I am certain she is going to be motherly to you, Miral. She will not let anyone speak ill of you."

Agar laughed. "That's for sure! Not that it's a bad thing, but all that mothering is smothering at times! Seriously, though, Galena is a good woman. We are blessed to have her!"

"No cousins, or uncles, or anything?" she asked.

Justin shook his head. "Much like my brothers and sisters they all met an unknown and unfortunate fate. 'Twas thought that assassins had a hand; however, we never had proof. And Aunt Galena did not marry nor express a desire to."

Miral blinked in surprise. "I am sorry to hear that. Thank you for the lovely stories."

"Aye! Well told, brother!" he said swinging his arm out to Justin, slapping his hand hard on his brother's back with a hearty laugh.

Justin retaliated with a jab to Agar's shoulder, knocking him over. Agar laughed hysterically as he rolled onto his back, causing Justin to burst out laughing. Miral was giggling along with them.

"Prince Agar, you grew up with a royal family. How come you don't have the same sing-song, formal accent as Prince Justin?" Miral asked him.

"Pray, Miral, Agar is fine for now," he winked then laughed. "Are you referring to the whole 'tis and 'twas, and the aristocratic, slowly spoken, artistically flared words that blend together and sound like a melody whilst speaking?" Agar asked mocking Justin's accent and long embellished replies.

Justin released a booming laugh. "You sound ridiculous speaking like that! You are trying too hard!"

"Ha-ha, it's not for me, Miral! I never felt right speaking like that, so I keep my street mouth, as mother called it."

"They allowed him to have his way as long as he represented the family well at social functions," Justin replied. "This is no trial for Agar. He is a one-man play, after all. 'Tis not a bad thing, life would be dull without you, brother!"

Agar sighed looking up at the sky. Miral glanced up as well. The sun was setting and painted the canvas in an artful display of rainbow colors.

"Do you think Katenna is well?" Agar asked Justin.

Justin looked over at Agar with a sly smile. "I am sure she is swooning over you as we speak."

Agar glanced at him frowning. "Ah! Don't say that! I would hate to think she is anxiously awaiting a visit from me."

"Who is Katenna?" Miral asked him.

Agar smiled brightly in response, "Katenna Bastette, the beautiful Queen of Egyptalia!" he said in a deep tone with arms spread in the air. "She is a cat, long curly purple hair, golden eyes, brown fur, long bushy tail, and gorgeous human-like face. She is womanly, but she doesn't take crap from anybody! Tough girl; I like that!"

Miral smiled at him as he continued to stare at the clouds above, with a love-struck look on his face. The sky grew darker, and the colors muted. Agar's expression became solemn with the scene.

"There was an illness that spread through the land two years ago. Kat and her little sister, Artilone's parents passed away then. Katenna is the same age as I. She took the throne when she was eighteen years old. Artilone bears a slight resemblance to Katenna, but she has blonde hair and lime green eyes."

"We will have to journey to Egyptalia to see Katenna and Artilone soon," Justin said with a smile.

Agar looked over at Justin dejected. "We need to deal with Irana first."

Justin poked at Agar. "I will have a missive sent to Katenna when we return. We will need to unite against Irana while we learn what is necessary to stop her."

"Thank you, brother."

Justin nodded to Agar. Nightfall was upon them, the full moon and stars reflected in Lady Miral's eyes, giving the radiant blue they bore a glow. He was grateful for the light of the moon this night. Something to chase away the darkness and provide them with comfort. The stories told on the long journey were an excellent distraction. Though he knew the pain buried inside them would surface once they were left to their individual thoughts. They had each other, though, and together they would bring each other peace.

Agar yawned. "I don't know about the rest of you, but I'm going to try to get some sleep."

Justin nodded and stood. "I am in agreement, brother."

"I am sleepy as well," Miral replied.

"Very well then," Justin bowed slightly. "We shall get you settled into a room."

They descended a flight of steps and entered a large chamber. Justin pointed to the right. "Over there is the galley and dining area, and to the left is the meeting room and office." He headed down the stairs in the center of the lower level and turned to face them. "And these are the royal quarters. I pray we all sleep well."

"Aye, sleep well, brother, Miral!" Agar headed to the room to the left and closed the door.

"Just-I mean, Your Majesty—"

"As Agar said, my name is fine for now," Justin interjected. "We may dispense with formalities when 'tis just the two of us and Agar."

"Really? That feels so improper."

He smiled in response. "You are an Elemental of Light, Lady Miral. In that sense you are on an equal level with Agar and I. I only ask that you mind my title when around others in Arisdale and the ship crew."

"Ok, Justin," she whispered. "If I may ask, why did Agar make so many jests when things were so dangerous?"

Justin opened his jaws and stared at her a moment. "Ah, yes." He beckoned her to follow him farther away to the other side of the room. "He has a rather remarkable ability to hear even the lightest of sounds," Justin whispered, "although, he would not be angry with me for answering for him. Agar's childhood was terrible. The day he found his power and his reason for being tossed aside brought him much pain. As a result, Agar has a means of dealing with grief, fear, and especially anger in a way that makes him appear inappropriate."

"Oh," Miral replied.

Justin nodded. "He greatly dislikes adverse events and conversations, and will do his best to turn them lighter to avoid it. I know this about him, and so I either ignore the unfortunate timing of the jest or laugh with him."

"That is sad," she said folding her hands in prayer.

"Indeed, we all have our sad tale. They are hard to tell, but as Elementals, we can understand one another. Share yours with us if you wish, and I shall share mine." He paused, arching a brow as he noticed her pupils dilating. "That is if Agar has not already?" Lady Miral winced under his gaze, and he sighed. "He told you what happened." He shrugged. "I cannot say I am surprised. He loves to talk."

"He told me, and I am so sorry."

"Ah well, 'tis difficult to live with. I try my best to make up for it every day of my life. For every soul I save, I pray perhaps my own soul will be redeemed. Five people died that day. The earth elemental before me had departed for the World of Light as we were visiting the mine. No one was aware that the gift would be granted to me," he scoffed. "Of all the irony, and of all the moments in one's life, it had to happen then!" He sighed once more looking away. "'Twas a family-owned mine, they left Arisdale and moved to Volga since my father refused to have me exiled. I wonder if the people might choose to deny me the kingship; they have that right, and I could not fault them for being afraid of me. Though I would love the job and I would like the opportunity to make my mother's dreams a reality."

"I hope they, at least, give you a chance to prove yourself. That wasn't really your fault, and things have been good since, haven't they?"

Justin turned his eyes back to her and smiled warmly. "They have been, and I have not quaked the ground in anger once till this day. I thank you, Lady Miral." He gestured to the door they stood beside. "This room was my quarters; however, I offer them to you. They are far more comfortable than the crew quarters, and frankly, I am not certain I trust them to be alone with you."

"Thank you. Where will you rest?"

Justin glanced at the main door in the center and nodded to it. "My parents' room," he replied softly. "I would rather be close to them in some way, whether it bring me comfort to rest or not." He lowered his head and squeezed his eyes shut. He opened them and looked into her eyes. "I am sorry I cannot offer you the same."

"That is ok," she ran her hands over her dress then tapped the brooch. "This belonged to my mother, my father gave it to me."

Justin nodded. "Then I am glad you do have something." He bowed low at the waist. "Milady, I wish you a good rest. Pray, do not hesitate to wake either of us should anything be amiss."

"Thank you, Justin, I pray you sleep well too."

He bowed his head and turned, walking to the room in the center and going inside. Once in his parents' room tears flooded forth in a torrent. He wiped his eyes and removed his armor, setting it down on the red and gold carpet. He curled up on the bed, picking up the scent of his parents, and stared absently at himself in the mirror against the wall.

Chapter 12 - Friendship

Miral opened the door to the room and crawled into Justin's former bed. Sleep would not come easily this night for any of them, but this was by far the most comfortable bed she had ever laid on. Her mind swirled with thoughts that were difficult to ignore as she stared out the window of the ship to the sea of stars. Since her mind insisted on thinking, she decided to focus the thoughts on something more pleasant.

Her mind turned to Justin at that moment, and the soft look his eyes displayed whenever he smiled at her. She wondered in awe at how wrong the stories and she had been. She was terrified by his appearance at first. Frustrated with how he toted her around. The frightening look no longer existed; however, she was still uncertain of how she felt about him, especially after witnessing his rage. His softhearted character that was revealed in all the stories told was truly a beautiful thing. She hoped that was his true nature. She may not have liked the means of which he acted in Delphi, but she didn't know him, and she misinterpreted his actions. He had been concerned for her well-being and saved her life twice.

She thought about what else she has been told that might not be right. Anything that didn't seem to fit in her mind she would ask in question to Agar and Justin later. They seemed willing to answer all her questions. She wanted to know the whole of every story. The elder races were a mystery to her. Now she would get to learn more about them than she dared to dream.

Her thoughts turned to her father then. If only he were still with her. She cried softly, not wanting to wake Justin or Agar were they asleep. She wanted to see the world, but she felt afraid of living in Arisdale. Justin towered over her in height, and she wondered if all Arisdalians were that tall. The thought of being the only little human in a kingdom of giants was more frightening to her now than before. Even though Justin and Agar were friendly and kind, it did little to ease her nerves. Her father was with her mother Sonya in the World of Light now. The comforting thought brought an end to her tears. She closed her eyes, and sleep overtook her.

Miral awoke to pleasant smells of food in the air. She got up from the bed, stretching the stiffness from her body, and headed to the ship's galley. It had been a day since they left Delphi. Justin said the voyage to Arisdale could take a couple days with a good wind.

Justin waved to her from his seat at one of the galley tables as she stepped through the archway. "Good morning! Sleep well?"

"Good morning, Justin! I did sleep well. What of you two?"

"Well enough," he replied with a smile.

Agar waved at her from in front of the iron stove that was bolted to the ship wall. "Aye!"

"You can cook as well?" she asked Agar with a tilt of her head.

"You bet I can!" Agar replied with a wink. "Justin and I learned to do a lot of things ourselves!"

Justin nodded. "Having all my affairs tended to is nice; however, there are times I would rather not. Besides knowledge is power, even if that knowledge is cooking an egg properly," he chuckled.

Miral took a seat across from Justin at the table and fidgeted with her fingers together in her lap. They were dressed casually in tank tops, pants, and half boots. She noticed that they both wore a large gold pendant around their necks. Miral peered at Justin's necklace. The bird of Arisdale was at the center, and four words were inscribed around the outer edge, but she could not make them out. Justin tilted his head slightly to the right drawing her attention from the pendant to his eyes.

"Care for some tea, Lady Miral?" he asked her, lifting a steaming pot next to him.

Miral glanced at the teapot and then at Justin. "You drink tea?"

Justin blinked before replying. "Ah, yes. Arisdalians such as myself consume meat primarily. However, there are nutrients that meat alone cannot provide. We predator types find plants to be distasteful and honestly I have no means to chew or digest them," he said grinning slightly. "This is where a particular tea blend will suffice perfectly, and frankly I rather enjoy it, especially with a spot of honey."

Miral smiled. "Pray, I would love to have some."

Justin nodded and poured a cup for her. "I would like to train you in the use of your magic, and some basic self-defense. If that is all right with you, Lady Miral?" he asked handing her the steaming teacup.

She took the cup carefully from him, her hand supporting the bottom. "I would like that, the magic, I mean. I don't think I am apt to be a fighter." She set the cup down as her hands trembled a little. "I don't want to hurt anyone ever."

Justin nodded to her while smiling. "As you wish, and there is nothing wrong with that, Lady Miral," he said.

Miral smiled back and stared deeply into his sun-filled eyes. Since they had first spoken, Justin's words always seemed carefully chosen to say exactly what needed to be said. He also had long-winded speeches; however, she found them intriguing to listen to.

Agar broke the exchange of stares, placing plates of food before them. "Breakfast is served!" he said before returning to the kitchen to grab himself a plate and sat next to his brother.

Agar had the same array of foods he served her. Eggs, rice bread, and a serving of mustard greens. Justin's plate only contained eggs and fish.

"Justin, I was just thinking about how we met. I wanted to know more about how you were able to find me."

"Ah, yes," Justin replied. "I followed the pulse of your magic, your inner light. 'Tis very radiant, more so than ours by far," he said while pointing at her.

"Can you teach me how to do that too?" Miral asked with wide eyes and a smile.

Justin jabbed a chunk of fish with his fork. "Of course I will. One only needs to seek out the power of the other Elementals. I imagine you are at least aware of how your energy feels since you know it exists."

Miral nodded to him in reply.

"Excellent. Greater focus is required the farther they are from you. You do not need to know what element they are because the presence of the energy will feel the same. Once attuned to the power of other Elementals, you will be able to pick them out quickly. 'Tis how I found Agar for the first time!" Justin said pointing to his brother.

"How did you learn all this so young?" Miral asked him sincerely.

"Heavens, you are a curious one, Lady Miral."

Miral shrunk back in her seat and folded her hands together in her lap. Justin had acted so casually towards her since yesterday that she forgot he was royalty.

His eyes creased and his brows lifted. "Do not worry, Lady Miral. I will answer any question you have, within reason of course."

Miral smiled and nodded. He knew that she was worried. She remembered being told by her mother that most animals had keen senses, and they were more aware of your emotions than you were. She wondered if he had the same ability to detect emotion. Hiding how she really felt was something she was used to doing in Delphi. Even when she was upset, she would not yell, nor make a face, but just silently bare it within her. She could no longer hide, Justin's piercing eyes saw right through her each time.

"I had an excellent teacher!" he said. "Sara Phoenix, the Elemental of Fire."

"With a temperament that matches her element!" Agar interjected.

"Ah, ha-ha, indeed she does!" Justin chuckled. "She is kindly, though, and sage! I will send for her when we return. I would like her to aid you in learning some new spells. I have no idea what kinds of feats you will be capable of, and would, therefore, lack the ability to properly instruct you beyond the basics," he shrugged.

"Thank you, I look forward to it."

"You are most welcome," Justin said with a bow of his head.

"What are those glowing gems on your armor? I have seen them used as lights, but never like that."

"Ethereal crystals," he replied with a firm nod. "They are harmonized to the frequencies of magic. Some are broad spectrum and work with any element, and others are attuned to one kind. The magic contained within them is what causes them to glow. Ethereal obsidian is a crystal that resists all magic penetration. They are exceedingly rare, and can be set onto any surface, such as a shackle to block the prisoner's ability to use magic. However, they are limited in range, and can only protect an area its size from magic. Shackles are effective because they block the hands, and thus prevent magic from being used." He paused and sipped at his tea before continuing. "The gems on my armor are attuned to earth only, which is why they are green. Although color doesn't always denote which power is present," he said pointing at Agar's helmet on his head.

"What? I like the color combination!" Agar said proudly patting his helmet. "Lightning is orange, but I prefer the two smaller yellow ones to them all being the same color!"

Justin shook his head at Agar.

"Hey, what can I say? I'm fashionable!" Agar said shrugging.

Miral giggled at Agar. He seemed to be a jolly man; very childlike in his expressions and mannerisms. Something about that gave him a charm all his own.

Justin chuckled. "Ah, well, where was I? Oh yes, the crystals. How much of your magic have you cast so far?"

"I have only tried small things, like filling a glass with water. I'm too scared to go beyond that." She wanted to talk about the day she lost control but stopped herself as tension gripped her chest.

"Splendid!" Justin replied. "When you cast that spell often, do you feel yourself grow a little fatigued each time?"

"Yes, I did notice that."

Justin nodded. "Magic has two costs to pay, one to the world, and the other to you. When the element is used up or changed, the cost of energy used directly affects the world. When I cast that rock wall in Delphi, the ground was forever altered," Justin explained. "I cannot restore the land to the way 'twas before. Once you expend all the natural energy the element has, the extra cost needed for the spell has to come from somewhere. That power is pulled from you. The crystals provide better focus for casting and an alternate source of energy, allowing magic to be less draining." He held his hands wide. "The larger the spell, the greater the focus, energy, and strength required to cast it."

Miral nodded her understanding. Magic sounded dangerous, but she was still interested in mastering her water.

"Tell me about your abilities," she asked, gesturing to Justin and Agar.

Justin motioned for Agar to speak first and finished his breakfast.

"Let's see, you already know about stealth. When we were in trouble, I used a channeling spell I call thunderhead. That is the largest in my arsenal. Thunder rains down from the sky and the power of the lightning when it connects with the ground can repel a being with a pressure wave," Agar said pounding his fist into his hand, then spreading his fingers as he lifted his hand back up. "A single bolt of lightning is also a channeled spell, and I call it a lightning stroke. I can infuse my daggers with a confined ball of lightning, which is known as spark. It can stun, and if driven in deep enough could kill. Lightning flash is bright and leaves the assaulter temporarily blinded. Then there is thunderclap. The sound alone will leave your ears ringing, which is disorienting, but it also repels anything in a 10-foot radius from me."

Miral stared at Agar with awed wide eyes. "You name your spells?"

"Ha-ha, yes we do! Justin and I thought it was wise to do this. Now we can work out strategies if we are ever in battle. This way he can say, 'Agar, cast thunderhead,' and I'll know what to do."

Justin laughed. "Do you remember the day Sara was training you, and you missed your focus target?"

Agar's mouth fell open into a laughing fit.

"What happened?" Miral asked.

"Ah, ha-ha, well—" Agar attempted to speak but laughter stopped his words and brought tears to his eyes.

Justin calmed himself. "He was asked to cast lightning stroke and to hit the target dummy to the left of us. The bolt landed behind us near the stables. General Dilos Manning was thrown from his mount and into the water trough," Justin chuckled.

"Oh boy, was he ever angry!" Agar laughed and rubbed his eyes. "That crude man got what he deserved, though!"

"Yes. We were forbidden to practice magic within the castle gates from that day on." Justin sighed and closed his eyes briefly. "I am sorry that you will have the displeasure of meeting him. He is not fond of humans at all, I fear."

His words made her feel uneasy, but she would be a fool not to expect a lot of that in Arisdale.

"Have at it, Justin," Agar said with a wave of his hand.

"Ah, yes, magic! I have a vast arsenal of abilities at hand, and a passive strength that earth provides me. The green glow you have seen several times is earth shield. It resists all earthen elements, and other elements as well. It expires with time, and that time is accelerated when an object or spell contacts it. However, I can only recast it after it has faded and 'tis not instantaneous . . ." Justin's voice trailed off as he lowered his head and a frown took the place of his smile.

Earth shield was the magic glow that protected her father until the blood demon ended its duration by poking at it. Justin wasn't able to shield him again fast enough then. Miral wore a frown as well but nodded at him. "I believe you did all you could, Justin."

Justin replied with a nod of his own before continuing to talk about his magic. "Magnetic reversal and earthen control can be summoned quickly or channeled into a larger spell. I used these to stop the sword and repel it, the same for anyone wearing metal or earthen things. When I jumped from the wharf, I used it to float," he said gesturing with his hands raised.

"Oh! So that's what you did! Have you done things like that before?" Miral replied with bright eyes.

Justin laughed, "Ah, yes. I stirred a bit of trouble with that ability when I was young, certainly caused the guards to panic when I used it to soar over the castle walls."

Miral giggled in reply.

Justin smiled and continued. "Quake, tectonics, and shatter are channeled spells I have. These spells can be altered in intensity, and size, as I will them to. Given the requirements to cast spells that modify the nature of the element, they take longer to shape. This process is called channeling. You witnessed quake and the rock wall, which were formed by using tectonics, which leaves shatter. The name implies the action. I can fracture an earthen element into smaller parts. The size of the fragments can be controlled by will. Earthen control then allows me to turn the pieces into projectiles, but I can also do this," Justin raised his hand and the utensils, cups, and plates lifted off the table and hovered in the air. "If I wanted I could use these all as projectiles now that I have them." All the objects set down on the table except for a single fork. Justin thrust his hand before him, and the fork zipped forward into the wall behind her and lodged in the wood.

"Wow! That is amazing!" she said with a clap of her hands.

Agar laughed. "Ha-ha! Yeah, learning what we could do with our abilities made childhood fun. I have to admit that I am a bit jealous of the big guy here. The things he can do are so much fun. He would jump out the highest windows of the castle and float down just to get out of doing something."

Justin chuckled in response. "Ah, yes and scolded fiercely afterward."

"It was amazing to float like that! I bet it's more fun to do that on your own as if you had wings!" Miral said holding her hand over her heart.

"'Tis indeed and it uses a lot of physical strength to cast magnetic reversal to float in that manner."

"Magic requires physical strength?"

"Not required, but it surely helps. If I wished to quake a large area, I could do so! I would feel the strain in every muscle from the force of splitting the rock in half, to sliding the broken halves against each other until they catch, and continuing to push them until they break under pressure, releasing the quake. The greater I make that quake, the more it takes from my own energy, and can even injure my body. Do you understand all that?" Justin asked her.

"Yes, I understand!" Miral replied. "How long does it take to wear yourself out, and can you die?"

Justin stared at her with wide eyes and a slightly open jaw. "Heavens! Those are some good questions. I am not sure how much spell casting it would take to be in danger. I never needed to use it to that degree." He rubbed his jaw while thinking. "Hmmm. Sara said that how much one can cast is dependent on their health and physical strength. Could you die?" He paused, glancing upwards as he rubbed his lower jaw again. "Yes, I imagine you can certainly push yourself to the breaking point."

Miral folded her hands together and held them before her. It all sounded dangerous enough before and now she regretted asking that question.

"Fear not," Justin said with a tilt of his head. "As you learn the feel of the spells, you will know how much you can withstand. Just listen to what your body is telling you."

Miral nodded. She wasn't certain she liked the sound of all that; however, what was the chance that any of them would need to fight to that extent? Irana is into something dark and vile, but no one on earth is so powerful that they can't be stopped with force. Justin was certain the other elder races would revolt against Irana in a heartbeat. She would lose.

"Is your magic the reason why nothing on this table is moving with the ship?" she asked Justin. "I can feel energy all around us, but I wasn't certain till now."

Justin smirked. "'Tis indeed."

Miral smiled at him, his magic was certainly useful. All that talk stirred yet another question in her mind. "Have you ever seen a god?"

Justin stared at her, looking as if the question took him aback.

73

"Where did that come from? What are you thinking about in there?" Agar chuckled, tapping Miral lightly on the forehead.

"No, sadly I have not, and I know not of anyone else seeing one either," Justin replied. "I do still believe, though. There are too many wonders in the world to think otherwise."

"That is exactly what I think too!"

"Truly? 'Tis a beautiful idea to share," he said placing his hand over his heart. "Any more questions, Lady Miral? Pray, keep them coming if you have them."

"That pendant," Miral said pointing at his neck. "What does it say?"

Justin lifted the pendant with his hand and held it out a bit closer to her. "Love, faith, justice, and honor, the creed of Arisdale. Perhaps 'twill include equality as mother wished, one day." He smiled wide. "These are given to royalty, the Elder Council and the eight leaders of the royal guard."

"Only two left now," Agar said.

Justin nodded. "I will have to promote six of the best from the soldiers. Those who meet the creed with a fiery passion. Their worth is not only measured in feats of strength but also in the qualities that make a good leader."

"I still don't know how Dilos became a general!" Agar interjected with a shake of his head. "I am glad that Captain Severos stayed behind, though; those poor soldiers and new recruits will need his kindness."

Justin sighed heavily. "I am glad as well. Dilos was promoted long before I was born. I would like to think that he was a better man then. Who knows, he is a brilliant tactician, and that may be why." Justin turned his attention back to Miral and smiled. "If you are ready, we can go practice magic, and teach you how to use the crystals to pass the time. 'Twill be easy for you out at sea. Tomorrow we will arrive in Arisdale."

Her heart beat faster with excitement to see what Arisdale looked like. "Ok, I am ready," Miral said standing from her seat, pushing it back to the table.

"Very well then," Justin replied with a nod before standing to join her.

"You two go ahead. I will clean up," Agar said with a smile.

Justin reached for Agar's helmet and took it from his head. His long black bangs tumbled out from under it covering his face.

"Hey! What are you doing?" Agar huffed in protest.

"I am giving Lady Miral your helmet to practice with. My armor is earth attuned after all, and far too big to fit her at that."

"Well, all right. Anything for Miral!" Agar said, followed by a wide grin.

Miral blushed. "Thank you, Agar."

"Sure thing, pretty lady!"

Justin rolled his eyes at Agar and chuckled. He gestured to the doorway. "After you, Lady Miral."

She bowed her head, went out the door, and up the stairs to the upper decks with Justin following behind her.

Chapter 13 - Magic

Once they ascended Justin stood in front of her and placed Agar's helmet on her head, grinning at her. "Not a bad look for you," he chuckled.

"I'm sure it looks terrible!" Miral said giggling. The ship crew watched them briefly before turning back to their duties. The sky was clear and vast with a deep and radiant blue. The breeze was cooler now than a day ago, but the warmth of the sun on the open deck chased away any chills.

"Let us start by finding Agar's magic energy. You may sit or stand, whatever is more comfortable for you."

The bobbing motion of the ship made her feel unstable, so she sat on the deck. She closed her eyes and searched for the magic energy of Agar. She could see her own blue energy all around her, and then she could see the green glow from Justin standing beside her. Between them, their colors merged and blended into an aqua shade. She had never seen that before and wondered what it meant. She continued and reached out to Agar. She imagined herself walking down the flight of steps to the lower decks. She saw an orange glow moving about ahead of her and drew closer to it. She could feel the static of his electricity around her as she got close to him. She opened her eyes and smiled at Justin.

"I could feel the lightning magic and the color of it!"

"Excellent!" Justin exclaimed. "You certainly have an accelerated learning. I have no doubt Sara will be fascinated."

"I do?"

"Indeed. It took me quite a few tries to be able to distinguish the magic type let alone see the color of it. Agar took even longer than I did."

Justin extended his hands to her. Miral placed her hands in his, and he helped her to her feet.

"Jus—," she paused remembering that the ship crew was all around her. "Your Majesty, I saw an aqua color between us where our powers merged."

"Did you now?" he asked with an arched brow and broad smile. "Splendid, we can work on that as well. What you saw was the combination of two coexisting main elements. The aqua color is holy magic. 'Tis created when life-bearing earth and life-giving waters combine into one. The power of healing and light."

"I can heal someone with my magic?"

"Only if we cast our magic together," Justin corrected. "Let us move on to some spell casting. Once you are more comfortable, we can try combining our powers." He approached the deck rails and spread his arms wide. "You have all the natural energy you could ever need to pull from out here; however, I will get you accustomed to the feel of the crystals."

"All right."

Justin removed the helmet from her head. "We will start with what you know already. Then you can try the same with the helmet on."

"Ok." Miral cast the one spell she knew, pulling glowing bits of water from the air into a small sphere with her mind. Once she collected enough, she let it fall into the sea below. She recalled Justin saying that one can feel a bit drained, and she did feel that, but it quickly faded once the channeling was complete. Justin placed the helmet back on her head, and she could feel a surge of energy around her.

"Cast it again. Draw from the crystals as well as the water this time."

She did as he asked and pulled water together once more while drawing energy from the yellow crystals. She formed the sphere and released it into the ocean.

"I didn't feel the drain this time!"

"Splendid! The crystals draw in magic continuously so they remain charged; however, you could draw from them to the extent that they are unable to recharge. As I said, I never had to do such a thing. Sara though, she will experiment with every factor. She said the crystals fail if overdrawn and will fracture. Now then, I would like you to try extending that spell's channel time. Get used to the feel of making the spell larger until we can speak with Sara."

She smiled at Justin and pulled at the water and crystals once more. She focused on the sphere allowing it to grow in volume. She monitored her body for fatigue or discomfort as she did. The sphere grew to the size of a human's head between her outstretched hands. She willed the orb to fall away, but it remained in place. She froze.

"Is something wrong?" Justin asked staring at her wide eyes and then the sphere.

"I can't release it the way I normally do!" she said in a raised tone.

"Try casting it forward," he replied, gesturing with a pushing motion.

Miral did as he asked willing the conjured liquid ball forward. A column of water erupted from her hands, taking her by surprise with its force, and causing her to stumble backward. Justin moved in a flash, catching her before she hit the deck.

"You all right, Miral?!" he asked helping her to her feet.

"Yes . . . I am," she said blushing.

Justin frowned. "I am terribly sorry for that."

"It wasn't your fault. Don't worry about it."

"Your simple water spell was actually a complex channeled spell. There was a lot of force behind that column!" Justin chuckled. "I would not want to be hit with that."

"That was a channeled spell?"

"No doubt."

"Did I miss anything?" Agar asked as he exited the double doors.

"Indeed, Miral here channeled a column of water that knocked her off her feet."

"Really?!" Agar said grinning. "I'm sorry I missed it!"

Justin bowed his head to Miral. "We can continue if you wish, Lady Miral. If you are feeling uncertain, then we will take it easy for the rest of the day."

"I think I will take it easy. Thank you for the lessons."

"As you wish, Lady Miral. 'Twas a pleasure," he gestured for her to walk with him to the helm.

"Thank you for letting me practice with your helmet, Agar," she said handing it to him.

"No problem, Miral! Did it help?"

"Yes, I could feel the difference with the gems. Even with that column of water."

"Good to hear!" Agar said smiling wide.

Miral laid on the deck of the ship and looked up to the sky. Her first channeled spell. The feel of it was intense and a bit frightening. Now that she had experienced it she was certain she could do it again. She wasn't sure if she wanted to, though. Justin was right, the force of the water column was powerful, and she could feel it rip through her muscles.

"Are you feeling well?" Justin asked looking down at her.

"Yes. It just feels good to lie in the morning sun. Tell me about Arisdale! What is it like?"

Justin smiled and sat cross-legged beside her. "Arisdale is a coastal kingdom in a temperate climate zone. The castle and outlying village sit on top of cliffs that are two thousand feet above the sea. This was a tactical location chosen by the first King, Hardaric Arisdale, about three thousand years ago, prior to the absence of Fandia. Arisdale has grown since 'twas established. The central keep, devotion chamber, and two of the front towers were the first constructions. Over the years, walls were built to surround the castle commons. A thousand years later two more towers were constructed. Five hundred years ago a housing quarter for staff and the Elder Council members, a banquet hall and ballroom were added. Arisdale is the largest of the remaining kingdoms in size and tracts of land that we govern. The village has about two hundred and fifty thousand people and is slightly over one square mile."

"That all sounds amazing! Temperate zone, so do you get the . . . um . . . the frozen water from the sky?"

"Snow?" Justin asked.

"Yes, snow!" Miral replied with a raised tone, staring at him eagerly, waiting to hear more. The last time she had seen snow she was far too young to really remember what it was like. The faint hint of childhood excitement lingered in the background, though.

"Indeed, we do," he nodded. "Soon 'twill be the winter season, then 'twill snow one day. How much varies; however, being so close to the sea often gives us far more than the center lands."

Agar laughed. "Ah, yes, for an island dweller that would be a sight to see! We take it for granted. I remember my first snowfall! You will love it, Miral."

She beamed at Agar. "I can't wait!"

Justin smiled at her with that soft look. "I would like to ask you a question, Lady Miral."

"Sure," she replied.

"Tell me about your mother, if you are up for it."

"My mother? Her name was Sonya. She had fair skin like mine, and blonde hair. She was from a small village to the northeast of Arisdale called Fovran. Father met her there, and that is where I was born. We moved to Delphi when I was three. My mother died when I was ten years old. She got very ill," Miral sniffled, fighting back tears.

Justin frowned at her. "Oh, I am sorry, Lady Miral."

Miral nodded. "It was so long ago, and I know they are together in the World of Light now."

"Yes, the World of Light, praise be to Fandia for that. There is no end, only new beginnings."

Miral stopped sniffling and stared at him. Their beliefs were the same. She knew there was a shared religion of Fandia and the Silver Dolphins, but to hear it from an Arisdalian as well was grand.

"One more day at sea," Agar groaned.

"What do you do to pass the time?" Miral asked him.

"Justin and I would spar or play games, and sometimes they let us navigate the ship! Good thing we paid attention!" Agar said elbowing Justin.

"You paid attention? I believe the correct answer is, I made you pay attention." Justin laughed and looked at her. "Agar has the attention span of a gnat."

"I do not!" Agar huffed in protest, crossing his arms.

"Surely you do."

Agar glared at Justin and waved his hand in dismissal. "Yeah, yeah."

"What about yourself, Lady Miral? What was life like for you?" Justin asked her.

Miral sat upright and frowned. "I . . . uh . . . things were hard for me. My father and I struggled for years just to live. We were lucky that . . . I mean when Irana was still a nice Queen, she gave us jobs in the castle. We were well fed but never truly well off. My father was my only friend and family. So, there isn't anyone I have left behind."

Justin wore a wide-eyed expression of disbelief. "Why is that? Not a single other person cared for you in Delphi?"

"Well . . ." she replied in a quiver, fiddling with her fingers. This part of her life she didn't want to share, but Justin's piercing eyes were studying her once more, seeing through to her core. Agar had told her Justin's sad tale. Perhaps it would make her feel better to share hers with them. She buried her face in her hands. "The other Delphinians are afraid of my family. My mother's illness spread and killed other people. They said it was a plague, but Father and I never caught it. Then I was angry about what they were saying about her. It began to rain, and the water hovered off the ground in large spheres all around me. I rose in the air with the water, almost like we were one. The rain . . . it fell in torrents, flooding everything. It scared them! It scared me!"

"Heavens, 'tis such a tragic thing to hear, Lady Miral. I am sorry about your mother," Justin said placing his hand over his heart. "These diseases have come in waves throughout Flourisha, often unexplained and occurring oddly. If such a disease were truly a plague then many would succumb, and yet the illness seems to choose victims at random," Justin said shaking his head. "That reaction with your magic was certainly elemental rage. For some reason, our magic reacts to rage in a way that takes it out of your control and self-feeds more rage. We are not sure why. As you know, I cause quakes and earthen objects to lift upwards as you had with your water. Sara Phoenix ignites anything near her on fire. Agar generates a significant amount of static, and emits electricity from his body."

Miral pulled her hands from her face and looked into Justin's sincere eyes.

Agar hung his head and looked away from them. "Just because it's an uncommon gift, it shouldn't make you feel that you're defective." Agar drove his dagger into the wood of the deck with a hard thrust.

Miral stared at him with drooping eyes. Agar knew all too well what that feeling was like. He was abandoned because of magic. There was something more to it, though. His enraged magic was deadlier in an instant than hers or Justin's.

Agar stopped stabbing at the deck and looked at her. "Well, Miral, you have friends now. Right, big brother!"

"Yes, of course!" Justin said smiling warmly at her.

Miral returned a smile. She wasn't alone anymore, and she was grateful for that. A loud sickening thump rocked the left side of the ship, and Miral placed her hand over her heart. Justin was on his feet in seconds and peered over the railing to the left as Agar looked to the right. The helmsman glanced between them then hailed the lookout. Miral watched Justin as he scanned the ocean. She saw his head feathers standing on end and quickly got to her feet. "Justin, what is it?"

"Don't worry, Miral. It's probably just a sea dragon, they are harmless!" Agar shouted still looking into the water.

Miral trembled in fear as a large blue-scaled tentacle wrapped around her chest from behind and pulled at her. "Justin!" she screamed.

"Damn!" Justin shouted. He ran to her and wrapped his arm around her. He grabbed hold of the helm with his other hand and fought the creature in a tug of war. "Get below deck!" he shouted to the crew. The helmsman leapt from the top deck and scurried away with the rest of the crew.

"What the hell?!" Agar exclaimed, running to them. "Have to get her free before I can shock this thing into the next life!" Agar drove his daggers into the giant tentacle, but they barely penetrated the surface. "This is some tough hide!"

Miral jerked her head back as a loud roar erupted from behind her. Another tentacle grabbed hold of the deck rails, slowly tipping the end of the ship towards the ocean.

"Whoa!" Agar shouted losing his footing, sliding towards the sea. He grabbed hold of Justin's leg and clung to him. "Don't let go, brother!" he hissed, his fur standing on end as he stared at his greatest fear, the water below.

"I do not intend to, Agar!" Justin replied in a strained voice.

The ship was tilted dangerously, and the three dangled helplessly from the helm like bait on a hook. Miral stared wide-eyed as the enormous head of a sea dragon reached into the sky. The ship leveled out as it rose, and the monstrous beast peered down at them with glowing yellow eyes. The creature pulled on her harder, and Justin tugged back, fighting to keep her on the ship. Agar continued to slash at the creature, but he didn't seem to be winning. Miral struggled for air as the dragon tightened its grip on her.

"Dodge left!" Justin shouted as the creature swung its free tentacle at Agar.

Agar dodged to the left disappearing into stealth, and Justin pulled her low, ducking as a tentacle swung overhead.

There was a warming presence that she became aware of as her vision faded. A brilliant white light and the comforting glow of aqua filled her mind. *Is the aqua light holy magic, the power that exists between Justin and me?* She stared pleadingly into his eyes, desperate to tell him she couldn't get enough air.

Justin noticed the look in her eyes and his breath caught in his throat when she fell limp. "Miral?! Agar, free her, she cannot breathe!"

Agar remained in stealth cutting at the tentacle. "I don't think I can hack through this, brother!" Agar replied in alarm.

Justin's feet slid forward as the dragon tugged harder on Miral. "Grab the helm, then grab me!"

Agar grabbed the helm then wrapped an arm around Justin. "Man, this thing is strong! How can you fight it?!"

Justin sent his will into the ocean, finding and dislodging a chunk of the seabed. He grabbed hold of it with his magic, swinging his arm in an arc towards the creature and a large boulder flew forth from the water, slamming into the creature's head with a loud crack. The dragon appeared dazed and released its hold on Miral.

"Do it!" Justin shouted hopping over the helm and into the double doors below with Miral in his arms. Agar ran and hid behind the main mast and channeled his thunderhead.

"Time to take that big nap in the sky!" he said as he released the rain of lightning over the sea dragon.

Justin heard the loud crack and rumble of thunder followed by a roar, loud splashing of ocean water, and then silence. He laid Miral down, listened to her chest, and sighed in relief with the sound of her heartbeat. He picked her up from the floor. The crew that had taken shelter here stared in silence. He carried her down the next flight to her room and laid her on the bed. "I am sorry, Miral."

"Is she ok?" Agar asked in an unsteady tone as he ran into the room.

Justin looked back at him and nodded. "She is alive, somehow."

"That is a relief!" Agar took a deep breath. "Damn, I wonder why that thing was so interested in her! I'll get the ship and crew back on course. You stay with her," he said placing a hand on Justin's shoulder.

"All right, brother," he replied as he sat on the edge of the bed.

Agar nodded and ran off, gathering the fearful crew.

Justin watched Miral carefully and pondered the event, rubbing his lower jaw. Sea dragons were often content enough with their own food supply. Collisions with ships that resulted in holes and lost vessels have been reported, but never an assault. It was evident the dragon didn't want to eat them, as it did not fight back with its mouth. What did it want?

Chapter 14 - Sanctuary

"Miral."

"Hmmm," she groaned.

"Miral, wake up."

She opened her eyes wide, her breath rapid, the memory of her father when he woke her in Delphi in a panic flooded her mind. She gripped the bedsheets tightly over her heart as it raced. She looked to the left and sighed deep in relief when she saw Justin sitting on the edge of the bed, fully dressed in his armor. She closed her eyes and took a few deep breaths.

"Are you all right? Did I frighten you?" he asked.

Miral shook her head and released her grip of the sheets. "No, it's just . . . my father woke me when the attack started and that dragon—" she replied, tears welling up in her eyes.

"Oh, Miral, I am terribly sorry."

"It's ok," she murmured stifling the tears. "I'm happy that you are all right. Is Agar?"

Justin smiled at her. "As I am that you are, Lady Miral. He is fine as well."

"I thank you both for saving me!"

"We are friends, Lady Miral, and as such, we always protect each other."

"How long was I out for?"

"About a day. I woke you because we have arrived. I thought you would like to see the view of Arisdale from the ship. 'Tis quite breathtaking!"

Miral beamed and her heart quickened in her chest. "We have?!" She got up from the bed and walked with Justin to the stairs of the upper deck. He gestured for her to ascend first. The brightness of the sun caused her to squint as she exited the doorway. Once they adjusted, she stood transfixed. The sight that unfolded before her was beyond what she imagined.

"Welcome to Arisdale!" Justin said standing by the deck rails with his right arm stretched out in presentation.

"Wow!" Miral said in awe, approaching the left side of him. Her wide eyes took in the majesty that laid before her. Waterfalls cascaded down the sides of the cliffs in various places. A flock of white-colored sea birds flew by, drawing her gaze to a rainbow that stretched gracefully across the mists of the falls. Arisdale Castle sat proudly upon the towering cliffs like a king on a throne of stone.

Justin stood to her right looking out at his home with a content smile. His crimson cape and head feathers were billowing in the crisp breeze. Miral shivered when a strong gust blew past. Arisdale felt drastically cooler than Delphi. She folded her arms in a self-embrace, rubbing them with her hands. Her dress was made of light fabric, suitable for cold days in Delphi, but not the temperate climate of Arisdale. She saw Justin's crimson cape being draped over her shoulders and stopped rubbing her arms.

"Cold?" Justin asked her in a concerned tone.

"Thank you, Justin." His cape was a thick, soft cloth and felt warm around her.

"A pleasure, Lady Miral."

Justin and Agar were both wearing sleeveless suits of armor and didn't appear fazed by the chill. Agar had fur, and Justin had thick scaly skin. They must be better suited to the colder weather. She looked back at the scene before her. Arisdale appeared to be a kingdom of might and splendor from her vantage point.

"Good to see you up and about, Miral!" Agar shouted from the helm.

She turned and waved to him. "Good to see you too, Agar!"

Agar grinned and ordered the helmsmen to guide the ship into port.

"All hail the Princes of Arisdale," a royal guard in white and gold armor ordered as he drove the end of his spear into the ground with a loud clack. The soldiers present saluted Justin and Agar as they descended from the ship plank. Her eyes were drawn to a guard behind the one that spoke. He had smoky-colored scales with red stripes and red head feathers with yellow tips; however, what actually made her take notice of him were his red eyes lined with brilliant yellow around the pupil. He looked more intimidating than Justin with the dark scales and piercing eyes.

The royal guard who commanded the others behind him, briefly took note of her standing between Justin and Agar with his orange eyes, before looking past them toward the ship. "Highnesses, where is—?"

"Captain Severos," Agar said placing his hand upon his shoulder and leaned to whisper to him.

Severos had light green-colored scales with a cream color from his lower jaw down his neck. The array of bony plates from his head down to the base of his neck was a tan color with orange and black stripes. His tail had four large spikes sticking out of the sides near the tip. Miral thought he looked kindly in his face and expressions; however, his tail spikes gave him an intimidating air.

Severos's face shifted as Agar whispered to him. The corner of his beaked muzzle sagged into a frown and he squeezed his eyes shut. He nodded to Agar and clasped Justin on the shoulder, bowing his head and remained silent. She knew Justin wanted to address this sensitive subject carefully, making the announcement to the masses as a whole rather than allow hearsay to warp the truth.

Severos removed his hand from Justin. He turned to her and bowed at the waist. "Welcome, milady Miral." He stood and gestured out with his hand. "Highnesses and Lady, there is a carriage waiting to take you to the castle."

"Thank you, my friend," Justin said holding his hand out palm facing down.

Severos, Agar, and Justin clasped hands atop each other before parting ways. She swiveled her head as they walked. The docks of Arisdale were certainly more impressive in size and upkeep than the ones at Delphi. She expected to find all of this kingdom giving that same impression.

Justin paused in front of the gilded carriage before turning to her. "After you, milady," he said, offering to take her hand to help her into the large red-cushioned carriage. She accepted and entered, taking a seat in the back. Justin and Agar sat across from her.

"What are those animals?" Miral asked pointing to the two-legged feral dinosaurs attached to the carriage.

"They are called Galli," Justin replied. "Very hardy, loyal, and noble creatures."

The green and peach-skinned Galli had large black eyes, and long yellow feathers streaming from their heads and tails. She thought they were adorable.

The carriage lurched and rolled forward from the dock then along a winding gray cobble road. The path took them up a steady incline from sea level to the two-thousand-foot high cliff tops.

Miral's mouth hung open when they crested the top of the emerald green hill. "The trees!" she blurted out with bright eyes and a broad smile.

Justin and Agar stared at each other in bewilderment.

"I heard about the colored trees of autumn from traveling merchants! I've dreamt about what they looked like, and wanted to see them with my own eyes!" The landscape was speckled with a carpet of brilliant yellow, orange, and red-colored treetops. "They are grander than I imagined!" she sighed. Feral species of long-necked dinosaurs and Triceratops roamed the fields grazing on colored vegetation. She could see Justin smiling at her as she absorbed the scene.

They passed the large iron gates to the village, and she watched the well-kept town of Arisdale as they rolled by. Arisdalians of all kinds were about their daily chores.

As they passed the village center square, she could smell various baked goods, and heard children laughing while they played in the streets. Some citizens stopped to watch the royal carriage as it went by, waving in the excitement of their sovereigns. In the distance the castle sat at a higher elevation than the enormous village, giving it the appearance of being a watchful protector.

The architecture of the buildings was unlike Delphi's. They appeared to be made of white granite stones with dark brown wood framing the structure and vertical boards decorating the faces. Many of the buildings were two stories and were likely the homes of the rich folk and merchants. The size of the village made Delphi appear as small as she felt around Justin.

The carriage reached the iron gates of Arisdale Castle and Miral's jaw dropped. The feeling Arisdale presented from the sea continued into the grand gothic-style castle; gray granite walls sparkled in the comforting sunlight. Four massive keeps, two on each side of the main road reached for the heavens. Red flags on top of the towers and royal banners hanging from the walls waved as if in greeting.

"The four keeps are the first line of defense for the castle," Justin said. "They stand sixty feet tall, and the walls are thirty feet thick. There are openings for archers and other siege defenses. This alley we are in now has become known as the gauntlet; 'tis a dangerous trek and attackers are unlikely to reach the central keep without a lot of casualties. The towers are also the soldiers' quarters, strategy rooms, and training halls for the royal guards' platoons. The round building ahead of us is known as the devotion chamber. 'Tis a place dedicated to the worship of Fandia."

Miral looked at the round marble chamber with a gilded silver door and roof. She wondered what the inside of the odd shaped building looked like. Behind the chamber was a massive keep, centered between two other smaller stone buildings.

"The central keep houses the throne room, council room, prison cells, and living quarters for the royal family and honored guests, which is where you will be staying," Justin continued. "To the left are the banquet hall and ballroom, and the stables. To the right are living quarters for the Elder Council and castle staff, and the grand castle gardens."

The castle gardens were a lovely sight from her vantage point. She was eager for a chance to look at all the plant life she had never seen before. They came to a stop before the main keep. In front of the pair of gilded oak doors, stood a beautiful elder race Arisdalian bird. She wore a large pointed helmet of gold, with one large pink ethereal gem, and two small round aqua gems on the sides. Her white dress blended with her body feather color. She did look remarkably similar to Justin's mother, Queen Anelda.

Agar and Justin exited the carriage. Justin turned to take Miral's hand and help her down. The lady who must be Galena greeted Justin with a warm hug. She was shorter than him by about a half foot. Most Arisdalians appeared to be taller than the average human. What she feared was looking to be true; she was a tiny helpless human woman in a world of giants.

"Justin dear, welcome home!" she said as she stepped back from him. She looked over to Agar and greeted him the same. She smiled warmly at Miral and approached her. "Greetings, milady. Welcome to Arisdale. I am Galena Shanahan."

"It is a pleasure to make your acquaintance, Lady Shanahan," she curtsied. "I am Miral Akemi."

"Oh, how lovely!" Galena replied, hugging Miral. She pulled back from her and lifted her brows. "I can feel her magic, water to be precise!"

Miral smiled at her. "Yes, Lady Galena, I can use water magic."

"A human Elemental?" Galena replied quizzically. "Well, you left to talk to King Charles and Queen Irana about a peace treaty, and returned with a water elemental! How splendid!" she said with delight and a clap of her hands. Her expression quickly shifted to concern when she glanced to the carriage. "Justin? Where are Yarway, Anelda, and Johanas?"

Justin approached his aunt hugging her tightly. "I am sorry," he said with a choke in his voice.

Galena's eyes filled with tears.

"They are in the World of Light now."

She cried in racking sobs, squeezing Justin tighter. "Why?!" she wailed, fighting to get her breath. "What happened?"

"I do not have all the answers yet," he replied, firming his embrace. "Irana has gone mad, and she commands a magic of dark origin. She killed them all, and Miral's father," he said through gritted teeth. "The entirety of Delphi are mindless slaves to her will." Justin released his aunt from the embrace.

After a long cry, Galena looked over at Miral, tears still streaming from her eyes.

"I'm sorry for your loss, Lady Galena," Miral said bowing her head.

Galena approached Miral, and embraced her once again. "As I am for you, child." She released Miral, looking her over. Her brow wrinkled, and she touched her four-clawed hand to her beak. "Oh, dear!" Galena said. "This is going to make things quite difficult!"

Justin placed an arm around his aunt. "Yes! I will need your help formulating a strategy to handle this!"

Galena patted Justin on his arm. "I will set to work on that," she said, her expression shifting to a frown. "Speaking of, the elders are chomping at the bit! They want word on how your visit went. Given the nature of the matter, it cannot wait! My best advice for you at this moment is honesty."

Justin sulked and threw his hands up. "Bah! I really do not want to deal with them after just returning!"

Agar wrapped his arm around Justin's back. "Them or General Dilos?" he asked.

Justin's eyes narrowed, his back hunched and he sighed heavily. "Both!"

Agar pulled on Justin's arm. "Come on, big guy! Let's get this painful process over with!"

Galena tsked. "Justin! I will show Miral around awhile, get her situated with a room. Then I will take the young lady to town and get her some clothes from Adra!"

Justin abruptly spun around toward Galena and Miral, pulling free from his brother's grip. Agar stumbled but caught himself before he fell.

"That would be splendid, Galena!" Justin replied while jogging to them. "No need to be stingy with the purse either! Get her a good wardrobe of various dresses, and whatever else she needs," Justin said smiling at Miral. He bowed to her. "I must take my leave, milady. I shall see you later."

She didn't feel she deserved so much. All she had was her mother's dress, though. Winter was around the corner, and Arisdale would only get colder. "Thank you, Your Majesty," she said, curtsying to him. "See you later then."

Justin bowed his head and turned away with Agar. Miral clutched his crimson cape in her hands and drew it tighter around her as he disappeared into the keep.

"Well then, Miral, come with me and I will give you the grand tour!" Galena chirped with delight.

Chapter 15 - Kindness

"I knew it! Did I not say thusly?!" General Dilos bellowed with conceit while addressing the Elder Council.

Justin sighed at Dilos. The large room felt drastically smaller and stuffy since he shared his report on the events in Delphi, giving the illusion that the world was closing in on him, and as he had expected, Dilos's ego had grown.

In attendance were the five men and women of the Elder Council, the remaining heads of the Arisdalian Royal Guard, General Dilos Manning and Captain Severos Miragaia.

He really didn't want to be in this position. Three days ago his mother and father were alive and well. How life can change in a heartbeat. Regrets followed. *One never thinks today will be the last day. Someone who was there is now gone. The old saying that every day should be lived in the present and to its fullest was clear. Mother taught me that change is part of the natural flow of life. To resist change is to suffer. Accept that change will happen, accept change when it comes, and learn to flow with that change. Turn change into a positive experience. That is what she taught me. All things happen for a reason. Life is ever changing. Even the seasons do not remain the same. Why would you?*

Elder Nyros, a Parasaurolophus, and Headmaster of the Elder Council stood and addressed Dilos. "Yes, general, you clearly voiced your concerns of treachery to the king and council when last we conversed. Our sovereigns were resolute and adamant. 'Twould seem we all bore false hope."

Justin fumed within. General Dilos, the snide, olive, and cream-skinned Dilophosaurus, never failed to be openly vocal of his hate of humanity. *By far the biggest weed in the garden.* Dilos believed peace treaties were a trap and begged them not to go. Justin had to admit there was a possibility Queen Irana had set a trap; however, there was no proof.

"Be that as it may, general, the acts of Irana alone do not speak for the whole of Delphi!" Justin said. "Were you not so focused on the fact that she is human, you would have heard me speak of the helpless, mindless citizens! I highly doubt they allowed that to happen to them just so they could kill us!" Justin snapped, gesturing with his clawed hands turned upward.

General Dilos's orange eyes narrowed. "How is it you are so certain the human citizens were helpless? Do you now have the power of foresight?!" he quipped with derision and raised arms.

Justin felt his blood boiling, growing in intensity with heat spreading through his body. He took a few deep breaths in an attempt to calm himself.

"No, no that is right . . . faith, yes?" General Dilos said, rubbing his tan, orange and yellow-striped head crest. "You have always acted on that principle, and one of these days that means of action will bring you death!"

"Dilos!" Agar shouted, "that is enough!"

Elder Nyros narrowed his light blue eyes at Dilos. "Drop your arrogant attitude, general or I will have you removed!"

"Elders, forgive me in my grief," Dilos replied bowing to Elder Nyros.

Justin shook his head. *Dilos ought to be a drama actor not a general.* He had despised Dilos all his life, and similarly, Dilos hated him just as much. He felt a knot grow in his gut. He still had to tell them about Miral. "One other matter, Elders . . ." Justin said, running his hand through his head feathers. "We encountered the Elemental of Water on our travels."

"Excellent!" Elder Nyros replied with enthusiasm. "You seem nervous. Why is this a matter of concern?"

Justin shifted his weight, the amount of dread he felt towards the words he was about to utter made him feel heavier. "She is . . . Delphinian." He tensed ready for the onslaught that was sure to come.

"Heresy!" Dilos bellowed with flared nostrils. "The goddess would never grant a human such a gift! This surely is another trap! I wager you brought her with you because you sensed she is innocent. Just like you did with that human thief! Am I right?!" he snapped. Dilos's gaze was locked on him, and Justin stood rigid and silent. "Unbelievable!" Dilos huffed, throwing his arms up, then running his hand through his orange head feathers.

"'Tis no trap! Her inner light is pure and blindingly bright, there is no darkness in her! She is no liar either, her words are truthful! Just like that human, that was not a thief!" Justin crouched with hands out, head feathers standing on end sickle claws erect, ready to pounce.

Agar reached for him grabbing his shoulder and arm and pulled him back. "Justin speaks the truth. She has a soul that seems untainted. You also know that he was right about that man being falsely accused, and you were the one who did so, Dilos!"

"I concur with the prince and acting king," Severos said bowing.

Dilos's face twisted into a glower but he remained silent.

Elder Nyros stood, his greyish-blue scaled hands tucked into his white long sleeves. "We have much to consider, and a coronation to prepare for," Nyros said with a nod. "Given the uncertain danger that Delphi poses, 'twould be best to proceed with the ceremony sooner than is customary. The human woman is granted a stay for the time being, although we will be keeping a close eye on her! I want a royal guard by her side at all times," Elder Nyros said to Justin.

Justin nodded to the Elders. He certainly didn't want Dilos to watch over her. It will take time, but he was sure Miral's gentle nature would warm their cold hearts.

"Allow me, sire," Severos said without hesitation, bowing to Justin. "It would be an honor to have that responsibility."

Justin smiled wide. "I am pleased, Severos, you are hereby assigned to watch over Lady Miral. If you are required for action or meetings, then I ask that you leave her with Galena."

Severos stood and saluted Justin. "As you wish, sire."

Elder Nyros nodded. "Very well then. We will break for the moment and reconvene within the hour to plan our address to the realm, and begin our evaluation for new recruits into the royal guard."

"You may all be excused," Justin said gesturing to the door.

The Elders and General Dilos left the conference room and closed the door behind them.

Agar sighed heavily while leaning against the gray granite wall of the council room by a window. "Why did the water elemental have to be human?"

Justin shrugged and approached Agar. "'Tis by the goddess's design, brother. She may wish for us to stop fighting amongst each other for once. What better way than to force our hand." He looked out the window and saw Miral sitting on a bench in the castle gardens. "She is a unique human. So pure and free of malice," he said while rubbing his lower jaw. "Truly makes me wonder if we have simply misunderstood each other terribly. The actions of a few cynical souls should not contaminate the whole population."

Agar joined him at the window. "I have to agree with you, brother. She fills me with hope for humanity. Maybe she will be the one who brings this ugly business to an end."

Chapter 16 - Wisdom

Miral hummed her mother's song happily as she enjoyed the sights of the castle garden. The fragrant scents from an array of multi-colored flowers filled her nose with joy. The strongest aroma came from the red roses. She had never seen them before, and every archway in the garden had vines of them intertwined through the lattices. Rows of the beautiful flowers lined the gray granite walls of the castle. Roses were her favorite among the garden flowers of Arisdale.

A large rectangular pond with what Galena said were water lilies sat before her. She had no doubt this area was used in gatherings and looked amazing at night. Ethereal crystal lamps sat in the pond and on decorative poles throughout the garden. She peered through an opening in the castle wall at a massive cliff in the distance. She hugged Justin's cape to herself as she continued to hum. She smiled when a flock of golden birds of Arisdale perched on the castle walls. They peered down at her and looked eager to come closer but hesitated, shifting their stare past her.

"Greetings, Lady Miral!" Justin's voice called out from behind her.

The golden birds watched him carefully as he approached.

Miral turned her head to look at him. "Hello, Justin!"

"What have you been about while I was suffering?" Justin asked in a sarcastic tone before taking a seat beside her on the bench.

Miral giggled. "Lady Galena showed me around the main keep, and where I'll be sleeping," she replied beaming. "Arisdale is splendid! I love it here in the garden the most!"

Justin sat up straight and smiled. "Thank you kindly!" He ran his hand through his head feathers. "I am sorry to inform you that the elders wish for you to be watched for a time. I think it best for your safety. Captain Severos Miragaia will be by your side when Galena cannot. He is a good friend. He will keep you safe."

"Oh, I understand," she said looking down at her feet. But it hurt that they didn't trust her, and also the fact that she could be in danger here. She really couldn't blame them though, not after what Irana had done. She glanced at Justin and noticed his searching stare was focused on her the instant her eyes met his. He was reading her and likely already knew what she wasn't saying, and that made her feel uneasy. "Those birds, they are the ones on your royal crest, right?" Miral asked pointing to the wall where more had gathered.

"They are indeed," Justin replied, staring at them with his jaws slightly open. "I have never seen them gather quite like this. I wonder what has their interest."

"Birds seem to like me. All animals actually."

Justin took his eyes from them and gazed at her quizzically. "Truly?"

"They approach me if no one else is around."

"'Tis a wonder indeed." He leaned a bit closer and spoke in a lowered tone. "Perhaps 'tis your charm, Lady Miral."

Miral blushed with the deep tone of his voice. "My charm? Oh, um, I don't know about that," she fumbled with her fingers. "How did they become the royal crest symbol?"

"An excellent question," he exclaimed in reply. "When Arisdale was first founded these birds made their homes among the cliffs. 'Tis said that King Hardaric Arisdale admired them for their beauty, grace, and resolve to roost in this manner. They can only be found along the coast as far as our domain reaches north and south. 'Tis what defined our boundaries thousands of years ago."

"Oh! I agree that they are lovely," Miral replied with a smile. "What is that tree up there?" She pointed to a cliff that sat a good thousand feet higher than Arisdale, and on the tip was a bare tree.

Justin stared at the tree, his expression shifting between softened eyes and a frown to smiling. He closed his eyes a moment then looked at her. "Mother and Father planted that tree after their wedding. 'Tis a symbol for us to stand tall and firm, beautiful and true, despite all that surrounds you. No matter how difficult or dangerous, be like that tree, exist as you are and not as others want you to be."

"That is beautiful!" Miral said folding her hands together over her heart. "Can you show me that tree one day?"

"I would love to. The view from the cliff is inspirational! I thought carefully about life looking down at Arisdale from on high," he said while gesturing towards the cliff. "The kingdom looks so small, and the world is expansive. Personal issues seem insignificant when you realize you are but one," Justin said with a smile and silently stared at the tree for a time. "The tree has pink blooms in the spring. Best to view it then; however, we can certainly venture there before winter."

"Great, spring then!" Miral said smiling wide. She imagined what a tree with pink blooms would look like. The vision her mind conjured was glorious, and she couldn't wait until spring came.

Justin nodded to her. "As you wish, milady."

"Justin?"

"Pray what?"

"Well, um . . . what do you fear?"

Justin stared at her with narrowed eyes, blinking a few times.

"You seem like your element, resilient, strong, and fearless. I don't know how to be."

"Ah, well," Justin replied scratching his head, "'tis an illusion, milady. Even the strongest of mind and heart will fear something. The secret to overcoming fear is to challenge its truth. To allow oneself to experience negative things and feel safe. One must feel fear without allowing fear to control. It takes courage to stand tall and say enough is enough." Justin sighed before answering her question. "What I am afraid of? I have more than one fear; however, I do fear the same as you."

Miral stared at Justin, unable to make her mouth speak the words in her mind.

"I saw your fear, Miral," Justin said with a frown and lowered head. "Your father, when he died, your concern was evident, in scent, in actions, in your eyes, and in your voice. You do not want to be alone, am I right? You have managed to convince yourself that you will always be alone without him, yes?"

Miral frowned and nodded. She felt tears pool in her eyes. Her mind played out a scene, head hung low, shuffling through life as people walked by, as if she was invisible to them. *My life has always been that way, hasn't it?* She rubbed her eyes and looked up at him. "How is our fear the same? You're a prince. There are so many people in your life."

"Sometimes loneliness goes beyond who is around you, and is about . . . who is not," he muttered staring off towards the cliffs once more.

"Your parents?" Miral asked him.

Justin looked at her with solemn eyes. "That is part of it now. Least until I accept what has happened. Despite that, I have good friends, and even if they should all pass, I know I will never be truly alone. In time, I will find others to call friend. There is just, well, something is missing, and that is where my fear of being lonely lives. I have yet to find a way to not be afraid of it."

"What is missing?" she asked.

Justin's head feathers spiked causing him to run his hand through them as he turned his head away from her.

Miral scolded herself and replied, "I'm sorry, you don't have to answer that!"

He turned his sunny eyes back to her and took a deep breath. "'Tis just . . . not something I like to talk about." He smiled at her, his brows lifted and he chuckled. "Ah, where is Galena?"

"Lady Galena will be coming to take me to town soon. She was needed to heal someone, and asked me to wait here."

"I see, very well." Justin shifted his weight, leaning back with elbows propped on top of the bench. He fixed her with a skeptical glance. "Has anyone been discourteous to you, Lady Miral?"

Miral leaned forward with hands on the edge of the bench, swinging her legs back and forth. She was too short for the bench that was designed for taller-in-stature Arisdalians. "Not directly," she replied. She heard whispers and saw stares directed at her, but that was all. Justin watched her closely once more, no doubt analyzing her.

"I will take that with much relief." Justin leaned forward slumping with head down and sighed.

Miral stopped swinging her legs and looked him over in concern. "What's wrong?"

He focused on his hands a moment, then glanced her way with a frown. "I am not certain I can do this, be a King, I mean. 'Tis overwhelming, and I do not know how to get all the madness in line." He sat back up and looked ahead, throwing his hands up in frustration. "Irana made such a mess of things, and made life here difficult for you! The humans Arisdalians speak of so hatefully, you do not fit those descriptions at all, Miral. Negativity, crude behavior, violent aggression, thieves, and killers," he said while looking at her sincerely. "'Tis not fair to judge everyone equally, based on others' indiscretions!" he shrugged. "How do I mend this? How do I get the people to understand what I can see?"

Miral reached for his right wrist and pulled his hand closer to meet hers. Holding his hand flat to hers, she stared in awe, her small hand fitted entirely within his. "What do you see?" she asked.

Justin leaned close to her and craned his head to see her hand against his.

"Hands, yours and mine. They appear different in size, in the number of fingers, and color. Despite that, both are capable of doing the same things. Even if they are done in different ways, one is not greater than the other. 'Tis all the same."

Miral smiled at him warmly and released his wrist. "What you said about humans is what humans say about Arisdalians. I think if you want to get through to them, you need to show them. Let them see the similarity, and they will learn to see life this way. I think the more one preaches, demands, and pushes, the more they lose in turn."

He stared intently at her with gentle smiling eyes as she spoke. Only this time, there was the light of fire in them as well.

"Justin, you are the perfect man to be king. You see things for what they are. Be true to yourself. Your natural being is what will lead you to success."

Justin wore a big smile and raised his arms. "Milady, that was positively brilliant! You truly are a wonder!"

Miral blushed at the compliment and found herself speechless.

"I thank you for being true to yourself. Because of you I see the world in a way I never have before!" Justin stood, and offered her his hand. "Pray, come with me! I want to show you something! Galena will not mind waiting."

Miral reached to take his hand, letting him help her off the bench. He released her hand and extended his arm, elbow bent to her. She had seen the nobles in Delphi escort ladies around this way before. Certainly never herself, and now that she was being offered an escort in this way, her blushing grew till her face felt on fire. She placed her hand on his arm and with a bow of his head they walked past the red rose bushes. That is when she realized he wasn't alone. Two guards stood at attention a few feet beyond the bushes. They were wearing a uniform similar to the one Captain Severos wore only the gold was a gray-colored metal, and they had no gemstones. The guard on the left who held a spear was familiar to her. She had seen him down at the docks when they arrived. She could never forget those sharp eyes against the dark scales. Now that he was not blocked by anyone, she could see that he had sickle claw talons like Justin's only they were smaller in size. Behind him was a tail lined with yellow tipped, red feathers at the base. It remained still as he stood stiffly in salute. She wondered what he was like as a person since his appearance generated assumptions she forced herself to ignore.

Justin bowed his head to them before he passed. After a few paces, the clanking metal of the guards' armors and their talons could be heard behind them. She thought about what it must be like to have guards around you all the time, as if they were your shadow, ever a part of you.

"I am taking you to the devotion chamber. I wager a guess Galena has not shown you yet," Justin said pulling her from her thinking.

"She told me you would want to!" Miral replied.

Justin nodded. "'Tis my favorite place to be. History claims that the chamber was constructed sometime during the Age of Fandia, between five thousand and two thousand AOF. The chamber was here when Arisdale was first founded. There are others like this. I have seen one in Egyptalia and in Volga. The room is filled with murals of Fandia, the elemental diamond of balance, and the Silver Dolphins."

Fandia, the Goddess of Light and Love, was the creator of life on earth roughly five thousand years ago. What the Silver Dolphins actually were is unknown, and the races all have their opinions. Some say they are Fandia's source of power, while others liken them as a higher-level god than Fandia. Some say the eight Elementals are the embodiment of the Silver Dolphins.

Justin stood before the silver gilded door of the devotion chamber, waiting. The dark-scaled guard stepped forward and opened the door; it emitted a loud squeal in protest.

"Gods, I must have someone fix that!" Justin said sounding annoyed. "Pray, one of you kindly remind me later?"

"As you wish, sire," the dark-scaled guard replied with a salute.

The other guard entered the chamber and shortly returned. "All clear, Your Majesty."

Justin smiled, bowed his head in thanks and gestured for her to enter first. "After you, milady."

Miral looked about the circular white marble room. Murals depicting Fandia lined the walls. The Goddess Fandia was always painted with blue and white skin, human-like face and hands, long fin-like ears, three clawed toes, and a long tail that ended with a flipper like that of a dolphin. Her hair was a mix of blue and aqua highlights, her eyes a shade of blue as well. She is depicted as a stunningly beautiful and elegant woman, her eyes looking full to bursting with love. The squeaky door was closed behind them, and the room grew a bit darker. Her eyes gazed at a rainbow of colored lights on the ground in the center then moved to the silver and marble ceiling. There were rainbow-colored ethereal orbs of crystal set in a silver diamond shape, and the Silver Dolphins were at its core.

"The diamond of elemental balance," Justin said standing close to her. "'Tis made of pure silver, a sacred metal in our world as I am sure you are aware."

Miral nodded in reply. She has seen the diamond of elemental balance before, a religious symbol along with the Silver Dolphins, but never so large and on the ceiling of a building. Nor had she seen that much silver in one place before. The blue orb representing water was at the top of the diamond, green to the left for earth, aqua orb of holy centered between water and earth. The element of fire had a red orb on the bottom tip, with the yellow orb of nature between earth and fire. The element of wind to the right had a purple orb, with the orange orb of lightning between wind and fire. Between wind and water was a light blue orb for the sub-element of ice.

"Justin, why are the elements aligned this way exactly?"

"The diamond shape alignment displays how they contrast and complement each other," he said moving his hand in an arc through the air. "Each primary element is connected to the others with a line. A similar line runs between two main elements and their coexisting sub-element. One element dominates another and is weak to another. Earth holds the seas and is the master over water, water puts out fire, wind erodes earth, and fire controls the wind. All is ever in balance."

"It's truly beautiful!" Miral said in awe.

Silence fell over the room for a time. She shifted her eyes to Justin, who was staring at her intensely with softened eyes.

"Lady Miral, there is something I wish to give you," he said in a deep tone. "'Tis a symbol of my oath and to others that you are welcome here." Justin reached behind his neck and unfastened the pendant that he wore, the creed of Arisdale. "There is a wealth of meaning in these words, and in the bearing of them as a gift."

Miral smiled as she watched Justin's head feathers rising and falling as he spoke.

"My name is inscribed on the back, of course, this one has my old title," he said turning the pendant over. "All who see this will know that I have given it to you, and, therefore, you are under my care. My oath is to be your protector, whether or not I am the one mentioned in your prophecy. I believe 'twas defined from the day we met, and I will continue to be so, Lady Miral," he said with a bow of his head.

"Justin—" Her voice caught in her throat as her face flushed. He had a charm that she couldn't deny. His words were delicate and purposeful. "Thank you," she said as she took the pendant from his hands.

The squeaky door cried out again, and Galena entered.

"Pardon me, I had a feeling you would be here, Justin," she said. "When are you going to fix that door, dear?"

Justin's head feathers spiked, and his eyes grew wide at the sound of Galena's voice. He ran his hand through his feathers and chuckled.

"Did I interrupt something?" Galena asked Justin in a motherly tone.

He waved his hands in front of him. "Ah ha, no. I was just showing Miral the room!" he said with a grin and ran his hand through his head feathers again.

Galena looked at him uncertainly for a time. "I would like to take her to town now if you are done with her, Justin."

He sighed. "Very well, I must take my leave. I had only been given a small break in the royal affairs before needing to attend to the rest." Justin hung his head. "I still need to address the public."

Miral felt pity for him at that moment; she was glad not to be in his position. Miral clutched the crimson cape to her tightly and squeezed the creed within her hand. Life will become more difficult for her after he delivers the news. She will be sure to keep the pendant on and visible.

Justin's gaze fell to his aunt. "There is much to do before the coronation in two days." He turned to Miral and bowed his head. "I pray you will be in attendance, Lady Miral."

"I wouldn't miss it for the world, Justin!"

He smiled at her, nodding his head. "I will be busy for the rest of the evening, and likely will remain so until the ceremony, I fear," Justin said with a solemn voice, frowning and bowing to her. "I will do my best to speak with you at least once in a day. Fare thee well, and I pray you have a pleasant evening."

"Thank you, Your Majesty. Have a pleasant night."

Miral watched Justin walk to the door and open it. He paused in the doorway to look back at her, smiling wide before he left.

Galena smiled warmly at the sight. "Oh my! He is positively glowing of late. You are good for his spirits, Miral."

Miral looked at Galena, and swayed back and forth on the balls of her feet. "Thank you!"

Galena nodded at her and gestured to the door. "Let us be on our way, dear! We must get you some clothing. Not that his cape is not a flattering color for you," she giggled and noticed the pendant in her hands. "Did . . . did Justin give you that?" she asked blinking and with a tone of surprise.

Miral nodded. "He said it's his oath to protect me."

Galena arched an uncertain brow and a slow smile grew from the corner of her beak. "An oath to protect you," she repeated. "Well, allow me to help you with that then." Galena took the pendant and circled behind her. She placed it around her neck and fastened it. "We will have to get you a thinner chain, though, this is far too masculine for you, dear," she said while looking her over. "We will head straight to the seamstress Adra Overa. She will have chains there as well. Come, dear," Galena said with a hand against Miral's back.

"Ok," Miral replied. She wasn't certain but Galena's reaction to the pendant was a bit odd, and it seemed the woman knew something she didn't. She thought back to Justin's words and one line stuck out more than the rest. *There is a wealth of meaning in these words, and in the bearing of them as a gift.* She wasn't certain, but she felt as if Justin had given her a riddle of sorts. One she would no doubt be thinking about throughout the day.

Chapter 17 - Address to the Realm

Horns trumpeted cries into the dusk, the sky's colors were muted and solemn as if they knew the weight of the words to be spoken. Justin was about to give the address to the realm. Miral stood to the right with Galena on the upper balcony of the main castle keep. Agar was on the left.

The new blue dress she wore was simple and made for shorter Arisdalian ladies. The hole for the tail was stitched up in a hurry so she would have warmer clothing for the chilly days. Miral looked out at the massive crowd of Arisdalians waiting anxiously below them. Every inch of the castle grounds was filled with people.

Justin walked to the balcony edge and held his arms high. The crowd grew silent, staring up at their prince, concern filling their faces.

"Good people of Arisdale," Justin said. His deep, powerful voice loud and crisp, cutting sharply through the air and easily heard across the courtyard. "'Tis with a heavy heart that I stand before you this day. In these times 'tis best to remember your sense of justice, your faith, your honor, your love, and the creed of Arisdale which makes our hearts beat and our resolve strong." He paused briefly and murmurs spread through the crowd with his silence. Justin raised his arms once more and they hushed.

"Before I explain why you are gathered here, I need you to understand events as they occurred. We arrived in Delphi on the fourteenth of October. I separated myself from my family to find an Elemental." He gestured to Miral, causing her to flush as thousands of eyes turned quizzically to her. "The Lady Miral is the Elemental of Water."

The crowd instantly grew loud, sounding appalled and chatting frantically among themselves.

"Silence!" Justin bellowed.

Miral jumped slightly with his booming voice and placed her hand on her heart. Instantly his roar of command was heeded, and they all stared silently at him.

"'Tis true that she is the first human in recorded history to possess magic; however, that is only due to our limited knowledge. She has been chosen by the Goddess Fandia to be a wielder of her light. This means that humans have the love of the divine light, and thusly, they deserve our respect in return."

Murmurs spread through the crowd.

"The Lady Miral is from this day forth a member of the royal guard, as an Elemental of Light. She is an honored guest and friend. I ask you to treat her with compassion, despite the announcement I have yet to give. Any and all unjustified behavior towards her will be met harshly, and seen as an insult to me! Am I understood?"

Treat a human with respect. Such a thing must be difficult for them, for they stood staring at Justin and her. All too afraid to be the first to speak, she imagined.

Justin's face bore a deepening scowl as he waited for a reply. "Do I make myself clear?!" Justin bellowed in agitation, his fist hitting the balcony rail with a loud crack causing it to fracture.

The crowd jumped and replied, "Yes, Your Highness."

"Very well then," he nodded. "The King of Delphi passed on from natural causes during our journey to the kingdom. For reasons unknown, the Queen of Delphi is now in possession of dark magic. Her behavior that day is in contrast to whom she was proclaimed to be, a kind and caring woman. When I arrived at the castle . . ." Justin paused and looked to be fighting his emotions. "'Tis with the greatest remorse that I say these words, Queen Irana Delphi had already murdered all the royal guards, their squads, and Yarway, the Elemental of Wind."

The people talked among themselves, some angry, some numb and silent, and others crying. Justin gave them a pause, allowing them to mourn before he continued. Miral pondered the two guards he didn't mention that were being controlled and not dead as far as she knew. Politics and the lies to cover what happened; that was something she couldn't see herself being able to do.

"We are not the only ones to suffer losses this day. Lady Miral's father was also killed, not by the queen but instead, by a demon Irana called a Virabis."

Miral's eyes watered with the mention of her father. The crowd gasped, and the jumbled noises of conversation resumed.

"The queen was mortally wounded but stood firm, and was somehow able to control the will of multiple people at one time." Justin paused taking a deep breath. "Your king and queen were wounded beside Irana and with her accursed magic, she formed a scythe that she used to—" Tears formed in his eyes as his voice quivered.

Once more Justin appeared to be fighting it all back. She lost that battle soon after he started talking.

"Your king and queen are in the World of Light now," he said with a croak, hanging his head.

The crowd, in shock, stared blankly. Slowly heads dropped along with Justin, Agar, and Galena, and Miral followed suit. The head priest of the temple of Fandia stood before the crowd leading them through the ritual of mourning.

"Goddess of Light, Fandia, to you we pray. Lead the souls of our lost loves to your light, where they may rest in their new existence, watching and guiding us from afar, by your divine grace."

Heads remained bowed for a time until the priest spoke once more.

"To you and your divine essence, the Silver Dolphins, we pray, in this our time of mourning."

In reply the people sang the song of mourning. The melody was the same one she sang in Delphi with her father, and to Justin and Agar on the ship.

"Silver Dolphins, light of the world, free my heart from sorrow. Silver Dolphins, I am in mourning, take my heart and lift up my soul."

So much of what her people believed was shared by the world. All that divided them was judgment. Unfair accusations made thousands of years ago that may not be true.

Elder Nyros stepped forward and joined Justin on the balcony. He raised his arms high. "Due to the unknown threat that Queen Irana Delphi poses to us, the coronation of Prince Justin Arisdale will be held in two days! We are recruiting for the royal guard, and other positions in the army. We ask that you all remain vigilant, and do not travel beyond the protection of the guards across our territories. To do so is to risk your own life. You may return to your homes. May Fandia bless Arisdale."

With that Justin and Elder Nyros turned to depart the balcony. Agar followed, then Galena and Miral behind them. Now that the address had been given things would become interesting for her. With a hand over the creed around her neck, she hoped in silent prayer to the Goddess of Light that the people heeded Justin's words and let her be.

Chapter 18 - Refined Life

The sun shone brightly through the windows of her new room. Miral laid lazily on the fluffy bed, covered in a heap of warm blankets. The bed on the ship was grand compared to the stiff mat she had in Delphi, but this bed was by far the most amazing ever. The warmth and comfort were hard to leave, and she had no real reason to get up other than the gripes of her stomach. No chores to be done and no Madrelin to scold her. Despite the rejections she may get from the people of Arisdale today, coming here had been paradise so far. Fears of what may come after the address of yesterday gave her pause, though, and she rolled over onto her belly and resigned to stay put. As she drifted back to sleep, a knock came at the door. She fought to open her groggy eyes and blinked towards it.

"Miral, dear, are you awake?"

The voice belonged to Galena; they were to meet with Adra in the morning. The coronation was in a couple days, and she now needed a ball gown as well. She was eager to get and wear such a dress, excited for another chance to speak with Justin and Agar; however, the fear of the unknown was stronger.

Miral pulled herself from the warm protective shelter, wrapping a robe around herself as she shivered in the cold room. She stumbled to the door and pulled it open. Galena smiled briefly before her face shifted to concern. Captain Severos had his back to the wall beside the door.

"Heavens, Miral, are you all right, dear?" Galena asked her.

Miral rubbed her eyes. "Yes, I was so comfortable I didn't want to get up."

Galena giggled. "Ah! I can understand that. When I first moved into Castle Arisdale, I had a similar reaction. Of course, I am far more used to the cold from being born and raised in Mystia in the Mystic Mountains. The beds here are wondrous, though."

Miral smiled. "I am sorry that I am not ready yet. I won't take long." She paused. "I would like to know more about Mystia, pray, could you tell me about it while I dress?"

"I would love to!" Galena replied entering her room and closing the door. She took a seat on the bed as Miral changed behind the folding panels. "Mystia is a spiritual community of elder race birds and others who wish to join us. We believe in the words of Fandia and the value of life whether 'tis elder race, human or animal. Being disconnected from every major kingdom left us to make our own decisions, and as such you will find no hatred toward human beings there."

Miral slipped her blue dress on and peeked around the panel at Galena in disbelief. "Really?"

She nodded. "My sister Anelda was so vocal and adamant about uniting the races in peace. I often wondered if she actually loved Johanas at first or if she knew 'twas the only way to bring about the change she wished for. However, she laid on the charm when he, as a young prince at the time, visited Mystia with his father, King Roryian. She captured his heart with ease." Galena smiled at her fond memories; however, as Miral expected, a frown soon took its place.

She walked over to Galena while brushing her long silky hair with a comb that was more useful for grooming fur than hair, but worked for the time being. "I am sorry."

Galena looked up at her. "Oh my, thank you. 'Tis so hard as you well know. We have nothing to bury, no real means of coping. Your father, Yarway, all the good men and women of the guard, my sister and Johanas," she sighed. "We all still have each other, though, and I know what my sister would do if she were here." Galena stood and looked Miral over. "You appear in order. Let us get you to the washroom so you can finish your preparations and get you something to eat. Then we will meet with Adra."

"Ok!" Miral replied.

Captain Severos bowed to them as they exited her room. In the guest washroom, she used the marble basin of warm water provided for her to clean up before returning to Galena and Severos. The young dark-scaled guard that she had seen twice the other day joined Severos in the hall and accompanied them. She still didn't know his name or species, but she would ask him when she had the chance.

Morning breakfast had already been served early for Justin, Agar and the elders and so they were not present. She was disheartened to have missed them, but she knew with the elders around there would be little chance for conversation.

The foods the castle kitchen served were far better than anything provided in Delphi. Gourmet meals, luxurious bed, beautiful clothing, and soon a ball gown of her own. Miral's life had gone from poor and simple to wealthy and refined, and all because she had magic. Something she never thought possible a few days ago.

The streets of Arisdale were not as cheerful as they were the day she arrived. A grim mood hung in the air, evident in drooped heads, half-mast flags, and silence. Even the sky wore a gray cloak of clouds for the occasion.

All who noticed the procession of the four locked their uncertain gaze on her a long while before returning to their business. The lingered stares made her feel smaller than she already was. She didn't know what they were thinking, but her mind imagined the worst, causing her to shudder.

"There! That is the one!"

Miral jumped slightly and held her hands over her heart when an elderly Arisdalian pointed at her. She trembled when the crested guard beside the man spun to face her. He had armor like Severos; however, his had more jewels. His orange eyes were narrowed into a sinister cast as he approached her. He had a wicked look to his skull that made Justin appear gentle in comparison. Severos stepped out ahead of her to meet the man halfway.

Galena placed her hands on Miral's shoulders protectively. "I do not know what this is about, dear, but you need not say a word."

The mean looking royal guard strolled past Severos without pausing to acknowledge him and approached her. "Miral Akemi, you are under arrest for the accusations of theft."

Miral gasped. "What? Why? I haven't stolen anything."

The dark-scaled guard wore a wrinkled brow and without warning ran as fast as he could back to the castle.

"Thordin?! I had not excused . . ." Severos sighed and turned his attention back to her.

Galena folded her arms. "General Dilos! There is no way Miral has stolen anything. The girl is not capable, and she has been under guard since she arrived here by either Severos or myself," Galena protested.

General Dilos. Justin and Agar had warned her about him. He looked as awful outside as they made him sound inside. She wondered how she wound up in this position. Had another Delphinian come to town to steal from an Arisdalian and she was just an easy target for blame? Fate seemed to conspire against her often. She was scared about what would happen to her now. A sickly feeling swept through her. Justin wouldn't let her be imprisoned, would he?

Chapter 19 - Disobedience

Justin glanced at each of the elders in the council room, tapping his foot in agitation. They were meeting to discuss plans and preparations for dealing with Queen Irana. However, someone was missing.

"Where in the hells is Dilos?!" Agar exclaimed, breaking the silence.

Justin smirked at Agar. He wanted to know the same thing but had not wished to vocally express his agitation. The council room door flew open and a young dark-scaled guard of Severos's platoon stood in the doorway hunched over and breathless.

Justin's head feathers rose with the racing of his heart to the sudden and loud entrance. "Heavens, soldier! Whatever could be so dire?!"

"Forgive me, sire," he said bowing his head deeply, speaking between breaths. "A villager is accusing Lady Miral of theft! General Dilos is there. I thought it best to inform you immediately, sire."

"Hells!" Justin growled.

Elder Nyros narrowed his eyes. "Majesty, regardless of what occurred I want you to bring her to us. We wished to speak with her anyway and given the circumstances, now is an excellent time to do so."

Justin groaned inside as he turned to face Elder Nyros, his head feathers relaxing as he took a breath. "Very well," he said bowing. He faced the guard that had barged in, his scowl returning to his face. "Where in the village are they?!"

"Dilos! Justin will be furious! Why is our word not enough?!" Severos barked.

"I trust the word of another Arisdalian before a human, and therefore, your word is flawed as well!" Dilos sneered, wrenching Miral's hands behind her back and binding them together in shackles.

She winced in pain with his rough handling and glanced up at Severos who looked back at her solemnly. He craned his head up with the sudden sounds of excited murmurs from the crowd. His eyes found what they searched for, and his face looked as ashen as a dinosaur's possibly could.

He knelt quickly. "Your Majesty, I am sorry."

Dilos released his grip on her hands and Miral spun around. She looked right into Justin's menacing glower and trembled in fright with his threatening expression. His teeth were bared beneath his deep-set scowl and fluffed feathers. His eyes were not focused on hers though, they were locked on General Dilos. He took a few deep breaths, no doubt trying to stifle his anger as his head feathers indicated with their repeated rise and fall. His gaze turned to her, shifting down to the creed around her neck then back to her eyes, his face expressing remorse as he did.

"Remove these shackles at once!" Justin bellowed while turning his attention back to Dilos. The crimson cape he wore danced wildly with a gust of wind as if it shared the frustration of its owner.

"She will be taken back to the castle, and a trial will be held for the claims made against her, as is the law, Majesty," Dilos said reaching to grab her once more.

Miral watched in amazement as Dilos's arms froze in mid-air and he was only able to move his hands. The general whipped his head towards Justin and scowled at him. The prince stood resolutely with his hand up and stepped forward. Miral stepped back to make room as Justin approached to place himself between Dilos and her.

"Hand over the keys!" Justin demanded as he released Dilos from his magical hold on his metal bracers.

"Justice is to be held the same for all! You cannot get her out of this because you are about to be crowned king!"

Justin growled. "You pretend to know the meaning of fair justice! Had you not beaten an innocent man near death once? Surely you recall the day you did and thusly imprisoned him! I have never seen you treat an Arisdalian thief that way!" Justin said pointing at Dilos. "No, you have wanted this since I brought her here! You never wished to see me a king either! I find it highly unlikely that these accusations are simply by chance and not an orchestrated lie on your part!" Justin growled as he paced. "What will you do once your attempts to smear my good name fails? Will you try to assassinate me next? Can I trust you, general?" Justin glared at Dilos for a moment, then his face shifted to a smile and he extended his hand, palm up to the side.

Agar materialized next to his brother, holding a set of keys up and wearing a grin on his face. "Right where you always keep them, Dilos."

Dilos growled at Agar. "Filthy cat!"

Justin lurched forward locking eyes with Dilos's and growled fiercely. "Perhaps some disciplinary action is in order, general! You seem to forget yourself before your monarchs!"

Galena wagged her finger. "General Dilos, I am appalled by your disloyal tongue! Fandia be blessed! Miral is innocent! Heavens, what would Johanas think of all this?!"

Dilos looked away from Galena and marched off with heavy stomps.

"Severos, take the general back to the elders and see that his discipline is carried out." Justin paused. "We are all angered by my parent's deaths, 'tis no excuse to be irresponsible. Also, find that soldier of yours who came to inform me as well. I wish to speak with him further."

"Yes, sire," Severos said saluting him and chasing after Dilos.

"Sorry, Miral! Let's get you out of these things!" Agar said unlocking her shackles.

Once they were removed she curtsied to Justin. "Thank you for believing me, Your Majesty." She turned to curtsy to Agar and said, "Thank you, Your Highness."

Justin acknowledged her with a bow of his head. "Of course, Lady Miral."

Agar put his arm around her shoulder and gave her a tight squeeze. "I believe I said this once before, but anything for you, Miral," he winked.

Justin smiled warmly at her a moment before looking out into the crowd of people. "Who here claims to have been robbed?" he asked in a commanding tone.

The crowd of onlookers remained silent, staring at Justin with unwavering gazes. Justin slowly met the eyes of everyone in the crowd and lingered with the group to the left of her.

He scowled and spoke once more. "Well then?! Do the people of Arisdale not think their acting king has more important matters to attend to? Should he not be planning the defense of the realm, rather than scolding children?!" Justin barked with a forceful rise in volume.

People were trembling as they watched him resume his search. Justin turned his head sharply and pointed to an elderly Arisdalian man who flinched beneath his glower. "You must not be aware that little gets by me. Everything about your posture, eyes, and pheromones are telling me 'tis you, sir."

"Forgive me, Your Majesty, I . . ."

Justin relaxed his posture, and his face took on a more concerned look as he shook his head. "Be honest with me or you shall bare your thief's punishments with him." He knew there was not a thief, per se. General Dilos's reaction provided doubt, and this man's sudden unwillingness to speak of the crime against him deepened that suspicion.

"Yes, Majesty."

"'Twas not the Lady Miral, or a human for that matter, yes?" Justin said while gesturing to her.

"Y . . .yes, Your Majesty."

"Tell me why, after I had clearly expressed the other day that the Lady Miral was to be treated with compassion, did you accuse her of theft?"

The man remained silent, dropping his head.

"Ah, the truth shines forth. If you wish, we can speak in private. I have already warned you of the consequences of failing to answer, and I have wasted far too much time on this matter! I pray you see now that you would have been wise to come to me directly! That goes for all of you! Change is upon you, and 'tis best that you accept and flow with it!"

"Yes, Your Majesty," the people said in unison.

Justin had a keen awareness of what was, and he had a way with words knowing what needed to be said. The more she witnessed his truth-seeing ability, the more she was fascinated by it. Of course, after their talk in the garden, she knew it was hard for him to do that for himself.

"Very well then, we shall return to the castle," he said gesturing for the elderly Arisdalian to head there. "Galena, when you are finished with Adra bring Lady Miral to me. The elders wish to talk to her today, and I would like a chance to speak with her alone before that."

Miral frowned with his words. Talk to the elders. She imagined it would be far from an enjoyable conversation.

"Oh, all right, dear," Galena replied.

Justin bowed his head to Galena and then to Miral. "See you then, milady."

He turned and headed back to the castle. Agar patted her on the back and followed Justin.

Galena hugged her tight. "I am sorry about all that, Miral, dear. I do hope this is the last time you will be treated poorly."

The crowd began to disperse as Galena talked, going back to their business. A few glanced at Miral as they walked away. She was prepared for troubles. She just hadn't expected this.

"Is it true? Is General Dilos trying to keep Justin from the throne?"

"That is a possibility," Galena said in an exasperated tone. "Dilos has hated him for years ever since Justin freed the human man that Dilos imprisoned for theft by proving him wrong. I cannot tolerate the man at times."

"What made him hate humans so much?"

Galena shook her head. "I do not know, Miral. None of us do."

Chapter 20 - The Study

On the fourth floor of the castle keep was the royal quarters. Only the royal family was permitted to enter this sector without the king's decree. The largest room at the end was the royal suite, the bedroom of the king and queen. Justin's former bedroom was to the right of the wide hall, Agar's to the left, the other four bedrooms stood vacant as they had for years, and a private washroom for the royal children was between them. The last room, closest to the stairwell was the private study.

Justin enjoyed spending time reading here. A fireplace on the left wall warmed the room with its comforting embrace of amber glow, a red-cushioned couch sat before it and was a fine place to consume a book in the cold seasons. Shelves with literature lined the wall. He was proud to admit he had read each and every one. To the right of the doorway was a desk where he was seated writing a letter in formal script. The quill was one of his father's long head feathers.

A knock came to the door, and familiar scents entered through the cracks. Without raising his eyes or halting his writing, he replied, "Enter."

The door creaked open and Galena entered with Miral behind her.

"I brought her straight away as you asked, dear. I do hope the elders go easy on her. May the Goddess of Light bless you both," she replied with a hand over her heart.

Justin stopped writing and lowered his quill to the desk while his eyes searched his aunt and then Miral. The lady was fidgeting and exhibiting scents associated with nervousness. He nodded his head. "All will be well," he said in a lowered and softened voice. He knew this tone was more likely to initiate feelings of relaxation and comfort. His years of study and education to be groomed into a king had provided such lessons. The ability to have a golden tongue to charm and manipulate was the sharpest blade a king could carry.

He offered a reassuring smile as he stood from the desk and gestured to the lone chair in front of it, speaking once more in a softened tone. "Lady Miral, you may have a seat here if you wish."

Miral curtsied and walked past Galena to sit before him.

Justin nodded to his aunt and she closed the door on her way out. He took his seat once more and turned his attention back to Miral. From his time with her he knew she was easily frightened, worried, and anxious; however, despite those traits she had what mattered most: a heart of gold, a calming presence, and wisdom in her words.

He smiled, being sure to use the same calming voice. "Lady Miral, first, I would like for you to take a deep breath and calm yourself. Surely 'tis serious business; however, with stillness, certainty in your personality, and carefully chosen words, you will get through this just fine. 'Tis why I called you here to speak. I will guide you on what to say and what to omit."

"I will have to lie to them? They scare me, Justin," she said in a wavering tone.

"Not a lie so much as selective truth," Justin said in reply. "A good king knows what is best for his people. Often the best things are colored facts. 'Tis a job with significant responsibilities and risks and a king knows he must live with the consequences of his choices. However, if that choice brings the most harmony to the world and to his people, then that is without denial the wisest choice."

Miral nodded. "I see. Then I will do what you think is best."

"I thank you, Lady Miral," he nodded. "Now then, I did not tell them about the forbidden word. I did not tell them about the prophecy, and I did not tell them that the sea dragon appeared to be after you," Justin said. "Each of these factors alone will give them pause to question your character and ensure that you will be imprisoned until this matter with Irana is settled, which could be months. Years even," he shrugged. "I do not wish to see this happen. I have seen you and heard your words up to this moment. I trust you, Lady Miral."

"How can you have that much faith in me after everything that has happened?" Miral asked with a frown and bowed head.

"Because I am keenly perceptive as you heard me explain to the crowd in town. There are cues given, and if one knows how to watch and listen carefully, they can see a lie in the expression and scent of another. The reaction is instantaneous. Many have tried and failed to lie to me. They try to keep their heartbeat even, their face neutral, their mind resolute. They manage to hide a lie well. What they cannot hide is that instant recognition by the mind that a lie exists and is given shape as scent or in the eyes and body," he said tapping his head. "Though with the amount of anxiety you have over talking to the elders, no one in that room will find the lie behind the scent of that fear. They are similar." Justin paused watching her for a moment. "Lady Miral, I have seen the full range of your emotional expressions, the varying tones of your words, and your body language. I have no doubt of your innocence. The problem will be convincing eight elders who already have a dislike of humans, and now have hatred for Irana and Delphi, that you are innocent and have not spelled Agar and I. This is going to be impossible if the truth is added. I ask, for your sake, to only talk about what you know as if you were utterly unaware of what actually happened that day. No prophecy, and no unusual book with the forbidden word." He leaned closer to her, his voice returning to a soft tone. "Can you do this, Lady Miral?"

"I can," she said looking down at her hands in her lap.

He frowned slightly at the soft and sad-sounding tone to her reply. This lady's life was turned upside down more than the rest of them, and she was now at the mercy of the judgmental Elder Council as well. "Lady Miral, I am deeply sorry for all this trouble. Once this talk is over, there will be no more doubts, and hopefully no more altercations. General Dilos and the man who accused you are both being made an example of. The king's law, once affirmed by the Elder Council, is not to be broken by anyone."

"What is disciplinary action?" she asked raising her head to meet his eyes.

Justin arched a brow and shook his head. "Lady Miral, this is the second time I have witnessed your concern for the well-being of those who meant you harm. 'Tis a noble trait when applied correctly, but also a danger to yourself if your kindness fails. I take the steps to ensure a fair treatment with minimal discomfort, whilst still being capable of reinforcing authority."

Miral crossed her arms over her chest and remained quiet.

He noticed her discomfort and preceded to answer her question. "Disciplinary action in Arisdale begins with imprisonment without luxury. If the offender reverts to their old ways stirring trouble once more, they are returned and the sentence is harshened. Fewer opportunities for time in the sun, warm meals, and so on. Without punishment for consequences, how will one who thinks they are in the right learn they are not? What if I was not a good king? What if I made my choices selfishly? Should I not pay for my chosen cruelty in some form?"

Miral sat in silence staring into his eyes then nodded slowly to him.

"The severity of the first punishment is determined by what they have done. If I were to be tried for killing another, I would receive a far harsher punishment than the general has now. I do believe in second chances, Lady Miral. I give them where I can."

"What about Queen Irana? What will you do to her?" Miral asked folding her hands together over her heart.

Justin grimaced. "Lady Miral, that is a difficult question to answer at this juncture. You say she was a tender queen once, and she is now a monster. Perhaps 'twas the forbidden word that caused her to fall victim to madness," he shrugged. "Perhaps not. I am not yet certain what to feel for Queen Irana. She has proven herself to be gravely dangerous; however, I will do my best to apprehend and keep her detained without harm. Fair treatment demands this, a trial to bring closure to the families of the lost. We do not have any records of the madness being cured, nor do they mention one having such incredible power as a result, and as such, I know not what can be done if Irana is indeed trapped. All this is utterly unknown. I pray that satisfies your concerns."

Miral nodded. "Yes, that does. I am sorry for doubting you." Her cheeks turned red and she placed her hands over her face. "I don't know what even gives me the right to question you! Forgive me."

Justin sat back in his chair and ran his hand through his head feathers. "Worry not, Lady Miral. I will be sure to stop you if I truly do not wish to be questioned on a matter," he said with a smile. "I do pray that we get another moment to talk that does not involve a political policy."

"Yes, I would like that," Miral replied.

Justin nodded. "They may want a demonstration of your skills as well. I have informed them that you had not been trained and that your knowledge is limited, which, of course pleased them. I mentioned to you before the power of our combined magic. I know we have not a chance to practice this yet, but I do believe showing them what we could accomplish together would strengthen your value in their eyes," he paused and lifted his brows. "That was phrased in a way that was terribly demeaning, milady, and I am sorry; however, the elders are what they are," he said shaking his head. "I wish to help you find respect where I can. Becoming a healer with my aid is certainly a grand way to be a productive member of society and help to Galena as well. Of course, have you any other ideas do share them. Generally, projects to give aid to the people are run by the queen. Mother had a few that need management. I know Galena is operating them now. You may assist her if you like."

"Oh! I would love to," she replied with a smile. "Will the magic be difficult?"

"Not at all; however, should it be a challenge for you, 'twill only reinforce the fact that you know little about using magic and would be in your favor either way."

"Ok, Justin."

Justin nodded. "I will have Galena and Severos escort you to the meeting room. I will greet you there shortly," he said with a smile gesturing to the door.

Miral got up and curtsied before walking to the door. She looked back his way with a smile then opened the door and left.

Chapter 21 - The Elders

Miral sat twiddling her fingers in the castle meeting room. She avoided being arrested thanks to the guard Thordin and Justin; however, she felt like she was still on trial for a crime. Sweat beaded on her forehead as the door opened spilling light from the hall into the stuffy room. Eight Arisdalians wearing white robes with gold trim, strips of gold cloth, and red gem embellishments entered the room in a line. The one in the lead she recognized from the address to the realm, Elder Nyros. All took places to the right of the room and stood to face the door.

"All rise and hail the acting king of Arisdale," the guard said with a salute before sidestepping out of the entrance.

Miral stood. The elders and Severos returned the salute, and Justin entered the room stopping in front of her.

"Hail, Your Majesty," they all said as one.

Justin bowed his head. "Greetings Elders and friends. Shall we commence?"

Elder Nyros bowed his head. "Indeed, Majesty." He approached Justin, and the other elders took their seats. He turned to face her. "We called you here today to speak with and understand you better, Lady Miral Akemi. As a guest in our homeland from a now-hostile nation, we must act with caution and care. We have accounts from both the king and prince, and while we honor their views and opinions on what occurred, we wish to hear your side of the story. Begin with the earliest recollection of trouble in your homeland."

Miral took a deep breath. Even with Justin's reassuring words, and now his comforting stare locked onto her, her words caught in her throat. All the elders were watching her intently like vultures waiting to pick her bones clean.

Justin's kindly stare turned to wrinkled concern with the prolonged silence. He spoke with a soft tone. "Lady Miral, we understand this is a lot of pressure on you, away from your own kind in a kingdom you have grown to fear; however, I assure you no harm will come from answering these questions." He wore a warm smile and nodded to her.

"Thank you, Your Majesty, Elders," she said with a curtsy and swallowed hard before attempting to speak once more. She thought about Justin's advice; speak only of what you know from the eyes of one who knew not what was happening. "My first recollection was the morning the royal family arrived. I lived and worked in the palace with my father. When he woke me, everyone was running around in panic. Blood painted the walls and floors," she trembled at the memories. "There was a creature inside that dissolved people when it touched them. It killed my father after Prince Justin tried to help me save him. Then we faced Irana. I knew without a doubt that she was not the same queen she was just a day before, the one that gave us love and shelter."

Elder Nyros arched a brow. "You say Queen Irana was acting normal the night before all this occurred?"

"She was grieving the loss of King Charles, but other than that nothing seemed out of place."

Elder Nyros took a deep breath and seemed displeased with the account she gave.

"Surely the queen had some motivation to call us there and then kill the royal family and others. You know not what that was?"

"I am sorry, Elder Nyros," Miral said hanging her head. "I truly don't know."

"We are suspicious of your involvement in all this. Seems highly coincidental that you have an elemental magic and were caught up in the middle of this by chance."

Justin's head feathers spiked and his expression grew sour as he stared at Elder Nyros.

She tried her best to speak past her throbbing heart and winded breath. "I . . ."

"Elders, forgive my interjection; however, I object to this line of questioning," Justin said. "'Tis nothing more than chance, and that can be proven with her limited knowledge of magic and how to use it. Also, she was not there when Irana killed the guards and Yarway! She was by my side the whole time! Even when—" he paused, "even when mother and father were killed."

"Limited by choice or as a ruse?" Elder Nyros asked.

Justin's jaws hung open as he stared at Nyros. "I cannot believe I hear this. You sound like the general now! 'Tis my word and trust not enough?! I was there! I saw her genuine fear as clearly as I see it now!" Justin said pointing at her. "Surely if she meant me harm she would have done so on the ship!"

"Perhaps the intention was to plant her in the middle of us, a way into the heart of Arisdale and the people."

She felt faint with the flood of emotions, nausea rose in her gut with the churning of the room.

"'Tis all speculation, Elders!" Justin replied. He turned his attention to her. "Miral?"

She sat, placing her hands on her face and cried.

Justin turned to the elders with a scowl. "You can see that, yes?" he asked with a raised tone while gesturing toward her. "She is scared."

Miral stopped crying and looked up at Justin.

"Everything in her life became fear. You can say she is playacting, but the truth is that these are genuine emotions. They run too deep to be anything more than truth. They are not a constructed lie to bring us down."

"You place all your faith in these words, Your Majesty?"

"I do, Elders. Should I be wrong then I shall take the fall alone," Justin replied with a hand to his heart. "I trust her and her innocence. As does Agar."

Elder Nyros stared between them for a time before turning to the seated elders. They all nodded to Nyros. He crossed his arms, tucking his hands into his long sleeves and sighed. "Very well then, we will place our trust with her for the time being."

Justin relaxed his head feathers along with his muscles. He nodded to the elders. "I thank you. You will not regret this."

"I pray we do not, Your Majesty," Elder Nyros stated firmly. "To be sure, though, we insist she wears the binding cuffs to restrain her magic till we are confident she is not a threat."

"Magic restraints?! Are you serious?!" Justin said thrusting his hands in the air.

"Considering everything that has occurred thus far, we feel 'tis not too much to ask."

Justin stared at them with jaws wide then glanced her way.

She was scared, but if doing this would allow her to be free without suspicion she would do it. She frowned and nodded to Justin. "It's all right. I will comply. I don't like my magic anyway."

Justin's expression grew solemn with hers. "As you wish then, milady." He turned to the elders. "Allow me to place them."

Elder Nyros nodded and approached the seated elders. He took two gold bracelets with a black stone in the middle and handed them to the king.

Justin approached and bowed his head to her. "The bands have a stone of ethereal obsidian as I explained to you on the ship. They are to remain on at all times," he sighed. "Removal of these bands will result in chained shackles and imprisonment."

"I understand, Your Majesty."

Justin gently placed the cuffs on her arms, snapping them shut until they were secure but not tight. She stared at the keyhole, the only means of removing the bracelets. At least they were not too cumbersome in weight or comfort. She could bear this for as long as necessary. She looked into Justin's regretful eyes and gave him a smile of reassurance.

Elder Nyros nodded. "Thank you, Your Majesty. Lady Miral, we are grateful to you for your cooperation in this matter. We shall take our leave and reconvene in a few hours for more affairs of state."

With that, the elders stood and bowed their heads to Justin. He returned the gesture. Once they left the room he released a lengthy sigh.

"I promised you all would be well," he said with a shake of his head, honest sincerity burning in his eyes.

"It will be, Justin. Better to have some trust with this than be a prisoner, right?"

He smiled. "You are right. The cuffs are not that dreadful. I was forced to wear them for a time after the incident with my rage," he said, closing his eyes a moment. "Once Sara Phoenix arrived here for the first time, they were removed and I began training with her."

"It's better this way. Now I won't have to worry about causing any trouble by accident." She looked down at her hands then back up at him. "Justin, to be honest, I just want a normal life," she said in a wavering tone, squeezing her eyes tight and lowering her head.

Justin kneeled. "Pray, Miral," he said, placing his finger under her chin to lift her head and peer into her eyes, "once things are calmer here, I would love to show you the beauty in what you were chosen for. The good you will be able to do with training."

While kneeling he was about the same height as her, and that made it easier to take in his sunny eyes. "The way you say that does make it seem better than I see it."

"Well 'tis so I swear it," he said with a warm smile. "We cannot practice the healing magic as you are now; however, I think you would agree, the ability to cast such a vital gift is a marvel. To save a life, 'tis something I was eager to try. The day I discovered you, 'twas the first thing that filled my mind."

"Save a life. One day we will, Justin," Miral replied with a wide smile. "I would like that."

"One day then," he nodded. "As much as I would love to speak with you more, I regrettably have matters to attend to before the next meeting," he sighed and returned to his full height. "Captain Severos will take you back to Galena. On the morrow, I will see you at my coronation," he said with a bright smile and fiery eyes.

"See you then, Justin. Thank you for standing up for me today."

"Of course, Lady Miral, as I swore to you the other day," he said with a glance and gesture towards the pendant around her neck. "I will do the best that I can to be your protector."

He reached out his hand, and she placed hers in his. He bowed and led her to the door. He opened it and hailed the captain, "Pray, take her to Aunt Galena, with my regards."

"Yes, Your Majesty," Severos replied with a salute. "I have the guard you wished to speak with here as well if you are ready, sire."

"Ah, yes! Send him in then return to me once Miral is with Galena. Fare thee well, Lady Miral." Justin bowed his head at her then returned to the center of the room.

"Fare thee well," Miral replied with a wave.

Severos hailed the young guard whose rounded eyes were now wide with concern. She watched the guard enter the room and kneel before his king. She hoped Justin wasn't angry with him. Severos shut the door and led her away.

Chapter 22 - Loyalty

Justin looked down at the unsteady guard kneeling before him. He was confident in his trained royal duty, certain he was raised to uphold this position adequately and perhaps better than those before him.

"Speak your name and your rank, soldier."

"Thordin Martanz, new guard recruit, sire," he replied with a wavering but firm tone.

"A new recruit," Justin replied with an arched brow. "That would explain a lot. How long have you been training?"

"About four months, sire."

"Ah, still earning your wings then," Justin said with a smile. "Thordin, I called you here to speak about your actions this day. Firstly, due to your growing worry, I wish to thank you for coming to retrieve me. I am grateful that I was able to intervene and make an example of the general and his accomplice before the people of Arisdale."

Thordin lifted his eyes to gaze at his king, a smile growing on his face as he did.

Justin focused on the friendly eyes that peered up at him. "However, one thing all guards must remember and uphold is obedience."

The smile vanished from the guard's face, and he lowered his eyes once more.

"You abandoned your captain. Though the action for such a noble cause is appreciated, 'tis dangerous in the wrong circumstances. In the midst of battle, the option to disobey an order to save a brother over following the order and letting him fall can lead to more casualties due to the failure to comply. Then you doom more than the one, yes?"

"Yes, sire," he replied.

"Total obedience is always expected even in the direst of situations. Orders are in place to protect you as well as others. We all have desires of the heart, but we must be careful not to allow our hearts to come between us and duty, or even your own life," Justin said closing his eyes with the memory of his parents beside Irana. He opened his eyes once more. "If your captain excuses you or if you ask to be excused first, then you are following the chain of command. Is that clear?"

"Yes, sire."

"Very well then. On this day, king's law was broken, and you, through the wrong action, brought about the resolution and made your king proud. In this instance I am giving you a pardon to your disobedience; however, do not think that I will always be so forgiving."

"Yes, sire. Thank you," Thordin replied, a smile returning to his face.

"A pleasure, my young guard," Justin said with a nod of his head. "Today you demonstrated the qualities of the creed. I will be keeping my eye on you from this day forward, Thordin. I pray you continue to become what I see in you. Live by the creed," Justin said placing his hand over his heart.

"With honor, faith, justice and love, sire."

Justin smiled. "Splendid, you are dismissed and are to return to duty."

Thordin stood and saluted him before turning to depart the room. He opened the door to leave and paused. Captain Severos had returned. The young guard saluted his captain and waited to be dismissed by him as well.

Severos returned the salute. "Hail, Thordin. Report to Galena in the main hall. You are to accompany her and the Lady Miral."

"Yes, captain. Right away, sir," Thordin replied, hurrying off to his assigned task.

Captain Severos smiled and shook his head as he entered the room, pausing before Justin to salute him. "Sire."

"Severos," Justin replied with a nod. "Your young recruit shows a lot of promise. If we can separate the kindness of his heart from his obedience, then he would make a fine royal guard, do you not agree?"

Severos blinked in surprise. "Sire?"

"You have trained him since he began. What do you make of him?"

"He is strong-willed and confident, good with a spear as well. His father is one of my top-ranking members."

"Taking after his father then," Justin said with a smile. "Captain, I wish for you to train Thordin harder. Put him through the trials of a royal guard and see if he can manage, without making him aware, of course. I want to know if he is capable."

"Yes, sire, but are you certain?" Severos asked with an arched brow.

"I am, Severos," Justin nodded. "What I need now, with Irana looming in the distance, are guards I can rely on to uphold my law. Not my father's or my ancestors. All I have is you, Severos. Dilos will never take my side," he sighed. "I am not entirely certain what to do about him. I need a general. Firing him now will place Arisdale in danger."

"Agreed, sire, then I shall do as you ask."

"Keep your eye open for more like Thordin, those who hold no hatred of humans. Irana caused this, 'tis her alone, not the humans of this world. This battle ahead must be fought with that understanding, or all my mother has done will be lost."

"I shall do so, sire," Severos said with a nod.

"I thank you, my friend. Keep me informed of his progress." Justin nodded. "Now then, captain, on to the next trial of the day. My general locked in a cell, no doubt fuming with hatred of me, and a conflict of unknown troubles to deal with."

"Sire, I will do my best to fill his boots in his absence, and I have faith that Arisdale will rise above this."

"I thank you. To faith then, may the Goddess Fandia bless us," Justin said closing his eyes and praying.

Chapter 23 - Gowns and Gossip

"Praise to the Goddess Isis, you look glamorous in that dress, dear!" Galena said sounding ecstatic, her yellow-feathered tail swaying with her joy.

Miral blushed and ran her hands across the front of the white silk ball gown. The dress was designed around the theme of water with white sleeves and three-tiered gossamer blue fabric cascading down the dress looking like a waterfall. Excitement rushed through her and displayed on her face in a wide, bright smile in the mirror. Today is Justin's coronation, and this is her first ball gown. "Thank you, Lady Galena! Goddess Isis? Who is that?" Miral asked.

"The Goddess of Holy!" Galena said with a smile, which faded into a neutral expression. "Unfortunately, the sister to the mischievous God of Chaos, ruler of fire and wind. She is lucky to have a good brother, though: Osiris the God of Water. Perhaps one you might pray to!" she said, followed by a sigh and a hand on her heart. "Fandia bless this girl."

Miral tilted her head slightly. "What is the God of Chaos's name? I never heard of him."

"Oh, be glad you have not. I am superstitious, I believe in the old texts that say a god can hear you if you call their name, and so I will not. I do not wish to call upon a chaotic god that can manipulate weather," Galena said with a resolute nod.

She wasn't sure what to make of that. A god who can manipulate weather, who is also mischievous, sounded like trouble. Best to not be on his bad side. Delphinians did pray to the God of Earth, Andeos, and Eva the Goddess of Nature for fertile grounds and crops. How many other gods were there?

"What accessories do you have for this gown?" Galena asked.

Miral watched as Adra turned behind her and fumbled around. Adra Oviera was an Oviraptor, and she didn't seem to mind humans. When Galena asked the tailor if she would be willing to customize dresses for her two days ago, she was thrilled and grateful for the challenge. She also needed shoes, her other ones were stained with blood. Though that was a problem, as Arisdalians do not wear shoes. Adra was eager to figure it out, though. The kind seamstress studied her ginger shoes and promised to come up with something for her. She upheld her promise and made rather comfortable white dress shoes to go with the ball gown.

Adra turned around with a bauble in her dark gray-scaled hands. It had white gossamer fabric in four pointed strips, each ending with a large pearl. She circled the counter and approached her.

"I think this one will do nicely! I mean no offense by this, dear, but given your small head, this bauble will look grand on you!" Adra said smiling brightly. She handed it to Galena and gathered Miral's hair into a high ponytail. Adra giggled as she did. "I never felt a human's hair before. It's so soft, silky, and tickles." She took the bauble from Galena and fastened it to Miral's hair. She took a step back and angled her crested head slightly to the right. She clasped her hands together and the corner of her beak upturned into a smile. "Grand, grand! Positively radiant!"

Miral blushed and held her hands together, draped down in front of her.

"Indeed, Adra! You have gone beyond my expectations! I extend the future king's thanks to you as well. He will be pleased!"

"There isn't a thing I wouldn't do for that boy," Adra replied. "He has always been such a dear to us. He will come to town and spend his free time playing with the children in the street, or helping this old lady carry some heavy loads of fabrics from the cart!" Adra laughed and looked her over once more. "So lovely for a human! You're utterly charming, young lady!"

Adra turned to Galena grabbing hold of her arm and pulled her to the counter. She glanced back at Miral, who was looking herself over in the mirror. She whispered, "You know, I'm failing to see what all the fuss over humans is about. She is delightful! Sure, the Glennoldian bandits cause a great deal of grief, but there are thieves amongst us as well!" she sighed. "You have your hands full with this, don't you?"

Galena glanced at Adra with slightly narrowed eyes. "Yes, quite! I think Miral will change their minds in time, though. She is so soft spoken, mannerly, and loving, a unique lady. 'Twill not be difficult for her to show us all how wrong we are."

"Well, I certainly hope so!" Adra said beaming, her face twisting into disgust a moment later. "Those blasted cuffs! They completely clash with her gown. The poor dear."

Galena frowned. "Ah, yes, 'tis a sad sight to see; however, 'tis in her best interest for now."

"Aye. Now then, down to business. First, I want to be her head tailor from now on."

"Granted, I am sure Justin would agree."

"Excellent! I thank you kindly!"

"How much for all the dresses and accessories?"

Adra rubbed her red head feathers. "I used the finest fabrics for the gown, as you had requested," she replied in a near whisper.

"Oh, out with it, Adra! Justin instructed me thusly, he made no limit for the price," Galena said placing a large coin purse on the counter.

"Gracious, he is generous!" Adra replied. "Very well, I ask for two thousand gold pieces for the gown and ornament, two hundred gold pieces for the casual dress, and one hundred gold for the shoes."

Miral's eyes went wide. "Oh, my . . ." she gasped, intertwining her hands in front of her over her chest. Standard dresses back home were ten gold, and even that was hard to afford.

Galena smiled at her. "Best get used to it, dear! You are a member of the royal court now!"

"Speaking of the court, any idea whom Justin will choose for the king's dance?" Adra teased, smiling scandalously.

Galena shook her head. "Not that I know of. He has not expressed any interest in a lady for years. He has avoided courting entirely."

"Eh, it's because of that arranged courtship with Razamarea, isn't it?" Adra asked in a gruff but mellow tone.

Galena shifted uneasily. "Yes, but I do not want to speak of that wretched woman. She has not been seen in a year, but he is afraid of her showing up again now that he is king," Galena shuddered. "I feel like talking about her will make her come back. I know that is not possible, I just—" she sighed hanging her head.

"Oh, that poor boy! I'm sorry, Galena!" Adra said shaking her head. "Well, if he has no one in mind I will gladly suffer her wrath for a dance with him!"

"Thank you, Adra," Galena smirked. "Well, we best depart. We must get ready for the coronation!" Galena said with her hand on Miral's back.

"See you then, dears!" Adra said waving.

Chapter 24 - Coronation

Agar locked his arm around hers and escorted Miral to the throne room. She steadied her gaze on the long crimson and gold-lined rug, which led to the gold and mahogany throne. The backrest of the chair was shaped to look like the bird of Arisdale and cushioned with red fabrics. The carpet and marble floor were speckled with colored lights from the large circular stained glass window of the Silver Dolphins behind the throne and was surrounded in drapes of crimson cloth.

She trembled slightly, making her steps unsteady. She didn't like the idea of being at the front of the room in the presence of all the nobles of Arisdale. She was an Elemental of Light, an honored member of the royal guard; however, the gold cuffs around her arms made her feel less than welcome to be alongside the king.

"You all right?" Agar whispered to her.

"Just nervous," Miral whispered back.

He smiled. "Don't you worry! Anyone gives you trouble I'll personally pay them a visit!"

"Thank you, Agar," Miral said with a shaky smile.

"My pleasure," Agar replied with a wink.

She focused her mind on other thoughts, distracting her from the glaring eyes that she felt watching her. All those beside the king would dress in similar colors. The women would be wearing white, and Agar wore a red and gold open jacket that fell to his knees with a red and gold collared vest and black pants. He didn't have his helmet on, and his long black hair was no longer braided, but pulled back midway in a ponytail, and had been preened nicely for the occasion. She thought he looked more dashing now than he had before.

Agar led her to the right of the throne beside Galena, bowed to her and took his place to the left of the throne. The band played a triumphant song. She was told they would be playing the anthem for Arisdale and listened intently. It was a vibrant tune that reflected the majesty of the kingdom. Trumpets called forth in succession as the song increased in intensity, the drums beating faster.

Her heart matched the pace of the rhythm when Justin entered the hall from a side room. He was dressed in a knee-length black open coat with gold trimming on a black and gold vest, black draped pants, black and gold half boots, and a red and gold-lined cape fastened around him with gold clasps and red gems. His outfit for the coronation changed the look of raw power and intimidation, that armor gave him, into a strikingly handsome, kind, and regal appearance.

Justin's eyes met Miral's as he marched up the aisle to the throne with a proud strut. His expression shifted from serious to a wide-eyed, bright smile. Head held forward, his eyes watched her for as long as they could.

"Galena . . ." Justin whispered to her taking his place before the throne.

"Yes, dear," Galena whispered in reply.

"You have outdone yourself."

Galena looked at him concerned and asked, "Whatever do you mean?" She followed his sideways stare to Miral beside her and chuckled softly. "Oh! She looks positively radiant, does she not? I truly was impressed myself! Adra did a lovely job!"

Justin fidgeted, trying to change his focus, and not let his head feathers display what he was feeling before the gathered crowd. They would misunderstand.

Galena watched him carefully and giggled.

The music came to an end and Elder Nyros approached Justin from the left side of the room accompanied by two attendants. Justin sighed, grateful for the distraction.

"Sirs and ladies, I here present unto you, Justin your King. To all in attendance this day, are you willing to acknowledge the truth of this?" Elder Nyros said with his arms outstretched beseeching the people in the throne room.

Justin studied the eyes of the nobles. General Dilos was the only individual wearing a scowl. He prayed that the man would not be a fool and make a scene now.

"We the citizens of Arisdale do recognize Justin as our King."

Justin lowered to one knee before Elder Nyros, relieved by the general's silence and happy for the acceptance of his people.

"Will you solemnly promise and swear to govern the people of Arisdale and the allied dominions beyond with honor, loyalty, faith and love, by the light of the Goddess Fandia, according to their respective laws and customs?" Elder Nyros asked.

"I solemnly promise to do so," Justin replied.

"Will you cause law and justice, in compassion, to be executed in all your judgments?"

"I will."

"Will you maintain the laws of the Goddess of Light and the divine grace of the Silver Dolphins?" Elder Nyros asked arms held high.

"The things of which I have here before promised, I will perform and keep. So help me, Fandia."

"Then by the power invested in me by the realm, under the eye of the Goddess Fandia, I hereby decree thee King of Arisdale!" Elder Nyros said bowing to Justin and stepping back.

The throne room erupted with cheers as Justin took his seat at his father's throne for the first time. His cape draped down to the left and the tail to his right as was customary.

"Long live the King!" the throng shouted.

The weight of his title became apparent to him as he sat on the throne that first belonged to King Hardaric Arisdale three thousand years ago. The painted portraits of past kings and of his father hung in succession, alternating between the columns down the walls; a long legacy of beloved rulers that reigned over the proud and prosperous kingdom, and he would not fail them.

Justin stood once applause and cheers faded. "Good people of Arisdale, to you I make another oath! I promise to uphold the light of life and love! I promise to continue to fight for unity in the honor of our fallen sovereigns, family, and friends!" He held his hands out in a presentation to Agar, Galena, and Miral. "With the aid of my companions, the Elementals of Light, the royal guard, and the noble soldiers of Arisdale, I promise to fight to defend this realm from the darkness looming on the horizon to my last breath!" Justin said with fervor. "To you, I give my honor, my loyalty, my heart, my soul, and my life!"

Cheers erupted once more from the throng. "Long live King Justin!"

Justin walked down the flight of steps to stand before his subjects. Galena motioned for Miral to join his side, guiding her to stand to his left with her, and Agar stood to Justin's right. The king stepped forward, and Galena directed Miral to begin walking, keeping just one pace behind him.

They exited the throne room and out the double doors of the main keep to an awaiting cart. The celebration continued in town in the form of a parade and the royal marching band. Events of this magnitude were rare, and the people enjoyed the chance for revelry, as did he.

"Well done, Justin, dear! A genuinely moving and passionate speech!" Galena said.

Justin's eyes turned to Galena. "I thank you." He shifted his gaze to Miral, who smiled brightly at him, his own growing with hers. As he had come to expect from his few conversations with her, she was blushing under his softened stare. Agar jabbed him in the side breaking him from his thoughts and caused him to take his eyes from her.

"You made it difficult to compete with that oath, brother! I will have to think hard to be as cunning in my speech!"

Justin chuckled and said, "I am sure you will think of something, brother. When are you going to propose anyway?"

"I'm . . . I will!"

Justin grinned at Agar. "You said that the last few times I asked."

"This time, I will!" Agar said.

Justin nodded. "Of course you will." He had a feeling that his brother hesitated in asking Queen Katenna for her hand in marriage for a reason. Though Agar never said it, Justin knew his brother didn't want to leave him, not yet.

The celebration in town was a grand sight, costumed outfits, people dancing, and the band's melody raising the merriment of his people, reigniting the liveliness of the city once more. Justin returned waves to the crowd as the canopied cart rolled through the village center. The honest and heartfelt excitement on their faces was a relief to him. To be forgiven for his past was more than he could hope for. A chance to be a great king was a monumental opportunity, and he would not waste it.

Occasionally, he would steal glances at Miral to observe her bright smile and wide blue eyes as she watched the decorated carts of colorful flowers and performances. It was a beautiful smile, and when worn on her radiant face, it meant something greater to him.

Chapter 25 - Trust

Miral looked about in wonder as they entered the ballroom. It was decorated beautifully for the event with clear ethereal crystal chandeliers, flower arrangements, and candelabras. A large table with red and gold cloth stood at the top of the mirror-walled ballroom on a small dais with several rows of smaller tables sitting horizontally on the other side of the dance floor. Grand embellished columns of marble lay between each pane of reflective glass.

The nobles from the coronation entered the room behind them with the Elder Council at the lead. Despite its grand size, the ballroom couldn't possibly fit the whole of Arisdale. Celebrations for the other citizens were carried out in the village.

Once all entered, the doors were shut and Justin motioned for everyone to be seated except the guards, who stood by the doors, and the two behind Justin; one was Severos, and the other Thordin. Servants appeared from a doorway to the left carrying trays of Arisdalian foods and drinks. Her palate enjoyed the unique flavor and cuisine of this kingdom. She missed Delphi, but Arisdale was quickly growing on her. Once all were served, Justin gave the order for the feast to begin. After the third course was finished, royal attendants announced the king's dance to commence.

Galena told her the first dance is only for the king and whoever he chose to dance with. Traditionally the king's choice was a lady he wished to court if he was not already wed; however, from discussion in the dress shop, she knew that things were different for Justin. She was curious to know what had happened, but it was not her place to ask such a personal question.

Miral was interrupted from her thoughts when she realized that everyone in the ballroom was dead quiet, and all eyes were focused on her. She was so deep in thought that she hadn't noticed Justin standing beside her chair. She gasped, her face flushed, and her palms began to sweat. He was bowing deeply at the waist before her, offering his right hand.

"Lady Miral, would you do me the honor of sharing this dance with me?"

Miral felt her heart pounding hard in her ears. "Dance? I don't . . . I never . . . have danced before!" She knew she must sound like a babbling fool, she felt so overwhelmed by his proposal. She took a deep breath. *He is just doing exactly what I suggested a couple days ago, which was to show them.* Galena's words about the traditions of the dance were filling her mind in protest, though.

"Pray, Lady Miral," Justin asked with pleading eyes, dancing head feathers, and a silly smile.

Everyone was watching intently. Agar and Galena were smiling at her. She could see whispers passing between people and mixed expressions of anger, confusion, and happiness. He had just made an oath to uphold the law. He wouldn't dance with her for love. He would lose his kingship, and possibly be exiled. They wouldn't hesitate to banish her, and she didn't want that. She took a deep breath and placed her hand in his. *Trust him.* She smiled at the symbolism of it all when they touched, two different species, but both had hands.

Justin smiled and led her to the highly polished white marble dance floor. They bowed to each other, and then came closer together hand in hand. Justin placed his left hand on her back, and she put her left hand on his arm.

"Feel the flow of the music," Justin said in a whisper to her. "Follow my lead and you will be all right."

"Ok," Miral replied.

Justin moved slowly at first guiding her a step at a time. "To the back, to the left, to the right, and forward."

She fell into the rhythm of the dance, stumbling slightly at times; however, Justin adjusted his footing fluidly to counter her missteps.

"Now I will add some motion," he said. "Step back, turn to the left, step left, turn to the left, step right, turn to the left, step forward, turn to the left, and repeat. Excellent, you are a natural, Lady Miral."

"Thank you, Justin," she said with an uncertain laugh. Once she relaxed into the dance, she could feel all eyes on her again. She could hear muffled chatter, and caught glimpses of various reactions she noticed earlier. Her already frayed nerves had gotten the better of her as her mind fabricated its own words from their mouths.

"You are trembling," Justin said, studying her with a tilted head and softened eyes.

"Oh, uh . . ." she replied in a wavering tone.

She saw him looking about the room for a moment, before turning his eyes back to meet hers, regarding her with a tender stare.

"Just ignore them! My dance, my decision!" he said with resolution and a deeper tone. "Focus on me. At this present moment, we are dancing, nothing else matters."

Miral looked into his sunny eyes and felt a wave of comfort fall over her as her mind pulled away from the imagined danger of unheard words. She noticed then that they appeared dreamy. She felt lost in his beautiful, compassionate gaze, and the world around them melted away.

"I am regretful that I had not another moment to converse with you as I wished to. Seems this may be my only opportunity for a while. I pray you forgive me."

Miral blinked. *He wants my forgiveness?* He has a duty to his kingdom, and while she missed his company as well, she understood. "Of course, I do, but you needn't feel guilty about that. Galena and Adra have been so good to me, and Severos has been watching over me. I know you and Agar have many responsibilities right now."

He smiled at her. "Thank you, Lady Miral. I am glad to know you have been well."

Time seemed to slow to a crawl as they danced. The entirety of it was an enchanting experience she would not soon forget. The melody was a beautiful tune of harps, piano, flutes, violins, viola and cello played lovingly with tender hands.

"Thank you for this!" Miral said. "I've always wanted to dance at a ball!"

Justin angled his head slightly to the right. "'Tis my pleasure, milady! Care to go for a spin?"

"Ok."

He took his hand away from her back and sent her into a spin in time with a flourish of music. After a brief pause, arms extended, he sent her into another spin guiding her back in. His arm was around her, catching her, pulling her in close while he twirled them around.

She could feel her face flushing with heat. He had drawn her in so close, that there was no longer space between them. His strong hand held her firmly against him, not allowing them to separate as she expected. She didn't know what to do with her free arm, and wrapped it around his waist, pressing her hand to his lower back. With his towering height and being so close, she could no longer look into his eyes. She laid the side of her head against him. The warmth of his body and the soft cloth of his vest felt soothing against her face, and he smelled pleasantly of roses and jasmine. She listened to the sound of his heart beating. The beautiful rhythm of life playing in her ears made her feel alive. Then a strange sensation that felt like falling ran through her core. She froze. *What am I doing?!* Her thoughts screamed that this act is improper, to stop, but she couldn't pull her head away. She didn't want to. She wasn't sure when or how it had happened, but a fire was burning within.

As the torrent of conflicting thoughts raged in her mind, she realized that Justin had remained silent, whispering no questions or objections to her laying her head on him. Her first thought that this dance is a show for the people changed, and now wondered if there was something more. She scolded herself for her thoughts. Her generally quiet mind was chatting away frantically, and she found it difficult to ignore. She breathed in deep trying to calm the storm in her head. All this worrying is stealing from the beauty of the moment. *Why are you questioning what it means? Just let time tell the story on its own.*

The thought did little to comfort her. She had fallen in love with him, and her mind was now frantic with new worries. *Does he feel the same? Is he just being kind? Was it all an act? What are you thinking, Justin? His pendant!* She remembered his words from a couple days back, and Galena's odd reaction to him giving this to her. A gift of something personal was a nobleman's way of claiming a lady for courtship. She never had a man express interest in her before, so the gesture was overlooked. Perhaps she was overthinking things. *Was that what he really meant with his words, though?*

The song was coming to a close, and she didn't want it to end just yet. Justin guided her into a dip, and she giggled in delight. A beautiful and fun end to what was a grand moment. They stared into each other's eyes for a short time. As she did, she realized how truly handsome and

143

charming he was. He brought her upright and took a step back while holding her hand. They bowed to each other, and he guided her back to her seat.

"Thank you, Lady Miral," Justin said while releasing her hand. "I dare say that was the most enchanting dance I ever had. You say you never danced before, yet you were flawless."

Miral smiled at him. "Thank you, Justin."

Galena approached them quickly, rubbing her hands together. "Justin, forgive me, but you have a mob of angered elders!"

The dreamy look on Justin's face vanished in an instant, changing into a glower.

Galena frowned and glanced over to the table where the Elder Council was seated. Agar let out a groan in reply. Elder Nyros was wearing a deep scowl with arms folded before him.

Justin grumbled. She was unsure of what he said, though his tone was that of frustration to be sure.

He took Miral's hand and bowed to her. "Forgive me, Lady Miral. I best calm the hornet's nest before they decide to sting," he said with a smile and sounded like he was holding back a laugh.

Agar chuckled in response to him.

"I understand."

Justin, Agar, and Galena headed to the Elders who stirred with aggression when they approached. Miral watched as Justin gestured for them to settle down. All this distress was over the fact that she was human. Feeling guilty for her feelings, she turned away from the ball and went out the side door to walk in the fresh air and clear her troubled mind. She wanted to look about the area anyway. So much work went into decorating the castle grounds in a short amount of time. It was night and magic-infused crystal lights dotted the landscape making it appear as if stars had fallen to the earth just for the occasion. She spun as a loud commotion broke the silent night. The familiar dark-scaled guard stumbled frantically through the doorway she came from. His rounded night hunter eyes gleaming in the dark.

"Lady Miral," he said while saluting her. "I'm sorry, but I cannot in good conscious let you wander off unsupervised. As the king ordered," he said smiling.

"Oh!" Miral said. "Thank you, Thordin. I appreciate the company."

"My pleasure," he replied.

Miral turned from him and sighed heavily. She never thought much about love before. Flaws included, Justin was perfect in so many ways, strong, brave and altruistic. Everything she was not. Admirable traits, along with his formality, tenderness, compassion, friendship, and he made her feel safe. Now she was in love with him and prayed he shared that feeling.

She heard a loud crack behind her and turned. She felt something tighten around her neck and lift her off the ground. In a panic she grabbed desperately at the hand that held her. The assaulter was a dragon female with magenta hair, eyes, and inner membrane of her wings. Rage displayed in her white and black-striped face. Thordin was unconscious on the ground in a heap.

"Justin is mine!" the female dragon growled. She pulled hard at the creed around Miral's neck with her free hand. With a snap of the chain, his gift to her was removed and tossed to the ground. "How dare you bewitch him into loving you!"

"He does not love me!" Miral strained to say. She was helpless. The locked cuffs on her hands prevented her from defending herself, though honestly, she was afraid to.

The woman's brow furrowed. "That is not what the entire kingdom saw, filthy human! That pendant proves my words as well."

Miral felt the woman's grip tighten on her neck. She struggled desperately for air.

"I returned from afar to comfort my love in his time of grief to see him dancing with . . . a human!" she said with disgust.

She was grateful when the woman released her, letting her fall to the ground. She breathed in deeply and then felt the woman lift her from behind and into the air. She flew her to the outer gates and far beyond the village. The female dragon stopped a far distance away and released Miral from her grasp ten feet in the air.

She screamed with fright and fell face first to the ground below. Pain racked her body on impact, ripping through her ribs when the woman pushed down on her back with a clawed foot.

"So you don't forget it, my name is Razamarea! I have the nerve to kill you, but I will give you one chance. Leave here and never return! If you do return, I will kill you!" she snarled before taking flight.

Miral couldn't move. The pain she felt was too intense. She cried, but that only made things worse. Razamarea was hateful and shrewd.

She wondered if that dragon did this to every woman Justin was close to. That must be what Galena was so upset about.

Justin had to deal with Razamarea all his life. Now he had angered the elders as well, all because they danced, and it looked like love. She could hear the footsteps of someone approaching her quickly but couldn't move to see who it was.

"Are you all right, miss?" The voice of the man who spoke was gentle and strangely familiar, but she couldn't place him.

"My ribs . . . they are broken!" she barely managed, finding it hard to speak through the pain caused by breathing.

The man placed his hands around her sides and began to talk in a language she never heard before.

"Lumine vita et amor, haec vulnera sanaret."

The pain melted away. She felt blessed, how odd to run into a healer at a time like this. "Thank you!" Miral said turning to face him, pain in her ankle making her wince.

The man reached down to her ankle speaking the same words. He wore a dark cloak that covered his face. His back was to the moon, and in the darkness, she could not see him.

"What does that mean?"

"By the light of life and love, heal these wounds," he replied standing and offering his hands to her. She took them, and he pulled her to her feet.

"I'm glad you took my advice!" he said sounding relieved.

Miral thought for a moment. His advice? Realization washed over her as she replayed the words and the familiar tone of his voice.

"Are you the prophet I met in Delphi?"

A strong wind gusted past them, removing the hood from his head.

"Somnus tutus es," he said.

Miral stared into the glowing yellow eyes of the elderly Glenn Woods wolf she met a few days ago.

"What does that mean?" she asked feeling weariness grow, her eyes becoming heavy, sleep suddenly trying to overtake her. She fell forward into his arms.

"Sleep, you are safe."

Chapter 26 - Egyptalia

Queen Katenna Bastette sat on her golden throne, which rested upon a three-tiered alabaster dais and sighed heavily, twirling her fingers through the curls of her purple hair. Peace is a blessing to be sure; however, along with peace came boredom, and that boredom came from being a queen. Every day was the same; bandits, thefts, murders, and civil disputes.

She was restricted from venturing far, and from being free to run about or have fun like the citizens. When she was a princess two years past, she felt free. Now she felt like a slave to the crown on her head. Everyone dreams of being royalty, and royalty dream of being like everyone else. That is what Agar had said, and she knew he was right.

One day I will be a real queen, left to just deal with relations and leave the politics to Agar. Katenna snorted at that thought and broke into rolling laughter that caused her guards to startle in concern. The realization filled her with a bit of dread. Agar is a man who was not built to be a king but a court jester. Things would become interesting around here for sure.

She was blessed to have her sister Artilone with her. Artilone rarely left her side and shared Katenna's burden. Today she had other matters to attend to with her priesthood, and that left Katenna alone with her thoughts and the guards who silently stared towards the single doorway to the throne room.

When will Agar stay with me? He told her once that seeing Justin happy was his mission. She imagined the day Justin was happy enough to be without Agar would be the day he found himself a lady, and that would only happen when Razamarea stopped coming around. Kat smirked. *If I were in Arisdale, I would give that wretch something to remember. Maybe then she would leave Justin be. He deserves better than this.*

She knew King Johanas had wished her to marry Justin, but the day she met Agar she knew that as good as Justin was, he was not for her.

"Kat!"

"Artilone? What is it?" Katenna asked concerned as she watched her sister run through the throne room to her.

Artilone was catching her breath and holding out a letter, her long yellow hair spilling out of her priestess hat in places. "We got a letter from Arisdale!"

"Let me see!" Kat took the letter from her sister. She hoped it was good news. Perhaps Agar was coming to visit. She missed him so much and smiled at the thought of him. He is charming, and she loved his sense of humor. He was always so dashing but terribly nervous around her. If he didn't say something soon, she would. She loved him and was certain of her feelings. Katenna broke the wax seal, unfolded the letter, and read aloud.

"Dearest Queen Katenna and Princess Artilone, it is with a heavy heart that I must inform you of our tragedy." Katenna trembled, a lump forming in her throat. Artilone stood wide-eyed with her hand over her mouth.

"We ventured to Delphi under the invitation of King Charles and Queen Irana to speak on peace arrangements. King Charles passed on before we arrived, and the Queen of Delphi has gone mad. She struck down six of the royal guards, Yarway, King Johanas, and Queen Anelda with dark magic."

Katenna froze. "No!"

"How terrible!" Artilone gasped, followed by tears.

Katenna paused and hugged her sister, both crying for a time until they collected themselves enough to keep reading.

"The people of Delphi are acting as a mindless mass," Katenna stopped reading and shuddered. "Justin and I barely escaped with our lives, rescuing the Elemental of Water in the process." The letter was from Agar, she was grateful that he and Justin were all right. She wondered who the Elemental of Water was.

Katenna continued to read. "Be wary, dearest Katenna. We do not yet know of Irana's intentions. I pray this letter finds you both well. How I wish I could come see you! We may yet meet. Justin believes we need to unite to fight back against Irana. We will be in touch. Until then, my love, know you are always in my thoughts. Signed Prince Agar Sabier Arisdale."

"Kat . . ." Artilone said in a quivering whisper, "what in the World of Life is happening?"

"I wish I knew, sis! Chin up! We will be all right! Queen Irana may have some dark powers, but what can she actually accomplish against an army of elder races!" Katenna paused feeling some regret for her words. "I feel sorry for the humans, though. I know Queen Anelda was hopeful of bringing the conflict to an end, but this . . ." Katenna said shaking her head, and clenching her hand in a fist. "This will not sit well with any elder race, a threat to one is a threat to all. As queen, the people will expect that of me, despite what I feel myself," Katenna said followed by a sigh. "Justin will be king now, how ironic that we share the fate of early rule." Katenna descended from her throne. "Come, sister. We best begin preparations."

Though she never showed it, her body trembled as she walked. Her mind churned with panicked thoughts as reality and fear merged into one.

Chapter 27 - Existence

Miral dreamed of her dance with Justin, though her strong focus on the images stirred her from slumber. Her eyes fluttered open, her mind hazy and drowsy. As she lay trying to reclaim consciousness, she remembered falling asleep in the arms of the prophet. Her eyes slowly wandered over her wooden shelter, a cabin of sorts with the fragrant scent of cedar all around her. As the memory of Justin returned she awakened faster. She was lying in bed in a white night dress that was not hers and sat up in a flurry.

"Ah, you're awake!" a lively woman's voice rang out from her right.

Miral turned to face the woman who spoke clenching the sheets close to her chest. She looked human but with long pointy ears. Her vibrant red hair was short and spiky, with two sections on the sides that were slightly longer with large purple clasps around them.

The woman stood, her black and yellow collared robe, which split open with a V-shape at her chest exposing a purple shirt that ended before her belly, unfurled as she did. She approached and looked Miral over. "You have been asleep for three days. How do you feel?" she asked.

Miral looked into the intense purple eyes while scanning her own body with her mind. "I feel all right, but a bit groggy." The stranger before her was only a few inches taller than she. It was comforting to finally see someone closer to her height again.

The woman clasped her hands together. "Excellent! A Glenn Woods wolf brought you here today. He said he found you beaten some ways outside of Arisdale." She leaned in close, squinting her eyes and waggled her pointer finger at Miral. "What in Fandia's blessed light are you doing by yourself in Arisdale?! Didn't anyone tell you it's not safe for a human to be alone . . ." her face scrunched, she leaned back, and her fisted hand tapped the bottom of her chin. Her expression shifted to high browed enlightenment. "Wait! You're the one Justin mentioned in his message! You have magic restraining cuffs on, they are Arisdalian, so you must be the water elemental, right?"

"I am."

The woman raised her finger to point up. "Allow me to introduce myself, Miral Akemi. I am Sara Phoenix, Elemental of Fire!"

She felt relieved at the familiar name and smiled brightly. How ironic and fortunate to be rescued by the prophet and brought to Sara.

Sara waggled her finger at Miral. "I take it from that look that you have heard of me," she said shifting her posture into a stance of pride and wearing a wide grin.

"I hear someone singing her own praises!" a tall light blue and white-skinned dragon said while entering the room.

He looked to be the same height as Galena and had large white horns pointing out from the back of his skull. Sharp angular beige bone plates ran from his forehead to the base of his neck. He wore light beige draped pants, white shirt, and a purple cloth hung from his belt.

Sara glowered at the dragon. "This big oaf is my husband, Talos."

He pulled his arm out from under his wings, which draped over his shoulders, and waved at her. "Greetings, young lady."

"Hello, Talos. My name is Miral Akemi."

Talos grinned at her with wide eyes. "The Miral?!" he said enthused. "What happened to you?"

"Hush!" Sara scolded Talos as she turned to the bookshelf, grabbing a quill and book with blue binding. She set them down on the table then turned to what appeared to be a kitchen. She grabbed a goblet and a small plate with bread and cheese and handed them to Miral.

"You must be starving! Dinner will be ready shortly."

Sara turned and pulled out a chair at the table so she could sit in front of Miral. Talos pulled a chair out as well and sat next to Sara. She scribbled words on the page then stopped writing and glanced at Miral.

"Let's hear the story of how you met Justin, and work your way to now," Sara said with an eager grin.

Miral recounted the story to Sara and Talos. She told them about the prophet and his warning, and how he was the one that brought her to them, and then told them about her encounter with the Virabis. Sara

151

feverishly scribbled down every word, while Talos stared at Miral wide-eyed.

She described her emotional run in with Justin, meeting him for the first time, and told them about her father, and how they failed to save him. She talked about Irana and their desperate escape from Delphi.

Sara looked up from her book at Miral. "Goodness! What a tale! How in the world did Irana come to learn dark magic? I never heard of any mortal wielding it before," she said scrunching her face.

Miral blinked at Sara as she rambled off questions and comments to no one in particular. She looked to Talos and he shrugged at her with a mischievous grin.

Sara was staring off into the distance, her eyes narrowing, fisted hand tapping her chin. "The legends speak of light and dark, the two powers of life and how everything is always in balance. Fandia disappears mysteriously, and at the same time people slowly became darker in nature, according to documented accounts through history." Sara sat up, raising her finger in the air. "The balance shifted that day. Light is fading and darkness growing. Perhaps Irana received her knowledge of the dark arts because of this phenomenon."

Talos had been making faces and mocking Sara while she spoke. Miral could no longer hold back the laugh that was building inside her with the show Talos put on and burst out a giggle.

Sara spun out of her seat lunging at him. "Talos!"

Talos laughed hysterically when Sara pounced on him knocking them to the floor. Miral stared at them with her hand over her mouth.

Sara rose and sat in her chair, picking up her quill and book from the carpet. She turned to Miral and smiled smugly. "Pray, continue!"

Miral glanced down at Talos, who was pulling himself off the ground with a smile on his face. She continued her story and told them about the voyage to Arisdale and how a sea dragon attacked them.

"Wait?! A sea dragon attacked you?! I have never heard of one attacking before. That is strange, and its focus was on you from the sounds of it." Sara peered at her closely. "I am uncertain. The only thing remarkable about you is how unusually bright your elemental light is. That must be what attracted it." She shrugged then tapped her hand to her chin. She stopped and gestured to Miral. "Pray, continue!"

She described with wonder the beauty of Arisdale, and all that happened while she was there. She told them about the coronation, pausing briefly with the memories of that enchanted night. A bright smile formed when she talked about her dance with Justin. Her expression shifting to a frown when she mentioned the angry elders. Then told them about how she wandered off to think and encountered Razamarea.

Talos and Sara both shot Miral wide eyes and open mouths that contorted to frowns and wrinkled brows at the mention of Razamarea's name.

Sara shook her head, slapping her palm to her face. "I should have known!"

Talos nodded to Sara. "I agree that we should have seen this coming."

Sara leaned back in her chair and sighed. "Razamarea. She has the idea in her mind that Justin is hers, despite his rejections. Any woman Justin attempted to court was too afraid to even speak with him the next day. He stopped courting women in hopes of sparing others the same fate."

Talos clenched his fist. "She brings shame to the dragons."

Sara stroked Talos gently on the side of his face. "You got the worst of it by far, Miral."

"I don't think I can go back to Arisdale," Miral replied, fidgeting with her hands. "I really want to, but she promised to kill me if I return." Tears welled up in her eyes, a cold drop rolling down her cheek that she wiped away.

"Nonsense! She will not be able to get away with it a second time! We will help make sure of that!" Sara said standing with her fist in the air.

Miral sat up straight and smiled. "Thank you."

"It's settled then! We will be going to Arisdale tomorrow anyway. It's Justin's birthday!"

"It is?!"

"We are lucky enough to have the best gift he ever could receive," Talos said pointing at Miral with a sly smile.

Miral blushed and looked away. She glanced back at Sara and Talos, who were holding each other tenderly. They looked like a happy couple. "Galena told me about you two briefly. May I ask, how did you meet?"

"You most certainly may!" Sara replied with a jubilant tone. "First I need to tell you about my heritage. My father was a phoenix and my mother was human."

"Was?" Miral asked concerned.

"Being a phoenix can be dangerous to one's life and others. Our bodies dance with flame. We cannot be touched in our pure state, other than by another phoenix or in this case Talos. Every time we use our phoenix fire, we lose time from our life."

Talos leaned in close to her wrapping his arm around her shoulders.

"My hair grows with the use of the phoenix magic because time is drained from me. If my hair falls to my waist, that means I lost half a year, the ground one year. I'm actually twenty-nine years old, but I'm aged to about thirty-one now. Phoenix fire is slightly different from the element of fire, as it burns hotter and its use is limited. As the Elemental of Fire I can cast an array of fire-based spells that other phoenix cannot."

Sara reached to the clasps in her hair and tapped them. "My father designed these clasps I have to block the phoenix form. They are lined with ethereal obsidian. He initially made them so he could be with my human mother."

"Justin told me a little about obsidian," she glanced down at the cuffs around her wrists. "I'm all too familiar with it now."

Sara nodded. "Yes, there isn't a lot of it around. As useful as it can be, it poses a threat to us also; however, the range of its power is limited at least." She looked at Miral solemnly. "Knowing the elders and Arisdalians in general, along with the events that just occurred, I'm going to take an educated guess and say you earned those out of distrust."

Miral nodded to Sara.

Sara shrugged. "Well, Miral, they won't be on forever, I can promise you that!"

She smiled but didn't feel like debating her feelings about her magic. "Pray, go on, Sara."

"My mother and father were both outcast from Volga. My mom died giving birth to me. My dad eventually died from overuse of his fire. He had become so disheartened with my mother's loss, that he could no longer live without her," Sara sighed.

Miral gasped, holding her hand to her mouth. "I'm so sorry, Sara!"

"Thank you, Miral. Now then, how we met!" Sara said smiling again. "I journeyed to Arisdale from Volga in hopes of conducting research when I was sixteen years old. King Johanas and Queen Anelda were ecstatic to learn that I was the Elemental of Fire. They wished for me to tutor Justin in the ways of magic, and in return I could do my studies.

One day I had been performing a risky experiment with volatile compounds. The experiment failed and spiraled out of control quickly, ready to explode. My only chance of survival was to shift to my phoenix form; however, in the haste I had to fry my favorite robes," Sara paused looking at Talos. "I'll let him continue the story."

Talos nodded to her. "I had my eye on her from the moment she arrived. Sara is a beautiful sight and I worked up the nerve to ask her to court that day. I knew that law forbade such a relationship, but I didn't care. I entered the room an instant before the explosion. Sara had been launched back by the force and I intercepted her path. I knew she was dangerous in that state, but I'm a dragon, these scales are fireproof," Talos grinned proudly tapping his chest. "I cared about her so much that I took the chance to save her. The force threw me back against the wall as I caught her. Sara was in a panic! She placed her hair clasps back on and turned to see what she collided with." Talos looked to Sara briefly then back to Miral. "She was relieved that I was ok, and then instantly turned red. She was naked, all her clothes burned away in her rush to transform. The front of my clothes had fared no better!" Talos chuckled. "I kept my eyes locked on hers, though, and covered her with my wings. She was speechless for the first time in her life!" he said sounding like he was holding back a laugh.

"Talos!" Sara erupted, slapping him on the head.

Miral giggled, it was funny to watch them. They loved each other, which was evident, and yet tormented each other.

Talos chuckled rubbing his head. "Ah-ha, as I was saying. I told her that I was in love with her since she arrived. Sara stated that she felt the same way about me. Being a perfect gentleman, I carried her back to her quarters so she could dress."

Sara's jovial expression faded into a frown. "Then as the elders learned of our relationship, they revoked our citizenship to Arisdale. The elder Arisdalians didn't want us to tarnish the minds of their youth. King Johanas argued with them for days, but the elders would not relent their position, proclaiming that they would be willing to seize the throne from him and abolish the kingship. I didn't want to see that happen. Johanas and Anelda were the sweetest and kindliest royalty I had ever met. Rather than see them lose the ground they were slowly gaining with humans and half-breeds, Talos and I agreed to leave. We are permitted to visit, but we may not display any affection to each other."

Miral frowned. The same thing would happen to Justin because of her. It would be best for him to be the one to express any feelings for her if he had them, and she did not want to manipulate him in any way, despite how she felt about him. "I'm sorry to hear that," she said. "That is a lovely story, though. I thank you."

"You're welcome!" Sara said. "It is nice to remember moments like that. As far as your magic training, we shall wait until we arrive in Arisdale! I will train you there, ok?"

"Sure, that will be fine, but will the elders even let you?"

"I'm sure they will after a little intellectual convincing and a promise to return the cuffs to your arms afterward," Sara said with a grin. She got up from her seat yawning. "Dinner should be ready." She turned and walked towards the kitchen, but paused mid-step. "Talos!"

His eyes went wide in response to her voice.

"I have a thought!"

Talos visibly cooled and turned in his seat to face her. "What's new, hun?"

Sara glowered at him and crossed her arms before her.

"What is on your mind?" Talos said, correcting himself.

Sara walked back over to Miral pointing at her. "She needs a dress! Her other one is far too dirty." Sara placed her fisted hand to her chin tapping it and turned back to the kitchen.

"Talos?" Miral whispered.

"Yes? What is it?"

"Why do the Arisdalians have a law that forbids your love?"

"Ah," he replied with a nod. "The Arisdalians are a proud group of races. For generations they only ever mated with each other. Some go further than that and keep the bloodline pure. The Arisdales were like that too until King Johanas. Justin is very much like his father's species in appearance, though his jaw has a slight beak look to it compared to his father. These laws are a way to preserve themselves. Surely you noticed how our hands are shaped compared to other elder races, like Agar?" Talos asked her holding his four-clawed hand up. "This is one of the traits of the old bloodline, same for the feet and our heads," Talos said while tapping his snout. He shrugged. "Maybe it's out of fear of change, or just pride. If your love is greater than the preservation of your species, you must leave the kingdom. I was once a lieutenant of the royal guard of Arisdale, Miral. Till I met Sara, then I quit my job."

A rustling noise came from beside the bed. Miral and Talos jerked their heads to the sound and saw a bag on the floor wriggling about. Talos slowly stood from the chair and inched towards the bag. "The prophet left this with you."

Miral watched the bag carefully as Talos drew closer to it. "I didn't have anything with me when I was forced out of Arisdale."

The bag stopped moving for a moment, and a small light blue and white-furred creature popped its pink jeweled head from the opening. It gazed at Miral and Talos with big black eyes and squeaked. The creature looked like a tiny rabbit, but its ears were large and rounded.

Talos bent down and picked up the little furry thing. It allowed him to scoop it from the bag, fitting perfectly in the palm of his large hand. Talos gently pet the creature with the side of his claw. It erupted with a purring sound to his touch. Talos chuckled at the fluffy animal and handed it to Miral. "I have never seen anything like it before."

The fur felt silky soft as she stroked it. "You need a name! I'll call you, Delphia."

The little animal squeaked and hopped up and down.

Miral giggled. "She likes it!"

Talos smiled and turned his head to look at the bag. He knelt and picked it off the ground setting it beside Miral on the bed. "It's heavy. I wonder what else he left for you."

Delphia leaped off Miral's lap and onto Talos's head. He was still kneeling on the ground and stayed there. She could hear Sara in the room muttering to herself about stopping in town to find a dress shop. The sounds of dishes could be heard clanking down on the table. Miral reached into the bag and felt soft silk beneath her fingers. She pulled at the cloth in the bag and drew it out, gasping at the sight before her.

"Looks like we won't need to find a dress shop after all!" Talos said with a broad smile.

The sound of glass shattering rang out behind them. "Let me see!" Sara yelled sprinting up behind Talos. Delphia leapt off Talos and onto Miral's shoulder mere moments before Sara drove her hands down onto his head.

His head impacted the wood frame on the side of the bed. "Ugh!"

Sara reached over Talos and touched the dress. "Wow!"

Miral was speechless as she looked at the dress. It was an elegant azure blue and white ball gown adorned with silver metal and threads.

Blue and crystal ethereal gems were attached to the sleeves, belt, and down two strips of silver cloth that hung from the belt. The dress is beautiful and looked fit for a queen. "I don't understand," Miral said. "How did he afford this? Why did he do all this for me?"

Sara stood raising her hands in the air. "Must be the work of the goddess! Come on, Talos! Help me get dinner on the table!" she said marching out to the kitchen.

Talos stood shakily. "Oh . . . noes! Nows . . . theres . . . fives of her!" he said incoherently while pointing at Sara. He shuffled to the kitchen rubbing his head.

Miral looked back at the dress and Delphia squeaked softly in her ear. "You know why, don't you?" she asked, petting Delphia on the head. Delphia squeaked and purred in response. "See you tomorrow, Justin!"

Chapter 28 - Birthday Ball

Miral stood before the enchanting azure gown. She touched its silky surface tenderly with her hands. Today was Justin's birthday, and she was lost in thoughts about him. Sara and Talos made their relationship work so well. She appreciated the time she spent with them and reconsidered her feelings for Justin by watching how two unique species interacted with one another, how they expressed their love, how they kissed.

Sara walked into the room wearing a long purple gown and smirked. "Not dressed yet? Let me help you get that on." She held the dress out for Miral while she stepped into it, then buttoned up the back. "You look beautiful!" she said, wearing a wide grin. "We will be working hard to keep Razamarea away from you after this!"

Miral looked herself over. "I never dreamed of wearing a dress like this. Not that the other ball gown I had wasn't more than I was used to."

"Life has a way of providing us with the unexpected," Sara replied. "It's the actions you take in the face of uncertainty that make you who you are. Fear or fearless, dark or light, the choice is always yours."

Miral stared at Sara.

"You know what I'm talking about!" she said winking. "You decided to face it! That is the right decision. Live in your own heart and light no matter what! Don't let that Raza get in your way," she said adjusting Miral's belt and tying it into a bow in the back.

"Sara, how did you know?"

"Miral, we found you in a ball gown, Razamarea beat you up while you were in it because you danced with Justin. I know him well. The only logical conclusion is that you have caught his interest and she knew it. So, let's not keep him worried and waiting!"

Talos stood beside a carriage with Delphia on his shoulder squeaking happily. He helped them into the carriage, closing the door, and sitting up front to drive it.

Despite having their company, and despite their words, Miral's mind spun with worried thoughts once more as she stared out the window. Between Irana, Razamarea, the elders, General Dilos and the citizens, her life in Arisdale was challenging. She fidgeted in her seat while stroking Delphia. Her attention was drawn to Sara when she leaned out the carriage window.

"Can't you get this thing going any faster?!" Sara barked at Talos.

"Don't you worry, we will get there in plenty of time. Besides I can't push the Galli any harder."

Sara glowered at him. "Then we are too heavy! Why don't you fly there and let me drive!"

"In your dreams, sweetheart!" he said with a chuckle.

Sara flopped back into her seat pouting. Miral giggled softly, and Sara looked at her with a smile.

The journey to Arisdale took several hours. Miral preoccupied herself by playing with Delphia so her mind wouldn't wander further. Once they passed the iron gates to the castle, her heart fluttered in her chest with anticipation. She hugged Delphia tightly as Talos helped her from the carriage. Together they entered the banquet hall and ballroom and saw Galena speaking to Severos and Thordin.

"Galena!" Sara yelled as they approached her.

"Oh, Sara, Talos! I am so happy to see you two well," Galena said hugging Sara.

"Likewise! It's been a while hasn't it," Sara replied. "Severos, how are you?"

"I am well, Lady Phoenix," Severos said with a nod of his head.

Galena's eyes widened when she hugged Talos. "Mi . . . Miral?" She left Talos and wrapped her arms around her squeezing tight. "Thank the goddess, you are all right! That dress, my heavens!" she said while releasing Miral from the motherly hug. "Who is this sweet thing?"

Miral smiled and looked at her new friend. "This is Delphia. A kind stranger gave her and this dress to me."

"Those are quite some gifts, goodness!" Galena said petting Delphia.

"Thordin? You're a royal guard now?" Miral asked him, noting his armor matched what Severos wore.

"I am still being evaluated, Lady Miral, but I have been given the position for the time being," he said.

"He was promoted for fitting the creed and going above and beyond the call of duty regarding you twice, earning him Justin's favor," Severos said. "After the first incident, Justin had me train him secretly. Thordin proved to be quite capable, but certainly needs more training."

"I have been assigned as your personal guard, Lady Miral," he said while bowing. "I am sorry for letting Razamarea hurt you, though," he frowned and hung his head.

"Ah, Thordin," Severos said shaking his head. "We already told you that not one of us hasn't been upstaged by Razamarea. That is why Justin had to cease courting. No matter what we did, she was clever and patient enough to pounce at the right time. He wasn't courting this time, least that we know of, and she still went after her."

"Well, that dance was certainly a display of much magnitude to the elders," Galena sighed.

Miral's cheeks turned rosy with the conversation, though she hoped everyone thought it was due to the chill in the air.

"Justin went looking for you after settling them down. Music was playing, everyone was dancing," Galena said with her hands in the air. "Then we all heard the most deafening roar ever followed by a small quake! 'Twas positively dreadful! My heart nearly leaped out of my chest," she said placing her hand over her heart. Galena wagged her finger. "We do not roar much anymore aside from young children that love to make a racket. 'Tis uncivilized and unnecessary."

"It was a troubling sound," Severos said.

"We all ran to the courtyard and saw Justin. He looked so angry. The ground was still quaking, just enough to rattle things, not enough to hurt anyone. He was clenching the creed and the bauble you wore in your hair while holding Thordin up. Oh, my heart sank!" she said. "Justin does have a very powerful voice, and when I realized he was the one who roared, well, I never want to hear that again!" she said. "Oh, my heavens!" Galena gasped, placing her hand over her heart again.

Agar appeared in front of Miral, slowly becoming visible out of stealth and threw his arms around her, hugging her tightly. "Miral! You're back!"

She hugged him back laughing.

Galena scowled at Agar. She grabbed hold of his ear and tugged at him. "Agar! I have been startled enough this week! Just because you can hide like that, does not mean you should! How many times must we tell you this?! Honestly!" she huffed.

Agar winced in pain. "I'm sorry, Mom! I won't do it again!" he said with sarcasm.

Galena released his ear and folded her arms in front of her with a scowl on her face.

Agar clasped hands with Talos. "Talos, my good man, a pleasure to see you again!"

"Likewise, Agar."

Agar turned to Sara and hugged her. He stepped away from Sara and nodded at Severos and Thordin. "Sorry to interrupt! I couldn't wait any longer to say hello! If I may interject, Galena?"

Galena nodded to him. "You may."

"Razamarea's scent was hanging in the air like a bad fart!" Agar blurted while fanning his nose.

Talos burst out laughing, then Severos and Thordin laughed as well. Galena's mouth hung open and she glared at Agar. Sara wore a satisfied smirk, and Miral giggled softly.

Agar grinned at Miral. "She reared her head the next day. Justin was livid. She denied knowing what he was talking about."

"Lady Miral, Thordin and I will do everything in our power to keep her away from you," Severos said bowing to her. Thordin bowed as well.

"Thank you both!"

Agar draped an arm over Miral's shoulder. "We looked for you every day! Justin refused to go home, even at nightfall! It took a lot of effort and insistence to convince him to come back for his birthday. I have never seen Justin act that way in all the years I have known him. There is no talking to him about it! He is about as entertaining as a wall with legs right now! He just left his own party and wandered off!"

Sara tapped her chin. "He is a very resolute man but that elusive distance is unlike him. Couldn't you find her by her magic?"

"We couldn't detect her magic aura at all," Agar said with a shrug.

Sara arched an eyebrow at Agar. "You couldn't sense it?"

Agar nodded to her and Sara tapped her hand on her chin.

"That is odd. I could feel her magic pulsing once she woke up," Sara shrugged. "I must think some more on that."

Galena placed a hand on Miral's shoulder. "We held you up long enough, dear! Justin will be so happy to see you! I believe you will know where he is, no cheating now!"

"The devotion chamber!" Miral replied without hesitation. "He said it was his favorite place to be."

"Come, dear. We will walk you there to make sure you arrive safely."

Chapter 29 - Reunion

They arrived at the devotion chamber stopping outside the door.

Sara hugged Miral then pulled away. "See you later," she said winking at her.

"You're all leaving?" Miral asked, her face blushing.

"Yup, you're on your own! We think it's for the best!" Agar said grinning at her.

Delphia sat on Talos's shoulder and squeaked to her. They all waved a farewell. Thordin remained behind nodding to her.

"I'll be right here waiting for you, milady," Thordin replied with a salute.

The two guards beside the chamber doors nodded to her as well. Miral smiled at Thordin before taking a deep breath and pushing the door to the devotion chamber open. It let out a wailing squeal that she swore was louder than last time. Apparently the door was not fixed yet. Justin spun at the sound, staring at her wide-eyed. She closed the door behind her and smiled at him, tears filling her eyes with her failure to contain them.

"Miral!" Justin exclaimed, running to her.

Miral ran to him, tears streaming down her cheeks. Justin quickly lifted her off the ground causing her to feel butterflies in her stomach and twirled her around in a circle while laughing. She giggled in delight. He lowered her to the floor and bent low to embrace her in a tight hug. Miral felt the warm fire within her again. She felt consumed by his massive hug, comforted and safe.

"I am so glad to see you!" he said with a soft quiver in his voice. "Are you all right? Did Razamarea hurt you?! Where have you been?" Justin asked his questions without taking a breath. He released her from the embrace and backed up. He walked a circle around her while studying her. "Where did you get that remarkable gown?"

Miral was reeling from all the questions. She wanted to be honest with him, but it was probably best to not tell him how badly Razamarea hurt her. "I'm all right, Justin! Happy Birthday!"

Justin blinked. "Ah, yes, 'tis so!" he chuckled, his tail swayed happily behind him, sweeping his crimson cape with it. "Miral, your return is the best gift I could have asked for! In fact, I had prayed so."

She blushed at his words. He looked incredibly handsome in his white jacket and vest. The contrast between it and his dark scales complemented him nicely. "The prophet from Delphi found me! I had fallen asleep, and he left me with Sara and Talos."

"Sara and Talos are here? Excellent! Pray, continue, Lady Miral."

She looked down and placed her hands on the gown. "The prophet left behind a bag that had this dress in it!" She raised her head to lay her eyes on Justin's. "Also, a very cute creature I named Delphia! Talos has her right now."

Justin rubbed his lower jaw with his hand. "The prophet? I must thank him in person!"

He continued to stare at her as if waiting for more words about what happened. She looked away and sighed. She bit her lower lip in frustration. Her mind wanted to release her emotions to him. She could feel them weighing her down like a thick blanket of fog.

"Sara told me about Razamarea . . ." Tension rose within her, silencing her words and causing her to fidget nervously with her fingers in response.

Justin grabbed hold of her trembling hands with a firm squeeze. His piercing, knowing, soft eyes displayed deep worry.

She found it impossible to resist those eyes and blurted, "She threatened to kill me if I returned." The trapped emotions spilled forth like the flood of tears from her eyes.

A pained cast washed over Justin's face, his head feathers lifting and falling in waves. He embraced her tightly once more and spoke in a quivering voice. "She will not hurt you again! I swear to you she will not!"

Miral stopped crying and sniffled. Justin was afraid. She remembered what Sara said. Everyone hurt by Razamarea was too scared to even speak to him afterward. *How long had he endured this rejection from women before he gave up?*

"I am so very sorry you had to encounter her," he continued. "She had been away for so long. I assumed she would not be returning." He released her from the hug and gestured wide. "Somehow word of all this reached her! I instructed the guards to be on the lookout for her if she returned. Just in case." He released a lengthy sigh. "Little good that did!"

"It's all right, Justin. You all tried," Miral paused. "Who is she anyway?"

Justin frowned and scrunched his face. "She is a lady of an influential noble family from Volga. Father arranged a courtship between us for relations when I was thirteen; however, I could not tolerate her rough-edged personality. She hates so deeply the things she loathes, humans being one of them. I wanted to fulfill mother's wishes, and with Razamarea, that would not have happened. I am grateful father did not press me about it. Surely, he could have forced me. I know he was desperate for me to marry and secure the bloodline, among other things." He shook his head. "Arisdales have sat on the throne for three thousand years. The fate of my family name lies solely on me now."

Justin paused for a time, his eyes distant, deep in his thoughts. He locked his eyes onto hers. "I chose long ago, that if I marry, 'twould be for love, for what good is a miserable king to his people. She did not take that well and tormented any woman I courted. I knew 'twould be best for me to cease courting until I was certain I found the heart that beats with mine. Once I found it, I swore I would fight for that love to the end of my days. This began nine years ago, and honestly, I had given up hope of finding true love. Instead, I decided to let it find me," he said while staring at her intently. He shook his head. "Oh, but the fool I am for dancing with you, Lady Miral," he said with a quiver in his voice. "I am a bigger fool for not telling you about her and giving you a choice that night. I had no right to put you in that position unwillingly. I pray you can forgive my foolishness," he said bowing his head low.

Her heart sank as she listened to yet another of his sad tales. *Justin is a good man and doesn't deserve to be plagued by an angry woman. However, had it not happened, he could have been married before we met. What am I thinking, as if I really had any chance with him? He is a king, and I am a human nobody.* He was just kind to her, but deep inside she hoped that kindness wasn't the reason he took a chance to dance with her.

"Don't be so hard on yourself, Justin. I don't regret the dance, not even after what happened."

He stared at her as she spoke, his sad sunny eyes shifted into the dreamy look she saw during the dance, and a smile grew on his face. She felt herself blushing as she stared back at him with her own yearning eyes.

Justin ran his hand through his head feathers and spoke in a lower tone. "Lady Miral, there is something that I needed to say to you that night."

Miral's heart was beating louder in her ears as it picked up pace with his deepened tone. She had become accustomed to feeling a spark for him on hearing the sweet and silky smooth voice that carried his poetic words fluidly. The feeling like she was falling was in her core once more. She held her hands together in front of her as she eagerly waited for the words she longed to hear.

"I had a lot of time to think things through and I . . ."

A blinding blue light filled the room and Justin's gaze shot up to the ceiling. His mane of feathers and sickle claws rose from their relaxed positions. His once dreamy face was awash with wide-eyed alarm.

"So sorry to interrupt!" said an unknown woman, who floated beneath the elemental orb of ice.

She felt Justin's hands grab hold of her shoulders, gently pushing her back while he stepped in front of her.

"Who are you?!" Justin demanded followed by a growl.

She could feel the deep resonating growl vibrating in her own chest, and found it to be unnerving. She clung to his crimson cape and peeked past his arm at the intruder. The woman before them was cloaked in black. The only visible features were glowing red eyes and light blue furry hands and feet. Miral wondered how this woman got into the chamber. She didn't recall hearing the door squeak.

"The lady is late for a prior engagement. Let us be going now, Miral. Come peacefully and he won't be hurt," the woman said, disregarding Justin's question.

Justin growled again, stooping into a fighting stance. "If you want her, you will have to go through me!" he bellowed.

The woman laughed with delight. "I am happy to oblige." Her hand rose and a light blue swirl formed, gradually taking the shape of a spear.

Justin tensed. His earth shield surrounded them just as the spear reached them. It was deflected, hitting the ground and shattering on impact.

Miral watched the woman, searching with her mind as Justin instructed her on the ship. She saw a light blue glow, the same shade as the elemental orb of ice.

"Uhh!" she whined. "That was no fun, dearest Justin!"

Justin arched a brow and his mouth hung open in recognition of the familiar phrase. His face hardened with a scowl, bared teeth, and his head feathers tensed upward. "Irana?! You dare assault me in my home!"

Miral felt stunned by the force of his voice.

"Happy birthday, dearest!" the woman laughed.

The two guards that stood outside the door burst into the chamber. The woman launched spears at them. The sharply pointed ice pierced through their armor with ease, dropping them lifelessly to the floor in the middle of the room.

Justin raised his hand towards the door as Thordin entered the chamber.

"Thordin! Stay back!" Justin commanded, thrusting his hand.

His magic repelled the guard by his armor out the door, and he disappeared into the dark of night. Justin reached his left hand back and gently grabbed hold of Miral's arm, and inched them toward the open door.

"I will not let you take her!"

Miral clung to him trying to calm her trembling hands, shifting her feet in a side step along with him.

The woman shrugged. "I need her alive, but as for you," she said with a smirk, "I care little of your fate. I will kill you if that's what it takes."

The woman extended her hand, launching a long channeled spell to the door slamming it shut and encasing it in a solid block of ice. She looked about the room, jerking her head back and forth wildly and screamed, "Arrrgh!"

Miral shuddered and her legs locked. The bloodcurdling cry sounded like an eerie mix of distorted voices. The woman launched blocks of ice towards every mural and statue of Fandia while screaming.

Justin dropped into a squatting position, pulling her down with him, narrowly dodging a block of ice that sailed overhead. He placed his hand against the wall and channeled a spell into it.

"No! Damn it!" he cursed.

"What's wrong?"

"I cannot use shatter to break through the wall! 'Tis repelling the magic!"

He moved to the door and reached for the block of ice. He channeled a spell into it. The ice block over the door shattered. He reached for the knob, but it wouldn't turn. Justin reached for the door once more channeling another spell, but nothing happened.

"Quake is not responding!"

Justin stood and rammed his shoulder into the door, but it stood firm in defiance. He punched the wall but made no dent.

"Ethereal obsidian!" Justin cursed under his breath. "My spells are being stopped by the door, wall, and floor! I cannot get shatter to connect to the ice that seeped to the outside!"

Miral looked over the scene, her lips quivering, clinging to Justin tightly. The element of wind was the dominant power over the earth and ice was made of wind and water. They were trapped. Irana intended to kill him if she didn't come peacefully.

Her heart ached. He was going to tell her something important. Now they were in danger, and no matter the outcome, they would lose each other.

Justin roared and she released her grip on him, staring in shock. Galena was right, it is dreadful to hear him roar. He launched into an attack, sickle claws raised. Miral folded her hands together in prayer in front of her. Justin was risking his life to protect her and all she could do was watch, the gold cuffs on her arms a searing reminder. Even if she knew and could cast magic now, she imagined there would be little she could do against the Elemental of Ice.

The woman dodged his assaults, floating about the room laughing.

"Fight fair, no magic!" Justin bellowed.

The woman stopped moving and sighed, "Oh, very well then!"

She landed on the ground and pulled the hood of her cloak back revealing a young and beautiful human-like face. The light blue fur covered all but her mouth down to her throat and chest, which was white. Her hair was the same shade of blue as her fur, lightening to

169

white at the tips. It was pulled up into a high ponytail, with two sections looking like tall rabbit ears that looped up and draped downward. She had very long ears that stuck out of the side of her head.

"I will play this game your way for now," she grinned, removing the cloak and letting it drop to the floor. "After all, you have no chance of winning!" She drew out her twin-bladed fans and stood in a defensive posture.

Miral watched as Justin and the ice elemental sparred. The snow hare looked naturally acrobatic as she flipped to the side dodging his charges. The cream-colored fur collar that wrapped around her chest and arms billowed with her movements. Her purple and silver armor and intricate silver leather belt with clear ethereal gems was light and form fitting, allowing her to move with ease. Her fan-fighting moves appeared more like dance than a battle. She was small, looking to be only slightly taller than Miral giving her an advantage over Justin's taller bulkier size. He was unable to disarm her with his magic. The woman must have no earthly elements on her. She managed to cut him several times with her bladed fans as she dodged his attempts to subdue her.

The woman launched into the air again. "I'm growing tired of this!"

Her hand rose and she formed a spear of ice. Miral's breath caught in her throat as it headed towards her as her earth shield faded. Justin dove at her wrapping his left arm around her waist. He twisted them around and hit the ground first. She was sprawled on top of him, with his arms tightly around her. He let go of her and she pushed herself to the side of him. Justin got to his feet and helped her up, then stood in front of her once more.

"I thought you wanted her alive!" he shouted in frustration.

"Oh, I do, but I don't care what condition she is in when I get her. Since you insist on protecting her, you will have to suffer!" She laughed and formed multiple small sharp ice shards before her. "Your shield is about to fade, and I know you can't cast a new one until it does!" she said in a playful mocking tone.

Justin spun to Miral, his face filled with a dread she had never seen before. His earth shield faded, and she could feel him casting another while he grabbed the sides of her shoulders, pushing her back and against the wall. He stood in front of her in a lunge, planting the top of his head against the wall.

Fear clutched at her throat, threatening to strangle her. He was shielding her with his towering mass. "No!" Miral cried out to him.

He released a howl of agony as the barrage of shards drove into his back, the earth shield failing to form. He fell to his knees, pulling her down with him.

"Justin!" Miral cried.

He was wheezing and moaning, blood dripping from his back to the floor. She placed her head on the side of his, crying. Her shaking hands cupped his cheeks. He was casting his shield again and moved his hands from her shoulders to the wall.

More shards drove into his back. His pained howl was more intense, and the protection failed yet again. Justin cast once more, the shield formed, blocking the next round of shards. He coughed blood and his wheezing increased.

"Arhhh!" The Elemental of Ice whined.

Justin wouldn't be able to hold the shield forever. When it failed, he would be in danger. She moved to crawl out of his protection and go to Irana. Justin grabbed hold of her shoulder and pushed her back to the wall.

"No!" he said, wheezing. "Thordin . . . they will . . . come!"

Miral clenched his white jacket in her hands, resting her head on his shoulder and cried. "Let me go, Justin!" she pleaded with him. She didn't want him to die, not like this. He looked so weak now, and a large pool of blood was forming around him. "You can't take another attack like that!"

Justin looked at her through his drooping right eye. "I will . . . never . . . let you go!"

The woman was attacking again. The energy of his shield was beginning to wane. Miral squeezed her eyes tight sobbing and held her head against his. "What good will it do me if you die?" she pleaded with him. "These stupid cuffs!" she groaned while tugging on them. "I can't help you heal either!" She stopped crying when she heard strange voices inside her rising in intensity and urgency.

"Give us control."

She closed her eyes and heeded the voice. Miral placed her hands on his. The cuffs around her arms broke free and fell to the floor. Justin's earth shield faded, and she redirected the ice magic Irana threw at him to his hands and arms, freezing him to the wall.

"Miral! What are you doing?!" Justin asked in alarm.

"Forgive us!" Miral said in two distinct voices, one male, and one female. "Live to fight. Seek and find."

Justin's mouth hung open, staring into Miral's eyes with confusion. He could feel the power of holy magic flowing through him, easing his pain. Irana's attacks stopped coming.

"Well! It's about time!" she sneered.

Miral's eyes filled with tears. "Justin, what's happening?!" She looked at his frozen hands and then into his weary eyes. "Why did I do that to you?!" she asked with a quiver in her voice. "Those voices . . . what were they?"

Justin closed his eyes. "I do not know, but . . . go . . ." he said, wheezing between words.

Miral cried tears of relief that he would not be killed, and yet feared having to go.

Justin stared at her intently, his eyes glossed over. "I promise . . . I will find you!"

She nodded and crawled out from under him.

"Miral, I need you . . . to know . . ."

She spun around to face him, desperate to know what he wanted to tell her. He sounded so weak and paused, wincing in pain. The sight of him made Miral tremble and place her hands over her mouth. His back was mangled, but no blood was dripping onto the floor now, partly healed by whatever it was she did. His crimson cape that had brought her so much comfort was in tatters.

He opened his eyes again. "I . . ."

Miral gasped as his jaws were frozen shut.

Justin turned his head to glare at the woman, growling at her.

"That's enough chatter!" she said smirking at him, wagging her finger like a scolding mother.

Miral placed her hand gently on his face, drawing his attention back to her. "I'll be waiting," she said in a whisper.

"I'm glad you decided to cooperate," The woman said glaring at her.

Miral took a glance back at Justin, who was watching her. She turned to face him, her hands in prayer as she cried. She felt the woman channeling a spell and saw ice form at her feet. She panicked as the deep stinging cold of the ice climbed her body. She was shivering violently and locked her focus on Justin in hope of ignoring the pain.

Justin's eyes grew wide. He turned his head forward and kicked wildly at the thick ice over his hands with his toe claws, desperately trying to break free.

The ice reached her face covering her head and all went dark. She could feel the bite of the cold. Somehow, she was still able to breathe, to think. The image of Justin struggling to break free filled her mind. *She will keep her word, won't she? She won't kill him, right?* She was deathly afraid now, but what other option was there? At least this way, she wouldn't see his death if it came.

Chapter 30 - Aftermath

Sara Phoenix fidgeted with impatience. She stood and headed to the ballroom door.

Agar leaped in front of her with arms out. "Let them be."

She scowled and poked at his shoulder. "Agar, something isn't right. I can't see Miral's light, and Justin's looks faint." She pushed him aside and walked faster. "Let's just take a peek to be sure!"

Talos and Galena jogged up next to her. Delphia was still perched on his shoulder and squeaked excitedly.

"All right, just a peek," Agar replied.

Thordin burst through the door nearly colliding with Sara. "The king! Someone is attacking and they have magic!"

"What?!" Agar growled running past him out the door.

The devotion chamber door and outer walls were encased in a thick block of ice when they arrived. The guards were hacking away at it; however, the magic ice was more resistant, and the blows did little to break it.

"Justin?! Miral?! Can you hear me?!" Agar hollered. Only the wind howled in reply. "Dammit!" Agar cursed under his breath.

Sara reached to unfasten her clasps.

"No!" Talos said stopping her hands.

Sara closed her eyes and sighed. "We need to get in there now! In this weather it will take days for that ice to melt, any other means will be far too long to risk!" she said looking at Talos.

Talos released her hands. "You're right."

He handed Delphia to Galena and turned back to Sara. Talos blocked the others' view of her with his wings. Sara slipped out of her dress and

Talos handed it over to Galena. She removed her clasps and was engulfed in her own flames as she transformed into her Phoenix body. Her hair danced wildly above her like a candle, her legs and feet were bird-like, and two fiery wings protruded from her back. She placed her hands close to the ice, melting it fast. She pushed the squeaky door open and was met with a horrible sight. Justin was on his knees, his hands frozen to the wall, his mouth frozen shut. Blood darkened his tattered crimson cape and white shirt, and a large pool was on the ground around him. His head hung down, and his partly closed eyes looked at them.

The room was in ruins, every beautiful image of Fandia destroyed. Justin's two guards lay lifeless in puddles of their own blood with holes through their chests.

"What in the world happened here? Where is Miral?" Galena cried, running to him. She examined the gaping wounds on his back, bones were exposed in places, some broken. He was no longer bleeding and appeared to be partly healed. She knelt to cast more healing spells on his back. *Oh, this poor boy. Trouble loves to find him, she thought.*

Delphia was sitting on Galena's shoulder and squeaked sadly.

Sara knelt next to him carefully melting the ice from his muzzle and stared into his regret-filled eyes. "Oh, don't you dare apologize! I'm not sorry! You don't need to be either! Understand?" The ice melted away and his jaws were freed.

"Thank you, Sara," he replied.

"That is better!" Sara said smiling and moved to free his left hand next.

Delphia leaped from Galena's shoulder and cautiously approached Justin. She hopped along the ground past Sara and Talos. She stopped at the wall and gazed up at him.

Justin looked at her and smiled. "Delphia?"

Delphia hopped up and down squeaking.

Justin chuckled. His laugh cut off as he shuddered and moaned in pain.

Delphia squeaked sadly at him.

Agar returned from looking around the room and reached down to support Justin's left arm. Talos stood by Sara's side watching her and holding the clasps.

Galena finished mending his surface wounds. She was not certain how well his back would heal. No doubt there would be scars. She looked deeper at him with her mind to be sure nothing unseen needed healing. He had broken rib bones and bruised organs. She could mend the wounds, but only time could heal the other traumas he suffered.

Sara stood and moved to free his right hand.

"Despite the obvious, are you ok, brother?" Agar asked.

"I will be all right," Justin replied.

Delphia hopped up Agar's back to his shoulder and looked into Justin's eyes.

"I am Justin," he said.

Delphia squeaked while bouncing up and down excitedly.

"A pleasure . . . to meet you too."

Once his other hand was freed from the wall, Galena stooped in to support him on the right. Sara turned to Talos, who blocked her from the others with his wings. She returned her clasps to her hair, which was longer now and tumbled down slightly past her shoulders.

Justin failed to push his trembling body upright. Galena and Agar helped lift him, and supported his weight between them. He was wobbling and barely able to stand on his own.

"'Twas, Irana," Justin murmured, pausing to breathe. "She took Miral."

They all stared at him in disbelief. Justin's eyes closed and he fell limp. Galena struggled against his dead weight, nearly falling over as his body shifted to the right. Agar strained to keep Justin and himself from falling over with her to no avail. Talos caught Galena while stepping in to relieve her of the burden. Severos and Thordin jumped in to help Agar and together they carried him out of the chamber into the main keep.

Chapter 31 - Desperation

Sara scribbled in her journal. She was seated beside Justin's bed in the royal suite. The room was lit by the orange glow of a warm fire that crackled in the fireplace. Delphia stayed with him the entire time, cuddled up in a ball next to him while he slept.

Agar took command in Justin's place, preparing the defenses in Arisdale. They didn't know where to begin looking for Miral. He thought she would be taken to Delphi and sent scouts to keep an eye on Irana from a distance. He wanted to look for her himself, but the elders put their foot down; until Justin awakes Agar had to remain.

What did she want from Miral? Between Irana and the sea dragon, and being the first human with magic, there was something important about the Elemental of Water. Sara hoped Justin knew something more.

She looked up from her journal when he stirred. He let out a groan and slowly opened his eyes.

"Justin. I'm happy to see you awake! How do you feel?"

He focused on her through heavy eyes, blinking several times as if trying to comprehend her words in his newly awakened state. Then his eyes went wide and he flew from his bed in a flurry, pulling the bed sheets around his waist. He stumbled a few times as he made his way to his clothing cabinet, still groggy from his long sleep.

Sara flushed and caught Delphia as she flew through the air from his haste and kept her eyes towards the bed, blinking in shock. "Justin! You really shouldn't be . . ."

"How long have I been sleeping?!" Justin interjected with a panicked voice, tearing through his wardrobe.

"Take it easy, Justin. You just woke up. We need to evaluate you fir—"

"Sara!" Justin bellowed. "How long?!"

Sara spun with a scowl. Justin had pants on and was putting an arm through the sleeve of his vest. She frowned, his back was riddled with rounded scars, like craters on the moon. "That won't help right now! You need to calm down and sit tight until Galena gets here!"

Justin pulled his jacket on and froze. His head feathers spiked in waves, his toe claws erect, and his tail whipped wildly back and forth. He jerked his head in her direction, and his eyes squinted in a tension she had never seen before. Objects in the room that were made of earthen elements lifted from their resting place and hovered in the air.

"I asked a question, and you will answer me now!" he barked.

The castle shook, nearly knocking Sara off her feet. Bits of dust and rock rained from the ceiling. She blinked, no longer feeling brave enough to combat him with words and shrunk back. Thordin and another guard entered the room looking about for a possible intruder.

"How long have I been sleeping?!" Justin barked to them in a commanding tone.

Thordin looked at his king with large rounded eyes and moved his jaws to reply, but Agar stepped in placing a hand on his shoulder.

"Leave," he said walking past them towards Justin.

"Brother! Will you deny me as well?!" Justin growled.

Agar's ears swiveled back. "Hey, big guy. We are only looking out for your health. What good will it do her if you die from anger now?" he asked moving closer.

Justin glared at him. "Answer my damned question then!"

Agar sighed. "If it's the only way then fine, but you have to know that we have been doing all we can, and you have to stay calm."

He looked further agitated by the words. "I have to?!" he bellowed. "I will not be ordered so! Now get on with it!" he grumbled.

"It has been fifteen days, brother," Agar said drooping his ears.

Justin stared at Agar. A growl grew in his throat. The earthen objects in the room began to move slowly rotating around him as they picked up pace. He released a roar, and the earthen objects zipped away from him with blazing speed. One shattered the large balcony window behind him. A metal poker from the fireplace embedded itself into the wall, nearly hitting Agar and Sara. Agar's fur was standing on end, and his face was dread filled as was hers. Delphia squeaked sadly.

Justin's expression shifted to concern as he stared at them. He looked to be crying as he spun toward the balcony.

"Justin!" Agar shouted chasing after him. Justin leaped off the balcony edge, and Agar watched him float down to the cliffs and run fast away from the castle.

Sara joined him at the balcony. "Agar, I'm not so certain it's safe to be standing here. The castle will need to have its integrity checked."

Agar backed away nodding at her. "I . . . I never . . . that was . . ."

Sara hugged Agar once they exited the royal suite. "I know, Agar. I know." *That was terrifying!*

No doubt Justin knew that. He had been trapped in elemental rage. She knew that feeling, it happened to her once after her father died. She returned to her mother's old hometown, and burning anger at the people who ridiculed him and her mother caused her to fall into the rage. There was no reason, only blinding anger. Every home in the village ignited into flames. When she came to, she looked at the smoldering village in fear and fled.

She cursed herself for defying Justin, but she feared that this would have been his response if she had told him. The best thing Justin could do for his kingdom was to leave until he calmed down. "Let's get the others and go after him. We will watch him from a safe distance until he is ready to come back."

Chapter 32 - Meeting

Sara looked around the dimly lit room at all in attendance to Justin's royal proclamation. Her gaze settling to the Elder Council who looked appalled by the king's words, but remained silent, fidgeting in their seats. They were deathly afraid of him right now and didn't wish to catch his ire.

Honestly, we are all afraid of him.

Standing in Justin's way, as he was now, was akin to willingly standing in the path of a charging Triceratops. No one had ever seen this side of him before. Once he cooled off and returned to Arisdale, he told them what happened and called a meeting to discuss what occurred.

Sara pondered the facts in her mind as he gave them. The most puzzling thing was the male and female voices Miral spoke with. Justin said the voices spoke without emotion as if they were two entities. She thought about the unnatural multi-voiced scream that Justin said came from the Elemental of Ice before she proceeded to deface every image of Fandia. The rage-fueled hate for the Goddess of Light was a concern in itself.

Then there was the chamber. Justin said the Elemental of Ice appeared out of thin air with a blinding light, and left with Miral under the orb of ice, disappearing within the same light.

Justin also said the walls, floor, and door would not bend to his will and repelled magic as if they were made of ethereal obsidian; however, magic could adhere to it. The chamber's structure was not earthen at all. Irana must have been aware of this. She also knew that they were in there at the time, and used the Elemental of Ice in her assault. She had set the perfect trap. She scolded herself for never researching the chamber's structure and elemental properties. Frankly no one did. We either all assumed they were typical buildings and never investigated them or a higher power sought to erase all knowledge of them from memory.

"I'm going after her!" Justin said with resolution, his back to everyone present, staring out the window of the council room into the dark night.

"You would abandon your kingdom to chase after a human girl?!" General Dilos said. "You have no way of knowing that she is not as much of a threat as Irana! This could all be an elaborate scheme!" he said, sounding like a preacher, arms outstretched. "You willingly throw yourself into the trap, yet again, because of your disgusting and misguided feelings for her!" Dilos snapped at him. "You cannot even rein in your own power, rocking the kingdom with quakes like a damn child!"

Sara saw Agar's eyes go wide and his fur stood on end. He immediately moved his hands to cover his slumped ears. Galena had done the same. Justin's head feathers spiked and his tail whipped wildly behind him. He spun around, his face set in a menacing glower.

"Hoo boy," Agar groaned to Severos, who nodded in agreement.

"General Dilos!" Justin bellowed.

Everyone jumped and straightened in their seats as Justin's expected, but powerful voice flooded the room. Sara wore a small smile on her face, and Delphia hopped up and down squeaking on Talos's shoulder.

Justin moved swiftly towards Dilos. "You dare speak to me so!" he growled. "Human or not it makes no difference! What I do is not for one human, but for the world! I also have no particular feelings that would ever hinder my decisions for this kingdom! Although that is none of your concern!" he said standing tall before Dilos, glaring at him.

"General Dilos!" Elder Nyros said while standing. "You will refrain from further provoking the King, is that clear?" he warned with a grave expression. "Pray, continue, sire."

Dilos remained silent with a scowl of indignation on his face. Justin nodded to Elder Nyros and turned, walking to his desk.

"Irana must be stopped! My parents, friends and guards avenged!" He turned back to face the room. "If saving Miral is the key to undoing Irana, then that is what I will do!" Justin said slamming his fist down on his desk with a loud crack, splintering the wood table on impact. "I am not only your king but an Elemental as well. My duty is to this world as a chosen warrior of the Goddess of Light," he said with a nod. "Given that earth is also the dominating element of water, I must go on this mission. If the choice arises to save the world or to save her, I will . . ." he paused, regaining his composure. "I can make the right choice as is my duty." He stood resolutely before them in silence looking into every eye present, stopping at Elder Nyros. "I know you all fear for my safety, but even if every stone in this kingdom should crumble, the heart of Arisdale will live on in the people!"

Elder Nyros sighed and rose from his seat. "Much to our regret, your arguments are valid, sire. Irana is able to bend the mind of an elder race, assault us in our own home, and nearly kill you, all to capture one Elemental who, by coincidence is human," he said looking at Dilos and folding his arms together. "The reasons are beyond our understanding at this juncture; however, the gravity of the event has escalated beyond racial issues. Irana has defaced the Goddess of Light in her assault, and commands dark powers unseen in the World of Life." He bowed deeply at the waist. "This fight is beyond mere men. Despite our hesitations and fears for your life, Your Majesty, you have our blessing to take your leave to rescue the Elemental of Water and stop Irana. If at all possible."

Justin nodded to Elder Nyros. "I graciously thank the Elder Council for your grand wisdom."

Elder Nyros nodded and returned to his seat.

Sara knew Justin would have abandoned the kingdom and his position to save Miral, regardless of their decision. He never admitted to having deep feelings for her when he returned to talk to them; however, the amount of emotional change that he had undergone since she entered his life spoke highly of her importance to him.

"I will not leave Arisdale defenseless, therefore, Prince Agar will remain behind with the royal guard to take care of things in my stead until we can regroup and take down Irana."

Agar stood and saluted. "As you wish, brother!"

Justin nodded to him and turned his eyes back to the room. "I am taking Sara, Talos, and Galena with me. We set sail for the Harbor of Glenn at dawn." He paused briefly. "Lose not your guard, your heart, or your light. Lest you find Irana's knife in your back! You are all excused!" Justin said gesturing to the door.

The elders left the room first. Justin caught Dilos by the arm as he strode past.

"Mind yourself, general! I will have you removed from service!" Justin whispered to him.

Dilos glared at him, then continued out the door. Delphia leaped down from Talos and over to Justin. She hopped up and down in front of him squeaking loudly. He smiled at her, picked her up, and petted her.

Sara smiled and leaned over to whisper to Talos. "An excellent speech!"

Talos nodded to her. "Indeed!"

Chapter 33 - Secrets

The voyage to the Harbor of Glenn to the south would only take a few hours by sea. Their destination was Glenn Woods, the home of the honorable Wolves, who are well known for their compassion towards all living things.

Sara sat at a desk in the ship's cabin scribbling away in her books. She loved writing and knew that without a well-kept history, events became skewed and forgotten with time. She pushed herself from the cedar desk in the king's office and headed out the double doors to find Justin, and get his side of what happened when he met Miral. It was a cold November morning. She was grateful that Talos had flown back to their cabin to gather travel clothes. Justin was standing by the deck rails of the ship petting Delphia while staring at the sea. He wore a thick blue and gold-rimmed collared jacket that ended just above his knees, sleeveless high collar vest, blue draped pants, and a long blue and gold-trimmed cape. The jacket had blue oval cut ethereal gems on the bottom edges, on his gold belt, cape clasps and along the sides of his blue and gold boots. This clothing was less protective than his suit of armor, but it would not weigh him down or exhaust him as quickly. It would also serve better in any weather condition.

Sara smiled when she saw him stroking Delphia. The little rascal wanted to go with Justin and put up a real fight when he told her to stay with Agar. The cute critter had some magic, which she used to fight back. Sara laughed at the memory of them all being levitated off the ground when they tried to get her off the ship. Justin relented and told her she could come, but needed to stay with Galena if there was trouble. With that, she lowered them to the ground again.

"Hello Justin, Delphia," Sara said waving to them.

"Greetings, Sara."

Delphia squeaked happily in reply.

Sara leaned against the rail next to him, holding up her quill. "I would like to get your side of what happened for my books. I have Miral's words down already if you would like to read her story?" Sara asked while handing him the book.

Justin looked at the book blankly for a moment before returning to his distanced gaze of the sea. "Not now," he said, his face and voice lacking emotion. Delphia squeaked sadly at him. He glanced down and resumed petting her.

Sara arched an eyebrow. "Ok . . . would you care to tell me your side now?" To her knowledge Justin was awake all night, and the lack of rest and stress displayed itself prominently in his eyes.

"I will do so one day, Sara. For now, I do not."

Sara wore a forced smile. "That is fine!" In truth, she was feeling frustrated. Sara tapped her fist on her chin. "Why are we going to the Harbor of Glenn?" She knew why they were going, but hoped the question would get him talking.

"Miral told me about how the prophet she met in Delphi showed up to help her in Arisdale."

Delphia squeaked with the mention of Miral's name and Justin stroked her fur in response.

"I find it odd," he said. "She gave his description, and I intend to find this prophet wolf. I have a lot I need to say and maybe he can help."

Sara nodded. "It is a good start." He still wore an unreadable emotion in both his face and voice when speaking of Miral. Even his tail and head feathers remained relaxed and lifeless. Agar was right, he was a stonewall with legs. She wasn't going to get anything more out of him on the matter. "I'm going to go find Galena and bend her ear for a while too."

"Very well then, Sara."

She headed back through the double doors and down the stairs to the kitchen. Galena was sitting at a table reading a book, her gold helmet resting on the table beside her.

"Galena, I have to ask you about Justin and his attitude toward Miral before I knew her."

Galena looked at her, closed the book, and set it down. "Every time they were together you could see a light in his eyes. I have never seen that look before," she smiled. "He was always eager to escape the Elder Council meetings to spend time with her. More often than not he was not able and thusly sad. He acted positively smitten with her at his coronation. When they danced together, all you could see were two in love. Agar made a bet with Severos that they would be dancing close together before the song was over. That rascal knows Justin better than we do," Galena said smiling at the fond memory.

Sara put her hand on her chin in deep thought. "If he loved her, he would be upset, naturally, but this is beyond that. Feels more like intentional distance from everyone." She threw her hands up in frustration. "He refused to give me his view of what has happened at Delphi and on." Sara paused a moment. "I asked him if he would like to read Miral's words. He didn't wish to," Sara said handing Galena the book.

She took it from her, smiling. "I would love to read this!" Her face shifted to a frown. "Oh Justin, dear. I wish you would open up to us! I really do hope he is not suffering too much," Galena said while staring at the book.

"What is all this?" Talos asked from behind Sara. "What are you two hens clucking about?"

Sara spun out of her chair. "Talos!"

Talos ran from her laughing.

The double doors to the ship commons flew open with a bang. The commotion broke Justin from his meditated stare at the ocean. Delphia strained her head to see what was going on. She squeaked when she saw Talos. Justin watched Sara pursue Talos around the ship and he chuckled lightly in amusement.

Chapter 34 - Honor

Kedros walked through the forest of Glenn Woods in deep thought. The multi-colored fall leaves crunched beneath his dark brown leather boots, the smells of autumn filling his nostrils. It was a beautiful day to be alive. The air was crisp and cool but pleasant. Sun peeked through the trees casting beams of light to the ground. He was attuned to nature and enjoyed the presence of it in the woods. The feral animals enjoyed his company as well. Of all the wolves of Glenn he alone had the ability to understand them. He loved his home in Glenn Woods. There was nowhere else he would rather be.

He placed his hands over his teal tunic and rubbed his stomach that grumbled in hunger, searching his brown pants pockets but he found no snacks. Trea probably had lunch ready for them back in the village by now. He was grateful for his best friend Stan and Trea, his friend's wife.

Kedros grabbed hold of his feather necklace rubbing the polished aqua and yellow ethereal gems with his thumb. It was a gift from his parents when they learned of his power, the Elemental of Nature. He and his little sister Kara lost their mother and father to an illness that swept throughout the Earth two years ago. The responsibility of caring for his now ten-year-old sister fell upon him when he was fifteen. He didn't mind it though because he loved Kara deeply.

A new scent came to Kedros; the smell of smoke and blood. His ears perked up and he sprinted to his village.

"Pray, can anyone help us?!" Kara yelled. It was strange, the harbor of

187

Glenn was normally bustling, and now it was hauntingly empty. No shouts from traders hawking wears, no drunken laughter, no children playing, just empty stone homes, dense fog, waves breaking against piers, and cries of hungry sea birds who ate from unstaffed carts. As she approached the inn, two men came out. They appeared to be drunk, stumbling as they walked.

"What do we 'ave here?" the taller man said with a crooked grin.

"It looks to be one of them forest critters," the other said.

"Pray! My village is under attack! We are outnumbered! Can you help us?!" Kara pleaded with them.

"Sure, we can help!" the tall man said grabbing her roughly by the arm.

"Ow, you're hurting me!" Kara yelped.

"You 'ave yet to feel the pain I can give you." He grabbed her by the hair and pulled her off into a nearby alley. The other man was laughing wickedly. He threw her on the ground pinning her there. His bright eyes shifted into a black and haunting appearance. Kara screamed and kicked in terror. The man abruptly gasped and sputtered, releasing his hands from her shoulders to grasp at the huge brown-scaled hand around his neck, black claws digging deep into his flesh.

"One wrong move and you will slice your throat open," a deep male voice warned.

Kara backed out from under the man still quivering with fear. Once cleared from him, her hero slammed the man's head into the ground, the impact knocking him out cold next to his companion. The one who saved her was an Arisdalian man in blue and gold clothing, his golden eyes fixed on hers.

"Are you all right, young one?" he asked holding out his hand to her.

She took his hand, letting him help her off the ground. "Thanks to you I am!" she said throwing herself at him to hug him before he could stand. "My name is Kara Okami."

"A pleasure to make your acquaintance, Kara. I am Justin, King of Arisdale."

"King?! I was saved by the king!" she said in a sing-song voice, twirling her light pink hair around her finger while spinning around.

Justin chuckled at her.

Kara stopped turning and swung her arms out. "My brother Kedros will be so happy to see you!"

"Kedros, the Elemental of Nature, right? Kara, we have come to speak with your tribe."

Kara's aqua eyes grew wide and her tail wagged quickly from side to side. "Yes and right! We are being attacked! I came here looking for help!"

Talos scanned the town, sniffing at the air. "This mostly human city is awfully empty of . . . humans," he said narrowing his eyes.

Sara shot Talos a side stare. He replied with a shrug while smiling.

Justin shuddered as a haunting memory returned to his mind. His head feathers stood on end. "Just like Delphi was!" he said alarmed. "Kara, take us to them!"

Chapter 35 - The Battle of Glenn Woods

Kedros Okami scanned the frantic battlefield before him. He was back to back with his friend, the gray wolf, Stan. "We are far too outnumbered!" he said running his hand through his light brown hair. He couldn't help but be distracted as well, he hadn't seen Kara anywhere and no one else had either.

Stan raised his bow and released an arrow, his golden hair blowing in the draft from the shot. "It would appear that way, Kedros."

"Stan! Help me!" Trea screamed as she ran from a human with a raised sword.

"Trea!" Stan shouted.

Kedros moved towards her along with Stan. The field before him was thick with men, and getting to her in time seemed impossible. He stopped running to channel a spell but froze as a figure leaped across the battlefield toward Trea with lightning velocity. Whoever it was, launched into a forward jump kick hitting Trea's attacker in the chest with incredible force and sent him hurdling thirty feet back. The towering Arisdalian man dressed in blue turned to attack another human that was headed towards him. Three other people of mixed race and his sister appeared in the tree line where the Arisdalian had come from.

"Kara!" Kedros shouted.

Kara hopped up and down waving ecstatically. "Kedros!"

Kedros fought his way to his sister and hugged her tight. "Kara, where have you been? I was worried sick!"

"I went to get help, and I found a king!" Kara said while pointing at the Arisdalian man. "King Justin of Arisdale!" Kara said clasping her hands to her face while grinning like a love-struck teenager.

Kedros rubbed the top of her head. "You silly girl. You did well." He stood and watched Justin fight. The king cast a quake as a herd of villagers closed in on him knocking them off their feet. He remembered meeting Justin once before about three years ago. He and Prince Agar were headed to Lake Lunast for fishing when they sensed his nature magic. They talked at length and asked him to join them in Arisdale. He didn't wish to leave home, though, and they understood.

Kedros looked to Justin's companions. The Arisdalian woman was healing the wounds of the fallen. Kedros turned to the blue dragon and red-haired woman. He stared wide-eyed as the woman changed to look like a phoenix. The dragon standing beside her appeared to have no magic but fought furiously. The bird laid down strips of fire to block the humans from fleeing women and children.

"Get Kara and Trea to safety!" Kedros said to Stan.

"You bet!"

Kedros ran to Justin summoning up vines from the ground to wrap around a soldier approaching him from behind.

Justin turned to him and smiled. "Kedros, right?"

"Yes, Majesty," he said joining Justin's side.

"Elemental of Nature, 'tis a pleasure to meet you again."

Kedros smiled back at Justin and released a howl. A mix of wild animals streamed into the battlefield from every direction, joining the fray. Deerlings trampled the attackers while dodging his allies. Bears roared and gave chase. Birds soared from on high flapping and pecking.

"Justin!" Galena shouted.

His laugh at the frenzied sight was cut short by the sound of desperation in Galena's voice. He turned in her direction. She was kneeling on the ground before a fallen human woman.

"'Tis as you thought, they are the humans from Glenn! Men, women, and . . . children!" she said shuddering. Delphia was sitting on Galena's shoulder and squeaked.

Justin growled. "Dammit! This does not bode well! Irana is using humans against us."

He heard a voice call from behind. "Justin!"

Turning to face the familiar voice, his visage darkened, and head feathers rose when he saw her. "Razamarea!" Justin growled. "You best not have any hand in this, so help me!"

191

"No! I came to help. I'm . . . sorry! Pray, forgive me?" Razamarea said throwing her arms around his waist.

"I am willing to forgive if you prove yourself, and if you stop pestering me; however, you may not embrace me!" Justin bellowed.

"Pray, I just wanted to apologize . . ."

"You have, now step away!" Justin's eyes went wide and he grimaced. He felt a hot, gut-wrenching pain in his side, and then the dampness of warm blood soaking his vest. She had stabbed him with a short-bladed dagger. Razamarea lifted her head to meet his eyes. They now glowed the same haunting red that he has seen twice.

"No, Irana!" Justin growled, stumbling backward grasping his side.

"Hello, dearest Justin! You survived, I see. That is good! I would have been sad if you died too soon!" Irana cackled. "You didn't rest very long . . . not too smart of you!" she said wagging a finger at him.

"You were the one! You told Razamarea and brought her to Arisdale to hurt Miral!"

"You're right. It was my doing!" she sighed. "I wanted to play with you more, and while I couldn't care less about this woman, she is useful to me. She was so easy to take control of thanks to you," Irana said turning away from him. "Farewell, dearest! Don't die too soon! I await our next encounter with much anticipation!" she said, taking to the air and flying away.

"What the hell was Razamarea doing here?" Sara cursed as she stopped beside him.

"Justin, you are bleeding!" Galena said placing her hands on the deep wound. Her hands emitted an aqua-colored glow that flowed into the wound sealing it closed.

"Thank you, Galena. That was Irana, not Razamarea."

Irana enjoyed playing games; however, he wasn't certain what her goal was in all this. She appeared to take pleasure in simply tormenting and hurting people. Especially him.

"Should I go after her?" Sara asked.

"No. We will accomplish nothing that way. Obviously, Irana can control multiple people at a time. She does not care for Raza's life and would sooner let you kill her than stop her," Justin said as he turned to the wolves still fighting the Glennoldians. These people are innocent. He knew what needed to be done.

"They must be stopped here!" he commanded in a loud tone. "Spare as many lives as you can! Surround and push them together! I have a plan!"

All present took to the task as Justin ordered. He turned to Kedros. "I want you to entangle them in vines once they are bunched up. I need time to channel a spell."

"Yes, Your Majesty!"

"Goddess Fandia, forgive us for any innocent lives lost this day!" Justin said while driving the humans back with strong-armed shoves and kicks. He repelled metal weapons from the hands of those who bore them. Sara laid circular barriers of fire along the ground to prevent the humans from regaining ground. Talos lifted stragglers into the air, dropping them to the center of the closing ring.

Justin felt the humans were gathered up well enough and called to Kedros. "Now!"

Vines erupted from the ground trapping humans where they stood and pulled any outside the circle into the tangled mass. Kedros continued to channel vines to hold them in place.

Justin channeled a confined quake. He envisioned a circular rock wall surrounding the humans. The ground rumbled and cracked violently, causing some of the wolves to stumble and fall. He felt his muscles ache from the strain of the massive spell.

Sara had changed back and was next to him, her hair down to her waist. He could see her staring, brow creased with worry, as she gathered her hair and cut it short once more.

The spell was nearly complete, and he drew energy from Sara's ethereal crystals in hopes of not overdrawing his own. His hands were rising slowly, trembling from the effort of lifting the massive rock wall. Pain racked his body with great intensity, and he felt as if his bones were being torn from his muscles. There was an odd sensation that increased with the effort. Sickness rolled through him threatening to bring him to his knees. Everyone stepped back quickly as boulders jutted from the ground in a ring around the humans, rising to a height of about fifteen feet. The wolf tribe was cheering victory. Human arms swiped through narrow openings desperately seeking something to grab; the air thick with their moans and growls.

The sickness crippled Justin in agony and he fell to the ground.

"What happened?!" Sara asked alarmed while taking a step toward him.

An elder timber wolf intersected Sara. The wolves of Glenn dropped to their knees when they saw him.

"The victory is great, but the cost was too steep to pay," he said to Justin while reaching his hand out to him. "You were poisoned by that dagger as well. It spread faster with all that effort, as she knew it would."

Justin looked up at the source of the voice. "You are the prophet, are you not?" he asked accepting his hand. Power flowed from the prophet's hand into his. Justin could feel his strength returning, the pain subsided, and his weariness faded. He stared at the man with open jaws.

He smiled brightly and nodded. "Ah, yes, the Lady Miral!"

Galena approached and Delphia squeaked excitedly at the elder wolf.

The prophet turned to her. "Hello little one, happy to see you again too! Enjoying the company of your new friends, are you?"

Delphia squeaked in reply.

The elder beckoned them to follow. "Elementals of Light, come with me, and we shall talk."

Chapter 36 - The Prophet

Sara, Talos, Galena, Kedros and Justin looked to the elder intensely while taking seats in his hut. The wood, mud, and straw shelters were typical for wolves of Glenn. Far more simple living than Arisdale but their kind loved being close to nature. Delphia wanted to be with the prophet and sat in his hand while he stroked her.

"What is she?" Sara asked the elder.

"Delphia? She is the only one of her kind. One of Fandia's creations gifted with magic and intelligence. I had to be on the move a lot, so I decided to give her to Miral for safekeeping. I see she is as stubborn as always," he laughed.

Delphia squeaked happily in reply.

"Justin, Fandia forgives you all. It was no one's fault," the elder said shaking his head.

Justin's head feathers spiked briefly with the unexpected remark. "How did you know I was concerned about that?"

He smiled. "You did a brave thing to save many lives at great risk to your own," he said pointing at Justin. "That was a large spell, you had poison coursing through your veins, and you have not yet healed from your brush with death."

Justin stared at the elder wolf as he spoke. The man ignored his question, but once more proved he knew more than he should.

"Sadly, they will remain mindless slaves until Irana is stopped."

Justin frowned at the elder. "Is there some other way?"

"No, not that we can do, but worry not, Justin. I will tend to them until you can save them."

Justin tilted his head while pointing at himself. "Until I save them?"

The elder nodded. "With the Elementals of Light, under your guidance. The protector is the leader of the elements. With no Earth, there is nothing to hold the waters, no place for winds to blow, nowhere for fire to burn. No home for life."

Justin leaned forward, the wood chair creaking beneath him. "Who are you really, if I may ask?"

The elder's appearance changed before their eyes, his old and wrinkled face smoothing into a younger look. His short white hair grew long and sparkled as it fell to his waist. Yellow eyes changed to a glowing aqua. When he spoke, his voice was also different.

"I was told to be honest with you, although I can only disclose so much; your fate is up to you. I am here as a guide and nothing more," he said with a bow of his head. "Forgive me for having to hide like this. It is best that I go undetected for as long as possible. Given our nature, we cannot fight this battle with you anyway."

Sara arched a questioning brow. "Your nature?"

The wolf nodded to her and placed his hand on his chest. "I am Andeos, the God of Earth."

"Andeos!" They said in unison, mouths agape at him before standing and falling to their knees.

"That is not necessary. Pray, be seated," he replied.

"Why are you unable to fight with us?" Galena asked returning to her seat.

He lifted his hands. "It is our light. As beings of light, we cannot fight gods of dark, and they cannot fight us. We are also forbidden to interfere with the lives of mortals unless permitted to do so. I was allowed to approach Miral as a prophet in Delphi and to aid her in Arisdale. We do our duty for the world's balance, and that is all. The Silver Dolphins will not allow it to be otherwise as doing so would shift the balance."

"The Silver Dolphins?! What are they?" Sara asked radiating excitement.

"They are the heart of the world, master of both the creation of life and its destruction equally. They maintain the balance of light and dark. At . . . any cost." Andeos looked away. "They don't have the ability to feel emotion. They do what is needed without judgment."

Sara stood. "Wait! The way you say that, it has something to do with Fandia's disappearance from this world, doesn't it? She lives, though?"

Andeos nodded to her. "It has everything to do with that, but any more than that is not for me to say. She is well, though." Andeos looked somber, and glanced at Justin. "To answer your questions, I am the one who built the chambers."

Justin's face became unreadable and his gaze locked onto Andeos, following him as he paced.

"The orbs are infused with elemental magic and capable of being used as gateways for elemental beings and gods. The walls, floor, and door are completely lined with ethereal obsidian to keep the teleportation spell confined inside; however, magic can be used within due to the inner barrier of magic-infused ethereal crystal on the walls, which aides in the teleportation spell. Other chambers exist in specific locations where magic is concentrated around the Earth," Andeos said stopping before Justin. "We never imagined she would be able to capture the Elemental of Ice and use her and the chamber against you," Andeos sighed. "The ice did leach through the spaces around the door, because of the absence of obsidian shards in the gaps, and trap you inside as you assumed. Your spells are too broad to seep through the space between the door and wall, and thus failed. The ethereal crystals are celestial in nature and not of any element, which is why you could not influence the chamber in any way. As I said, magic can adhere to the crystals' surface inside, which is why Miral could freeze you to the wall. Irana knew all this, and it is why she used the Elemental of Ice. How she knew when to attack is uncertain at this time, but we have a theory. Fandia wishes you to know she is deeply sorry," Andeos said with eyes locked on Justin, who was tense with eyes narrowed, head feathers standing high.

"Pray tell, what is this theory? What is Irana for that matter?!" Justin growled.

Andeos's kindly face scrunched. "Things are not as they seem. Trust your senses, not your eyes. Question reality, for what you think is happening, may not be what is occurring." Andeos squatted to the ground pointing at Justin's shadow. "Beware of the things of darkness. For your foe is the Goddess of the Dark. Pay attention when you meet up with anyone she controls. You will see what I mean by it. Fear is her greatest power. I ask you all to mind your emotional states. She will try to use them to gain control of you by darkening your inner light as you fall victim to the fears that surround them. I would tell you more about her if I could, but I cannot speak of another god or goddess without drawing their attention to me. It is how we communicate. For you all, thinking of gods is safe, but there are gods you don't want in your mind. Never say their name aloud and you will be safe. This is why her name is the forbidden word. It was made so when she betrayed her duties long ago."

Sara shot up out of her seat. "You're saying that a goddess is behind all this?!" she gestured wildly. "We mortal Elementals are the only hope against a goddess in control of an army of innocent people?!"

Andeos leaned back against the oak wall of the hut. "At this moment, yes. All the other fail-safes the Silver Dolphins have to maintain the balance have failed. When this occurs, the Elementals of Light are all that remain. You need to save Miral to defeat the goddess, though. If any of you die, she cannot be stopped until the Elemental to replace you is located and trained. The power lies dormant inside a soul until called upon by the Silver Dolphins to awaken."

Sara arched an eyebrow in question. "Fail-safes, what are they?"

"I'm sorry, that is not for me to answer."

"Why did she come to Glenn?" Kedros asked.

Andeos clenched his fist tightly. "I'm sorry, Kedros, it is because of me. We are immortal, but we can be killed. That is why we gods have been hiding since Fandia had to leave the World of Life. It takes another being of great power, one that is neither of light nor dark, to kill us. She has such a being, the Virabis, and she is looking for the other gods and me."

Justin shifted in his seat. The situation had changed drastically and become more dangerous than he could imagine. "Miral spoke with two voices that acted for her in the chamber. What was that about?"

"I'm sorry, that is not for me to answer," Andeos said shaking his head.

Justin narrowed his eyes at Andeos, taking a deep breath. "Can you at least tell me why she wants her?"

Andeos looked at Justin a long time, he glanced away furrowing his brow. "That is also not for me to answer, I'm sorry."

A chilling silence filled the room while Justin glowered at Andeos with spiked feathers.

Andeos met the king's intense gaze once more. "Be careful with your anger. Emotions that are not expressed correctly become rage, which is an element of darkness. Your powers are that of light. Drawing upon darkness through rage will allow it to take control of you and then you lose control of your abilities. Reality will fade the longer you remain trapped until all that is left is the blinding rage that started it. Who you were before mentally will be forever gone, if you're not already dead from using too much magic. Without the Goddess of Light in the World of Life, there is nothing but your own will to keep dark things at bay in your mind. Make sure you attend to your feelings," Andeos said in a scolding tone. "Stop beating yourself up for what was out of your control," he sighed. "Besides, knowing why won't change things. Just understand that if Miral falls to the pull of darkness, the world will be forever lost to darkness, twisted and broken," Andeos said looking directly into Justin's eyes. "Do not allow that to happen."

Justin stood rigidly before Andeos, his face cast in a glower, feathers lifting once more. "You told her she would be safe with me!" he grumbled while pointing to himself.

Andeos maintained a straight face. "I did, and she is. But safe does not guarantee that you can hold on to her. She needs you all to protect her to the best of your ability. That is all you can do."

Justin visibly cooled, but remained where he was, staring deep into Andeos's eyes.

Andeos sighed heavily once more. "I helped Miral after Razamarea assaulted her, and I hid her magic aura from you because she had a path to follow, which led her back to you. What occurred after that was sadly unknown to me. I played the part of a false prophet. I cannot foresee things, as I am not the God of Time. I can only guide you with what I know presently which I receive from those who say my name or Fandia's."

"The God of Time?! What is he capable of?" Sara asked.

Andeos jerked his head in her direction, his ears perked up, and he gazed at her with an alarmed look. "He is dangerous, mad, and for now, he can't influence the World of Life directly. I pray that it remains this way! He can't change the past; however, those who speak his name, even into the future, give him access to all that they know in this present time. Knowledge has no limitations and can flow back and forth through time to him. Therefore, he can know the fate of the world and things to come. If he was free, he could influence the present course of time to his design. Fate is ever changing, though it is possible to undo his schemes and change the future. Outwitting him will be nearly impossible if people call him. Be aware that the danger to your life is monumental if you speak his name. Am I clear?"

Sara nodded. "What is his name, and what about you?"

Andeos looked away with a furrowed brow and frown. "Our minds were linked long ago. He is always aware of me, and I of him. His name, I will not say nor write in the World of Life, but it has already been spoken in Delphi. The book that claimed the forbidden word to be safe, he was the author."

Justin wore a deepening scowl. The Goddess of the Dark and the God of Time, both dangerous, both involved with what occurred in Delphi. "Explain the reason why you cannot disclose anything about Miral's involvement?" Justin asked wanting to direct the conversation back to the matters at hand.

"We are in the World of Life, and as such, speaking of the why is far too dangerous to you all, and the world. Too many unknown eyes and ears! Only Fandia may safely say why. The same applies to the God of Time, she will explain him."

"How do we meet with Fandia?" Justin asked.

"When you hear the cry. The call of the Silver Dolphins!" Andeos said.

Justin sighed deeply. "Then we had best be on our way. Miral has waited long enough!"

Andeos placed a hand on Justin's shoulder. "I know where she is. I went to look for myself, and she took her right where I expected she would. Go to Mystia in the Mystic Mountains to the north. The Goddess of Nature guards one of the transport chambers, and she will instruct you on its use. Miral is being held in the former Palace of Artichia, where she can keep her frozen. Save her and return to Arisdale. I will be waiting for you all there."

They stood to leave the hut and stopped when Andeos spoke once more.

"The greatest weapon in your arsenal is the light of love. When you call upon that essence to fuel your powers, you are drawing from Fandia. Never forget that!"

They all nodded in understanding and exited the hut. The wolf tribe gathered up provisions for their travels and provided them with six fur-lined robes, gloves, and three pairs of fur-lined boots for their venture to Artichia, and five Galli for their trip to Mystia.

Kedros bid farewell to his sister, Stan, and Trea.

"We will take good care of Kara for you while you're gone, Kedros," Trea said hugging him.

"You come back safe, Kedros!" Kara said embracing her brother.

"I will do so, sis. I promise!"

"Good luck to you, my dear friend," Stan said wrapping an arm around his shoulder.

"Thanks, Stan. Take care."

Andeos, who had retaken his elder form, exited the hut. "One last thing. The blood demon, as you call her . . ."

Justin spun looking at Andeos with concern.

"Avoid her at all cost! You cannot fight her! She is a summoned being from another world. Elemental magic is useless," Andeos said with a grim expression. "We don't know enough about her yet. I pray we can find a way to stop her."

"Understood," Justin replied with a nod to Andeos. "One last thing, if I may?"

"What is it, Justin?"

"Why did you not warn my family about these events in Delphi as well? Why did you not stop them from going to the castle?!"

Andeos grimaced. "If I asked your father to take Miral with him and leave due to the dangers, he would have sailed off without her, or never come in the first place despite your objections and you know that. Besides the Silver Dolphins forbade the interruption."

"What?!" His head feathers stood on end. "The Silver Dolphins permitted the death of my parents?!"

"Justin, this is difficult to hear, but it was their time to go. They would have died somehow on the trip back and if that were stopped, fate would have found another way to make it be that day still, and how would that have ended for Miral?"

Justin gritted his teeth but remained silent with downcast eyes, his feathers relaxing.

Andeos shook his head. "I am sorry, Justin. I truly am. You all have a journey in this world. Some roads are short and others long. Your parents raised you so you could best carry out your destiny, which was their purpose. Honor them."

Justin looked back up at Andeos and nodded. "Then I will make them proud, and save this world." He turned to gather the others, and they departed for the Mystic Mountains.

Chapter 37 - Forgiveness

The emerald greens of the forest trickled sparkles of sunlight to the blackened ground below. Birds sang their songs unaware of the darkness falling upon the lands. With every step set in resolute determination, Justin trudged on with his companions, only stopping to rest when he was begged insistently to do so. He would walk on until his body caved in, eager to reach Miral as soon as possible. In the seventeen days since she was taken, Miral was alone with the Goddess of the Dark, and he feared what that meant for her innocence and light.

They made camp near the northern end of Lake Lunast, a place filled with grand memories from fishing trips with his father and Agar. The recollection pooled tears to his eyes as he gazed upward. The looming peaks of the Mystic Mountains were taunting him in his mind. Tomorrow they would arrive, and tomorrow he would find her. He sat upon an old weathered log and stared at the snowcapped peaks beyond the trees as if doing so would bring him there faster.

Kedros approached cautiously and sat beside him. "Your Majesty, may I talk to you?"

Justin turned his eyes to look at Kedros and nodded. "Pray."

"I am sorry about everything you have been through. You care about Miral a lot, don't you?"

He looked back at the mountains and spoke with a lowered tone. "She is a good lady, and does not deserve all the troubles she has faced since the day I met her."

"You feel like you failed her then?" Kedros asked.

Justin opened his jaws slightly, staring distantly ahead before replying. "Yes, I do."

"I bet she doesn't think that. You did all you could," Kedros replied with a smile.

Justin reached into his pocket and pulled out the creed of Arisdale. "I gave her this. I did not get to return it yet," he said as he stared fixated on the gleaming gold of his family crest. "'Twas my oath to protect her, and I failed twice. I was useless in that chamber as if I had no powers at all. I did not like feeling that vulnerable."

"You weren't useless. You had your shields and strength from what I heard. You did the best you could and still are."

"No amount of shields or strength could keep her from being taken," Justin grumbled between gritted teeth. He glanced towards the Mystic Mountains and squeezed the creed tightly in his hand. "I promised her I would find her. When I do, I will return this to her and never fail her again." He closed his eyes and dropped his head.

Kedros sighed. No matter what he said Justin continued to blame himself. He picked up a stick and drew pictures in the dirt as he thought. He stopped and stared at the heart he made. "Andeos said the light of love is our weapon against the Goddess of the Dark so what happened to Irana? Did no one love her enough without King Charles around? Did she not love herself enough either?"

Justin lifted his head slowly, his head feathers rose slightly, blinking in surprise at Kedros. "By the gods," he replied in a near whisper. "Kedros, you may be right about that. We could have prevented all this, not just we but someone could have."

"Do you think it will help her still?" Kedros asked. "Maybe that is what we need now. We don't know her, but unconditional love can be given by anyone at any time."

"Then we will try." Justin paused as memories returned from his day with Miral in the study. He shook his head at the irony. "I was asked what I would do about Irana, what I felt about her. I did not know what to say then, but now," he sighed, "now I know that 'twas not Irana's doing. Now I feel sorrow for the woman and hatred for the dark goddess. Miral knew all along, hmm, she knew Irana better than we did."

"Miral sounds like a rather unique and inspirational lady, Your Majesty."

"She is indeed, and pray, you may call me Justin," he said with a bow of his head. "Whilst we venture 'tis best for those who know me not by sight to know me not at all."

"A good point," Kedros replied. "Justin, I swear that I will do everything in my power to help you save Miral and the world, and maybe even Irana if we are that lucky."

Justin smiled. "I thank you, Kedros. 'Tis good to have you with us on this venture. No doubt your spell song may help us, the one that pacifies another. Did that help at all against the people attacking?"

"It did but the range was limited and keeping it going would have worn me out and accomplished little," he sighed. "Andeos said we couldn't help them, our love wouldn't be enough."

"One individual, like Irana that we know to a degree through Miral certainly, but an entire village of humans that despise us," Justin shrugged, "that is an impossibility. Best we can do is end this quickly. They will all need our help to rebuild what they have lost. Spoiled foods, homes, and the like. 'Twill be a good sign of faith if we do. A way of making amends," Justin paused. "I wonder why the Goddess of the Dark is so interested in using humans in her games?" He huffed in frustration. "I would also like to know what exactly she is after in all this. Everything she does seems so random, but controlled."

"I hate to say this, but," Sara remarked as she approached them, "the mention of a God of Time makes me think that what seems random is in fact with a purpose. Whatever that is involves something that occurred between the Goddesses of Light and Dark long ago, and we are not allowed to know what that was yet. Frustrating!" Sara said with exasperation.

"'Tis indeed," Justin replied.

"Oh my, this all is frightening!" Galena said rubbing her arms. "Our lives have been flipped upside down, and we are in the hands of the gods. Fandia, bless us."

"The forbidden word, the name of a dangerous goddess capable of causing madness in those who utter it," Sara said shaking her head. "Opening your mind to her to see all your thoughts and feelings, trapping you in the webs of your own fears without you knowing why. I don't want to know what that feels like, but I have to admit I'm curious!"

"All I have to do is remember the day I married you," Talos quipped.

"Talos!" Sara replied.

Talos laughed and shrugged with a smirk. Sara silently eyed him and crossed her arms.

"Heavens," Justin exclaimed. "Certainly better ways to lighten the mood, my dear friend; however, well said."

"I can't believe you're encouraging him!" Sara said raising her arms.

Justin shrugged. "'Twas an excellent jest, true or not."

"Yeah, you're right," she replied begrudgingly.

"Justin, dear," Galena said, "you look exhausted. Pray, tell me you will get some rest tonight."

"If I do 'twill be from sheer exhaustion and not will," Justin replied.

Sara patted his shoulder. "You've got to regenerate your magic for tomorrow, Justin. Give it your best shot, ok? Miral would want you to," she said.

"I will do my best then," he said standing. "Thank you, my friends. Kedros, 'twas an excellent chat," he said with a bow of his head.

"My pleasure, Justin," Kedros replied with a smile.

He left his friends and headed for the small shelter that they constructed from branches and thick mats of leaves for the roof to shield rain should it fall. A blanket of soft mosses to lie on covered the ground. He had never slept outdoors like this before, and it would no doubt be a challenge, but the feeling of freedom it stirred was a welcome change from the enslavement a crown created. He returned the creed to his pocket for safekeeping and curled up on the moss using the fur cloak he was given as a blanket.

"Fight with all the light in your heart, Miral. I am coming," he said in quiet prayer, hoping his words would somehow reach her and find her safe.

Chapter 38 - Mystic Mountains

The snowcapped Mystic Mountains were by far the tallest mountain range of Flourisha. Its majestic stature in the horizon could be seen from Arisdale on a clear day. The shale rocks of Mystia gave the mountain a blue look from afar. The pleasant scent of pine trees filled the crisp and chilled air.

Sara ran her finger across fossilized remains on the smooth rock. She pulled her journal and charcoal from her pack and sketched the images she saw: seashells, trilobites, coral, and ancient plant life called crinoids. She loved to find rocks like these.

Her homeland in Volga was well known for its interest in science and magic, and she learned all she knew from the grand colleges there. The formation of fossils was still unknown. She was eager to understand how life could be forever trapped in stone in such a way. She would have to ask Fandia and Andeos of this later, along with her thousands of other questions.

Justin wore a frown as they walked along a narrow path up the mountain. He was near his mother's birth home, though there was no time to stop there, not now.

"Do you feel that?" Galena asked rubbing the sides of her arms.

There is a force in the air. It feels thick.

Sara stopped sketching. "It's protection magic."

"Welcome!" a young female voice said in her ear.

Sara jumped with fright. "Yahh!"

Talos erupted in uncontrollable fits of laughter. His eyes were tearing, his hand holding his abdomen as he hunched forward from the intensity of his laugh.

Sara swung her hand at him slapping Talos on the back of the head. "Talos!" she scolded.

The voice giggled and a young woman that looked the age of sixteen fluttered before the adventurers. She had rust-colored hair, olive eyes, human-looking body and head, and yellow butterfly wings.

"Welcome to Mystia, Elementals of Light, and you," she said pointing at Talos.

Sara grinned mischievously at her husband. "Ha, ha, ha! You're the fifth wheel on the carriage, hun!" she said while poking him.

Talos smiled and shrugged at her.

The young girl fluttered closer. "I am Eva, Goddess of Nature. I have been expecting you. Please follow me, and I will explain things along the way."

The group followed the goddess across the rocky narrow path.

"The world's winds converge here in the Mystic Mountains. From them I learn of the world's happenings," she said with arms outstretched. "Lately, the winds have been troubled, the messages muddled. Now I am receiving no messages at all," she said shaking her head and lowering her arms against her tribal outfit of greens, reds, and yellows.

"What would cause that?" Kedros asked.

Eva looked back at him. "A few possibilities exist. The Egyptian God of Chaos, Seth is a troublemaker. He has full dominion over winds and fire." She fluttered backward pointing at Sara. "He is a lot like you in his temperament."

Sara fumed to herself. She had heard about him before, but Eva's tone reaffirmed her feelings. She would likely hate the God of Chaos.

Talos chuckled. "A male version of Sara, and Sara in the same room together . . . hmmm."

"Talos!" Sara bellowed.

Talos sidestepped, dodging her slap. He wrapped his arms tight around her. "Love you, sweetie!"

"Love you too," Sara grumbled.

"The other possibilities?" Justin asked.

"The Elemental of Wind," Eva replied. "I know of Yarway's fall, and I am aware of the darkness controlling people, like the Elemental of Ice. I lost the messages from the wind shortly after her attack on you in the chamber."

Justin wore an expression of deep concern. "You think the Elemental of Wind has been possessed by her as well?"

Eva nodded. "Through the Elemental of Wind, she could disrupt the flow of messages with the sole purpose of stopping me from hearing them. I rely on them to care for the nature of the world. Disrupting that process alters the planet and keeps us in the dark about her plans. A dangerous thing for life, and the planet," Eva said shaking her head. "I can't speak for the other foolish things Seth does, but he would not be that much of a fool in this instance."

Justin ran his hand through his head feathers. "Do you know who the Elemental of Wind is?"

Eva stopped before a circular building that looked like a replica of the devotion chamber in Arisdale. She shrugged at Justin. "No clue, for some reason the Elemental of Wind has been difficult to find. I do have a suggestion about where you can look. I will explain inside," she said gesturing to the door.

Eva fluttered to the center of the room and spread out her arms. "Please stand underneath your element orb."

"What about Talos?" Sara asked concerned.

Eva fluttered to Talos and pointed at him. "Hold onto her tight, and you will be taken with her. Don't let go! I can't say what could happen. Some poor soul did one time, they disappeared and were never seen again."

Talos clung to Sara in an iron grip from behind her.

Eva nodded and turned to face them all.

"If you don't get it right the first time, keep trying until you find your destination. I feel you are all strong of mind and skilled enough with your powers that you should be okay. Just realize that this spell is highly taxing on your body. Be certain you have the strength to cast it when you do," she said. "What is your destination?"

"Artichia Palace," Justin replied.

"There is a transport close to the palace. During the age of Fandia, the chambers were built at the heart of an area's power. The element you are gifted with is based on your homeland of origin. Arisdale is the heart of the earth, Volga the heart of fire, Artichia the heart of ice, Glenn Woods the heart of nature, Mystia the heart of holy, Zeiram the heart of lightning, and Fovran the heart of water," she said. "If you laid the elements out on the map based on the lands they correspond to, the diamond of balance is visible as you draw lines between them."

Sara was wide-eyed with excitement. "Why did I never realize that?"

Eva smiled at her. "I may not know who the Elemental of Wind is, but your best chance is Egyptalia, the heart of wind."

Justin rubbed his lower jaw. "Eva, can you do me a favor?"

Eva fluttered to him. "What is it?"

Justin picked Delphia up and cradled her protectively in his hands. "Send word to Prince Agar in Arisdale. Inform him of what we know so far, and about the Elemental of Wind. I would like him to go to Egyptalia and scout that out."

"As you wish!" Eva said smiling. She turned to address them all. "Using the transport chamber requires the same principles used for any spell. Hold your destination in your mind as you channel your magic to the orb above you. It helps if you know well the image of the place you wish to travel." Eva fluttered back towards the door, turning to face them. "I wish you all the best of luck. I pray I will see you again soon."

They set to channeling their powers as Eva instructed. The force of it was monumental. To Sara, it felt heavy and thick as it whirled about her. Swirls of elemental colors washed over them until it was blindingly bright. As the light faded, they saw the same room, but Eva was not there.

"Now that's the way to travel!" Sara said enthralled.

Talos was clinging to her in a death grip, his face pale, and eyes bulging with panic. Delphia was squeaking happily in Justin's hands.

Galena walked towards the door. "I wonder if we got it right," she said while pulling it open. A strong gust of ice cold wind billowed past her. "Brrr . . ." Galena shivered pulling her cloak tightly around her.

"Appears so," Kedros laughed.

Justin tucked Delphia under his cloak at his shoulder and sprinted past them and out the door.

"Justin! Wait up!" Galena yelled pleadingly.

"I feel her!" he called back to them, not stopping or slowing his sprint. They chased after him into the biting cold of Artichia.

Chapter 39 - Hope

It was morning when they departed from Mystia, and yet it was now night. Streaks of misty green and blue lights danced in undulating waves in the black sky as stars flickered with brilliance. The world was in the winter season, which means Artichia would currently be under the effects of polar night. A phenomenon where darkness reigns for twenty-four hour periods and the duration of this endless night varied, lasting from a day to six months, depending on the location from the poles.

They ran for about a mile before the once-grand palace of Artichia came into view. Sara could feel the pulse of Miral's power. It was weak and Miral's light looked duller than it had been before in her mind's eye. The light from the Elemental of Ice was also present but terribly faint.

They entered the dark crystalline palace. The rising moonlight narrowly peeked through the large stained glass windows, shining in slivers on crystal faces. The palace had a haunting feel, which was enhanced by the fact that it stood empty after falling to civil war six years ago.

Justin stopped running up ahead, arms stretched wide, lit by a faint blue outline from his ethereal gems. They stopped just short of colliding with him in the pitch-black room. All Sara could see in the darkness were Justin's retinas, reflecting a golden yellow glow. Talos and Kedros could see better than she and Galena could at night also.

Kedros had the added luxury of a spell he called nature awareness. He told her the spell enabled all his senses to become heightened. Sara watched Kedros's glowing green eyes as they darted about the ceiling like a predator tracking prey. The yellow and aqua ethereal gem necklace he wore lit his face. Talos was sniffing at the icy air, puffs of steam wafting out with each breath. Justin reached back to Galena and handed Delphia to her. His eyes remained fixed on searching the ceiling. Sara scanned the room with her mind, but the Elemental of Ice was masking her light.

Kedros tugged on Justin's jacket to get his attention and pointed to a spot above. The king's eyes locked to the area and he nodded. He gestured for them all to back away from the ground around him as it began to crack and split. The rock broke away from the ground, and he hurled a massive stone block into the area he was watching.

Nightmarish laughter erupted from above while large chunks of ceiling rained to the floor with a deafening thud, letting a flood of moonlight in. Justin growled and head feathers fluffed at the Elemental of Ice as she floated down to the floor landing in the beam of light.

"Welcome, dearest Justin!" the Elemental of Ice said.

"How can someone so beautiful sound so . . . evil?" Kedros asked.

"I see you for who you are!" Justin said, pointing at the woman's shadow.

Sara peered at her darkened form on the floor. It was swirling and dancing as if it were black steam, and there were five long finger-like sections attached to each side of the head of the woman's shadow.

A new voice filled the room. It was a creepy, echoing, distorted mix of sounds that didn't come from the elemental's mouth.

"You know now? I figured as much. You did stop my hunting party from finding Andcos, after all. He is a sneaky one, but I will have him," she cackled.

Justin launched forward at the Elemental of Ice. "We need to restrain her!" he said while casting his earth shield to protect his companions.

Galena cast protection spells to reduce any physical damage they would take. Any other spell would be too dangerous to the Elemental of Ice. Talos and Sara took to the air after her.

Sara had the dominating advantage, but she had to be careful. Melted ice was water. She dodged the ice shards, but a few grazed her. She felt the pain, but there was no blood. When she changed back, though, she would bleed.

Talos moved in close to distract her from casting spells. The ice elemental slashed at him with her sharp-edged fighting fans cutting at his arms. Justin pounced at the elemental when she came close enough to the ground, but she dodged him and rose back into the air. The Elemental of Ice was graceful and skilled and able to keep them at bay.

"There are no plants here for me to draw on!" Kedros shouted.

Justin and Sara stopped and turned to Kedros. They combined fire and rock together creating the elements needed for nature. Kedros drew from the power, and vines extended from the flaming boulder. The Elemental of Ice madly dodged the vines as they reached for her. Sara and Talos took to the air again, attacking her from opposite sides. They closed in tight on her. She kicked Talos in the chest and sent him into a column. His earth shield failed and his wings were frozen by the elemental. He plummeted to the ground ten feet below.

"Talos!" Sara cried out.

Galena rushed to him and cast healing magic.

Sara felt the burning heat of elemental rage in her mind and assaulted The Elemental of Ice relentlessly, no longer caring if either of them sustained injuries.

"Sara! Mind your anger!" Justin called out as water trickled down from melting ice above.

Sara continued her assault and the Elemental of Ice was too distracted fending her off to notice the vines were upon her. She screamed as she was pulled from the air to the ground. Justin pinned her to the floor when she landed.

"Don't celebrate yet, dearest!" Shadow sneered. "I will not let you have her soul back! Then you will be unable to stop me!"

Kedros knelt to the left of the elemental singing a soothing tune and took her hand in his. He had the yellow glow of nature magic around him as he sang.

The elemental's eyebrow arched. "What are you doing?"

Kedros tenderly kissed the elementals hand. "You're so beautiful! I would love to see your light shine!" he said.

Shadow wailed, her scream sounding like pure agony. The elemental's eyes closed, she lay still, and Shadow's cry vanished. The elemental's shadow changed back to its natural state. Her purple eyes fluttered open and turned to Kedros, misting with tears.

"Thank you!" she said, reaching to touch Kedros on the cheek. "You're beautiful too!"

Justin smiled, removed his hands from her and stood. Kedros helped her to her feet. The elemental turned to Justin and threw herself at him. Justin stumbled back a bit, his hands awkwardly held at his sides.

"I'm . . . so . . . sorry!" she cried.

He gently patted her on the back. "'Tis all right, that was not your fault, ok?"

She nodded, wiping tears from her face. "My name is Snow, Snow Artichia."

Justin stared at her, jaws open. "Princess? You survived the war? I thought all of the Artichia bloodlines fell."

"I was sent away with my nanny when the civil war broke out. That is what she used against me!" Snow said while pointing at her shadow. "She showed me . . . horrible things! Nightmares that I don't know if I can ever get rid of! I couldn't tell the difference between what was real and what was an illusion!" Snow was quivering, tears forming in her eyes anew.

Justin gently grabbed hold of her shoulders, his face and voice displaying dread. "I am deeply sorry for all you had to endure, Snow. Truly, but, where is Miral?!"

Snow's face was ashen. "Oh, no!" she gasped. "This way!" she beckoned while running down the hall.

Chapter 40 - Earth and Fire

They followed Snow into what appeared to be the throne room. Justin watched her as she approached the clear crystal throne of her father and walked past it. She pulled on a lever and a rock wall slid away revealing a bright blue glow.

"The room beyond was used for practicing magic arts," Snow said. "It is strongly infused with crystals attuned to ice magic." Snow placed her hand to the glow and met a solid surface. She glanced away from Justin with a frown. "I cannot enter now that it is sealed, and I know not how to break it to get in. She set all that up and blocked my knowledge of it."

Sara approached and touched the wall and pulled her hand away quickly. "Ow! Elemental protection, as the opposite of water it would make sense that it caused me pain." Sara paused tapping her fisted hand to her chin. "Ice, the sub-element of wind and water, perhaps the elements that dominate both could enter as one!" Sara glanced back at Justin. "That would be earth and fire."

Justin looked at Sara with anticipation and a heavy heart. Her hair had grown to her waist after the battle against Snow. He thought back to all the times she had to use her gift so far. She had lost a year and a half of her life already to Shadow, and she would have to give more of her time till the battle was over.

Sara smiled at him. "I wager it's enough for us to hold hands and focus our powers as one. Let's give it a shot!" she said with a wink.

He approached the glowing wall beside her and took her outstretched hand. Justin placed his hand to the glow with Sara. It went through. He pulled his hand back briefly looking at it wide-eyed before he charged through the wall pulling Sara in with him. His heart sank at the sight before him and he released Sara's hand. There was a long white room with glowing crystals along the walls. At the end of a platform hovered a large crystal with Miral encased within.

"Miral!" He sprinted and touched its cold, smooth surface with his hands. She had a peaceful look on her face, eyes closed, and hands locked in prayer.

Sara stared at the crystal awestruck as she circled it. "She is alive in there, that's for sure. How though?"

"How do we get her out of that?!" Justin asked Sara, rubbing his head.

"I have a theory," she replied. "After crystals are formed, they have a tendency to split or break along definite planes of weakness. This property is called cleavage. A strike to one of these planes of weakness should safely shatter the crystal. Use your quake and listen for frequency disruptions."

Justin nodded to her and rested his hands on the crystal, casting a small quake onto the surface. He listened carefully to the resonating sound as the waves softly rolled through it. A distortion as a resonating hum could be heard in the center of the crystal. He stopped, pulled his hands away, and stretched his arms back wide. "'Tis right here!" he said driving his claws into the crystal's faces at full force, penetrating deep into it. He cast shatter and the crystal fractured into small shards.

Miral's limp body fell free from its grasp. Justin caught her in his arms and cradled her. He fought back tears, pressing his ear to her chest and listened to her heartbeat. He heard the beautiful sound within, his own beating faster in response to his joy.

"Fandia be praised!" Sara said relieved. She knelt beside Justin and examined Miral.

Justin barely heard what Sara said as he became lost in the feeling of Miral in his arms.

Kedros inched up beside Snow to speak to her. She was leaning against a far wall, hands folded before her and a deep frown on her face. Kedros shook, running his hand through his hair.

"Hey . . . um . . . Snow . . ."

"Yes?" Snow asked, her frown shifting into a smile as she turned to face him.

"What?!" Sara's voice erupted from behind them.

Snow and Kedros both jumped completely startled by Sara's loud voice and the fact that she was back. They turned to look at her. Sara had her hands around Talos's head and was shaking him.

"You take that back!"

Talos looked dizzy and was stumbling around.

"Are you about done, Sara?!" Justin asked.

Sara let go of Talos and stormed off. Talos stumbled a bit before regaining his composure.

Delphia squeaked and hopped over to Justin. Galena scooped her up and sat Delphia on top of Miral. She purred and cuddled between Miral's head and neck.

Justin smiled at Delphia briefly before shifting his attention to Snow. "Is there a village nearby, princess? We need to rest so we can use the transport on the morrow."

Snow nodded. "There is, just a mile to the north."

Galena knelt beside Justin helping him place the fur cloak, boots, and gloves on Miral. "Are you not worried about her coming for us?"

Justin sighed. "I do not want to place any innocents in harm's way, but we need to rest and get out of the cold. We should not use the teleports again till the morrow. I do hope it will take her some time before she is on us again."

"It is a tiny village, very few live there now," Snow said in reply.

"Very well. Pray, lead on, Snow."

Chapter 41 - Memories

Snow led the group to the nearby Glacier Inn located in the village of Frost Star. Her mind drifted back to her childhood on seeing the once lively village and snow-covered roofs. She had friends here, but she wasn't sure they were still around. Most people fled when Artichia was besieged.

She had no self-control in her youth and never acted the way a princess was expected to. She would sneak out of the palace to play with the village girls in Frost Star. Snow smiled at the memories, those were fun days. Her pleasant thoughts ended when tension rose inside her grasping tightly at her throat. She fought it, too afraid to let the others see her tremble, but that made it worse.

Justin had explained to her the plight of the world. She shivered at the thought, the Goddess of the Dark. That vile woman had taken all her precious memories and twisted them to cause her pain upon recalling them. She wondered if she would ever reclaim her mind as her own, and if her memories could ever feel joyful again. Her mind was so used to being afraid now, that it learned a new way of being. It swirled with terrifying thoughts as if the dark goddess was still in control. Now it was difficult not to respond to uncertainty with fear first. She hated that. It is not who she once was.

Tears formed in her eyes as she reached for the door to the Glacier Inn. She pushed it open and smiled. The lodge was lit by the welcoming glow of warm firelight. The alluring smell of food wafted through the air, making her tummy rumble. She was starving. Shadow hadn't bothered to meet her bodily needs. The Goddess of the Dark hadn't cared if she died.

"Snow, would you kindly take this coin purse and make arrangements for us. Pray, two rooms," Justin said handing it to her.

"M . . . me?" Snow jumped.

Justin smiled at her. "You can do it, go on."

Snow pondered his words. Why choose her? She swallowed hard and took a deep breath, reaching out with shaking hands, snatching the purse.

"Kedros, go with her," Justin said.

"Ah, yeah ok," Kedros replied.

Galena whispered to Justin as Snow and Kedros approached the innkeeper. "What is that for? She is terrified, and that purse does not have much in it."

Justin grinned at Galena. "'Tis good for her to interact with Kedros in this tricky situation. You can see the spark between them, yes?"

"Oh, that is clever of you," Galena said smiling.

"I would like two rooms for the night," Snow said to the crude looking Artichian Wolf Innkeeper. His odd appearance and scruffy fur gave her the shivers.

The Innkeeper gestured to her with two fingers. "Two hundred gold."

"Two hundred gold for one night?!"

"What do we have?" Kedros asked her.

"We only have one hundred gold pieces," she replied, her ears slumping downward.

The innkeeper shook his head with his hand out.

"Full price for two, or only one room! We are in hard times. You should know that!" he said pointing at her.

Kedros frowned and looked back at Justin with a questioning glance. Justin nodded to him, his face expressing a grin. Kedros turned back to her and shrugged.

"That's it, Snow."

She reflected for a moment. *I can do this! Be brave, Snow!* "I know! Can we make a deal?" she asked.

The Innkeeper shrugged. "Depends on what it is."

Snow raised one arm and kicked her opposite leg out.

"I'm a dancer! May I entertain your guests in exchange for the other gold pieces and food?" she asked fluttering her eyelids.

"I can help with chores that need to be done!" Sara hollered from behind Snow causing her to jump once again.

The Innkeeper nodded to them. "All right, you have a deal." He palmed the coins.

The group headed to the dining hall of the Glacier Inn. Snow thought it was a decent place, despite the look of its keeper. The warm and homey atmosphere was a welcome change from the cold it kept at bay.

The innkeeper abruptly leaped before Justin with hand up. "Is she ill?" he asked pointing at Miral.

"No. She is just tired from the journey," Justin replied taking a step forward and forcing the Innkeeper to move.

The man shifted in front of him again. He looked at Justin incredulously. "Wouldn't the lady be more comfortable in the room?" he asked while repeatedly gesturing to the stairs.

Justin's eyes narrowed into a menacing glower. "The lady does not leave my side, ever!" he bellowed.

The man trembled before him. "Very well, very well," he said, stepping out of the way.

Justin fumed to himself and covered Miral's face as much as he could with the hood of the fur cloak.

Chapter 42 - Passion

The patrons that were present stopped their jovial conversations and turned to stare at the odd grouping of races as they entered the dining hall, going back to their business after a time. The dimly lit gray stone inn was packed full of Artichian hares, polar bears, and snow wolves. A large fireplace in the center lit the room with a golden hue.

Talos sat to the right side of a large table with bench seats facing a stage. Justin sat to the left of Talos, leaving a small space between them. He lowered Miral's legs to his lap, pulling his hand out from under her and supporting her against him. Galena and Sara sat across from Justin and Talos. Kedros sat to Justin's left, and Snow sat across from him.

Snow watched the king as he stared at Miral longingly and frowned. "I hope she wakes soon. I worry about what she has seen," she said trembling.

Justin's brow creased as he frowned. "I am sorry for what you had to endure, Snow," he replied. "May I ask you about it?"

Snow grimaced and sighed heavily, drooping her long ears. "Yes, but I will not go into detail! Describing what she showed me makes it real, and I don't want that!" Snow said shaking her head.

"Very well then, Snow. I would not want you to do anything that makes you uncomfortable," he said. "How did this happen to you?"

"At first, I had nightmares. They would stick in my mind and haunt me throughout the day. I couldn't escape the visions that tried to terrify me, and they grew in intensity with time. There was a voice inside, which repeated the same words continually, begging me to give it control so my suffering could end."

Snow fidgeted with her hands on the table and hung her head. "Then I felt her in my mind! Making me move and speak! It was frightening to see myself doing things I didn't want to do!" she said glancing back at him. "Screaming inside, fighting her, and not winning!" She cried for a moment, pausing as she looked over at Kedros and smiled. "Until I heard your song and then your words!" she said placing her hand on top of Kedros's. "There was a brilliant light within me then, my inner light, and I felt her grasp loosening on my mind! So, I clung to the light, and drove her out!" Snow said, tears in her eyes once more. She rubbed her hand over Kedros's. "Thank you again, Kedros! You're my hero!"

"You're welcome, Snow!" Kedros replied with a broad smile.

"If I had known long ago, when I was lonely, depressed, and scared that all I needed was my own inner light, love, and comfort for myself to be happy, she would never have taken me!" Snow said. "I was never alone! I had the World of Life all around me, and now I have new friends! I am grateful for all of your light in my life."

Justin smiled at Snow and Kedros. "Thank you for sharing, Snow. I too am grateful for your light as well."

"Love—the light of life! That is what Andeos was telling us," Sara said nodding. "From the sound of it, Kedros's spell was able to pull your awareness from the hold she had on your mind and help you find your inner light. That will be useful in our fight against her."

"At least we know her weakness now!" Talos replied.

"Yes, but—" Justin stared at Miral, a frown creasing his face.

"Do not overthink it, Justin," Galena said in response. "Let us see how she is when she wakes. We know what that horrible woman is capable of. We can deal with it then. Miral's light is strong, dear. She will beat this!"

"You are right," Justin replied.

One of the serving girls approached and took their orders. Talos watched the girl leave and turned to his wife. "You have a lot of dishes to wash!" he said pointing at her.

Sara shot him a menacing glare. "You're helping!" she retorted, standing to poke him on the end of his muzzle.

"Am I?" Talos chuckled.

They all broke out in laughter and Delphia leaped onto the table, stretching her legs. She hopped back and forth between everyone, getting petted by each for a time.

Kedros ran his hand through his hair. "So, uh, how did you learn to dance, and fight like you were dancing?"

Snow smiled, and her ears perked upward. "I always loved dancing! I learned when I was a little girl and danced as often as I could every day! After I fled with my nanny, I used my skills to make us money to live off of. One day a stranger approached who offered to teach me a unique dance technique that could also be used to fight. I agreed to train under her. I wanted to be able to fight!" Snow said with fists clenched in the air. "The technique used war fans as a weapon. Mine are made of resilient Artichian birch wood sharpened and hardened to be resistant to steel weapons. Making it from wood keeps it light. The fans can be used to slice or shield me, and can hide a dagger or poisons that are released upon opening the fan towards the foe!" Snow said, her expression saddening as she glanced at Justin.

"Forget about it, Snow. That was not you," Justin said with a nod.

Snow smiled and nodded back to him. She turned her eyes back to Kedros. He was handsome and shy. She liked that. She hadn't known him long, but felt that Kedros was a gentle, loving soul. Fate had thrown them together. Of that she was certain.

"Great story! Thank you, Snow," he said staring back at her, trying hard not to blush.

"Tell me about yourself, Kedros." Snow asked.

"Ah me, well—" Kedros stammered rubbing his neck. "I'm from Glenn Woods. I'm seventeen years old, and I love nature." He said meshing his words together quickly.

"Your seventeen?" Snow smiled. "I'm sixteen!"

Kedros smiled at her and relaxed some. "I have a sister named Kara, she is ten years old. Our parents died when we were little."

"We all have that problem, don't we?" Snow said looking over the table. "I'm sorry, Kedros."

"I'm sorry, Snow. I can't imagine what it was like to be in the middle of war."

"Thank you, Kedros." She listened to the others laughing and exchanging humorous stories and smiled.

"Ha, ha, ha!" Justin laughed, trying to catch his breath. "Do you remember the day that—" He paused mid-sentence, his eyes widened, and he angled his head to look at Miral. She was staring at him through squinted, wet eyes, and her quiet convulsing sobs grew louder.

"Miral!" Justin said, pulling her close and hugging her tight.

Miral wrapped her arms around his neck and buried her face in his shoulder as she cried. "You kept your promise!"

"You are safe now," Justin said in a soft tone.

"Praise be to Fandia!" Galena exclaimed, fighting back tears.

"Delphia!" Miral replied in a voice choked with tears, as she squeaked excitedly and hopped onto her. Miral hugged her between herself and Justin. He was holding her in his lap, the realization made her blush. She loved being held by him like this, though, loved being so close. She wanted to stay in his arms. "This isn't a dream? You're really here, Justin?" Miral asked while searching his fiery eyes.

"I am really here, Miral, you are not dreaming," Justin said with a reassuring smile. He gestured his hand in an arc across the table. "Your friends are here, and we saved the Elemental of Ice."

Miral turned her head, smiling wide as she looked upon the familiar faces of friends. Her eyes lingered when they found Kedros.

"That is Kedros Okami, the Elemental of Nature," Justin said.

"Kedros!" Miral replied, nodding to him, still fighting back tears.

"It's a pleasure to meet you, Miral!"

Justin gestured to Snow. "This is Princess Snow Artichia."

Snow's eyes filled with tears. "I'm so sorry, Miral!"

"It's all right, Snow, it wasn't your fault!" Miral smiled, wiping tears from her eyes.

"How do you feel?" Justin asked her.

"Stiff, but all right."

"Are you hungry?"

"Starving!" Miral said with her hand over her stomach. She wasn't sure how long it had been since she was taken, but her hunger was telling her that it had been ages since she ate last.

Justin helped her to the spot between himself and Talos, who stretched his wings out blocking her from behind.

"Thank you, Talos!" Justin said.

"My pleasure!" Talos grinned. "It truly does my heart good to see your smile again, Miral!"

"I am so happy to see all of you again!" Miral replied while reaching for the hood on her head. She felt Justin's hand grab hold of hers. She let go of the hood and looked at him with concern.

"For now, 'tis best you leave your hood on," Justin whispered lowering his hand and wrapping his arm around her back. "Folks are acting skittish here."

"All right, I will."

He smiled at her and rubbed the side of her arm.

A serving girl approached with plates of food. Galena pushed her plate to Miral and asked the girl to kindly fetch another.

"Thank you, Galena," Miral said in response.

"Of course, child! I know Justin will offer you his plate in a heartbeat, but your body needs vegetables with that meat, dear," she giggled.

"Thanks, Mom," Justin said smiling at Galena.

Galena smiled back at him. "Oh, now you sound like your brother."

Justin chuckled in reply.

Delphia hopped around on the table taking a carrot from every plate that had one, squeaking with delight as she nibbled on them. Miral saw that Snow was devouring her food as quickly as she was. Whatever Irana had done to her, had to be the same. She left them starving. Delphia hopped over to Miral, and Justin stroked her fur making her purr.

"You were right about her, she is cute," Justin said.

Miral giggled. "I'm glad you brought her with you!"

He stopped petting Delphia and watched the Innkeeper intently when he approached to ask Snow to satisfy her bargain. The man stared at Miral with an icy glare. His face twisted with scorn. Justin glanced at her briefly. She was too busy playing with Delphia to notice. He leaned forward, blocking the keeper's view of her. He bared his teeth, his head feathers tensed, and glared at the Innkeeper with the unspoken threat. The man's face flushed, and he urged Snow along. She followed him to a room beside the stage.

"I don't like that man," Sara said, squinting her eyes. "He looks like a creeper!"

"Ah, ha, ha!" Talos burst out laughing, slapping his hand on the tabletop.

Kedros frowned at Sara and peered back at the doorway rubbing his head. Justin smirked.

Miral stared at Talos with an uncertain gaze then to Sara. "Hmmm, who is it you don't like?"

Sara looked to be forcing a grin, and waved her hands in front of her. "Ah, ha. Don't you worry about it, Miral!"

Snow took to the stage, and the small inn band played a fast-paced song. They watched her gracefully dance with her fans on the stage lit with candles and purple ethereal crystal lamps. She was amazingly talented, and her movements were fluid and poetic. Miral saw Kedros lean forward on his elbows, sighing deeply to himself. She smiled wide at the sight of him.

"He was the one who saved her!" Justin whispered.

"Really? How?" she asked intrigued.

"First, you need to know a few things. We met with Andeos and he told us we are fighting the Goddess of the Dark. She has control over Irana, and he warned us never to speak her name," he said while pointing at the shadow of a cup on the table. "The forbidden word."

"Andeos! He is real?" Miral whispered.

Justin nodded to her. "Yes."

Miral looked at the cup on the table. "I understand. That makes sense now," she said putting her finger on the shadow and tapping it.

"Good! We are currently in Artichia, which is where you were being kept."

Miral's eyes widened. "Artichia?!"

"Mmhmm," he nodded to her. Justin gestured with his hand in a downward motion. "We had Snow pinned to the ground. Kedros knelt beside her singing a spell song of pacification and picked up her hand. Kissing it, he told her she was beautiful, and that he would love to see her light shine." Justin mimicked his words with her hand in his, holding it to the end of his muzzle, his eyes peering into hers.

Miral blushed. His face expressed the same dreamy look she had come to love, the one he wore during the dance.

"Snow was free after that, because she found her inner light."

"Justin—" Miral said taking in his handsome features.

Justin lowered her hand and slowly leaned his head in closer to her. "Yes, Miral?" he asked in a deep soothing tone.

She froze, her face flushing wildly. The end of his muzzle was close to her lips. She stared longingly into his sunny eyes. Her heart pounded loudly in her ears, then a wave of dizziness washed over her.

Justin's smile dropped, and a frown took its place. "What is wrong?"

"Nothing's wrong . . . I just—" She fell forward, but Justin caught her and held her against him.

Talos noticed Miral falling forward and reached over to help support her as Justin stood.

Snow's dance was over and everyone in the room applauded, unaware of the commotion from the back table.

Chapter 43 - Consequences

Justin lifted Miral off the bench and cradled her in his arms. "I am going to take you up to the room so you can lie down."

"What is wrong?" Galena asked.

"I think she is just feeling faint," Justin replied. "Come up with us and look her over." Justin carried her out of the dining hall, and Galena quickly followed. He walked up the stairs and down the corridor to the room at the end. His muzzle curled with disgust as he entered the room. It was orderly but poorly kept. He shook his head. No surprise really, the Innkeeper mirrored the state of his inn. He laid Miral down on a bed and knelt beside her, holding her hand.

Galena examined Miral. "I cannot find anything physically wrong with her at least," Galena said with a nod. "My thoughts are that she is still suffering the effects of being in that crystal and malnourished. 'Tis difficult to say this under our current circumstance, but you need to take it easy. Do not let yourself get too stimulated, dear," Galena said, lightly touching Miral on her shoulder.

"All right," Miral replied.

"Thank you, Galena," Justin said.

Galena nodded and left the room, closing the door behind her.

Justin sat on the edge of the bed. He reached for the cloak hood, drew it back from her head, and gently brushed the hair from her eyes. "Rest if you need to. I will be right here. I will not leave your side."

"How long has it been?" she asked.

"Miral . . ." Justin sighed, averting his eyes a moment. "'Twill not do you any good to know things like that."

"You're right," she said, a frown creased her lips. She reflected for a moment with her hand on her face. "Andeos! What did he look like?"

"That is a better question! The answer will take you by surprise." He was pleased to see her smile return and never wanted to see it fade again. "The prophet was Andeos in disguise."

Miral stared at him, blinking rapidly. "Andeos has been helping me?"

"Yes!" Justin said nodding to her. "He has long white hair, aqua eyes, and looks a lot younger than the prophet."

"That means Fandia is real too!" Miral said, clasping her hands together. "I would love to see her in person!"

"You and me both!" Justin chuckled.

Miral smiled warmly at him then frowned once more. "What does she want from me?"

Justin shook his head. "Andeos would not say. 'Twas too dangerous to tell us why in the World of Life. I–" he paused, his face reflecting more than he was saying as he peered into her eyes. "We have to protect you, Miral. That is all he would say."

"You're feeling guilty," she stated in a quiet tone.

Justin's brows lifted, then scrunched as he frowned.

"You don't have to be. There was nothing more you could have done. I'm all right now because you're here with me," Miral said, her smile returning. She fixed her gaze onto his eyes, laying her hand on top of his.

Justin smiled at her. He reached into his pocket and pulled out the creed. "I wanted to give this back to you."

Miral looked at the creed, tearing as she placed her hand over it.

"My oath remains, Lady Miral," he said with a nod.

She blushed and took the creed from him, fastening it around her neck once more. "What was it you were trying to tell me in Arisdale?"

Justin's peaceful expression vanished and a wide-eyed, dazed look took its place. His voice was quivering as he spoke. "Miral, I am sorry, I cannot—"

A loud bang resounded against the room door. Justin scooped Miral from the bed into his arms. The door swung open hard, the knob cracking loud against the stonewall. Justin backed up to the outer wall growling. Miral trembled in his arms, clinging tightly to him.

The Innkeeper strode into the room. Red glowing eyes stared back. Justin adjusted himself to hold her with one arm, reaching behind him to the rock wall of the inn with the other.

"I warned you, didn't I, dearest Justin?!" Shadow said wagging the Innkeeper's finger at him. "I took you to be a smart man. I thought you would have taken my threat seriously and yet you nearly failed twice!" she cackled.

Justin glared at her, continuing to channel a spell behind him.

"I gave you a gift!" Shadow continued. "I let you save her from Delphi! I allowed you to have your fun before I took her back! I made it easy for you to save her again and this is how you thank me?"

Justin growled at Shadow, teeth bared, and head feathers flaring.

"Ah, relax, dearest! Since I arrived just in time, I won't uphold that promise I made you!" she laughed.

"How did you even know?!" Justin snapped at her.

The Innkeeper pointed to himself. "I will allow you to know that because I adore you so much!" Shadow said with a smirk. "I owned his soul long ago! I can hear all that he hears when I choose to!" she said inching closer. "Though the truth is that I knew you would come here, and I knew you would fail to keep the promise. How, that I sadly cannot say, not yet."

"What do you think you can do without a magic user under your control?" Justin sneered.

The Innkeeper raised his arms and many Artichians entered the hall.

"Power in numbers, my dearest!" Shadow said. "They were easy to get control of during the civil war, and I know how you feel about hurting innocents," she mocked followed by a wide grin. The keeper glanced back into the hall. "Your friends are a little too busy to help you!" He turned back to face him. "Now then, hand her over! Your time with her is done!" Shadow demanded with the keeper's hand outstretched.

"Never!" Justin bellowed. A loud bang erupted from behind him. Stone shards zipped through the air in every direction and the cold Artichian air rushed into the room. Justin launched backward out the hole he created in the wall, disappearing into the frigid night.

Chapter 44 - Nightmares

Justin sprinted across the snowy fields of Artichia, clutching Miral tightly to him as she shivered violently. A blizzard had rolled in blocking the moonlight and casting the world in near total darkness. He remembered seeing a network of caves on their trip to the Glacier Inn. He searched desperately for them with his connection to the earth, his eyes stinging from the frosty air. Going back now was too risky, and there was no way he could make it back to the transport chamber in this weather. The flurry of snow made it impossible to see, and Miral was a human. His skin was thicker and better insulated than hers. Even with the fur cloak, keeping her in the biting cold of a blizzard would be foolish.

He found one of the cave openings and ducked inside, sniffing the dwelling and was confident no animal called it home. Justin placed his back against the cold wall of the cave. He shivered and slid down to sit on the icy surface. He lowered Miral to his lap, drew his knees up, and pulled his fur cloak from behind him wrapping it around the front of his knees, and tucked it behind him. He rested his feet on top of his cape to keep them off the cold ground. He held her shivering body tightly to him, hoping what heat he had would comfort her. He then took her cold hands in his to warm them.

"What happened?" Miral asked, her teeth chattering loudly. "What did she mean by her threat and her promise to you?"

Justin heaved a sigh. "I cannot. . ." he said in a broken tone.

"Cannot what?"

Justin shuddered. "Pray. I just . . . cannot!" he begged in a quivering voice. He heard Miral crying. Her beautiful face was dimly lit by the blue glow from the ethereal gems on his cape clasps and sparkled with teardrops. Justin wiped them from her face with the side of his thumb.

"My first snowfall and I don't even care to see it."

"Pray, Miral, do not cry," he said, placing his muzzle against her forehead. "I am so sorry! Just know that I will always be here for you. I will not let her get you again!" He touched the side of her face, wiping new tears away. "We will stop her! Then we can be at peace and talk about it, all right?" he asked in hope of reassuring her. He took Miral's hands back in his to keep them warm, then lifted his head, and rested it against the cave wall closing his eyes. "I am so tired," he said exasperated, taking a long deep breath.

He was still sore from Shadow's first assault and his extended rest, and things got worse with the strain of casting the rock ring in Glenn. His body was exhausted from lack of good sleep the other night, the fatigue heightened from the use of magic. Despite their desperate situation, his eyes grew heavy. With Miral safely in his arms, he knew he could succumb to his mind's pleas for rest, but doing so would leave them vulnerable. He was pulled from his thoughts when he felt Miral trembling harder, pained cries filling the air.

"I don't know if I can sleep!"

"Miral?" He could see fear in her eyes and remembered Snow had shared that same expression. His head feathers spiked. "No!"

"She showed me nightmares! I can see them when I close my eyes! They seem so real when I'm in them, and only when my eyes are open do I see they are not real at all!"

Justin's eyes darted as he searched her face, his heart aching. Tension welled up inside him. He let her go, he failed her and had forgotten all about Shadow's promise amid one spellbound moment. Everything was his fault.

"Fear . . ." Miral said in tears, "it surrounds you, the darkness . . . picks at you, wearing away your spirit until you become its prisoner . . . until you break. Anger builds turning into rage and then . . ." Miral gasped. "The wave . . ."

"What wave?"

"When I was ten . . . when I became enraged. It was so big! I couldn't stop it! I killed them all!" Miral sobbed.

"There was no wave, Miral. You told Agar and me thusly."

"I'm not sure what is real anymore! It's so dark in here! I feel like I'm trapped again! I don't want these feelings, this fear. I don't like it! I'm so scared, Justin!" she wailed.

He wrapped his arms around her and hugged her tight, his head against hers, rocking her gently. "Miral! Stay strong! Keep your inner light shining bright! 'Twill be all right, I promise! 'Tis safe to feel fear. 'Twill pass. I told you this before. Do not let it control you," Justin said. He cursed Shadow and himself in his mind.

Chapter 45 - Storm

"They are not in the room! There is a huge hole in the wall, he must have gone out into the blizzard!" Galena said descending the stairwell.

Delphia whimpered and squeaked on Talos's shoulder.

"Terrific!" Sara grumbled shaking her head, tying a few living people together with rope. She looked out at all the unconscious Artichians lying in heaps on the floor. They fought waves of them for what seemed like hours. "She planted them here, waiting for us, waiting for Miral to be separated from us!" Sara fumed.

Snow looked out the window; the blizzard was howling fiercely. "I hope they will be all right."

Kedros stood beside her. "I'm sure they will! Justin and Miral seem strong-willed, I don't think anything could ever take them down!" he said. "They have each other too. Their light will keep them safe!"

Snow turned to Kedros with a warm smile. "You're right! We need to have faith!" Snow said throwing a fist into the air.

"We are stuck here until this storm passes," Talos said. "What is our plan?"

"We go back to Arisdale as Andeos instructed," Sara said. "Justin will do the same if he hasn't already."

"Oh, dearest Fandia and Andeos! Pray, help them and bring them back safely!" Galena prayed aloud.

Sara fidgeted, pacing back and forth, her arms flailing about as she walked. She fumed to herself in quiet contemplation.

"Is Sara claustrophobic?" Kedros asked Talos.

"No, no, just angry!" Talos replied. "When she gets like this, it's best to keep your distance and wait it out," Talos said watching her pace about.

Sara stopped. "All right, Seth, that's about enough! You hear me! Knock it off!" Sara hollered into the air with indignation.

The wind subsided, shutters stopped banging, and the building was no longer creaking.

Snow leaped up to look out the window. Her ears perked up, and she looked back at Sara. "It . . . stopped!"

Sara stood tense and began to tremble. She seemed like a volcano about to erupt. Talos bolted to his feet and over to Sara.

"That son of a bbrrhh—!"

Talos put his hand over her mouth just as Sara was about to sling a tirade of obscenities. She writhed about in his grasp, still yelling muffled words.

Galena and Snow's eyes were wide, and Kedros blankly stared at her.

"Why did you have to go and say his name, hun?" Talos asked letting her go once she settled down.

"I don't care! He did it, see!" Sara said pointing wildly to the window. "If that dirty dastard tries to enter my mind, I'm gonna give him what for!" she said stomping out the inn door. The snow outside hissed and steamed beneath her feet.

"Dear Goddess Isis, bless us! Wait up, Sara!" Galena called out chasing after her.

Talos shrugged running after them with Snow and Kedros in tow.

Chapter 46 - Mistakes

Justin was no longer tired, adrenaline raced relentlessly through his veins keeping his mind sharp. He choked back his anger the best he could, though. Artichia was not a wise place to cause a quake.

He consoled Miral while he listened for signs of the blizzard letting up. Once it did he departed the cave and made the trek to the transport chamber at a full sprint. He didn't know how much more abuse his body could take, but there was no time to stop. Shadow was done playing games, he was certain of that. Her words echoed in his mind, feeding hatred, forcing rage to continue to fuel him. He needed that. The moment it subsided he would likely collapse, and Miral would be in danger.

She remained quiet with a distanced look on her face. Her beautiful blinding light was a lot dimmer now; her smile gone. He wanted to save her, to return her smile. He desperately wanted to tell Miral and his family about Shadow's words to him, the promise she made once Miral could no longer hear them. He couldn't though, not to Miral, not to them. That was part of her threat to him. Justin cursed Shadow in his mind again as rage boiled in his blood.

He reached the transport chamber exhausted, breathing heavily, and darted inside. Miral glanced around the room. Her face displayed deep sorrow as she looked at him.

"This looks like the same place," she said.

"'Tis in appearance," Justin said while catching his breath. "Andeos said . . . many of these . . . were built long ago." He took a long deep breath. "The gods would . . . use them to travel . . . and we can as well."

Justin sighed, he wasn't sure if he had the strength to cast the monumental spell needed to travel. He desperately wanted to return home. Perhaps the others made it back already, and they could get some rest before having to fight Shadow. Of course, they may still be on their way here; however, he was certain it wasn't wise to sit here and wait, not after what happened in this chamber in Arisdale.

He made up his mind and took his place beneath the Earth orb. "I am going to cast the spell for both of us. I do not want you to try this as you are," he said while looking at Miral.

She nodded, wrapping her arms around his neck tightly. Justin focused his mind to Arisdale, channeling energies into the earth orb. The room glowed with green bright light, and slowly faded away. As it began to come into view once more, Justin felt a rush of confusion and panic. It wasn't in ruins.

He lowered Miral to stand on her feet. "Stay here. Something is not right." He reached for the doorknob. It felt scorching hot to the touch. He pulled his hand away and clenched his fist. "Damn it!" he groaned and blinked his weary eyes. He removed the fur cloak and set it on the ground, then reached for the doorknob once more turning it quickly and swung the door open. The bright sun was blinding, his eyes were still used to the darkness of Artichia. It felt deathly hot to his currently cold-adapted body, and his thick winter clothing was not helping. He squinted at the sun and moved his hand to block it from his eyes, then felt sharp objects poke his chest and neck.

"Move and you die!" spoke a familiar voice.

Justin's rage burned anew as his head feathers and sickle claws rose with the threat. "Dilos?!" Justin bellowed. "What in the hells are you doing?!" His eyes adjusted and his heart sank at the sight before him. A giant pyramid sat in the distance, proudly reaching for the heavens. "Egyptalia?!" Justin exclaimed.

"Indeed, now turn slowly, and do not try fighting your way out of this!" Dilos sneered. "Unless you want to die, that is."

Justin unwillingly did as he was told. The weapons pointed at his throat held small shards of ethereal obsidian. There was a small army with weapons and arrows aimed at him. None of them wore earthen armor. He had no way of using his magic to disarm them and remain uninjured. Dilos knew that. He turned around and his eyes fell to Miral, who stood trembling with her hands clasped together. He felt deeply regretful as he stared at her, desperately wishing things could have turned out differently. The teleport spell was another mistake to add to his book of blunders.

"Why are you doing this?" Justin asked Dilos.

"Shadow promised me Arisdale in return for my service," he said. "I am king now!" He laughed and clasped Justin's hands behind his back in shackles set with ethereal obsidian stones.

The instant they snapped shut, Justin could no longer feel his magic pulse. He jerked his head to look back at Dilos, eyes tensed and narrow. "You would betray your king and homeland to her for your own self-gain?! Do you really think there will be anything to rule when she is in charge?!" he bellowed.

Guards knelt to clasp his legs in chains, and metal boots were slid cautiously over his toe claws.

"How is that any different than what you did? You left us behind to go on this mad crusade!" Dilos said with disdain. "Shadow came while you were gone! The people were being turned into mindless slaves! 'Tis through my actions that they will be spared that existence!" Dilos motioned to the Egyptalian guards. "Take him to the Queen."

"Queen?! Katenna?" Justin asked dismayed. Shadow had her, and Agar would not be pleased to learn of this. He wondered if Agar was all right, and hoped in silent prayer his brother was on his way here.

"Of course!" Dilos said clutching Miral in his grasp.

She was screaming, crying, and fighting against Dilos's tight grip. Justin lurched forward growling and straining against the chains the guards forcefully pulled back on.

"Do not hurt her!" he roared.

"Hurt her?" Dilos asked. "That is not for me to do!" He motioned forward to the guards and they pulled him to the palace.

Justin looked over the unusually quiet streets of Egyptalia as he was tugged along, wondering what Dilos meant. He frowned; for once the place that brought joy on family vacations, and where he met Agar, now brought pain and hopelessness. The warm and tightly packed sandstone homes of noble houses stood tall and fought back the sun, providing some shade as they marched to the palace. He thought about the promise Shadow made, the one that was not only threatening his heart, but also the world. His eyes fell to Miral, who no longer struggled as Dilos pushed her along, her head hung low. He promised the elders that he could make the right choice and do his duty to the world, but in all honesty, he couldn't bring himself to choose to save the world over her.

Chapter 47 - Confessions

"Dearest Justin!" Shadow's voice sang out. "I'm so pleased to see you again!"

Miral watched Queen Katenna rise from her golden throne decorated with Egyptalian water lilies and precious gems and minerals. She wore a long white dress with gossamer sleeves, a wesekh collar consisting of lapis lazuli, turquoise, carnelian beads, and a crown set with similar stones.

She walked in a way that made her appear to float gracefully down the steps of her throne to stand in front of Justin and Miral. She was as beautiful as Agar described her back on the ship. Only her golden eyes were glowing red and set into a wicked glower.

"Why did you run from me?" she asked, stroking her finger across the top of Justin's chest. "All that energy you wasted, the sleep you lost, for what?" Katenna arched an eyebrow at him. "Ah, the same old silent treatment. That is rather rude of you!" she said while taking a couple steps away from him. "I'm honestly going to miss you, dearest! You have been delightfully fun to play with!"

"What are you going on about?" Justin grumbled.

She turned back to him grabbing hold of his arms. "I want to take you to the World of Dark with me so I can torment you more, but . . . you won't let me!" she whined.

Justin stared at Katenna wide-eyed.

Miral trembled and raised her bound hands shakily to her heart.

"You left me no choice!" she said shaking her head. "You are too much of a threat, and so you must die!" Shadow hissed.

Miral collapsed to the ground and cried in racking sobs. "No!" Fear swirled in her head exhausting her as she lost the will to fight back. There would be no life for her without him.

"Miral!" Justin cried out as he was jerked back when he attempted to kneel beside her. A deep guttural growl rolled through his chest with the rise of his feathers, his sickle claws restrained by the metal boots. He released a hissing screech of threat and strained against the chains. More guards joined in to pull back on the restraints to keep him from moving.

Miral shuddered at the noise Justin made as he fought to free himself. The growls, the roar, and now this new sound, the screech. They were terrifying, but they were Justin's cries, how his kind expressed feelings of threat. Tears formed in her eyes as Katenna walked over to her. She kneeled in front of her, drawing her head up with a finger under her chin.

"Does that hurt?" she asked gently with Katenna's voice. "I can make your pain go away if you wish! I can end the nightmares that haunt you."

"Miral! Do not listen to her!" Justin shouted, renewing his struggle to free himself from the guards. "She is trying to trap you in an illusion!"

Miral's lips quivered, and she felt her body trembling violently as she fought back feelings that were rising.

"Oh dear, you don't see it, do you? I am your only friend in all this. What hurts you now will end once you hear the truth," Shadow said helping Miral to her feet. She turned her to face Justin. "Look at him!"

Miral locked eyes on him, tears streaming down her face. She was gasping for breath between sobs.

"Your heart is aching for him, isn't it? You want him! Adore him!" she cooed into Miral's ear. "Do you even know how he really feels? What he really wants?"

Miral stopped crying and stared blankly at Justin. His face no longer looked at her with worry, and he no longer fought to break free. *What does she mean by that? Why is he not fighting anymore?* She blinked, uncertain when things shifted as if she drifted off and missed something. Or perhaps, she was dreaming all along.

"Oh, I'm so sorry. He hasn't told you! How cruel of him, hmm? If he had been honest with you, he could have spared you this pain! Isn't that correct, Justin? Be honest . . . you have no real feelings for her!"

Miral continued to stare at Justin; however, he wore an unreadable expression.

"She is one of you, an Elemental, but you had to tolerate a human in your presence because your hateful Goddess Fandia forced her into your life!" Shadow said, her hands braced firmly on Miral's shoulders from behind. "Tell her she is a fool to believe she could ever be loved by you!"

"You can read me like an open book, I see," Justin said shrugging. "You have it all figured out. I am Arisdalian, she is a human; I am king, she is a commoner. I cannot love her, and I do not love her! That is what I have wanted to say since the dance!"

Miral was reeling, her heart pounding, aching, and tears flowed forth. "The dance . . ." she replied in a barely audible tone.

"'Twas a show, nothing more! The people really enjoyed mocking you! Truly the most enchanting dance I had ever had!" Justin said smugly. "Nothing that you have been experiencing was real. 'Twas all an elaborate game. Even the pendant I gave you was nothing more than a mark that I own you," he smirked. "I always wanted to be king. My father was a fool, my mother weak! I found the perfect way to be rid of my parents and have a far greater power than I already possess. I must admit I will miss you. You were a fun human to play with. There was so much more I wanted to do with you first." He looked her over. "Hmmm, yes. However, I do keep my word, and I promised you in exchange for my new position."

"That is the promise you made to her?! Why didn't you just bring me back to her in Delphi?!" She trembled violently through her body as she spoke. She resisted the terrifying feeling, trying to push it away, but that only amplified the sensation.

"She needed you to be broken, so I took you with me. I made you feel like you belonged. Made you believe you had my affections. All so I could break my promises in front of you and watch you fall. The pain in your eyes is delightful!"

Miral's heart ached deeply as if a knife stabbed her. *He doesn't love me? All those times we were together, talking, laughing. He was always so warm and tender, paid me so much attention. Held me close, so close. Have I been mistaken?! He was only tolerating me?! Playing a game?! I don't know what's real anymore! I don't want to feel anymore!* Miral turned away unable to look at him, crying and screaming in pain-filled sobs. She pulled at the creed, breaking the chain and tossed it aside.

241

Chapter 48 - The Promise

"Miral?! Whatever she is telling you 'tis not the truth! I . . . "Justin felt
several hands grabbing at his muzzle, forcing his powerful jaws shut. A
guard pushed a leather sheath onto his snout and fastened it tight. He
watched with an aching heart as Miral tossed the creed away.

"Ah, ah, ah!" Shadow scolded him wagging her finger. "You want me
to uphold my promise, hmmm?" Shadow asked while staring into his
eyes. "Oh, I see, that is noble of you. Do you want to know what she
would think about that when I tell her?" she grinned. "It's over, Justin! I
have her now thanks to you," she laughed triumphantly. "Take him
away! It will soon be time for you to die!"

Justin was hauled off by the guards and forced into a cell. He sat
dejected on the golden sandstone floor of the palace prison. His head
hung down, his lower jaw resting on his knee. The guards removed the
muzzle, but his shackles and chains remained. He thought about Miral.
He loved her so much and refused to think of her as she looked
moments ago.

"I remember the day we first met. You were so scared of me, and I
was rather enchanted by you but uncertain. I grew up with my kind
avoiding humans. In law 'tis improper to love outside of the Arisdalian
species, so I tried not to think about how beautiful you were. How
lovely your blue eyes and silky hair are, and of course, how alluring your
scent is to me. Over the days since our meeting, that pure enchantment
became admiration and love. Your smile is like the moon and stars at
night, guiding and comforting." He sighed heavily. "Even given the
terribly sad circumstances of your past, Miral, you always smiled. I love
your smile and never wanted to see it fade." He stopped his speech and
cried. "Now that smile is gone, and I failed you. I wonder what a life of

love would have been like with you, Miral. I wonder if I will have the chance to find out." He paused as he recalled past events, things said and shared. "I was going to ask you to court but the—" he shook his head. He didn't want to remember that. The day everything went to hell. What was the point of these thoughts, other than to torture himself? It was too late now.

He cursed Shadow and her threat to him once more. She had a foot in the door of Miral's mind and caused her to faint in response to his foolish attempt to kiss her. His single greatest mistake made in the heat of passion. So many mistakes, all of which will bring the World of Life to its end.

His mind refused to accept what was, refused to let go, and generated obsessive thoughts that looped endlessly. Faintly in the background of his mind was a voice.

"Let me end your suffering. Give me control."

"Justin!"

He sat in his protective posture on the floor, not acknowledging the familiar voice of Artilone when she spoke. The panicked urgency of his thoughts held his focus as he fell deeper into the darkness within.

"I'm going to get you out of here," Artilone whispered, fumbling with a ring of keys.

Once more Justin didn't even flinch. He was consumed by the image of Miral huddled on the floor screaming and wailing pain-filled cries. Nothing he said or did made Miral feel better, feel safe. If he couldn't do it then who could? *I am not good enough. I never was. Why do I bother? I am not a hero.*

She frowned when he didn't reply to her. "Justin?" She tilted her head and studied him a moment. "It's all right, you're just thinking too much and not feeling," she replied in a soothing tone.

Justin blinked, ceasing focus on his swirling thoughts as her voice triggered a memory. In his mind, he saw his mother comforting him when he was younger, advising him not to overthink. Galena has said that too lately. He was doing it again. He ignored his thoughts, letting them play in the back of his mind, disinterested in what they had to say as he focused more on the image of his mother. The positive

243

environment she created for him, the love and comfort she gave. She was gone now, but he could give himself that same love and support anytime he needed it. He looked up from his knees and tilted his head to her, taking a few deep breaths. "Artilone, you are not under her control?" A smile grew on his face, and the feelings of dread dimmed slightly as he took in his good friend's bright expression. "Well done."

"A lot of good it did her too!"

"Dilos!" Justin growled as the man grabbed Artilone from behind.

"We will be having two executions this day!" Dilos said binding her hands together. He shoved her into the cell causing her to fall forward. Justin shifted to the side to keep Artilone from falling face first onto the stone floor.

Dilos looked them over with a smug smile of satisfaction and left.

"Damn it! Curse that damn fool to the hells!" Justin fumed. He turned his eyes to look at her with remorse. "I am sorry, Artilone."

Her eyes watered. "What is going on, Justin?" she beseeched him.

He sighed, "'Tis a long story. Simply, we are at war with a goddess, and . . . we may have already lost. Because I am a bloody fool," he said dejected.

"That doesn't sound like the Justin I know!"

"Agar?" Justin asked in disbelief, blinking a few times to be sure he was still awake.

"What are you doing beating yourself up like that?!" Agar asked as he materialized in front of the cell with a huge grin on his face. "Is that really my brother or did someone replace him with a doubting, self-torturing look-alike?"

"Agar. . ." Justin replied with a groan. His brother was right, of course. What was he doing to himself? What good would it do the world or Miral to wallow in the past and what may never come to pass? He shook his head, closed his eyes a moment and breathed in deep breaths as his mother taught him.

"I got your message!" Agar said dropping to a knee in front of the cell door. "And I met Andeos!" He fumbled with his pockets and pouches. "He got me out of Arisdale before she came." He stopped the mad search of his blue tunic and pointed to his shadow on the ground.

"You are up to speed then, good!"

"Let me get you two out of here!" he said reaching into his travel bag and pulling out a set of lockpicks.

"No!" Justin replied.

Agar arched an eyebrow in question to Justin. "No? Why?!"

"She might not be aware that Artilone is locked up to be executed," Justin explained. "Too busy with Miral—" Justin's brow furrowed as his face wore an expression of sorrow and anger. "She is weak against love. Things need to stay in place so we can free—" Justin's mouth hung open. He sighed, closed his jaws, and averted his eyes from Agar.

Agar grabbed hold of the bars tightly. "Don't you dare say Kat!" he growled.

Justin looked back at Agar with a frown. "I am sorry, Agar."

"Damn it!" Agar said standing and pacing about the room.

"She is the new Elemental of Wind," Justin replied.

Agar stopped walking and glared at Justin. "No way!" he frowned and sighed heavily.

"I am hopeful that seeing Artilone will free Kat from her grasp; however, if that fails, we will need you to get us out of trouble. Then it will be up to you to save her. All you have to do is—" he paused taking a breath, "tell her how you really feel." Justin drooped his head.

Agar turned and arched a brow at Justin. "You haven't told Miral how you feel yet, have you?" Agar replied.

"I cannot."

Agar placed his hands on his hips. "Can't or won't?"

"Cannot," Justin snapped in annoyance while looking away from his brother.

"Man!" Agar said rubbing his head. "What the hell did she do to you to make you act like this?!"

Justin looked at Agar with narrowed eyes. "Take a look around and make sure no one is in earshot. She can hear through the . . ." he pointed at his shadow a few times, "of corrupted people."

"All right," Agar said walking to the hall cloaking himself with his magic. He turned back and appeared before Justin. "All clear. What is so dire that you can't tell the woman you obviously love how you feel?" Agar asked pointing at him.

Justin sighed. "After crystallizing Miral she swore to never let me speak the words I wanted to say. If I did, Miral would be broken and would be useless to her, and if that occurred she would kill her," Justin replied in a quivering voice.

"Damn!" Agar said shaking his head.

"She would not hesitate because what she wanted from Miral would pass from her to another. Her life was meaningless. That other would be a child. An innocent but easily corrupted child," Justin said.

Agar stood with his jaw hung open. Artilone gasped and covered her mouth with her hand.

"I cannot tell Miral how I feel because I love her and cannot knowingly let a child suffer!" Justin said standing. "Though by not telling her, the entire world is still in danger! There was not a better option," he huffed. "I am hurting inside, Agar, conflicted with what to do. Follow my duty as king or protect the lady I love. I thought 'twould be ok to be with her the way I wanted, secretly loving her, being there for her, and to be close to her. I believed I could save both her and the world at once. I am a damned fool! I just made things worse, made her question what she meant to me!" he stopped, resting his head against the warm sandstone wall. "'Tis all my fault," he whispered in a quivering tone, tears forming in his eyes. "I have lost her and 'tis all my fault! I should have pushed her away, kept my distance!"

"What do you mean you lost her? I can feel her. She is here in the palace."

"Here, but not!" Justin said while facing Agar. "She is breaking inside; 'tis because I failed! I could not help feeling love for her when she was with me again! I nearly kissed her in the inn while Snow was dancing! The Goddess of the Dark took my feelings for her and twisted them to hurt her! She is down there somewhere probably dreaming of me telling her I hate her or something! Nightmares that were instilled in her as she dreamt in the crystal remain, haunting her and growing stronger! The line between reality and the dream blurred entirely until they break, and the Goddess of the Dark takes over. The same thing happened to the Elemental of Ice . . ." Justin said trailing off and looking away again. "Nearly happened to me before Artilone arrived."

Agar growled, his anger becoming palpable as static and electricity pulsed from him.

"I am sorry, Artilone. We can still save Kat. She will be all right," Justin said. "Snow, the ice elemental, she is in good spirits despite the fear that lingers." Justin turned back to Agar. "I was hoping to tell Miral how I felt after we stop the Goddess of the Dark! She pushed us so hard, though. I have not slept in two days. I have little strength left in me between that and all the magic I had to cast," he said. "Now everything has become dire! If Miral is corrupted the world is lost, if she dies the world is lost!" he exclaimed in a rising tone. "What was I to do?!" he sighed. "I failed Miral and the world!" Justin said hanging his head, his tirade coming to an end.

Agar shook his head and squeezed his eyes tight and clenched his fists. "Justin! Stop! Just stop blaming yourself!" he said through gritted teeth. "You couldn't have known this was going to happen! You're the last Arisdale! It was a hard decision to make, but you're only a living being, we all make mistakes, brother!" Agar stood tall. "Being true to your feelings is never one of them! There may still be hope! Let's go on believing that and stop this damned goddess!"

Justin sighed and looked into Agar's eyes. "By the gods, what has happened to me?" he frowned and took a deep breath as he turned to his emotions inside. His greatest fears were about love. After Razamarea's torments, he believed he would never find a woman to love. Would never have a family of his own. He thought he had control of that fear, changed the feelings about it, but it was clear that he didn't. Once he fell in love with Miral, his new fear was losing her, being alone without love once more. Shadow knew that. "She was trapping me in my fears, it happened so quick and subtle. Curse it all." He hung his head a moment before locking his eyes back on his brother. "No more!" he said with bared teeth. "You are right, brother. 'Tis not over yet!"

Chapter 49 - Wind

Agar watched in stealthy silence as Dilos returned to collect Justin and Artilone for the execution. They were led down the halls of Egyptalia Palace to the courtyard to the gallows. The guards refitted Justin with the leather muzzle once he was in place. Agar assumed they feared getting bitten when they put the noose around his neck. Artilone trembled in fear beside him.

"It'll be all right, Artilone! Have faith!" Agar whispered to her from behind.

Trumpet fanfare played and Katenna strode out to the throne across from them. Agar tensed at the sight of Kat, her beautiful golden eyes glowing bright red. He felt a surge through him with his rising tension. She wore a casual sleeveless, short white and aqua accented dress with a golden collar around her neck, a small yellow ethereal gem on its surface. Her gold belt and gold and aqua bracer had purple stones. Her white, aqua and gold boots had both yellow and purple gems. She paused beside Dilos and squinted her eyes.

"Ah, my fair Queen, the execution is set as you requested!" Dilos said. "I have an added bonus for your pleasure."

Katenna's face twisted into a snarl and her words were strained. "Dilos! You damn . . . fool . . . I cannot . . ."

"Huh? I thought you would be pleased?!" Dilos replied as he turned to face Katenna.

"Oh, but I am, thanks!" Katenna growled as she swung her fist into the side of his head with a loud crack.

Dilos hit the ground and hollered to the guards, "Hang them!"

The guards moved to kick free the platform beneath Justin and Artilone. Katenna screamed and ran to the gallows. "No! Artilone!"

Tears of joy streamed down her face when she saw Agar appear on the top beam of the gallows cutting free the noose from Artilone and Justin.

Agar smiled at her briefly, before his eye caught the glimmer of sunlight reflecting off metal. He sent forth a blinding lightning flash as he dove at the guard closest to Artilone with daggers drawn, sparks of electricity were coursing across the blades. When they contacted the guard's metal breastplate, the shock dropped the jackal to his knees. Agar kicked him in the chest knocking him off the edge of the gallows.

"Agar!" Katenna cried out in excitement. She heard the roar of her people behind her and turned to face them as the mix of races plowed toward the gallows. Katenna stopped to channel winds. She felt them caress her as they swirled and churned growing in speed and intensity. She set the spell free and a large gust of wind bellowed forth knocking all in its path to the ground. Katenna smiled in satisfaction when no one got up. She dusted her hands off and turned to Artilone, Agar, and Justin.

She threw her arms around her sister and embraced her. "Oh, Artilone! I'm so sorry!"

"Kat! You don't need to be sorry!" Artilone cried. "Justin told me what happened! How are you?! Are you going to be all right?" Artilone asked.

"You know me, sis, I'm a tough girl! It will take more than what she did to bring me down! At least she taught me how to use magic, that churlish clot pole!" Kat grumbled. She said that, but she wasn't sure if it was true anymore. The powerful fears the Goddess of the Dark instilled lingered despite the brave face. She fought hard to break free from the nightmares but failed. The sight of her sister in danger was enough to help her find a light inside to fight back.

Katenna stared at Justin as Agar removed his muzzle, remembering the moment she helplessly watched as he and Miral were brought before her in the throne room. He looked pathetic in shackles and chains. The amount of restraints it took to stop that mountain of a man was unreal.

He also looked weary and exhausted, and not the powerful guy she had come to know.

"Justin, I'm sorry!" she said walking up to him.

Agar removed Justin's wrist shackles letting them fall to the ground as he moved on to free his legs and tail.

Justin stretched the stiffness from the freed limbs while looking at her. "I am sorry too, Kat. Though, these regrets are not yours to bear, all right?"

She nodded in reply. "I know, but what she was saying to Miral was . . ."

Justin fixed her with a wide-eyed stare, his head feathers fluffing. "What did she do?! What lies were told?!" he asked.

"She had you tell her in the illusion that you only tolerated her because she is an Elemental. That you hated humans, and that you didn't and couldn't ever love her because of who and what she is. Also, that you wanted to hurt her, and that everything was done to increase your power," Katenna said rubbing the side of her arm. The Goddess of the Dark was so cruel to Miral, more so than she had been to Katenna.

Justin growled. "Curse her to the hells!" he bellowed, his words echoing off the courtyard walls.

Agar removed the final shackles around his ankles, heaving the metal boots from his feet. "She has a lot of payback coming her way!" Agar said as he stood.

"Where is she?!" Justin asked.

"She was put in the . . . dark pit," Katenna said.

Justin's head feathers stood on end and his face looked more dread-filled than a moment ago. He jumped from the gallows and ran into the palace at full speed.

"Hell," Agar groaned running after him with Katenna and Artilone.

They followed Justin into the lower levels of the palace. The prison cells here were meant for the worst offenders. The dark pit was aptly named for the lack of windows, creating an atmosphere designed to break the will of the prisoner. Katenna lit a torch and they filed down the winding stairs.

She stopped fast in front of the first cell, drooped her ears and groaned. "She isn't here!"

Justin slammed his fist against the bars, denting them on impact. The rattling echo of metal resounded down the halls of the dark pit in an eerie symphony. He sighed deeply. "We will return to Arisdale then. Maybe Andeos can help us!" he said turning back to the winding stairwell.

Kat jerked her head to look at him. "Andeos?!"

"Indeed!" Agar said smiling at Katenna. "Come on, I will explain on the way," he said motioning back the way they had come.

Chapter 50 - Escape

Agar's ears twitched as he exited the dark pit. Katenna and Artilone also spun to face the same direction as him. The low rumbling sound of many feet and cries of people could faintly be heard.

"They are still under her control?!" Katenna asked.

"Yes, and they will remain that way until we stop her. Keep moving!" Justin urged.

They exited the palace and saw a wall of black in the distance headed their way. Agar froze in horror when he heard the familiar scream of the blood demon as well.

"Damn! She is here!" Justin said in panic scooping Artilone off her feet and dashing forward.

"She?!" Agar asked sprinting hard to catch Justin.

"Andeos said the Virabis was a female, a god killer, and to avoid her at all costs, there are no means to fight her."

"Terrific!" Agar groaned.

"Virabis?" Katenna asked.

Agar nodded. "Vile creature that seems to only consume blood and flesh. We first encountered her in Delphi."

The swarm of Egyptalians closed in on all sides.

"We must keep pushing forward, keep an eye out for a moving mass of blood!" Justin said as he stopped running.

Katenna channeled a chamber of gusting wind around them.

Justin released Artilone from his arms and knelt. "Artilone, climb on my back and hold on tight. I will be able to defend you better this way."

Artilone did as he said, and Justin lifted her while standing. Katenna set the wind free, knocking back the swarm of her people. She cast an enhancement spell of speed on them.

Agar finished his channeling and lightning rained down in a deafening roar around them. It streaked forward, clearing the path to the teleport chamber in the distance. While running behind the path of the lightning, they fended off attackers from the sides.

Agar saw Justin leap forward dodging an Egyptalian man who dove at him. He grabbed the man and tossed him back into a group of people to the left. He panicked as Justin stumbled slightly on landing and caught sight of trouble in the distance. "We got archers!" Agar called out. He could feel Justin's energies swirling as he cast a spell. "Justin! Don't use magic! You look ready to collapse, brother!"

"I will manipulate the wind to deflect arrows or weapons from overhead and around us!" Katenna said in response.

"Yes, mom," Justin replied while pushing against the chest of a man, sending him hurtling back.

Agar's smile shifted to a look of horror. "Hells! There she is!" he said pointing to the southeast. In the distance was the Virabis. She looked different now, taking on a taller, slimmer, curvy shape, like a woman.

"She is becoming more bipedal, probably from feeding off of living things!" Justin replied.

"She sure seems more interested in eating us than all those people!" Agar replied clapping his hands together at a group to his right, which repelled them ten feet away.

The Virabis glided after them, sounding as if she was cackling in delight. He saw her regurgitate a stream of blood into the air sending it towards them.

Justin cast his earth shield despite his weariness and Agar's plea that he does not use his magic. The shield reflected the blood, but some landed on the Egyptalians nearby. Their skin and muscles boiled and melted away, exposing bone as blood ate through flesh. Agar stared in horror at the blood demon. The fiend was a surreal monster of nightmares. "What in the hells is that thing?"

"I don't want to know!" Katenna replied.

The Virabis plowed straight through the Egyptalians cutting some in half as she passed through them, blood erupting forth like a psychotic rain shower, their half flesh, half bone bodies falling to the ground, guts spilling out on impact. They arrived at the transport chamber and bolted inside, slamming the door shut.

"Quickly to your element! Kat, you hold on tight to Artilone and she will go with you! Imagine Arisdale as your destination, channel your energy to the orb above," Justin said while dropping to a knee. Artilone stepped down and ran to Katenna.

"Unbelievable!" Katenna replied trying to shake the horror from her head so she could focus, wrapping her arms around her sister tightly.

"I'll cast it for us, Justin," Agar said hugging his brother.

"Yes, that would be wise."

The blinding light of orange and purple filled the room. The Virabis threw the door open and screamed in rage. Her bloody arms reached forward for Justin as the light grew brighter. When they could see again, the chamber before them was the ruined remains of Arisdale. They all heaved a sigh of relief.

"That was incredible!" Katenna said in awe, her expression shifting to wide eyes and an open jaw as she glanced about the room. "What happened here?!"

"Katenna, that is a long story," Agar said in a solemn tone.

Justin paused and sniffed the air. It was evident from the look on Agar's face that he smelled it too, the familiar scent of Miral.

"She is here!" Justin said running out the chamber door.

Chapter 51 - Of Life

Justin followed Miral's scent to the main castle keep. Arisdale sat in an unusual, eerie silence that was profoundly unsettling. He expected mobs of mindless Arisdalians to come for them, but there was nothing. Dilos said he spared them the fate as slaves in exchange for doing Shadow's bidding; however, Dilos had failed her, and he prayed that his people were ok.

Justin paused in the hall. Miral's trail was coming from the throne room, but there was something else. "They made it back," Justin whispered to Agar.

The scent of Sara, Talos, Galena, Snow, Kedros, and various others were coming from the prison cells stairwell to the left. They must have resisted to Dilos's rule and the poor souls were locked away.

Agar nodded in acknowledgment. "I will get them out! I won't be much help to you against Miral. Water and I don't mix," he said with a frown. "I don't think you should be alone, though, you look beat. Kat, would you mind going with Justin to back him up?"

"Of course, I will!" Katenna replied with a nod.

"Very well. Take Artilone with you, Agar. We will keep the Goddess of the Dark busy while I try to free her. If I cannot . . ."

Agar patted Justin on the shoulder. "You can! We will be along to back you up if it proves to be too difficult! Go get started!" Agar said pushing him, then turned to run to the prison cells with Artilone.

Justin eased open the gilded doors to the throne room. Miral was standing in the light of the Silver Dolphins stained glass window with eyes closed. She no longer wore the beautiful blue and white gown but was dressed in a low-cut light suit of silver and blue armor with a long blue flowing open skirt, with a rectangular cloth hung from the silver and blue gem belt. Large ornate shoulder pads with blue ethereal orbs set in them sat atop her shoulders.

He looked at her shadow on the ground and to his dismay could see the Goddess of the Dark, her long spiked fingers around Miral's head. Tears filled his eyes. He fought back the painful sadness growing inside. "You cannot have her!" he bellowed.

Miral opened her eyes, they glowed the haunting red of a mind-controlled victim. "Far too late for that, dearest Justin," Shadow said in her own voice. "It's all thanks to you! The agony you cause this one is delicious."

"Gods no . . ." he whispered.

"Humans are so easily corrupted, and I would know," she said while pacing across the throne room. She stopped after a few steps and spun to face him with her hands outstretched in the air. "I made them that way, after all!"

Justin was taken aback. That could explain why humans are prone to misdeeds. He shook his head. No, that is not it at all. It was just another lie, another mind game. Miral has exceeded typical human behavior. In truth he didn't really know humans at all, none of them did. They never gave them a chance back then, and they were blamed immediately for Fandia's absence.

"They are my pawns, fuel for my power, nothing more!" She waved her hand in dismissal. "That includes your precious Miral," she said smiling, sitting on his throne. "How do I look sitting here? This is what you wanted, right?" she smirked.

"Miral is not your pawn!" Justin bellowed, his head feathers standing on end.

"Do you like it?" she asked gesturing to the armor along the length of her body. "I do, you see, she will be my new host. I do need to look my best!"

Justin's anger raged forth and the ground quaked in response to his fury.

Katenna grabbed his arm. "Justin, not now! Try your best, ok?"

"Oh my! You need to learn to control that!" Shadow scolded in a mocking tone. "Does this mean I made you angry? I'm sorry, dearest!" She stared at him a long while. "That anger, you reminded me of something from Miral's nightmares. What happened to her mother, that was all part of the plan!" she sneered.

"What the hell do you mean?!" Justin asked. He took deep breaths to calm himself, though that was proving difficult.

"I mean what I said! Her illness, the plague, dark gods are beyond your understanding, dearest. As their creator, I rule them all."

"Dark gods?" Katenna replied wide-eyed.

The idea was frightening and yet made sense. *Was there a god of pestilence? What is lurking in the World of the Dark, and what could they do?* Fandia must have protected the World of Life from the gods of darkness once, as there was never any written word of them.

"Since she is mine now, I would like to have you too! Won't you join my side, then you can still be with her, and I can torment you for eternity!" Shadow cackled.

"I will never stand by you! I will stop you!"

Miral stood and grasped a poleaxe that was resting beside the throne. It had a dolphin-like appearance to it. He wasn't sure how she had the strength to wield the massive weapon with ease.

"How do you plan on beating me? Miral never liked to fight!" Justin said taunting Shadow.

Shadow bellowed forth a long laugh in her own voice. "Beat you?" she scoffed. "That doesn't concern me! All I need to do is force you to push yourself to death, and wait as Miral slips further into darkness," she said with confidence. "You know that she is consciously watching this! How much pain do you think it will cause to see herself hurt you! Even after what you said to her, she clings to hope! Foolish girl!" she cackled.

Justin shuddered and looked to Shadow on the ground instead of Miral.

She laughed wickedly. "Yes! Hurt her more! I desire it! I know you enjoy pleasing me! You have done well with that so far!"

A realization that brought much relief flooded him. Shadow was careful with her words; however, it was evident she did not fully have control of Miral yet. There is still hope! Justin grinned at her. "You like to talk, perhaps too much."

Miral glowered at him in disbelief. "A smile?! Curse you!" Shadow said in her own voice launching a column of water at him.

Justin dodged the water with a flip to the right. The spell was the same one Miral cast on the ship. Upon landing, he stumbled and was hit with another blast of water. The force of the impact was intense and drove him into the wall behind him. He howled in agony as sharp pain radiated up his back. He fell to his hands and knees groaning. Miral's spells were likely more lethal from a distance given their nature. He had to close the gap and do so without using magic.

Katenna had moved in to distract her from the side; however, Shadow reacted to the assault with blazing speed and nailed Katenna with the same water spell. She was hurled back into the wall behind her. Kat didn't move.

"No!" Justin roared, forcing his aching body into a sprint. As he neared, a spout of water rose from under him launching him into the air. Justin recovered his balance, landing shakily on his feet, but nearly fell. Another column of water struck and he was thrown into the wall again. The pain that coursed through him was more intense than before, he dropped to his knees wheezing, and coughing blood.

"Ha, ha, ha! You're not looking so well!" Shadow cackled. "Keep pushing yourself, though!" she said beseeching him. "I was hopeful that you would have killed yourself from exertion by now! So, you won't use your magic, hmmm?" Miral paused and arched an eyebrow at him. "Oh, I see! You're hopeful that your companions will be along soon to help you!"

Justin forced his face to remain neutral, but inside felt dread at Shadow's taunt.

"Abandon that thought, dearest! They will be preoccupied for the foreseeable future. Your royal guards and soldiers are waiting for them. That weakling is out cold," she said pointing to Katenna. "It's just you and me now!" She smiled, kissing her hand, then blowing it to him.

Justin glared at Shadow, anger rising as his muscles tensed.

"Do you want to know what Miral is thinking right now?" Shadow taunted. "She believes you are trying to kill her! That is what I am showing her!"

He fought back rage, not wanting to lose himself or his magic. He had to act now or Miral would slip further away from being saved, and the World of Life would fall. If he died trying to save her, life would go on, he would just be replaced with another earth elemental. His life was meaningless in the big picture, and he would make that sacrifice for her if it came to that. Justin growled and renewed his efforts to close in on her. He listened carefully to every sound, drowning out the unnecessary. Focusing his nose, a slight change in humidity was detected. He launched into a forward flip, narrowly dodging the waterspout that erupted beneath him, and landed wearily fighting to stabilize himself.

Shadow swung the poleaxe in an arc at him as he came in range, cutting into his side. Justin winced, blood staining his blue vest once more. He threw his hands out to repel the poleaxe, but the spell did not work. Shadow blasted him with water. Justin drove claws into the ground to stop himself before hitting the wall again.

He focused on her. Miral was not a fit woman and Shadow was having difficulty getting her body to move as fluidly as she had with Snow. All he needed was to be wary of her magic. Justin charged at her once more casting his earth shield; it no longer mattered. She had to be stopped at all costs. Shadow cast a column of water at him. He dodged the attack shifting his course to the right. She swung the poleaxe at him again, but the earth shield stopped it. He grabbed hold of the poleaxe and forced it from Miral's weaker grasp. Once in his hands, it dissolved into water, trickling to the ground. He tackled Miral, protectively holding the back of her head as they hit the ground together. He pinned her arms and legs down with his own.

"He, he, he! Well, isn't this fun! What will you do now?"

Justin's eyes flooded with tears. "Miral, I know you are there, I need you to hear me. The real me, not the illusion she showed you!"

Miral squirmed to break free from him. "You are wasting your time! She doesn't want to listen to you!" Shadow hissed.

Justin ignored her and moved in closer to Miral's face, the end of his muzzle by her ear. "Miral, you are the brightest light in my life, and I am sorry for waiting so long to tell you this . . ."

"You do this and I will kill her!" Shadow raged.

"I love you, Miral! I need you here with me!"

Shadow screamed and Miral's face twisted in shock and disgust before relaxing, her eyes resting closed. Tears shone on her face and streamed down as her eyes fluttered open.

Justin looked deep into the beautiful blue eyes he loved so much, fighting back sobs of joy. He lifted her off the floor and embraced her tightly. "Miral!"

"Justin!" Miral replied, crying in relieved sobs.

He felt something strike him on the head from behind, and his vision flooded with darkness.

Chapter 52 - Of Love

Miral watched breathlessly as Justin fell to his side and reached out for him. "Justin?! What have you done, Dilos?!"

"Get up!" he demanded, grabbing hold of Miral, wrenching her off the ground and bound her hands together in front of her. He pushed her forward to the throne. "I have been given a chance at redemption." Dilos reached to the lantern on the wall behind the throne. He pulled on it and part of the wall slid back. He shoved her through the doorway down a dark hall. "'Tis all your fault!" Dilos sneered.

"What is?"

"Razamarea, she deserves to be treated better than she has," Dilos said. "If she did not get so focused on . . . him!" Dilos growled with indignation.

"You love her?!" Miral replied in shock. "Why did you never tell her?"

"Do not dare preach to me, human!" Dilos snapped shoving her forward.

She stumbled but caught herself before she could fall. "Why . . . why do you hate humans so much?" Miral cried.

"Because human bandits killed my sister! I saw them laughing while they hurt her, and I could do nothing!" Dilos growled shoving her forward again.

"I am sorry!" Miral cried. "I truly am."

"This tunnel was built to allow the royal family to escape to the cliffs if the castle was besieged. Now it will serve another purpose," Dilos said ignoring her and pulling on another lantern at the end of the hall, which slid back to reveal the backside of Arisdale castle, and the edge of the towering cliffs it sat upon. The cold wind of winter gusted past and made her shiver in her new skimpy armor.

Dilos shoved her forward again. "You are broken now. Shadow no longer has any use for you!" he said guiding her to the cliff edge. "She promised Justin that if he told you how he felt, she would kill you."

Miral trembled in fear, she felt dizzy looking down to the rocky sea below. "Pray no, no!"

"Sure, I could end your misery quickly and cut that wretched human head from your body, but it seems fitting to watch you fall in terror into the sea you came from!" he said shoving her off the cliff.

Miral screamed in pure terror. She squeezed her eyes closed tight, not wanting to see the ocean rush towards her. It was a long way down to the sea from the cliffs, and she wondered how it could end this way. Justin confessed that he loved her, and she knew in her heart he did all this time, but she needed to hear the words from him. Were they never meant to be together? She cried in agony as she fell. She didn't know if magic would help her now. Shadow taught her to use it, but she was certain she saw spiky columns of rock in the sea below when she first arrived in Arisdale.

Miral stopped crying when she felt a force tug on her, abruptly stopping her fall. Then she felt the odd sensation of being pulled upward by her armor. Her back collided with something that wrapped her in an embrace. She felt gravity shift around her followed by the sensation of falling once more. Her eyes flew open. She was no longer falling face down and could see the sky above her. A blue and gold cape whipped wildly in the wind around her, and the feeling of soft leathery-scaled skin touched the side of her face.

"Justin!"

"I am here, my love," Justin said.

She felt his energies flowing around them, and their descent slowed, causing them to drift down like a feather on the wind. She cried with relief and kissed him tenderly on the side of his face. He worked with his claws at freeing the rope tied around her wrists.

"How did you . . .?" she barely managed over her sobs.

"I was moments away from stopping Dilos from pushing you. I used your armor to stop your fall and pull you up to me. Now I am drawing on the magic of the cliff rocks to slow our fall."

"What do we do now?"

"We need to combine our powers," he replied. "You thicken the water around us to slow our fall through it, if possible, ok?"

"Mmm, ok," she said.

"You can do this, Miral! I believe in you!"

Miral smiled, she could do this. She understood how it worked now.

"I am going to shatter the rocks beneath us like I did at the inn, but it will take much effort," Justin said sounding weary.

"Are you going to be all right?" Miral asked.

"We have not come all this way for nothing, my love!"

"I love you, Justin!" Miral cried.

"I love you, Miral!" Justin replied. "Now focus!"

She focused her mind on softening the waters. She could feel the ocean responding to her will, straining her muscles. She drew from the massive ethereal crystals on her armor to lessen the fatigue of the large spell.

"Hold your breath, now!" Justin commanded.

He released his spell and they fell faster, hitting the surface with a crack, and descended through the icy cold water. She focused her mind and could feel them slow as her energies churned around them. She sensed the intense pulses of magic emanating from Justin, pulverizing the sharp towering columns of rock beneath them into dust.

Once they slowed considerably, Justin kicked and paddled through the water holding her with his left arm around her waist. They breached the surface gasping for air and waded back to shore. With great effort she pulled her trembling, waterlogged body onto land. Justin struggled to walk on the wet sand and stumbled forward, knocking her down with him. She was momentarily jarred by the fall, but grateful that he caught her before she hit the ground face first.

"Sorry, Miral," he said, laughing lightly and letting go of her.

She rolled over onto her back, shivering as she lay in the cold, damp sand beneath him and giggled. "That's ok Justin!" She gasped, "Your crystals! You had to overdraw them! Are you all right?!"

"Oh, indeed they are shattered. I feel fine, love, truly," he said.

Miral looked longingly into his sunny eyes, she felt herself blushing intensely, her heart beating fast. Justin was looking at her the same way. He loved her, and she loved him. Their life together since Delphi had been an incredible journey, and now she, a common human woman, had found love with an elder race king. She wanted to share an intimate moment with him, and any kind would do. To be able to kiss or not, that didn't matter, she still loved him more than life itself. She reached up to his face, cupping her hands behind his jaw, and pulled downwards gently. She closed her eyes as his muzzle neared her lips. She could feel a warm fire burning inside her, taking away the cold. She waited patiently for the touch, but none came. Concerned, she opened her eyes to look at him. Justin's eyes were closed, and he wasn't moving. She saw his beautiful inner light go out in her mind, and a wave of grief rolled through her chest.

"Justin?!"

She watched in horror as he fell limply to his side onto the damp sand and lay still.

"Justin?!" Miral cried. She scrambled to him, an ache in her heart, tension choking her throat. *He isn't breathing!* She laid her head on his chest to listen for his heartbeat, but the beautiful rhythm of life was no longer playing within. She felt her body trembling violently, tears painfully flooding her eyes. "Pray love, breathe!" she pleaded, desperately waiting for him to take a breath. Nothing, only crashing waves and the cries of birds could be heard. "Justin?! No! You can't leave me! Not now!" she cried, clinging to him. "Not like this!"

He had pushed himself hard to save her, and now his body had given up, the effort too much to bear. *It's my fault! Why did I allow the Goddess of the Dark to trick me and why did I ever doubt him?! If I were not afraid, if I fought back against Dilos, then you would be alive now!* "Love . . . love . . . come back to me!" She laid herself beside him, holding him tightly. Denial flooding her mind, her body, unwilling to move.

Chapter 53 - World of Light

"Miral?" Justin called as he looked over the unfamiliar field of flowers he stood in. The air was comfortably warm and fragrant, and the feeling of inner peace was profound. "Miral?! Where am I?!"

A bright light appeared and grew closer to him, slowly taking the shape and form of a being, one that looked remarkably similar to the Goddess Fandia, only he had pure white skin and light blue sparkling hair. His face bore soft, yet handsome features and he smiled.

"Justin, I am Aurorus, God of the Heavens, Keeper of the World of Light."

Justin's heart sank with a heavy weight as he looked down at the shorter man. Tears flooded his golden eyes. "I have passed?!" he replied with disbelief.

Aurorus nodded. "You have. Come with me, there are others who wish to see you."

He lifted his brows. "Others? My parents, Yarway, everyone who has passed?"

Aurorus smiled gesturing for him to follow, leading him to a city of white buildings; a shimmering fountain sat at the center with benches around it. People of all sorts were laughing and enjoying lives in the World of Light.

"There is no end, only new beginnings," Justin muttered quietly to himself. He wasn't ready to be here, though, there was so much he wished to do, to feel. He took his sorrowful eyes from the people in the town center and focused ahead. They were approaching a large temple with finely dressed guards standing at attention. Justin wondered what need a god would have for guards in the World of Light. The thought that the eternal rest could be disturbed with troubles was discomforting.

Within the grand temple of pillars and silver metals, Justin faced his family, the fallen guards, and one other familiar man, Yarlin, among the crowd of other faces in the temple.

"Justin!" Anelda chirped as she ran to hug her son.

"Mother," Justin replied in tears, embracing her tightly. "Oh, how I missed you so."

"I know, Justin. We missed you too, and we have been watching over you." She stepped back for Johanas when he approached.

"Father," Justin said with a bow of his head, "I pray I have made you proud in my short reign."

Johanas wrapped his son in a tender hug. "You have, Justin. I am certain you will continue to make me proud."

"What do you mean, Father?"

"Young King," called an Arisdalian Velociraptor who approached him with a proud strut. He resembled his father and himself, though his eyes were a dark blue. "I am Mishiku Arisdale. I wish to extend my gratitude for all you have done and will no doubt continue to do for our home and world. You have the appreciation of all former kings," he said gesturing to the crowd of people.

Justin looked at them all, his grandfather, Roryian, the first king, Hardaric, all were there.

"For honor, faith, justice and love," they said with a salute.

Justin smiled and returned the salute. "I am greatly honored."

To be hailed by the former kings of Arisdale and addressed by his great-grandfather, the one who began the process of change by freeing the humans from slavery, was a joy to be treasured.

"Justin," Yarway said with a grin and a nod. He gestured to his right, where his wife and children stood.

Justin wore a broad smile at them all. "My friend, I am glad you have found your peace. 'Tis a pleasure to meet your lovely family."

"I'm glad you found yours," he replied with a wink.

"Uh, had, yes." Justin stared blankly a moment before turning his gaze to Yarlin when he approached.

"King Justin," Yarlin said with a bow. The blonde-haired woman beside him who looked remarkably like Miral in her features curtsied. "I want to thank you for trying to save me, but more so for protecting our daughter, and for loving her. There is no one I would be prouder of seeing her with than you."

"You have changed how we see your kind, King of Arisdale," Sonya said in a soft and songlike voice. A voice that reminded him of Miral as much as her smile did. "You're a man of honor, compassion, and we are moved by your love for her."

"The Lady Miral is a grand choice for a queen, my son," Johanas said patting him on the back. "Your desperate search for the perfect mate frightened me, but in doing so, you found the one that will not only change the world, but will also be the best for you in your struggle for inner peace."

"You have the blessings of everyone present, my son," Anelda added with a warm smile.

"Your blessings?" Justin smiled wide but then frowned. "I am here now. How will I—"

Aurorus approached and touched his shoulder. "Justin, I need you to listen. Can you hear the song?"

"The song?" he replied quizzically, quieting his mind and searching for this so-called melody.

Chapter 54 - Miracles

Miral heard footsteps crunching on the grains of sands behind her. She trembled in fear, praying silently that it wasn't Dilos or Shadow, but then again, she didn't want to live without Justin. She laid her head against his chest once more and clung to him, she didn't want to see who it was.

A brown-furred hand entered her field of view and touched Justin's head. "He has a lot left to do!"

Miral jerked her head up and stared right into the aqua eyes of a Glenn Woods wolf. She blinked, tears forming anew. "Andeos?" she cried throwing herself into his arms sobbing.

Andeos embraced her back. "The Goddess of the Dark knew he would fight hard for you, thus she pushed him to this. She believed she would have broken you by the time his body failed. We prayed it wouldn't come to that."

"Why did she want to break me?" Miral cried.

"You will know the answer soon enough."

Miral heard someone else approaching and looked to see who it was. A woman wearing a white dress, pink scarf belt, gossamer sleeves that hung from gold cuffs around her arms, gold collar with aqua ethereal gems, and Egyptian-looking headdress, kneeled in the sand in front of Justin. She was beautiful and radiant, and human. Her long white hair and two long pink-colored sections in front of her ears sparkled in the sunlight.

"I am Isis, the Goddess of Holy," she said embracing Miral. "Aurorus, the God of the Heavens, sent me. He said the Silver Dolphins called to him, beseeching our aid." She released Miral and stroked Justin tenderly across his matted, wet head feathers. "It is not yet his time to be in the World of Light."

"Goddess of Holy, you can . . . bring him back?" Miral said between tear-soaked breaths.

Isis looked at her with gleaming pink eyes and smiled. "Only when it's not a soul's time to leave the World of Life, and if they are worthy," she replied. "In his case, both are true."

Miral smiled, taking breaths to calm her tears.

Isis closed her eyes. Large glowing aqua wings shot out from her back as she sang a beautiful song. The ethereal tune was enchanting, and her voice unlike any she had ever heard. Miral watched with wide-eyed wonder as she sang, eager for Justin to open his beautiful golden eyes again.

"I am a being of light. Hear my cry, follow the guiding light. The World of Life and Love waits for you, return to life and love."

With the end of her song, her wings shot forward wrapping Justin in an embrace. The wings detached from her back and began to sink into his body until they were gone.

Isis smiled warmly at Justin. "Wake up, dear!" she cooed.

Justin's eyes flew open in shock and he drew a long breath. He turned his head to Miral, tears misting his eyes.

"Justin!" Miral cried with joy, throwing herself onto him, clutching him tightly.

"Mi-Miral!" Justin cried embracing her, burying his muzzle into her hair.

"Love," Miral replied.

"Welcome back!" Andeos replied with a grin.

Justin smiled at Andeos and turned his gaze to Isis. He reached his hand out to hers. "Thank you, Goddess Isis!"

"You're welcome, Justin! However, your thanks are not only for me. The Silver Dolphins pleaded for your life. That has never happened before," the goddess said shaking her head.

Andeos nodded. "It is strange. As I said before they are emotionless, but they have shown emotion toward you for the second time!"

"The second time?" Miral asked as she tenderly brushed away the moist sand that clung to the right side of Justin's face.

Andeos nodded. "Yes, but that is not for me to—" Andeos stopped himself and smiled at Justin. "Sorry, I know you are tired of hearing that."

"That is all right," Justin said straining to push himself upright with Miral's help.

Isis embraced him tightly once he got to his feet. "I am happy to have been able to save you!"

"I am grateful," Justin replied returning the hug. He glanced at Miral who was staring blankly into the distance. "Miral? Pray, what are you looking at?"

"Do you hear that?" Miral asked him, listening intently inside her mind. "Sounds like dolphins."

"I do hear them now," he replied, shifting his gaze to Andeos.

"It is time!" Andeos affirmed with a nod. "I will lend you some of my strength. You will be able to rest in safety once you arrive at your destination," Andeos said placing a hand on Justin's shoulder, restoring some of his power and energy by giving his own. "Now then I'll take you both top side." Andeos closed his eyes and gathered sea rocks into a platform. "Hop on!"

Chapter 55 - The Call

Sara glanced about the throne room. Agar and Galena were tending to Katenna, who they found unconscious. She gathered up her waist-long hair and cut it short. Two years lost so far, she thought.

Justin and Miral were no longer here and the room displayed signs of battle. The floor and red carpet were soaked with water. Blood lay near the right wall and close to the throne. Sara knew something dire had occurred. Shadow had set the perfect trap again.

The secret door behind the throne was open, but no one was outside. They felt a wave of grief wash over them, and could see in their mind's eye a light that went out. She felt it for herself the day Yarway died. The feeling was the same. Justin and Miral were the only ones not present; it had to be one of them.

The light returned in time, grief disappearing with it. She hoped the original feeling was a fluke and they were both all right. Sara paused and scrunched her face when she heard the sound of a dolphin. "Do you hear that?"

"Hear what, hun? You going mad on me?" Talos asked.

"Talos!" Sara bellowed, smacking him on the backside of his head.

"I don't hear it either, Talos," Artilone replied.

"I hear it!" Katenna said. She looked around at the other elementals. "Looks like we all do!"

"'Tis coming from outside," Galena said heading out of the throne room.

They followed the sound to the teleport chamber and went inside. They stood in awe and shared stares of confusion among each other.

"That figures!" Sara said staring at the ceiling.

From the Silver Dolphins in the center shone a bright white light and it was pulsing.

"What in the world is this?" Snow asked with her hand over her mouth.

"The call!" Andeos replied walking into the chamber behind them.

Delphia squeaked happily and hopped across the floor to Justin and Miral. Miral picked her up and cuddled her hard, giving her kisses on her soft furry head.

"Justin! Miral!" Galena cried, running to embrace them in a big hug. "Oh, I am so happy to see you, but why are you soaking wet? What are you wearing, dear?" she asked looking at Miral. "You did not . . . the cliffs!" Galena said with her hand over her heart.

"Ah-ha, well, that is a long story. I promise to tell you all later. Right now we have somewhere to be," Justin said pointing at the pulsing light.

"Miral, I'm so sorry for what she made me do to you!" Katenna said reaching to hug her.

"Thank you, Katenna! You don't have to be sorry, though!"

"You all right, brother?" Agar whispered to Justin. "You were so tired and I was worried when we couldn't find you. I could have sworn your light went out. Galena was frightened to death, we all felt it!"

"I am more than all right now, Agar!" Justin said smiling at Miral.

Miral blushed, smiling back at him.

"Ah, I see! It's about time!" Agar said jabbing Justin on the shoulder. "We are family for real now!" Agar hugged Miral tightly.

"What's going on over there?" Sara asked arching an eyebrow and squinting her eyes.

"Oh, nothing important, Sara!" Agar said grinning, which caused Sara to narrow her eyes at him.

"Anything special we have to do this time or is it the same old deal?" Sara asked Andeos.

"Just take your places and focus as a group this time," Andeos said. "Talos and Artilone, I'm afraid you won't be able to go along. They must face the Goddess of the Dark soon."

Sara stared blankly at Andeos and nodded. "I guess it's goodbye for now, my love," Sara said to Talos.

"Getting soft on me now, hmmm?" he joked.

"Oh you!" Sara said burying her face in his chest.

Talos embraced her tightly. "Don't you dare overdo yourself, you hear? Come back to me, sweetheart!" he said as his eyes misted with tears. They shared a tender kiss, and Sara took her place under fire.

The kiss made Miral's heart long. They had not yet shared a kiss. Fate had been in the way every time.

"Bye, sis," Katenna said hugging Artilone.

"I believe in you, Kat! You're going to come back!" Artilone replied with a sniffle.

"You know it!" Katenna nodded firmly.

Talos approached Justin and Miral and she handed Delphia to him.

"We'll be back, ok! Stay with Talos, and be a good girl!" Miral said kissing her on the head.

"See you later, Delphia," Justin said petting her.

Delphia squeaked sadly at them.

Talos headed towards Andeos and Artilone and turned back to wave farewell. "Good journey, friends!"

"Farewell!" Artilone said with a firm wave.

They each took their place under their element. Sara glanced to Miral along with Justin and noticed her expression had shifted to neutral visage.

"Miral? Are you all right?" Justin asked her concerned.

"Together we are one!" Miral said in the two voices.

"Is that the voices from the chamber?" Sara asked Justin.

"Indeed. Those are the same voices," he replied.

Miral smiled brightly. "I heard them again! They stopped speaking to me after she took me."

"You will soon learn of who the voices belong to, Miral," Andeos said. "I am glad they are speaking once more."

Each elemental cast the teleport spell, and they were bathed in a warm blinding light.

"Good journey and best of luck to you!" Andeos said, and then they were gone.

Chapter 56 - Light

The room that materialized before them was unlike any other teleport chamber. They stood with mouths agape at the surreal sight.

"Are we . . . under the ocean?!" Snow asked in a wavering tone, clinging to Kedros and causing him to wear a silly smile.

Sara looked positively terrified about being underneath the sea. She cautiously approached the large window looking up and jumped back when a large eerie looking fish swam by. Miral ran over beside Sara to look out the window. Rainbow-colored fish swam past the glass dome, and seaweed danced to the rhythm of the flow. "It's so beautiful!"

Justin stood next to Miral and wrapped his arm around her. "Well, I'll be!" he smiled. "How is this possible?"

"Anything is possible here," spoke a soft, loving voice.

The elementals spun to look behind them and stood rigidly transfixed at the beautiful woman who approached.

"Fandia!" they all said in unison.

"Welcome, my children!" she said, tears filling her eyes.

Fandia was more elegant in person than she appeared in the murals. Miral could feel her warm radiant light, and all negative emotions vanished from her heart and mind. Fandia's movements were graceful and she seemed to float more than walk with each step. Her revealing two-piece pearl gown flowed as if blown by the wind. She wore a large pearl bivalve helmet with ethereal gems that shone with rainbow lights. She was truly enchanting to behold.

Fandia tenderly embraced each of them. "I haven't seen another soul besides sea life out my window in over two thousand years," she said tears spilling from her sorrowful eyes.

"Why? What happened?" Miral asked.

Fandia smiled warmly at her. "I will tell you, but first—" she said approaching Justin to embrace him, "you need to rest, dear. The strength Andeos gave you will not last much longer. We simply cannot have you die again. Come with me," she said pushing him.

"D . . . die?" Galena sputtered. "By the heavens, what do you mean?!"

"I will explain when I return," Fandia said.

Miral stood with hands clasped in front of her watching Fandia push Justin forward. Fandia reached back with her free hand and grabbed hold of her arm, pulling her along.

"You too, Miral."

Fandia led Justin and Miral into a large circular room; in the center was a bed that appeared to be made of clouds. Fandia raised her arms in the air and glowed with a warm light. She turned to them holding two goblets in her hands. She handed one to each of them. Miral stared at the glowing blue liquid in the cups.

"Drink this. The waters of light will renew and heal you quickly," Fandia said.

Justin and Miral did as she asked, drinking down the fresh liquid, and Fandia then cast a warm light over them.

Miral felt warmth rush through her, drying damp hair and clothing. She looked over to Justin. He was no longer damp either, but appeared to be feeling the opposite of her, and looked ready to pass out. Fandia guided him to the bed.

"Rest, dear. Time flows differently in my domain. For every hour that passes in the World of Life, a day goes by here. Leave your worries behind."

Justin flopped down on the bed and lay on his left side. "Thank you," he said.

Fandia turned to her and smiled. "You may stay here with him or return to the others with me; however, I advise you to rest. Shadow was not kind to you."

"Fandia, the nightmares . . ." Miral said trembling.

"Worry not, Miral. The drink has cleansed your heart, soul, and mind. They will haunt you no longer."

"Thank you, Fandia!" Miral cried.

"Of course, dear. Though, you do need to learn how not to listen to fear, and not have a conversation with it. That is how Shadow digs herself in. The more you wrestle with her, the deeper she can go. When you chose not to listen or believe in what is said or shown, you will free your mind. Rest now," Fandia said walking past her and out of the room.

She took note of what Fandia advised; she would need it for the days ahead, then turned to watch Justin breathing deeply on the bed. He was sound asleep already. She removed the large shoulder armor and boots, then moved to the opposite side of the bed and crawled close to him. She had never seen him sleeping before and watched intently. He was beautiful even in rest. She ran her hand through his head feathers, curious to know what they felt like. They were soft and tickled her hand making her giggle. She settled down to lie on her back. The bed was as comfortable as it looked, and she fell fast asleep.

"They're both asleep now," Fandia said smiling to the elementals. She raised her hands and a table with goblets of glowing water appeared before her.

"Drink, the waters will restore your strength," Fandia said gesturing to the goblets.

They stood with stunned looks on their faces before reaching down taking a cup and drinking the glowing liquid.

"Wow, it's incredible!" Sara exclaimed.

Fandia raised her hands once more and chairs appeared. "Please sit if you wish. Katenna and Snow, as I just explained to Miral, the drinks will remove the nightmares Shadow implanted in your minds."

Snow's head jerked up. "Really?!"

Katenna smiled. "Thank you, Fandia!" She glanced to Agar, who was wearing a broad smile.

"So that you are aware, I can safely speak her name, and I will do so for clarity," Fandia said before turning to Galena. "About Justin. Shadow has a desire to make him suffer, because of his nature. He has a mind so powerful that she struggled to touch it. This angered her greatly. She does not like being denied what she wants, and what she wanted was to control him. She can only feel desire, not love, and she wants him because he resists her. Shadow has been pushing Justin hard since she attacked him in the chamber. She enjoys the torment he has to endure physically and mentally. She wants to take Justin's soul to the

World of the Dark so she can make him suffer for eternity. This is how she expresses love."

Galena gasped and covered her mouth.

"That is horrible!" Katenna said outraged.

Fandia nodded. "That is her being. Limitations are what drive her to act as she does."

"That's why she wanted to put on the execution show!" Agar said.

"Execution?!" Galena replied in shock. "My poor old heart, Agar! Pray, be more graceful with your words."

Agar smiled at her and shrugged.

Fandia nodded to Agar. "Yes, she enjoys making a dramatic scene, and because Justin will not let her in his mind, she tried what she could to get in. She pushed to keep him on his feet with no rest with the intention of watching him die from the effort or let her in," Fandia said in a lowered tone. "Justin fought to save Miral from her control and had to use magic. Then he had to keep her from falling to her death from the cliffs of Arisdale. The force required to protect them from the fall far exceeded what his body and the gems had left to offer."

Galena cried. "Oh, that poor boy!"

Fandia raised her hands in the air. "The Silver Dolphins cried out for his soul asking the God of the Heavens to spare him and return him to life. The God Aurorus sent Goddess Isis to return Justin's soul to his body. This can only be done when a soul is not yet to depart from the World of Life and deemed worthy to return."

"Oh, the Silver Dolphins and the gods be praised!" Galena cried out.

Sara tapped her fist to her chin. "Who is God Aurorus? I never heard of him before."

"I will answer that when they awaken, Sara," Fandia said with a nod. "In the meantime, you may ask me any questions unrelated to your current situation."

Miral stirred and slowly opened her eyes. She saw Justin's hand resting beside her head. He had his arm draped over her. She blushed, her back was pressed close to him. She wasn't sure how she wound up this way. She must have done so in her sleep. She also didn't know if he was awake and was afraid to disturb him by turning to find out. She loved the feeling of his warmth against her, she felt protected. She wanted this moment to last, just like she wished their dance could have gone on forever.

She gently placed her small hand on top of his and thought of how blessed she was to have him love her. She wondered if there was a future for them. Could they beat Shadow and live the rest of their lives together? Could they have children? What would they look like? Her thoughts were interrupted when she felt Justin move his hand beside her bracing his weight as he lifted his upper body. She turned her head to look at him and her lips met his muzzle. She was momentarily surprised by the unexpected contact. She felt his warm tongue gently and playfully tickling her lips, making her giggle. She parted her lips and pressed her mouth against his muzzle. She felt on fire and loved the sensation as their tongues met, and they kissed for the first time.

Chapter 57 - Truth

"Do you think the elder races will ever find a way to live in peace with humans?" Sara asked Fandia.

"I wish for this, Sara. I do believe that Justin and Miral will be able to make this happen."

Galena clasped her hands together and smiled. "They love each other, do they not?"

"Undoubtedly!" Agar said. "He told me he did!"

"Why the hell was he so quiet about it then?" Sara asked.

"The Goddess of the Dark told him she would kill Miral if he ever told her how he felt, or told us he loved Miral and why he couldn't tell her," Agar said. He paused and rubbed his head, grinning wide. "That made sense, right?"

Galena covered her mouth. "What?! How awful! No wonder he has been so moody."

"Aye, he was trying to keep his distance," Agar nodded. "Justin said she attacked the inn because he screwed up and almost kissed her."

Sara arched an eyebrow and flailed her hands about. "Wait! When did this almost happen?"

"When Snow here was dancing!" Agar said pointing at Snow. "Which I am eager to see, by the way!" he winked.

"Thank you, Agar!" Snow said blushing.

"Why would she kill Miral if Justin confessed his feelings?" Kedros asked.

"The whole reason will come to light soon," Fandia replied. "As you all know, Miral has something Shadow wants. To get it Miral's soul must fall to darkness. If Miral is filled with the light of Justin's love, Shadow will lose the ability to corrupt her. Justin needed to confess his feelings for that light to take root, it isn't enough that she thought he did. The power Miral has will pass to another if she dies. Then Shadow may start over with corrupting the child that gained that power."

"A child?!" Galena gasped. "Blessed light!"

"That will never come to pass!" Justin's deep voice rang out from behind them.

"Did you sleep well, dear?" Galena asked smiling at Justin, who walked with his arm protectively around Miral.

"I feel fantastic!"

Agar raised a suspicious eyebrow at Justin's goofy grin. "Well, glad you're in better spirits, brother!" Agar said winking at him.

"Hmm? Did I miss something?" Galena asked.

Justin ran his hand through his head feathers. "Ah ha! No, no, nothing at all."

Fandia stood. "If you are ready, I shall proceed with my explanation."

"We are," Justin replied, taking a seat.

Miral moved to sit in the chair next to him, but Justin pulled her onto his lap and embraced her. She blushed and giggled.

Fandia smiled at them and nodded. "To understand what is happening, you need to know how it all began," Fandia said. "Upon the creation of a planet by its core, its heart, gods of light and dark are also created to oversee the natural order of things. The Silver Dolphins are the heart of this world, and they created me to be a physical representation of their form. I was born to uphold the light of the world, and all other gods of light answer to me," Fandia said with arms wide. "Where there is light, there is also dark, and my shadow was born into the world. She preferred the irony of the name and kept it. She commands the gods of dark, who live in the World of Dark. She was devious then, but she did her role without question, and never tried to usurp me." Fandia looked downward and frowned. "That is until Andeos," Fandia said. "I fell in love with him."

"Gods are permitted to love each other?" Sara asked.

"They may love whomever they wish, but it's dangerous," Fandia replied. "Unity of a god and goddess can bring forth new gods. A god who beds a mortal creates a demi-god of which there are none at this time. The powers they possess can disturb the balance, too many hands manipulating the natural order of things."

"Like that God of Chaos!" Sara grumbled.

Fandia nodded with a frown. "Yes. Seth's parents are gods. He is often the only source of trouble for you, though."

Sara fumed to herself.

"Why is he chaos? Has he done anything that I'm not aware of?" Katenna asked.

"That is a long story, Katenna. Best saved for another time. He cannot do anything harmful as he is now, though."

Katenna nodded her understanding.

"Shadow was jealous of me," Fandia continued, "and felt she deserved love for herself. She approached me about her upset. She was angered that there were no means of giving her what she wanted, and she reached into my heart seeking to take the Silver Dolphins for herself." Fandia looked downward again. "I . . . was with child when she attacked me, a boy," Fandia said with tears in her eyes.

They all sat silent, allowing Fandia to continue without interruption.

"When Shadow touched me, her darkness entered in. I am of pure light! Darkness cannot live within me, and so it went where it could go, to my child. The power tore the child into two beings. Aurorus is a being of pure light as I am. He resides over the heavens in the World of Light." Fandia's visage darkened, as much as her pure soul could manage. She cried, "The other child." She composed herself, stifling her tears. "To understand what happened to him, you need to know that a being created from light cannot exist in peace without light. When the children were split in two, all the light went to Aurorus, leaving the other with nothing but darkness. He is insane from the lack of light, and he is the keeper to the gateway into the World of Dark," she said sounding remorseful. "The Silver Dolphins took my children from me when the darkness reached them, assigned them these roles, and set them to the realm as fail-safes to the World of Life, should it fall to one side or the other."

"Who is the other child?" Justin asked her.

Fandia breathed in deeply before replying. "The God of Time."

"No way! A mad god is in control of the flow of time?!" Sara asked.

Fandia nodded. "I am sorry . . ." she cried. "It's as I said, too dangerous for gods to partake of love."

Miral felt heartbroken for Fandia. Why did love always seem to have a price? "It's all right, you couldn't have known she would attack you and that this would happen. We must make the best of what we are given. Right?" Miral said.

Justin hugged her tightly in response.

"Thank you, Miral. You're right." Fandia composed herself. "He has been locked away somewhere by the Silver Dolphins to protect the World of Life. Although, I fear that he may be helping Shadow."

"Is that why she always seemed to know exactly where we would be and what to do?" Justin asked.

"That would be the reason. She isn't capable of knowing more than she can get from those she controls or from those who say her name. Shadow and I were both sealed away as well to protect each of us from each other. She could only rise to the World of Life now if my son found a way to help her," Fandia said frowning. "He must know the events as they would occur and directed her to do as she has; however, his goal is unclear to me. I know he wants freedom, and he needs the Silver Dolphins to allow it, but there are too many contradictions. Shadow is not one to take orders either. Therefore, the truth is hard to ascertain."

"That makes sense," Katenna said. "She took over my mind before I was aware that I was the Elemental of Wind. She told me that I was."

Fandia nodded. "This is troubling," she said closing her eyes and breathing deeply. "For your protection, I must make you aware of his name," Fandia said, and a parchment appeared before her. Gesturing with her hand through the air a name appeared on the paper before them. "Never speak it, never write it! Leave it only ever in your mind." Fandia said, and the paper vanished. "Destroy any written words you find and end all conversations. The more he knows, the more power he gains. As Andcos told you."

Miral flushed. "That name! He was the author of the 'Truth of Times'!"

Fandia nodded. "Andeos warned me of the book. He is spreading awareness, and at the same time that gave Shadow minds to feed off of and gain power from," she sighed. "We don't know how he got that book to the World of Life, though."

"Little can be done about that now, though we will be mindful," Justin said.

Fandia nodded to him. "Shadow must be returned to her prison. To rise to your world, she needs to feed off negativity and darkness of people's hearts. If she succeeds in entering the World of Life, she will open the seal to the World of Dark, and he will be free, along with the other dark gods and god killers. Not that life has a chance of being as you know it under Shadow's control, but I don't know what my son's madness would do to the World of Life."

"This is grave news," Kedros said shuddering.

"We will not fail!" Justin said to his friends and family. They all nodded to him.

"Fandia, what were the fail-safes that . . . failed?" Sara asked.

"The Silver Dolphins placed protections from imbalance. The first was Shadow and I being sealed away. Shadow is breaking free, and it has failed. The second fail-safe is called on when either light or dark become imbalanced. The Silver Dolphins send a being from the World of Light, known as a Lightress to the World of Life when darkness is too strong. The being is sent into an area where dark energy is concentrated. The soul of the Lightress is pure, and their very aura can pacify people near them unaware that she has quelled negativity within them. She has healing energies, can restore life, and her voice can calm and soothe, heal and purify. When they sing, the effect is magnified. They are an extension of me when I cannot be present."

"What happened to the Lightress?" Snow asked.

"She never came," Fandia said shaking her head.

"Never came? Why?" Galena asked.

"The Silver Dolphins insisted that they sent her and that her name is Tikal, but neither Andeos nor I could sense her. Andeos and the other gods searched for her everywhere darkness was massing and could find nothing. I don't know what became of her."

"I don't like the sound of that!" Agar said.

"Tikal," Justin said rubbing his chin. A being whose soul is of pure light. He wondered what could have happened to the woman. Shadow may have found her through the God of Time. He shuddered at the thought. "Is there an opposite to the Lightress?"

"Yes, the Darktress from the World of Dark. All is ever in balance. Light has yet to exceed dark. I would never tip the scales," Fandia said. "The other fail-safe is as Andeos said, you are all that stands in her path. The Silver Dolphins need your combined light to send her back. They can't generate enough on their own."

"What of Miral, why has she been her focus?" Justin asked hugging her tightly.

Fandia smiled and approached Justin and Miral. "Shadow cannot touch the Silver Dolphins because they are of light and dark, and yet of neither light nor dark and as such they are capable of killing gods, as they will. Shadow presumed she would be able to pull them from me; however, in doing so, she was injured by the light within me and by them in defense. They will not kill her nor me, as the World of Life will fail without us, and thus Shadow has been sealed away for disrupting the balance. She seeks the Silver Dolphins once more and to have them, she must corrupt them as they will not go to her willingly. To do so, she must corrupt and control the host they live in. When corrupted, the Silver Dolphins will tarnish to black, and the blue heart will bleed and turn red."

Miral felt flushed with Fandia's words. She knew Justin was anxious too as he was squeezing her tighter in his arms.

"In my absence, the Silver Dolphins hid within the hearts of humans. As Shadow's creations, they could hide behind the mask of darkness within them, but they sought to aid humanity at the same time. For every heart they lived in, that soul became more of light. Over the one thousand seven hundred years since Shadow's assault, the bloodline that bore the Silver Dolphins became instruments of light, leading other humans to act the same. The leader of the human rebellion was of this bloodline," Fandia said looking down at Miral and taking her hands. "Your ancestors, dear."

Miral's shock prevented her from speaking.

"The Goddess of the Dark was after her for the Silver Dolphins?!" Justin asked with fluffed head feathers.

Fandia nodded. "It was the Silver Dolphins that spoke to you that day, Justin. Pleading with you for your life. They were also the ones that calmed you on the ship when you fell into rage. They were the reason the sea dragon wanted her, they saw the light, and wished to have it." She looked to Miral once more. "They live within you, and you are the first of your bloodline to teach them to feel emotions!" Fandia said delightedly. "Miral is also the first human to be born with the purest light that can be within a human soul, giving her the gift of magic! That is why she is as she is."

"Unbelievable!" Snow said in awe.

"How do we stop the Goddess of the Dark?" Justin asked.

"The light of life and love!" Fandia said with a bright smile. "The Silver Dolphins told you before you came here."

"Together we are one!" Miral said in the two voices that were the Silver Dolphins. "Fandia, we are glad to gaze upon thee once more. We are saddened by your sorrow. We wish to free you from your protection. We know not how."

Fandia smiled warmly. "I am glad to hear your voices once more. I am happy that you can feel now!" Fandia said as she placed her hand over Miral's heart. "Weep not, we will find a way," she said.

Miral blinked then beamed. "I'm starting to get used to that!" she giggled.

Justin chuckled at Miral. "I feel better knowing who is speaking."

She felt better knowing that as well. She thanked them within herself for saving Justin's life two times. They responded with, "We are joyful!"

"The eight elements combined bring forth the light of life and love. That is your weapon, weaken her and send her back to darkness," Fandia said. "Shadow will try to separate you. She knows her only chance to succeed is to break you first. To dim your inner light and trap you in an illusion. Use that to your advantage. If she fails to break you, she will try to kill you. More Elementals will rise up against her, but remember if Miral falls there is little hope of stopping her. Stay together and remain resolute at all times!" Fandia said gesturing to the diamond of elements. "When you depart here you will be forced to face her. The chamber will take you to Delphi."

Miral frowned at Fandia. "I never saw a chamber there."

"It's hidden beneath the ground," Fandia replied. "It was once my home." Fandia held her hands out to Justin and light emitted from them. "I have something I wish to give you, as you have overdrawn all your crystals."

Miral stood and moved to the side allowing Justin to stand before Fandia. A gold helmet in the shape of a dragon's skull appeared in the goddess's hands. The helmet was decorative with green ethereal gems, one on the top and two on the sides. Justin took the helmet from her and placed it on his head.

"Thank you, Fandia." He looked at Agar, "What do you think?"

"That is a fancy helm, brother! You look very intimidating and stylish!" he said laughing.

Fandia approached Justin and laid her hands on his shoulders. "The battle ahead will be a tough one, and the armor is celestial in nature. It is light and will not weigh you down. Best to be protected as much as possible so that you may defend Miral. Be aware that it cannot fend off her magic entirely," Fandia said. "I would do the same for you all, but I have not enough resources here to do so."

Justin glowed with a bright light. When it dimmed, he was adorned with gleaming gold and green armor. Justin looked himself over smiling wide. A green and gold cape hung behind him with a golden bird in the center. The armor was elegant, covering his arms, legs, and tail, and appeared to be themed around his family crest, the Arisdalian bird. He looked at Miral with a proud demeanor. "What say you, love?"

"That armor looks beautiful on you," Miral said blushing.

Justin tenderly touched the side of her face. "Thank you, my moon and stars." He looked over his friends, his family, it was time to confront Shadow and end the long battle that began a month ago. He trusted them all. They fought with mastery when they were together and he knew they could do this. "What say you, friends? Are we ready to give her what she truly deserves?!" Justin asked in a rallying cry.

"I know I am!" Agar said punching his fist into his hand.

"No one messes with me and gets away with it!" Katenna said.

"She will pay for her cruelty!" Kedros said.

"You better believe it!" Snow replied.

"Let's teach this wicked goddess a lesson she'll never forget!" Sara said.

"For Anelda and Johanas, I will see her fall!" Galena said.

"For my father, for my friends, for all of life and love. I am ready!" Miral said.

Fandia smiled warmly. "Go with the light, my children. May it bring you victory.

Chapter 58 - Courage

They appeared inside a teleport chamber and exited the room. A dark cave lay before them lit by blue and clear ethereal crystals that lined the walls, ceiling, and ground. Miral felt a shiver run through her in the cold, damp cave.

"Amazing, so this is Fandia's lost kingdom!" Sara said her voice echoing off the cave walls. "I have never seen an ethereal crystal cave this massive before. I have to come back here and explore it!"

"It's so beautiful!" Snow said in awe.

They followed the wall of crystals to a winding stairwell and ascended. The end of the grey-stone stairs brought them to a sealed iron hatch. Justin motioned for them to back away and used his magic to shatter the metal into pieces.

"We are inside Delphi Castle," he said in a dull tone as he took in the throne room. He turned to take Miral's hand as she ascended. Tears and tension welled up within him as memories flooded his mind. His mother, father, Yarway and the royal guards were not there. As much as he wished to bury them properly, he did not want to see them as they would be now. He shuddered and cleared his mind of the disturbing thoughts.

"Back here . . ." Agar groaned.

"Welcome to your death!" Irana's voice rang out from a darkened hallway. "Think of all the trouble you could have saved yourselves if you would have died here the first time!"

"I do not plan on dying again, Irana," Justin said.

"I almost had you . . . curse Aurorus and Isis!" Shadow hissed. She gazed at Justin, her face scrunching with disgust. "She gave you that armor! It reeks of her stench! I will enjoy tearing it from you!"

"How do we save Irana?" Kedros whispered to them.

"Irana cannot be saved, she has given herself entirely to her torment!" Shadow said, followed by a laugh. "Your end lies here, Elementals. I have gained enough power to rise into the World of Life! Gaze upon me now in all my glory!"

Irana was engulfed in a swirling black and purple mist. Her haunting red eyes the only thing that remained visible, but they had changed shape. When the clouds settled, they gazed upon the darkened form of Fandia.

Her skin was swirling and wafted from the surface as steam. The black of her body draped her like clothing. She had streaks of black on her forehead and cheeks, and down her arms. Where there was no black she glowed purple. Her tail did not look like Fandia's. The tip looked similar to a sharp double-pointed halberd. When Fandia was brought into existence, her shadow was too, and she was just that in appearance.

"I am a greater beauty than my opposite! Don't you think?" Shadow asked with a smirk.

"Not at all!" Justin said with a shake of his head.

Shadow glared at him. "That is no way to treat your goddess! I have returned not her! I am the ruler of the World of Life now!" she hissed. "You will bow to my will!" Shadow outstretched her arms and the room went dark for everyone, but Miral.

Miral blinked as she scanned the room with quick turns of her head. Justin was gone, they were all gone. Her eyes reluctantly fell back on the Goddess of the Dark who bore a widening smirk. Miral wrapped herself in her own arms and bit her lip as her body trembled.

"You're broken, that is why you are still here, alone. The Silver Dolphins shine with the radiance of the disgusting love in your heart. I told Justin I would kill you if he broke you, and I am not one to break a promise!" She lunged at Miral with her shadowed scythe forming in her hands. "I will enjoy giving you a slow death!"

Justin could hear Miral screaming in terror, calling his name repeatedly.

He ran to her voice, out the throne room of Arisdale to the court. She was being pulled to a block with an executioner who was holding an ax. Elder Nyros stood before her.

"By order of the Acting King, this woman is to be put to death for her crimes against the Kingdom of Arisdale. 'Tis by her hands that we lost King Johanas and Queen Anelda."

Justin blinked in disbelief, fear constricted his chest and raced his heart. He wanted to run to her but stopped himself. "This is not right. I would never sentence her to death, even if she were guilty." Everything felt so real, but this is just an illusion, this was Shadow's doing. The vision vanished and he could hear the vile goddess speaking in his mind.

"Justin, you're a tough one! What can I do to make you play along, hmmm? Now that you have confessed your feelings, your greatest fear is losing her. What would happen to her if she lost you?" Shadow cackled.

Justin ignored her as she showed another vision, and sat cross-legged on the ground, closing his eyes.

"How dare you have the audacity to ignore me! You will play my game!" Shadow bellowed.

Justin remained still, silently reflecting within himself on his own light. His mother had taught him about meditation and mindfulness. How to sit with the thoughts and things around you without attaching to them emotionally. He realized now that it was his second greatest weapon against Shadow. The reason she failed to get into his mind all this time. He would not feed her with words and would not play her games, as Fandia advised. She was trying to break him.

"She will never be accepted among your people! You'll never live a happy life! You will regret your choices in the future!" Shadow hissed.

Whether or not anything Shadow said could be true, didn't matter. It was uncertainty of what may come, that people feared the most, and Shadow's greatest power against someone's mind. He remembered his mother's words.

"Living in fear of tomorrow or of what was, only causes you to lose what you have today. The mind likes to think, likes to question. Let the thoughts that do not matter hang out in the background until they leave. Thoughts are only thoughts until you give them emotion. All emotions bring a tidal wave to your shore, and fear and anxiety are the most dreaded. We shrink away, instead of standing firm and letting that wave hit us. You will find that as you bear it, fear loses power every time it returns and isn't so terrible. Ask yourself when gripped by fear, what is here right now, where are you, what are you doing, how do you feel, who loves you? That is what

matters. Let the future be, let the past go, and take in all that is good and bad equally, to learn and grow."

He understood. With that memory, he found new strength. Everything happened for a reason, even the worst things, and if one could accept and learn from that, forgive and let go, one could live a life of real power. He could become fearless and would thanks to Shadow. Then, in the stillness of his mind words from his dream returned. The dream that woke him the day before his family left for Delphi.

"Suffering will rise as the light fades. Seek the inner light."

He knew the voice belonged to the Silver Dolphins now. At the start of it all, they tried to reach him and were always taking care of him. He saw his own inner light burning ever brighter as he followed it in his mind.

"No!" Shadow screamed.

Justin's eyes flew open. He was back in the throne room of Delphi Castle and Miral was desperately running from Shadow in tears.

"Miral!" he called as he pulled on the earthen elements of her armor, zipping her across the room towards him.

Shadow hissed as the cursed weapon's swing narrowly missed Miral.

They embraced each other tightly a moment before he set her down, facing the goddess, ready for the next assault.

"You . . . you frustrate me so, dearest!" Shadow's voice screamed as she turned to face them, then vanished. "I will enjoy killing you first!"

He couldn't locate Shadow by her voice. It seemed to be coming from every direction at once. He jumped back, pulling Miral with him when he saw a black mist crawling down the pillar beside him.

"Run, Miral!" Justin commanded standing firm to distract the Goddess of the Dark. She wanted him now, and he wanted it to remain that way till the others broke free.

Shadow took shape as she emerged from the pillar, scythe in her hands.

"I will have this world and the Silver Dolphins!" Shadow screamed swinging her weapon at him.

Justin dodged her while tossing chunks of broken columns as she continued to swing her blade down at him. Sections of his armor dripped blood where she made contact.

Miral refused to hide as Justin risked his life once more for her. Not again. She sent a channeled column of water at Shadow, then ran to his side.

Shadow shrieked in pain when the water contacted her. "Arrhh! You may have escaped the nightmares of your mind, dearest, but you will not escape this one!"

The room was engulfed in darkness. Justin could faintly see tentacles of shadow as they streaked towards them. He gently pushed Miral out of the way with his magic against her armor and howled in agony when a searing pain ripped through his side.

"No!" Miral screamed. A brilliant light emanated from her chasing darkness away. It was the light of holy magic, the power that existed between them.

Shadow sent tentacles out to Miral in response, but she deflected them with a blast of glowing water. The goddess recoiled in pain from the light-infused magic.

"Your inner light!" Miral cried to him.

Justin drew from his inner light and sent it forth to the darkness inside. Shadow wailed in agony as it touched her.

Miral stood by Justin's side and spoke with the voice of the Silver Dolphins. "Together we are one, our light is stronger together."

Justin smiled at her, dropping to a knee. "Then let us fight as one!"

Miral quickly climbed on his back and they attacked Shadow together, combining earth and water into an aqua-colored light, the elements of life. Shadow shrieked in pain as the holy magic grazed her side. Justin and Miral then paused to channel healing energies to seal his wounds before the assaults began once more.

Sara stood in front of a mirror in shock. Her hair was now a mile long, her face wrinkled and pale. She was going to die like her father. She didn't want to leave Talos behind like this. She wanted a child of her own. There was so much left to do, it couldn't end like this. She turned away from the mirror, painful tears flooding her eyes. There was no more life left. She had to be a hundred years old now. She reached up to remove her clasps and end her suffering. She froze when an unfamiliar male voice filled her mind.

"What the hell is wrong with you, hot stuff? Don't let that psycho get to you! You're my girl, after all. Come find me when this is over so we can get . . . better acquainted with each other's bodies!" he said.

Sara fumed, her anger rising to a new height. The voice's street word use and accent were similar to Agar's, which meant he was Egyptalian. Seth must have finally walked into her head. "Get your perverted hands off my mind, you filthy dastard!" Sara bellowed. She blinked in shock when the room dissolved, and she saw Justin with Miral on his back, fighting Shadow with united magic. Shadow must have trapped her within her own fear, and to her dismay, Seth got her out of it.

"Guess I owe you one, Seth!" Sara said as she pulled the clasps from her hair and joined Justin and Miral.

"Sara! Thank Fandia!" Miral cried out.

"We must fight as one with our inner light!" Justin said dodging Shadow.

"All right then!"

Sara added fire to Justin's water-projected rock. The combined light of aqua and yellow streaked forth to Shadow. She screamed in rage as the threefold attack contacted her.

"You will not win! Your companions are becoming lost in their own fears!" Shadow hissed sending forth tentacles of darkness, charging at Justin and Miral with the scythe raised.

Katenna stared blankly before her. She was back in Egyptalia standing in the crypt of her mother and father. She felt tears pooling in her eyes as she gazed upon the carved stone names. She hated coming here. Why was she here now?

"My Queen, don't you wish to know how your parents actually died?" a priest said from the back of the crypt.

Katenna's eyes went wide. "What do you mean? They were sick."

"That is what you were told, but I know the truth!" he said. "They were poisoned!"

"What? Who?" Katenna said in shock.

"It was Agar!" he replied.

"No! That's impossible!" Katenna responded with resolution, though she could feel herself trembling.

"He was sent by the king and queen of Arisdale to assassinate them at the time of the plague. He has stealth, does he not?" the priest asked.

"You lie, he would never! I love him!" Katenna cried. She paused when she saw a glimmer of light and walked to it. The crypt vanished and Katenna could see Justin, Miral, and Sara. Katenna fumed in anger and ran to join them. "That witch, she did it to me again! I will make her pay for this!" she growled. She cast a gale of light-infused winds that swept away Shadow's tentacles.

"Welcome to the fray, Katenna!" Sara called to her.

"The others still trapped?" she asked combining her winds to drive the water and fire-infused rock faster, the friction generating lightning and chilling the water to give it the strength of ice. The four main elements were together, and their united power created sub-elements giving the attack a powerful white light. Shadow narrowly dodged the assault, her face for the first time expressing fear.

Justin grinned. "What is the matter? Are you afraid?"

Shadow screamed with indignation. "You will fail! The others will not be joining you!"

"That is where you are wrong! They are strong of heart! Your tricks will not work!" Justin said in defiance. To be honest, though, he was worried about Agar's fear, the reason he hates water. Shadow vanished from sight. Justin tensed as he scanned the room for her.

"Watch my back!" Justin commanded.

Katenna and Sara stood behind Justin and Miral waiting for her to attack.

Agar crept into the council room of Arisdale to hear what the king had to say. He liked his stealth just for moments like this. It was his second day in Arisdale and he wanted to know what the king talked about; there would be no secrets from him.

"The boy will make a useful tool in our arsenal," Johanas said.

"A tool? Nothing more than that?" Elder Nyros asked.

"Anelda wishes him to be a son to me, but I refuse to accept him on this level. He is an Elemental and is only valuable to me in that regard. After all, the cat is unstable, you heard what he had done. The reason he was rejected by his family?" Johanas asked.

"Very well then, Your Majesty. I will have it noted, and should anything happen to the royal bloodline, he will not ascend the throne," Elder Nyros said. "Is the prince aware of this, Your Majesty?"

"He is," Johanas said. "Justin dislikes the cat as well. He too knows that Agar is valuable in service only."

Johanas never felt that way about me . . . or did he? Justin wouldn't lie to me, he never—. He wasn't certain; he was in the room with Johanas, hearing his words, but something didn't feel right about it. Justin was his best friend, and you can't disguise that. But then, Justin knows how to read people. He can hide how he really feels. Agar sat dejected on the floor.

"I've never been wanted anywhere. What good am I?"

He decided he would leave. No one would use him just for his powers. He quietly exited the council room and saw Justin standing in the hall looking right at him through the stealth.

"You were spying on father!" Justin said.

"What do you care? I'm not staying! I'm not going to live a lie!"

"You already are. Do you not remember what you did?" Justin asked.

Agar stood wide-eyed as his past came rushing back in a wave of panic. He was being held underwater, desperate for air, thrashing to break free; however, all that was freed was the blinding light of his rage. The hand that held him under released its grip and he could breathe again. He was relieved, but the eyes of gathering people brought that relief to an end.

"He killed him! Did you see that?! He has magic!" an unknown voice in the crowd called.

Agar sat quietly with his shock. They didn't see the other boy bullying him, drowning him, they only saw the end results, the anger that couldn't be contained. But he killed someone. The look in his parents' eyes when they learned, when they promised him everything would be all right as he drifted off into a drug-induced sleep. The pain when he woke to find himself lost and alone. Justin was right, he was living a lie all his life.

"Brother, wake up! Do you not see the lies for what they are? What about Katenna? We all love you!" Justin said in a desperate tone.

"The . . . what? Huh?" Agar stammered. "Wait! This isn't real, I'm not a child anymore! My new family loves me, they forgave me!" He blinked in confusion as the memories faded and were replaced with the sight of his loving family fighting Shadow.

"Damn you!" Agar growled.

"Brother! Guess you heard me, huh?" Justin exclaimed.

"Sure did! Thanks!"

Shadow reappeared next to Katenna and swung the scythe towards her.

"No!" Agar bellowed diving at her pulling her to the ground.

Justin, Miral, and Sara spun and pelted Shadow with water-driven, flaming, shattered rock, making her turn back to them in fury. Katenna winced in pain and grabbed her leg.

"Damn it!" Agar cursed pressing his hands over the gaping wound. "You are going to be all right, Kat! Stay strong, my love!"

Shadow spun with Agar's words and sent tentacles at him.

Agar shielded Katenna howling in pain as the magic contacted him.

The dark goddess charged towards them with scythe raised. "All love will wither in my presence!"

"Agar! Send your inner light to her!" Justin yelled joining Miral and Sara in another trinity of power directed at Shadow. She recoiled from Agar's light, her tentacles retracting from him. The spell impaled her from behind and she screamed.

Agar lifted Katenna, used his stealth to hide them, and ran from Shadow.

Galena knelt before her beloved family. She had lost them all to the Queen of Delphi. Johanas, Anelda, Justin, Agar, and Yarway all gone. What was she to do now? What was the point of going on? The pain of loss was so overwhelming that she felt numb. Her spirit shattered into pieces. She could heal so many ailments and pain, but she could not mend her family, could not save them, and could not even heal herself. *What good am I with these skills if I cannot protect those I love.*

The young princes never got to live their lives to the fullest. Justin never found love. She paused, something about that didn't seem right. *Did Justin fall in love? Who was it?* She could have sworn there was someone and searched her mind for answers. The girl was gentle, sweet, and amazingly pure of heart. *How do you forget someone like that?!* She thought hard about whom the girl was. She had touched her heart and Justin's. She took her shopping for the coronation. The coronation. Justin wasn't dead, neither was Agar. *Miral!*

A new vision filled the throne room. Justin was wounded and looking weary with Miral on his back, and Sara was fighting and dodging Shadow. Agar and Katenna were on the ground.

"Blessed light! You are a shrewd woman!" Galena said as she ran to Katenna. Agar pulled his hands away and Galena cast healing light on the wound sealing it shut.

"Thank you, Galena!" Katenna said.

"Thanks, Mom," Agar teased with a wink.

"Oh, Agar!" Galena said giggling and cast healing on him as well.

Shadow lashed out with her tentacles to Justin, Sara, and Miral. Her scythe grew in length and width as she charged Galena, Agar, and Katenna.

"You are fighting a lost battle! Even if you are healed, you will never be whole! There is so much darkness in this world for me to feed on! I will run you into the ground with my hands or by your own exhaustion!" Shadow bellowed.

Agar helped Katenna to her feet. Galena joined her holy light to the wind and lightning. Together they sent it forward to meet with earth, water, and fire. The spell tore through Shadow, who screamed in fury.

Kedros's worst fear had come true. Glen Woods was aflame, the beautiful, enchanting forest burning to the ground before his eyes. All those he loved died in the fire, burnt beyond recognition. Ash and the hot stench of charred flesh filled the air. If only he had stayed, then he could have saved them all. No, nature magic didn't have the power to stop the fire from taking everything from him, his home, his sister, and his friends. He felt like he forgot something. Why did he leave here in the first place? What was so important that he would leave behind all he loved?

All he loved, he thought. Surely there was something more beyond the woods. Nature is everywhere, his love everywhere, but it wasn't just nature that he was missing. The thought of stopping the fire was on his mind once more. The ash that drifted like a darkened snowfall brought a thought to his mind. *She could do it. Snow, I love her so.* Kedros felt shocked when the forest dissolved and was replaced by the throne room of Delphi Castle. His friends were locked in unified battle against Shadow, but Snow was not with them.

"New blood, let us see how you fair!" Shadow screamed as she charged Kedros from the darkness behind him.

Kedros leaped to the side as Shadow swung her scythe. Blood soaked his tunic. She had cut deep into his side.

Galena rushed to him as Shadow screamed from combined magic assaults. She sealed Kedros's wound and grabbed hold of his hand to move him from Shadow before she recovered.

Justin saw that Kedros and Galena were clear and sighed in relief. He was feeling exhausted. He knew his friends were also, but he had been at this longer.

They attempted to launch combined assaults whenever possible, but Shadow was determined to no longer allow them time to channel. She was relentless, swinging her scythe while casting tentacles of shadow, creeping about the walls and floors in shadow form, eager to take Miral's life above all. Galena was moving between them as she could to stop the bleeding, as Shadow would turn to her whenever she attempted to heal them.

"That leaves Snow," Miral said biting her lip.

"She is easily frightened. I do hope she can pull herself together," Justin replied to Miral.

"Please hurry, Snow. We need you!" Miral cried out.

Snow trembled, staring blankly at her blood-soaked hands. She was in Frost Star, kneeling in the icy snow before the dead bodies of her childhood friends. They didn't flee from Frost Star as she thought. The truth was before her now. When Shadow stole her life, she returned here and killed them with her bare hands. She had no right to be happy. She was freed from Shadow's torment, only to find a real horror locked in her memory. There was no point in fighting anymore, no reason to push on. She sat in the stinging cold resigned to her fate and emptied her mind of all thoughts. She would die here with them.

Shadow stopped fighting to cackle manically.

"One of you has failed! I will be keeping her in endless torment in the World of the Dark! Time for you all to die!" Shadow said as she swung the enlarged scythe at them.

Kedros tucked away behind a pillar, heaving heavy breaths and turned inward to his light. "Please hear me, Snow. I believe in you!" he said, then quietly sang the same song he shared with Snow once before.

Snow sat silently staring into the distance. How long before she died? She paused as she heard a sound carried on the wind, but the howling of a blizzard drowned it out. This all seemed so familiar. Frost Star during a blizzard and . . . that song. Where was it coming from? She turned to look behind her and saw a yellow light in the distance. The corpses of her friends vanished. She shook her head then stood and ran to the light with desperation. It felt warm and comforting. The familiar tune filled her heart with joy. It didn't matter if those horrors were real or not because someone loved her, she loved herself, her life mattered, and she had the right to exist.

The Artichian landscape fell away and Snow stared into the aqua eyes of Kedros, who was singing that beautiful song. It was the second time he saved her life with that melody. She kissed him on the lips, squeezing him tightly, and he kissed her back.

"I love you so much, Kedros!" Snow cried.

"I love you, Snow!" Kedros said.

Shadow screamed with rage. "You will all die! I will have what is mine rightfully!"

Dark tendrils shot out from her in every direction. They all desperately dodged them. Justin was used to their contact and instinctively fought back when they touched him. Shadow kept her assaults coming, they all had to stay on their toes to avoid her.

"The time has come, goddess! You will be going back to your prison!" Justin bellowed.

"We shall see about that, dearest!"

Shadow sent her magic to the ceiling punching through it with ease. The elementals dodged chunks of the marble ceiling as they rained down.

Justin thrust his hands up stopping the largest pieces of the roof. He strained against the weight of them all.

"Get clear!" he commanded.

He watched his friends swiftly back away from the large chunks floating overhead. Shadow grinned wide and moved towards him with her scythe raised. The others cast channeled spells at Shadow, but she moved forward with determination.

"After the two of you fall, the others will die quickly!" she hissed.

"We need to focus our power into one force for the Silver Dolphins. They will use it to send her back," Miral said to Justin.

"She knows it, but I have an idea," Justin said in a strained voice. He released all but one of the large chunks of marble. They fell to the floor with a deafening thud. "Cast your water column now!"

Miral cast her magic towards Shadow, and Justin released the marble from his control. As the rock neared the racing column of water, Justin focused his magic into fragmenting the large rock into several medium-sized pieces. The force of Miral's power hit the marble driving it into Shadow. All eight elements hit her at once, weakening the Goddess of the Dark.

"Sara, put down a ring of fire! Kedros, snag her with vines! Miral, cast a spout of water under Shadow once he has her. Katenna and Snow, combine your power to freeze her in place!" Justin said. "The rest of us will do what we can to keep her busy in the meantime!" Justin commanded.

"Curse you!" Shadow screamed.

"You got it!" Sara said. She flew around Shadow in a wide arc dodging tentacles as they reached for her.

"You will fail, dearest!" Shadow hissed swinging her scythe out in an arc at Sara. The attack caught her on the leg, but she did not falter.

Katenna and Agar combined powers to form a tornado of lightning while Justin and Miral fought off the dark magic reaching for them. Shadow was enveloped in gusting winds, which cut off her tentacles before they could branch out again. She screamed in rage swiping at the tornado with her scythe. Kedros set forth to his part of the plan, entangling the goddess in vines. Miral along with Katenna and Snow froze her in place.

Justin smiled, the plan worked, now they had precious time to channel. "Now focus together as one!" Justin called out.

Miral slid down Justin's back and stood beside him. She and the elementals entered within their minds to their inner light and pushed it out. She could see the colors of every elemental's light converging at a center. She was jolted momentarily when she heard Shadow scream in rage. She was breaking free from the trap.

"Send me back and I will only return! Your efforts are wasted! You know not of what is to come!" Shadow screamed as she tore at the vines holding her.

Miral ignored her words maintaining focus on her task. The lights were together now and she could feel the Silver Dolphins stirring within her. Then a bright light the size of a fist shot forth from her heart, and Miral's eyes flew open.

Before her in the combined light of the elements hovered the Silver Dolphins. They looked exactly as they did in all the murals and depictions, but in person, they shone with a blazing radiance. Their beauty and grace were undeniable. Miral could see the eyes of her friends staring in awe at the sight before them.

Shadow's face lit with desire as she glared at the Silver Dolphins. "You will be mine!" she bellowed.

"We belong to all, and yet to no one," the Silver Dolphins replied.

"Why do you choose her then?!" Shadow hissed.

"Fandia knows this. Fandia respects the balance."

Shadow's face twisted with rage. "You're flawed! You will never understand your own failure as you are!"

"We are aware," the Silver Dolphins said. "Return to your realm, Shadow. Respect the balance." They glowed with intensity as they spoke.

"Never!" Shadow hissed with indignation.

A beam of warm light shot forth from them and enveloped her. Shadow screamed, flailing frantically at the light as it surrounded her, shrinking in size. Shadow's dark presence disappeared with the light.

"Shadow is returned. We are . . . happy," the Silver Dolphins said uncertainly.

Miral smiled. "We are happy too!"

The Silver Dolphins returned to light and entered back into Miral's chest.

"Happy! I'm ecstatic!" Sara said retrieving her hair clasps and flying to hide behind a pillar near some drapes. "No peeking now!" she called out. Sara changed back and pulled drapes down from the nearby window.

Miral gasped. "Your hair!"

Sara's hair was dragging a couple feet behind her on the ground as she limped to them. "Ah, yeah. I burnt about three years on that battle," Sara said. "Could have been worse, though!"

Galena ran to Sara and began to cast healing to her cut leg.

"She is gone! It seems unreal!" Agar said draping his arm around Katenna and giving her a hug.

Snow and Kedros were hugging each other tightly too.

"Blessed be Fandia!" Galena said delighted clasping her hands together in prayer.

Miral was glad to see all her friends and family safe. Her journey since Delphi had been full of emotion, and the love of life was the greatest of them all in the end.

Justin embraced her tenderly. "Let's go home!" he said.

"Yes, home!" Miral said returning the hug.

Chapter 59 - Oath

"So, how are we getting back to Arisdale?" Agar asked abruptly.

Justin arched a brow at his brother. "Well, after a battle that long we either rest here till the morrow or find a ship we can borrow."

Agar laughed at the rhymed speech then shook his head. "Pray, not a ship, not after what happened last time!" Agar groaned.

"I agree with Agar," Miral said gripping Justin's hand tighter as she thought about the sea dragon.

"Then we shall remain," Justin said in hope of reassuring her. "Besides looks as though we are needed," Justin gestured with his head as they exited Delphi Castle and saw a herd of confused Delphinians.

They had all been freed from Shadow's control now that she was gone, and stared in shock as the elementals came into view. Young children ducked behind adults and peeked out nervously.

"Oh boy, what do we do about this?" Agar asked Justin.

Justin removed his helmet, tucking it under his right arm, and stepped forward guiding Miral along with his hand against her back.

She saw them all; Madrelin, Helen, Jed and his father Harris. Everyone who made life hard for her. She resisted Justin slightly, her legs locking as her heartbeat pounded in her ears.

Justin turned his tender stare to her and a smile grew on his face. "Breathe, love," he whispered.

She relaxed slightly as she smiled back at him, but held her hand protectively over her heart in prayer.

He bowed his head to the crowd. "Good people of Delphi. I am Justin, the King of Arisdale. With me are the other Elementals of Light."

He gestured back to his family and friends, then looked at Miral with a smile.

She could see the people were listening intently as he spoke, trembling nervously while they gazed up at him. She smiled at the memory of her first encounter with Justin, and the feelings his presence invoked before she knew him.

"The Goddess of the Dark possessed your queen, which is why you lost control of your minds. Though on this day, the dark goddess has been sent back to her prison in the World of Dark and will no longer trouble you. At least, that is, if none of you speak the forbidden word again," Justin said in a scolding tone.

Smiles of relief grew on the faces of the Delphinians. Quiet murmurs passed between them until Justin spoke again.

"As you are now regretfully without a queen, I offer you sanctuary under the banner of Arisdale until such time when you can decide for yourselves how you would like to reform your kingdom. From there forth, I hope we will remain allies. I give you my oath that I will protect and serve the people of Delphi." He placed his hand over his heart with a bow of his head.

An elder Delphinian, which Miral recognized as Gostre, stepped forth. He bent low at the waist and addressed Justin. "Your Majesty, I am Gostre, the late queen's advisor. We thank you for your protection and aid. Your oath comes to us with great shock, although the queen truly did wish to talk with you about peace."

"Did she? I was concerned about her state of mind on the matter. Though I assure you 'twas our intention to make peace with Delphi that day," Justin said in reply. "'Tis a terrible tragedy that we were unable to save her. You have my deepest sympathy."

"Forgive me, Your Majesty, but how can we be certain of your word? Fear has gripped us for years! We dare not venture past the safety of our boundaries," Gostre said.

The Delphinians all mumbled and nodded in agreement.

Justin smiled and wrapped his arm around Miral giving her a light squeeze. "This beautiful lady is your reassurance."

The eyes of the Delphinians fell on her and their faces lit with recognition. Miral blushed and wanted to shrink back out of their sight, but Justin's strong grip held her firmly at his side. She wondered what they thought of her now under the protective arm of the towering King of Arisdale.

Gostre stared dumbfounded at Justin and Miral. "You worked in the castle, didn't you, child? Miral, yes, that is it. I could never forget you."

Murmurs rolled through the crowd as they stared at her. Miral couldn't make out their words but trembled with her old memories. He couldn't forget her, none of them could. She noticed Justin tensed, his hold on her tightening, and his gaze watched them intently. As the crowd took in his piercing eyes and scowl, the mumbles came to an end.

"Your Majesty, why is she our reassurance?" Gostre asked.

Justin turned to face Miral and dropped to one knee, setting his helmet on the ground beside him. He took her hands in his. "I wish it to be known before all of Delphi, that my word is all. That because of what you have taught me and because of my love for all that you are, I will also honor them always."

Miral felt her face on fire with blushing, and her heart beating a song in her chest as he spoke.

"Lady Miral, will you marry me?"

"Yes!" Miral replied excitedly once her shock dissipated. Tears of joy flooded her eyes as they embraced each other.

The shocked faces of Delphi watched with reverence as Justin and Miral kissed.

The elementals had no doubt the humans were awed at a sight that none of them dared dream possible. The end of their lifelong struggles was before them and existed in the love between an Arisdalian King and a common human woman.

Justin turned to face Gostre and reached out his hand to him. "A gentleman's agreement, friend?"

Gostre hesitantly reached for the large hand of the king, grasping it firmly. They exchanged a hearty shake and Justin smiled warmly.

"Then you are hereby under the care of Arisdale. Before we part to return home in a day's time, we will remain to aid you in getting reestablished. A month has passed since the troubles began."

"Thank you, Your Majesty, we are humbled by your generosity."

Justin nodded. "Well then, who wants to join me in fishing?" he grinned.

"You know I will!" Agar replied without hesitation.

Miral giggled. "I never have, but I would love to learn."

"Then I shall teach you, my love," Justin replied.

"I will go gather what plants I can," Galena said with a smile.

"I will help!" Kedros said with excitement. Snow joined his side and followed him and Galena in the search.

The elementals and humans of Delphi divided up to begin rebuilding and supplying their home. The first day of a new era started. One Justin prayed would last forever.

Chapter 60 - Change

Justin fumed with rage before the Elder Council. He slammed his fist on the cedar desk before him with a loud crack punching a hole into the surface. "You will stand there and deny me, even after all we have sacrificed to save Arisdale and the world?!" he growled. "Let us not forget that all the kings of Arisdale's past and my own father gave me their blessings!"

Miral held her hands together before her. She loved Justin dearly, but he was an intimidating sight when angered. One with the earth, his anger channeled to the rocks beneath him, responding in kind as a quake. Miral reached for his arm. "Love, pray! Calm down."

Justin turned his eyes to her, and like the first time on the ship, his features softened, and the quake dissipated. He frowned. "Thank you, love."

He approached the Elder Council about his oath to the Delphinians and his marriage proposal to her once they returned to Arisdale. He was hopeful that the battle to free the World of Life from Shadow would be enough to prove her worth as a queen. She possessed the sacred Silver Dolphins within her body and fought to save the world by calling upon them. Nothing that happened was enough, though. They refused to grant him the request to marry and were obstinate about giving extra aid to the humans of Delphi and Glenn.

"Regardless of your sacrifices, blessings, and the divine power that has chosen her, we will not break the ancestral law!" Elder Nyros replied stubbornly.

"Your refusal 'tis not about ancestral law and you know it!" Justin bellowed.

Elder Nyros stood firm with a scowl.

It was true. The elders still hated humans, despite the truth they now knew about Fandia's absence.

"Very well then!" Justin replied in agitation. "I hereby renounce the throne! I would rather live as an exile in Delphi with the woman I love than be a king to bigots and fools who fear change!" he barked wrapping his right arm protectively around Miral.

"Justin! Are you insane?!" Elder Nyros said in objection.

Miral clung to her love. She felt sorry for him. The pain it would cause him to turn his back on his father's throne and his ancestral heritage was sure; however, the Elder Council left him no choice.

"I have come to voice my opinion on the matter!"

Justin and Miral spun around to face the familiar soft voice that resounded behind them.

"Fandia, you're free!" Miral said in awe.

Fandia stood in the doorway of the council room smiling brightly. She glided into the chamber and approached the Elder Council. Andeos walked in the door behind her and joined her side.

The two gods stood before the Elder Council, who dropped to their knees.

"God . . . Goddess! You are real, you have returned to the World of Life!" Elder Nyros stammered.

"I have, and it is because of Miral that the Silver Dolphins decided to release me from protection!" Fandia said, placing her hand on Miral's shoulder. "She taught them to feel love, and they have become a greater being, now capable of emotion! A feat I never thought possible. You ought to be humbled by this woman."

"Forgive us, Goddess Fandia!" Elder Nyros said.

"It is not my forgiveness you ought to seek!" Fandia said gesturing to Justin and Miral. "I bless their union as well. Now that I have returned, the light will cleanse the world and balance will return," Fandia said with her arms held out. "Your accusations towards humanity have been unjust! When the humans came into the World of Life, they needed your love and guidance, not your disdain and hatred. From all the years of assumptions and persecution, you have made an enemy of a friend. The elder races have forgotten my teachings and me," she said with a frown and a shake of her head. "Through the years I wept in sorrow, unable to show you the error of your ways. Anelda knew this, as does your king.

What code you live by is a choice! It was not forced upon you! The light that is love! Living a life of love allows for forgiveness, unity, honor, and peace for others and yourselves. Those who act through darkness bring hatred, disharmony, disdain, and war. There will always be some darkness as is the balance, but it exists equally!"

"Yes, Goddess Fandia," the elders said in reply.

"King Justin, Lady Miral, we beseech thee. Forgive us for our narrow-sightedness, for our misguided fears, and for our unfair accusations," Elder Nyros said with a lowered head, speaking for all the elders.

Justin nodded to Miral, and she approached Elder Nyros offering him her hand. "Of course, we forgive you!" she said.

Elder Nyros took her hand and a look of awe filled his face. Miral could hear the Silver Dolphins singing out within her. She felt them sending warm energy down her hand into Nyros. They were joyful and wished to share this joy with him.

Miral hugged Elder Nyros and spoke in two voices. "Live your life in the light of love!" She released him from the hug.

Elder Nyros stood, blinking in disbelief. "What was that?"

"That is the Silver Dolphins speaking, Elder!" Justin said moving to stand behind Miral.

"What . . . she really is a delightful girl," Nyros replied smiling at Justin.

"I know. She is amazing!" Justin replied fondly, laying gentle eyes on Miral.

"Well, we have a wedding to plan then, do we not?" Elder Nyros said.

"I thank you kindly, Elders!" Justin replied embracing Miral from behind. He turned to smile at the gods. "Thank you, Fandia, Andeos!"

Fandia smiled warmly. "Of course, Justin."

"Congratulations!" Andeos said.

"Ah, if you will all forgive me, my lady and I have had very little time alone and need to get better acquainted." He faced the guards who awaited him in the hall. "If one of you would mind getting the fire started in the study for us, 'twould be most appreciated."

As he expected, Thordin's eyes lit up, and he bowed quickly. "It would be an honor, sire." He ran up the stairwell to the royal quarters, skipping steps as he did.

Justin laughed in response. "Ah well, at least he is ambitious. 'Tis a good thing in the right circumstances, Severos."

Severos nodded. "Oh yes, indeed, Your Majesty."

Chapter 61 - Thoughts

"Today is the wedding day of King Justin and Lady Miral," Sara scribbled in her book. "November fourteenth, the first day in a new era that is called KOA for the King of Ages. The title bestowed upon Justin, the leader and hero of the world. Justin was also hailed as the king of kings, and the right hand of Fandia. His new title is now the High King of Flourisha."

During their brief rest in Delphi before returning to Arisdale, the people of Delphi had come to revere Miral and wished for her to be the new Queen of Delphi. *She will make a great queen, Sara thought.*

"The humans of Glenn also expressed their gratitude to Justin for saving their lives. Peace was founded between Arisdale and humans. Justin's mother's dreams came true.

"Together Justin and Miral completed each other. She was the calming presence and peace Justin needed to maintain control of anger, and he was the strength and security Miral needed to feel safe and wanted.

"Queen Katenna allied with Delphi and Glenn as well, and an alliance of nations was born with Justin as the leader. Agar and Katenna planned to get married sometime after Justin and Miral." King Agar, Sara mused. He certainly liked the sound of that.

"Snow and Kedros discussed whether or not to rebuild Artichia. If they wished to do so, they had Justin's full support. Another kingdom that would look after the peace between people would certainly go far. On Snow's venture home, she found her old friends were still alive and well, and she was relieved that she had not killed them as Shadow showed her.

"The transition to world unity certainly did not go smoothly. Many refused to accept the terms of the new alliance. Justin stated that no aggression would be tolerated. If anyone disapproved, they could leave and find a new home. Things would take care of themselves in time, and they were not alone in the struggle. The gods no longer hid and aided people freely as they once had long ago. The days ahead would be challenging, but after all the elementals had done to save the world, politics were a small issue.

"Fandia's return greatly influenced people to set aside their intolerances. The Goddess of Light remained in Arisdale with Andeos to be near the Silver Dolphins. There wasn't a soul alive who didn't wish to live within the watchful eye of the Goddess Fandia. Arisdale's village would be expanded, but could not possibly hold the world's populous.

"Galena had become a surrogate mother to Miral and kept busy with wedding plans. Adra was certainly ecstatic to oversee the design.

"Dilos abandoned his position as general of the royal guard and had not been seen since the day he pushed Miral from the cliffs. We assume he is alive and may turn up one day. For now, though it may be best that he and Razamarea have not been seen."

Sara paused in her writing. As Fandia wished, she wrote in her books that the Silver Dolphins left Miral and returned to the Goddess Fandia. The truth is that the Silver Dolphins expressed a desire to stay with Miral. They had become attached to her. This would be kept secret from all other people to prevent anymore harm coming to her.

Sara resumed her writing. "As for me, I lost five years of my life, thirty-six years old now, but gained so much more in return. What a grand adventure this has been! Talos and I now live in Arisdale once more.

"I finally got to have a chat with Justin and get his side of the story. It was truly amazing to put their two tales together, seeing their individual thoughts and feelings. It was clear that they were destined for each other early on." Justin also told her about his time in the World of Light. A story that none of us will ever forget. "The World of Light was as the legends said, an alternate existence for your soul when it departs the World of Life." Sara smiled warmly at that thought. Her mother and father were together again as well, and she would see them once her journey was over.

Shadow's name was changed in texts and she would henceforth be called the Goddess of the Dark or the Mistress of Fear, to protect people from her. The book that began all the troubles in Delphi was found and secured by the gods.

The blood demon has not been seen since Shadow's imprisonment. Andeos said he could no longer sense her either. Sara wondered if this was the last they would hear of the horrible thing, though she wished she could have seen it for herself at least once.

Sara wrote, "I hope what occurred will be carried through time. It is important that the lessons learned over the last month never be forgotten. In the words of the Silver Dolphins, may you always live your life in the light of love."

"Hun! What are you doing? You need to be getting dressed now!" Talos said interrupting her.

"I know! I had to finish my thoughts!" Sara replied in annoyance.

"What? Did losing five years of life make you senile?" Talos mocked.

"Talos!" Sara bellowed while flying out of her seat at him. She laughed with delight as she chased him. Being home is good.

Chapter 62 – When Two Become as One

The wedding was held in the castle gardens, their favorite location in Arisdale, where his heart first beat for her. Justin stood rigid with a nervous smile. The day was unusually warm for November, and he was grateful for that. No doubt by the grace of the gods.

People from all lands that could make the journey in time for the day filled every space of the garden and beyond. They wished to bear witness to the grandest event in the history of the world.

Fandia and Andeos stood in the center of a red rose arch behind Justin; she would be the one to grant them the blessings of marriage. He had his friends beside him. Agar was best man, Talos, and Kedros, his groomsmen.

Stan and Trea were sitting in the front row to the right, smiling at him. Goddesses Isis and Eva were also in attendance, seated up front to the left. Two Egyptalian human men, one with green hair and one with black and red hair sat beside Goddess Isis. The green-haired God of Water was Osiris, brother of Isis and Seth. Justin gazed at the man with black and red hair who looked both annoyed and bored at the same time.

Justin fidgeted as he waited for Miral. He loved her, and the people had come to love her too. Kedros was jittery too and appeared to be just as nervous. *Must be the anticipation of the sight of the one you love, he thought.* He hadn't seen Miral since midday yesterday. It took considerable time to prepare for a wedding this monumental. In the days between Shadow's defeat and yesterday, he stayed very close to Miral's side, sleeping on the floor beside her bed at night to honor the traditions of marriage while remaining close. The separation yesterday caused him a lot of anxiety, even though he knew the girls were with her. Agar had to console him for hours. He felt the tense grip of fear overwhelming him if he was more than a few feet from her, and even that was difficult for him. Because of Shadow taking her away from him repeatedly, he now lived in a programmed fear of that happening again, and he hoped it would soon pass. The Goddess of the Dark was gone and the chance of her returning in their lifetime was slim. Fandia said it would take her centuries to regain enough power, and with light returned to the World of Life once more, that task would prove more difficult.

He was brought back to the moment when the band played a triumphant fair. Snow appeared in the aisle wearing a red-colored gown and walked gracefully down the crimson and gold-lined carpet. She smiled at Kedros before turning to face the aisle. Sara appeared. She left her hair long for the occasion, and Justin thought that the look suited her. Once Sara was in place, Katenna walked down the aisle smiling at Agar, and she took her position as Miral's maid of honor.

The song changed, the tune was the same he heard Miral humming several times before. The melody was hauntingly beautiful and suited her elegance. Justin became more aware of his senses as the scent of red roses became stronger. He was eager to see his beloved in her wedding gown for the first time.

Kara Okami walked down the aisle with Delphia on her shoulder, dropping white rose petals on the ground. Justin fought hard to not let his jaw drop when he saw Miral come into view escorted by Galena. The white gown was elaborate, silver embroidery, blue ethereal gems, ruffles, and lace. An intricate cloth hung from her silver ribbon belt and was decorated with the Silver Dolphins. She was naturally beautiful, but she looked majestic in her gown. Justin smiled wide when she reached the end and faced him. Her smile, the one that he never wanted to see fade, shone as brightly as the moon at night.

Miral blushed a deep red as she smiled back at him. She was excited for this day to finally come. The thought of being his wife and queen to Arisdale, and high queen to the world, felt overwhelming to her, but she knew there wasn't anything she couldn't do with him by her side.

"Children of light! We are gathered here this day to honor the greatest of all emotions," Fandia said with her hands outstretched. "Love, the light of life. Justin and Miral began their journey as strangers, thrown into a desperate struggle to save the World of Life. During their journey, they found within each other the light of love. Love so bright, that the Goddess of the Dark sought to destroy it, and the Silver Dolphins fought to protect it. Theirs is a love that shows us what it means to live life to the fullest of our being. Love that has set me free," Fandia said smiling. "Pass down their tale through all time, and may it never be forgotten." Fandia drew closer to Justin and Miral. "Please hold hands."

Justin took Miral's small and delicate hands in his. The memory of the day Miral took his hand and placed it against hers came to mind. What she said then was true. Here they were showing the world the truth of things.

"Justin. Do you solemnly swear by the light of life to honor her, love her, for all the days of your life?" Fandia asked him.

"I do!"

"Miral. Do you solemnly swear by the light of life to honor him, love him, for all the days of your life?" Fandia asked her.

"I do!"

Fandia looked to Agar and he handed her a ring. "A ring is the representation of love for it symbolizes the eternity by which love exists, and the cycle of life, as do the Silver Dolphins. What begins will one day end. What matters most in a life of love is the journey we take during that cycle," Fandia said holding out the ring to Justin.

Justin pinched the ring between his fingers. "Miral, with this ring I swear to you my undying loyalty, my life, and my love. You are my pillar upon which I will lay the foundation for our future. From beginning to the end, I will always love and protect you," he said sliding the ring onto her finger.

Fandia turned to Katenna, who handed her a ring, and she gave the ring to Miral.

Miral felt warm tears stream down her cheeks. She fought back against the quiver in her voice as she spoke. "Justin . . . with this ring, I swear to you my undying loyalty, my life, and my love. You are my protector. I will be the support and love for our future. From beginning to the end, I will always love you," she said placing the ring on his finger.

"To each other you have sworn your vows of love and by the divine light of life, I hereby pronounce thee man and wife, King and Queen of Arisdale and Flourisha. You may kiss your bride," Fandia said to Justin.

Justin wrapped his arm around Miral dipping her back slightly and leaned down to kiss her.

The throng of people erupted with cheers. "Long live the king and queen."

The future looked bright for the World of Life, and for Justin and Miral, a new adventure had just begun.

Chapter 63 - First Dance as One

Justin and Miral walked down the aisle hand in hand, followed by Katenna and Agar, Sara and Talos, and Snow and Kedros. The remainder of the wedding celebration was held in the castle ballroom, the place where Justin and Miral both said they fell deeply in love. Now they would have another first dance, this time as one. The love they shared shone from them as they danced, visible in movements and in their expressions.

Sara contemplated the words she would use to describe their love to the world as she watched them dance. She would do so in a manner that would teach all who read it a valuable lesson and call it "When Two Become as One."

The celebration was a grand event to be sure. A large feast was shared with the villagers and visitors from afar. Most of the guests brought food from their culture as gifts for the celebration. Sara watched her new family of friends as they celebrated the love-inspired day and let out a happy, content sigh. Talos had gone off to speak with the guys, but she felt content to stay at her seat and observe the rare sight. She found herself wishing she had her journal to jot down her observations. A feeling of warmth around her waist interrupted her thoughts. She heard a deep, husky male voice whisper in her ear.

"I finally found you, my little Phoenix . . ."

Sara jumped out of her seat with a start, her mind racing with thoughts. *That voice!* She jerked her head back and stared right into the deep red eyes of a rather handsome, dark tan, human man. His long black hair draped midway down his back, two red streaks from his ears draped down to his chest, and he had a small goatee under his lower lip. Several chains of gold and an ankh hung around his neck. Sara jumped back, but his arm tightened around her, his hand forcefully grabbing her shoulder.

He smiled at her mischievously. "Mmmm . . . much more beautiful in person."

Sara narrowed her eyes once her mind put the pieces together, those words and that voice. "Seth!" she scowled.

Seth chuckled with delight. "I was starting to think you'd forgotten me . . . but you were just stunned by my appearance, weren't you?" He grabbed her chin and moved in closer. "It's all right, I have that effect on women," he said.

Sara felt her blood boil with rising anger. He moved his hand from her shoulder to her chest. She reached to push his hand away, but he blocked her and wrapped his other arm around her pinning her arms to her side.

She struggled to free herself from his firm grip. "Get your hands off me right now!"

Seth beamed with delight. "Ohhh! You're a frisky one! I like that!"

Sara growled, her anger building into rage as he forced her closer to him.

"How about we leave this place and think of a way for you to repay me for saving you."

Sara glared at him. "I will not go anywhere with you, you arrogant, disgusting lecher! Talos!" Sara bellowed.

She saw Talos jump with a start, his usual response to his name being hollered. She yelled so loudly that even the band stopped playing, and everyone turned to look at her. Talos's expression took on a sinister cast when his eyes locked onto Seth.

The God of Chaos's face displayed a neutral visage as he watched Talos charge at him. "Hmm, what a pity . . ." he said looking her up and down, "for me." He grinned.

Talos swung his fist at Seth, but the god gracefully dodged the swing, jumping backward. His face bore a mischievous cast while crouching into a battle stance, his eyes wild.

"Finally some fun!" Seth said beckoning Talos to attack.

His hands glowed red, and Sara heard wind, rain, and lightning roaring outside in answer to his excitement. The windows blew open and gusts swirled with aggression within the ballroom knocking over candelabras, glasses, and other light objects. Women held their dresses tightly to their sides.

Sara then felt the ground rumbling with growing intensity and turned to see Justin glaring at Seth with rage-filled eyes over the distasteful interruption. Miral was clinging to him, her face bearing a wide-eyed expression. Sara couldn't hear what Miral was saying to Justin, but it had no effect on the king. He marched over to Seth growling, his head feathers and sickle claws erect.

"That is enough!" Isis shouted.

Seth raised an eyebrow as he looked at his sister, his face twisting with disappointment. "Ugh . . . here comes Madame killjoy . . ." he muttered under his breath.

The winds, rain, lightning and Justin's quake ceased as she grabbed hold of his hair forcefully and yanked him away from Sara and Talos.

Justin wore a grin of satisfaction at the sight.

Seth winced in pain, growling, "Ow!"

Isis dragged him away from the party ranting, "I can't take you anywhere!"

Fandia stood in the doorway to the ballroom with her arms folded, scowling at Seth.

"Are you all right, hun?" Talos asked looking her over.

Sara embraced him tightly. "Yes, I am all right. Thank you, love."

"Promise you will never say his name again!"

"That is a promise, the dastard!" Sara grumbled.

The band returned to playing music and the guests to their conversations. The girls approached Sara with concerned looks.

"That was the God of Chaos . . ." Katenna said sounding annoyed.

"What a pervert!" Snow said.

Galena frowned. "Oh, poor Goddess Isis."

"Mischievous god is an understatement!" Sara said grumbling.

Agar approached and draped an arm over Katenna. "Man, what a creep!"

Kedros stood beside Snow frowning. "He sure is. Sorry, Sara."

Miral approached her. "I'm very sorry, Sara . . ." Her words were cut off as Justin swept her off her feet and cradled her in his arms.

"Sara, you all right?" he asked concerned.

"I am, Justin," Sara said with a firm nod.

"I am pleased to hear that," Justin replied with a smile. "My friends, I pray you forgive my interruption. After all that, I am ready to retire. Have a lovely evening. I will see you all on the morrow." Justin turned towards the ballroom door with Miral in his arms. She pulled herself up to peek over his shoulder blushing a deep shade of red. She looked back at them and waved farewell.

Agar grinned wide and waved back. "Goodnight!"

Chapter 64 - Deceit

"Azan!" Shadow screamed with rage.

"No need to be so loud. I can hear you just fine," he sighed with exasperation. "I simply chose to ignore you for a week!" he said with a hint of amusement.

Azan approached the black crystal pedestal in the middle of the darkened room where the only source of light emanated. He was shrouded in darkness as he glared at Shadow's form within the sphere that sat upon it.

"What went wrong?! I did everything you asked of me!" she hissed.

"Nothing went wrong," he said. "You did very well, every piece has fallen perfectly into place."

"Then why . . . am I . . . in my prison once more?!" Shadow yelled.

"I don't recall promising you freedom!" he said.

Shadow glowered back at him. "What?! You used me?!" she hissed. "They are together! You had me push them to break so they could be happy?!"

Azan scoffed. "Not at all! But they had to suffer in desperation and be happy, as you say, for my goal to be achieved." He remained silent for a moment. "You let your hatred of Justin get the better of you, Shadow. Your selfish desire for the Silver Dolphins drove you to go against the plan; however, you forget me, who I am! I was prepared for your derailment, and as such, your attempts to break free without me have failed!" He smirked.

"You will pay for this outrage! I will make you suffer!" Shadow screamed.

Azan laughed. "You will never again be free from your prison!"

www.ingramcontent.com/pod-product-compliance
Lightning Source LLC
Chambersburg PA
CBHW020535020726
47494CB00006B/1772